PIRATE CONSORT

TELEPATHIC SPACE PIRATES

BOOK 2

CARYSA LOCKE

*P*lasma salvos breached the hull. Nitrogen and oxygen, life-giving and finite, vented into space. The ship's reserves dropped to less than sixty percent in a matter of seconds. It wasn't the worst damage *Razor's Deep* had taken in battle, but it was close. Even for the latest nanograph - an update Braxton purchased during their last space dock - self-repair had limits. The nanites could only do so much to mend the inner bulkheads of the ship before the air supply dropped below survivable levels.

The boy with no name sat hunched in his alcove, connected mentally to every aspect of the ship's systems. Before the nanograph, he'd only been able to connect with the ship's central computer. Now, it felt as though his mind touched every corner of the vessel. He knew the damage report without having to ask the ship.

He ran a tally through his mind in milliseconds: forward weapons offline, drive core cracked, hull breach across two decks and three bulkheads. Aided by the ship's computers, his human brain processed the calculations as fast as the most sophisticated AI. He hesitated for less than a second before shutting every blast door and vent to the aft section of the ship, isolating the breach across decks 3 and 4.

It saved the ship. And condemned twenty-seven men and women to die.

The nanograph wouldn't finish repairing in time to save them, but the rest of the ship would remain stable with...twenty percent of the air reserves remaining. It would be enough for them to survive, if the mechanics could fix the jump drive. Provided the pirates let them, of course.

The boy had heard many stories. In most of them, pirates didn't leave behind survivors.

"What the fuck are you doing, brat?" Braxton's voice was a harsh and unwelcome intrusion, blaring through the ship's comm system.

The boy flinched, ducking his head away from the sound. It was a reflex, one he couldn't help. The mercenary commander's accent made *fuck* sound like *feck*. But the boy had no trouble understanding him. Braxton was one of those people who shouted everything, whether speaking the words with his mouth or thinking them with his mind.

The boy struggled to move his lips, pulling back from the vastness of the ship to his own small body. It took several seconds to get his jaw to move in response to his wishes. Speaking out loud was difficult while he was connected so deeply with *Razor's Deep*. Every square inch of her was built of nanograph now, filled with nanites making it both self-repairing and malleable to whatever the crew needed. The boy was connected to every line of code, every nanite, and of course to the ship's central brain. He felt *Razor's Deep* like she was his own skin and bone, injured now, but still vital. Still alive. All he had to do was think a command, and the ship responded. Instantly. Faster than any human could hope to.

His own body felt impossibly sluggish by comparison. But when Braxton used that tone, it was best to answer as quickly as possible. So he made the difficult transition back to his own head and hoped he could answer fast enough.

"We were losing too much air." He forced his mouth to move, to form physical speech a null like Braxton could understand. Everything would have been easier if he'd been purchased by someone Talented, like him. But Braxton wasn't Talented. He couldn't connect his mind to ships or hear thoughts.

That was lucky, though. If Braxton could hear the boy's thoughts, he'd have spaced him a long time ago.

"I don't give a fuck. You just killed two dozen of my people!" The mercenary captain sounded angry. Fear clogged the boy's throat. He was too valuable a slave for Braxton to space, most days. But his owner acted rashly when temper controlled him. Sometimes he deprived the boy of food. Sometimes he beat him. Once, he'd dragged the boy from his alcove and all the way to the airlock, stopping just short of spacing him.

The boy considered his next words carefully. It was important not to disagree with Braxton. Even when that was what he was doing.

"Thirty-eight people are still alive." He made his voice as neutral as possible. "Forward weapons are offline. The first bombardment cracked the drive core. We have just enough air to make one space jump to the nearest waystation. If the drive can be repaired."

A dangerous silence answered him. The ship rocked as another salvo exploded, just missing the hull. A warning shot. The pirates knew they were badly damaged. Another hit could destroy the ship. They were just reminding Braxton of that, probably while they prepared a boarding party.

He held his breath; losing this battle would surely have put Braxton in one of his foulest moods. He would be looking to vent some of that rage.

On his worst days – in the darkest corners of his mind – the boy hoped it would happen. He looked outside at the stars and the cold black, and thought maybe it wouldn't be so bad to be out there. The vast emptiness held a certain appeal. Silence. Peace. No one to hurt him, no thoughts beating at his mind, no masters to be cruel or indifferent. No hunger pains.

He looked down at his small body, the spindly legs and arms. He wore an old cast off shirt from one of the crew. It was so big it dwarfed him. Braxton had him on nutritional bars for rations. "No sense wasting good food on a slave." He got one bar a day, and water to drink. If he did something extra spectacular, like help them win a major space battle, he got a plate from the regular mess as a special reward. He always ate the food slowly when that happened, savoring every bite. But that hadn't happened in a long time. Right now his skin felt stretched over bone, with little else in between. What little fat reserves he'd had were long gone, vanished as his body tried to grow in height.

The boy wasn't sure how old he was, exactly, but he thought somewhere around twelve. It seemed as though those dozen years stretched back forever, and sometimes he wasn't sure he wanted to live for twelve more.

On those days, when his thoughts seemed lost in darkness and despair weighed him down, he liked to put all of his consciousness inside the ship. Leave his empty body huddled in the tiny alcove in the engine room, a chain around one wrist attached to one of the bulkheads. He would let himself feel the frigid hull like his own skin, immersed in the silence like his head was under water. Soundless. Sightless. It was the most peaceful thing he'd ever experienced in his young life.

He imagined death was like that. He wanted to stay there forever, but no matter how hard he tried, his mind eventually fell back to his body, tugged by some invisible force he couldn't see or control.

"We're about to be boarded." Braxton's voice still sounded pissed, but there was grudging acceptance to it as well. A kind of capitulation the boy had never heard before. "Those motherless pirates are taking the ship."

Even as he spoke, the words faded from the boy's awareness. His thoughts were focusing back to *Razor's Deep* as another vessel connected to the airlock. He felt the bump of the link expanding to fit the conduit, the grind as it sealed into place.

The hatch was locked, but that didn't stop them. Heat sliced the locking mechanism. The outer door opened and he could do nothing to stop it. Unfamiliar boots thumped onto the deck.

Braxton and his people waited in the corridor for them.

If they hadn't suffered the hull breach, the boy could have urged Braxton to back off so he could seal away that part of the ship. He could have vented the air and suffocated the intruders. But he couldn't sacrifice the air that remained.

Still, he had a few tricks left.

Pull back, he told Braxton as the pirates cut through the inner airlock door. He could hear the Captain's thoughts, so loud they hurt.

The mercenary didn't like taking orders. Especially from a slave. Braxton hesitated, but then he pulled his people back to the nearest cross-corridor. It was almost too late. The pirates were already pouring into the hallway. Plasma weapons fired from both sides. Five of Braxton's people went down, but the pirates took no damage. Something the boy could neither see nor feel shielded them, absorbing or deflecting the mercenaries' weapons-fire. Intrigued, the boy focused his mind around that area for a heartbeat. But it told him nothing. They weren't carrying plasma shields. He could sense nothing touching the walls of the ship.

He didn't have time to solve the mystery. Braxton and his men were outnumbered. The boy triggered the ship's fire suppression system in the section of corridor around the pirates. The nanites responded, changing the shape of the nanograph walls to include openings and tiny nozzles. The foam sprayed all around the intruders, treating them like flames that needed to be smothered. It was sticky by nature, beginning in nearly liquid form, but quickly expanding to fill the available space.

So the boy didn't understand what was happening when the foam being sprayed onto the pirates built into a giant ball in front of them, instead of sticking to their arms and legs and filling the corridor. A second later, the growing ball shot down the corridor straight at Braxton.

The boy winced as it happened. *Impossible.* But the boy felt it happen. The ball and expanded and tangled up what remained of Braxton and his fighting crew.

"I'm going to kill you, you fucking—" Braxton's words cut off abruptly when foam filled his mouth. He gagged and spit, fighting to free himself from the sticky mess, still firing useless plasma bursts at the pirates. Most of the shots were wild, skimming off the nanograph walls. The nanites were already working hard at repairing the burns and scorch marks. The boy directed them to change shape yet again, to build a wall across the hallway and prevent the pirates from moving through. Nanograph was infinitely customizable, but it took time to form new shapes. It wouldn't be fast enough. He knew it in his heart, even as he urged the nanites to move faster.

And who have we here?

The boy froze at the sound of another voice in his head. It was unfamiliar, deep, and male. Someone like him – someone Talented – was inside his mind. He tried frantically to lock down his thoughts, to freeze like an ant that has just been noticed by a hungry spider.

No need to fear me, boy. We are alike, you and I.

The pirates were already moving past the partially formed wall. He couldn't think, couldn't focus to figure out what his next move should be. The voice in his head was such a shock it overshadowed everything else.

The boy couldn't help his curiosity. He'd never met anyone like himself before. Almost of their own accord, his thoughts reached out to the other mind. *Who are you?*

Dimly, he was aware that the fight was all but over. Braxton and his crew, snarled in the foam, were easy prey to the pirates. A few more fell, but most were disarmed.

A friend.

The boy doubted that. He didn't have any friends.

The pirates rounded up the surviving mercenaries and locked them inside the cargo hold. He could hear Braxton screaming that he was going to kill them all. But those seemed like distant events barely worthy of the boy's attention. All of his focus was on the mind connected with his. What did it want? Everyone wanted something.

My name is Kai. I'm a pirate.

The boy shrank away at those words, images filling his thoughts of everything he'd heard about the ruthless pirates who roamed fringe space. If even half of the tales were true, he'd be fortunate if they only spaced him.

Don't be afraid.

The boy could feel Kai's mind moving closer. He realized the man must be walking through the ship, trying to find him. Panicked, he started closing and locking every door, slamming them shut as fast as he could direct the nanites. He locked down the lift. What was he going to do? What *could* he do? He couldn't jump away with the drive core cracked. Besides, the pirates were already aboard. Braxton's people were locked up or dead.

Boy, stop.

The boy felt them cutting their way through doors. All of the locks in the universe would only hold for so long. He closed his eyes and began to count his breaths. A calming exercise a fellow slave once taught him.

Let me help you.

In his mind, the stranger's tone was insidious and deceptive. Why would anyone, especially a pirate, help a slave?

Even if by some miracle the pirates took what they wanted and left him here with Braxton, once the captain escaped the hold, he would blame the boy for this. For using the fire suppression system. For losing the ship.

Braxton would surely kill him this time. And the pirates would do worse. They took slaves, sometimes. He'd heard the stories. The mercenaries delighted in telling him every detail of what he could expect if the ship ever fell to pirate hands.

A fine trembling overtook his whole body. His teeth began to chatter in his skull.

Maybe he couldn't stop the pirates from getting to him, but he could stop them from hurting him. He turned his attention to the cracked drive core. It didn't have the same self-repair systems the walls and hull did. It was too complex. Emergency protocol shut it down when it took damage. But he could force it awake again. And if he did, he could start a feedback cycle that would destroy the ship.

We can help you.

It would kill him too, of course. But there was a certain peace in that.

Damn it, stop.

The boy coaxed the drive back to life, syphoning power from other systems.

Let me speak to him. Boy. This voice was new. Female. He froze, something about it so compelling that it broke through his frantic thoughts, scattering them.

My Queen, you should not be here. Kai did not sound happy, and this, too, made the boy pause and think.

There's more than one of you? The thought was a whisper that escaped his attempts to control it.

Feminine laughter filled his mind. *Of course.*

How many?

Why, all of us. The woman didn't sound mad, or worried, or coaxing. She sounded amused.

Something about her voice drew him. His heart thumped in his chest. He'd never been so scared in his life, and yet something about her calmed him better than the counting exercise. An old ghost of a memory surfaced. A woman's hand brushing his hair back from his temple. It was soothing in the way that this woman was soothing. His fear drained away. He stopped drawing power, but held the drive core poised to be flooded, just in case.

Who are you?

My name is Lilith.

Lilith. He tested her name out in his thoughts, mesmerized by it.

It is customary to exchange names when meeting someone.

I have no name. I am a slave.

Silence. The boy felt something, like a tremendous pressure. It filled the silence and he sought out the comfort of the ship's nanites in case the walls should crumple beneath the force of it. But nothing happened.

When her voice came again, Lilith sounded empty of amusement. Instead there was a complete absence of emotion. *No.*

Confused, the boy wondered if he'd missed a question someone had asked.

No what?

No, you are not *a slave. You are not nameless.*

But I am.

Not anymore. Lilith's voice held more command than any of the masters he had ever served. *You are one of us, and we do not tolerate slavery. You are free.*

The chain holding him to his alcove sheared and fell slack. He stared at it, uncomprehending as it clanged to the floor, hanging loose. It wasn't nanograph, but pure titanium, like the bulkhead it attached to. He couldn't manipulate it. Yet, something had sliced through it with the ease of a hot razor cutting wax.

A scuff of noise made him look up, and he found himself staring up at the most beautiful face he had ever seen. Two people stood before him, though the door to the engine room was still closed and locked. How did they get in? One of them was a man, tall and intimidating. He wore an armored chest piece similar to what Braxton and his mercenaries used, but it had a faint pattern the boy recognized: nanograph, but lighter and more flexible than the ship. The most expensive armor on the market. Nearly impossible to get.

The second person was a woman. Her dark hair fell in a long braid over her shoulder. She wore an armored vest and shirt, not nanograph, but the material fluid as only the most expensive armored clothing could be. Her face held a fierce, striking beauty. The boy met her startling green eyes and was enthralled. She reached a hand out to him, her skin a dusky bronze that made him think of sun-drenched planets.

He stared at her fingers, sitting immobile. His mind held to the drive core with a strange desperation. He wanted badly to take her hand. He wondered what would happen when he did.

These people have used you. Sold you for their own profit, abused your gifts. You don't belong with them. The woman's mental voice was soft, yet held more authority than all of Braxton's shouting. *You belong with us.*

Still, he hesitated. *A pirate?* His tone was dubious. He didn't want to do any of the things in the stories. He didn't want to space people or maroon them, or own his own slaves. He didn't want to hurt people unless he had to. He knew what it felt like to be hurt.

Her eyes gleamed, and he had the feeling she

was amused again. *Give us a chance. If you decide you don't want to stay, I won't force you.*

He stared into her eyes, wanting so badly to believe her.

I swear to you. If you don't wish to come with us, we will leave you here. She paused, glancing over her shoulder. The boy realized the man was speaking to her mentally. She gave a nod, then turned back to meet his gaze again. *We will even fix your drive core, so you can jump to a waystation.* Her expression hardened. *And we will remove everyone else from the ship, and give you a cut from our take.*

His suspicion deepened. No one helped a slave like him for free. *Why would you do that?*

You are like us. Talented.

He thought about that. He'd been sold for his abilities. For what he could do. If these people were like him, maybe they didn't need his Talent. Maybe they really would help him.

You don't want anything?

Only for you to be free. And safe.

He studied her. He could usually get a sense of what someone was like when he met them. But she was a contradiction. Hard, yet soft. Distant, but vibrant and warm. He thought about what she said. Even if she did everything she promised, and he made it to the waystation – even if he had credits or hard coin to start a new life – he had no idea where to go or what to do. He'd been a slave for as long as he could remember. And he felt drawn to this woman as he had never felt drawn to anyone before. She felt warm and safe. Like something forgotten, but right on the edge of his consciousness. Something he didn't know he'd been missing.

Or, you can come with us. Where, I promise you, no one will ever hurt you again. She was still holding her hand out to him. Waiting.

What would I have to do?

Her head tilted as she eyed him. *Why, learn. Learn your heritage. How to properly shield your mind and use your Talent more efficiently.* She paused, a smile widening her lips. *Learn who you really are.*

The boy swallowed. He wanted to do everything she said. But he was so afraid. He thought about the peace of the void that awaited him. His mind still held the drive core, ready to punch power into it with a thought.

Lilith waited, like she had all the time in the universe. The man behind her shifted, looking uncomfortable. His stance over the woman was protective. Worried.

She was important. Not someone who should be waiting on a nobody like him. Kai had called her a queen. The boy looked down at his own grimy fingers, his skin pale beneath the layer of dirt and bruises, the nails bitten to the quick. A tightness filled his chest and his breath hitched. For a horrible moment he thought he might cry, and he knew if he did he wouldn't be able to bear the humiliation.

"Sebastian," said Lilith.

The boy looked up, his eyes darting to the man, but he wasn't moving. She wasn't talking to him. "What?" he asked out loud. His voice cracked.

She smiled at him, and it was the most glorious

thing he'd ever seen. "Your name. It will be Sebastian, if you like."

The man behind her made a noise. His chin lifted in obvious surprise.

"It was my father's name." There was something in Lilith's voice. An echo of sadness. "A good name for a strong man."

The tightness in the boy's chest expanded.

"Sebastian." It felt strange as his tongue shaped the name. *His* name. Tears blurred his vision, and he dropped his hold on the drive core, letting it go silent and dead once more. When he moved, it was in a clumsy lunge forward to grasp Lilith's fingers before she changed her mind. Her touch was warm, firm, but not painful. She took his hand like he was an equal.

"I like that name," he said, ducking his head so she wouldn't see his tears.

Lilith pulled him to his feet. She smiled at him as though he was the most important person in the universe.

"Welcome home, Sebastian."

Mercy nursed her drink and tried not to fidget. She didn't want to risk moving too much and getting any of the sticky, unidentifiable residue clinging to the table and chairs transferred onto her. Even a place as shady as the Birn waystation had access to cleaning drones. Why the hell didn't they use them? It might not officially qualify as a colony, but that didn't mean they had to live in filth.

The cheap ale hit her tongue, a wash of bitterness with a sour aftertaste. Mercy glared down at the glass, wondering how long she'd have to continue drinking it. The pirates and their high quality goods were clearly making her soft.

"Try to act less like you hate every second of this." Her best friend, Atrea, eyed her from across the table, a glint of amusement in her blue eyes. "I can remember a time when a trip to Birn was exciting."

"When we were fifteen, sure." Mercy forced herself to relax back into her seat, trying to look as casual as the handful of people scattered at similar tables around them. "The thrill has faded."

Atrea covered a laugh by sipping her own questionable glass of ale. She didn't even grimace, a feat Mercy couldn't quite manage. The two of them were in the spaceport bar, a place characterized by its bad beer, worse food, and the lingering smell of unwashed bodies, layered with the more prevalent burnt-metal odor that clung to any ship venturing through space. Most spaceports and stations had air recyclers that dealt with the worst of the smell, but this place either didn't have any, or hadn't bothered servicing them in a few dozen years.

Birn was positioned in the Toth system, on the furthest edge of Commonwealth controlled space. Little more than a waystation, it officially existed to provide refueling and a few supplies for the sanctioned merchants who traveled out this far, those few who ventured to trade with the Commonwealth's most distant colony worlds. Unofficially, it provided refueling and a thriving black market for smugglers, mercenaries, and pirates.

It was a pit, a place where dubious deals were made and mercenaries went to be hired. Which made it the closest thing to neutral territory between the Commonwealth of Sovereign Planets and pirate-controlled space. But it still technically fell within Commonwealth borders. A fact that made a lot of the less official visitors uneasy. Including Mercy.

Fortunately, this wasn't her first time visiting a place like this. She'd lived for several years as a smuggler beside Atrea and her father, Wolfgang, before rejoining her pirate family a few months ago. Both she and Atrea wore armored clothing, and were visibly armed. Every so often, Mercy would meet the gaze of one of the shadier sorts sharing the waystation, and tap her fingers on the grip of the disruptor holstered against her hip. Just to let them know she was aware of them.

No easy marks here.

Atrea was armed to the teeth, of course. And not with a standard disruptor, either. She preferred weapons of her own design, antique metal throwers she'd built herself. They were limited in ammunition, but the wounds they left were messy, bloody things. Getting hit with one tended to shock and terrify people, even if it failed to kill with the first shot. As a backup, Atrea carried a disruptor modified to be deadly. She wore her weapons openly, in holsters that had the worn look of long use.

When she wanted to, Atrea could appear completely guileless and non-threatening. She was small and delicate looking, with an ethereal beauty holo stars paid a lot of hard coin to try and achieve. Her blue eyes could be hard and steely, or wide and naïve. Men often seemed driven to try and protect her, which Mercy found amusing. But right now, Atrea's blond hair was braided back, and she occupied her seat with a casual confidence. From the moment they'd stepped off the ship and onto Birn's soil, she'd radiated a dominance that clearly said "fuck with me at your own peril".

Mercy wasn't quite as good at projecting that aura as her friend, but she had something Atrea didn't. With her Talent, she could put pressure on the minds around them to turn their attention elsewhere. Once, it would have taken all of her concentration. But she'd spent the last few months working hard on her telepathy. She found that now she could maintain the pressure with little thought, so that most of the furtive glances skipped right past them and landed somewhere else. No one was mistaking either of them as targets of opportunity, if their gazes lingered at all.

Of course, maybe the location wasn't entirely responsible for Mercy's nerves.

"You want to talk about it?"

Damn, Atrea knew her too well.

"No." Mercy moved her gaze over the room, but she still didn't see or sense any other Talented individuals. Only Atrea and herself. Everyone else was head blind. Nulls with no psychic ability at all.

"Sure. Just wallow in misery and tension over there." Atrea took another drink.

"I'm not tense. Or miserable." Mercy forced her fingers to relax where they gripped her glass.

Atrea laughed, a low sound that didn't carry past their table. "Please. You hate this place. Part of you hates what we're about to do. And you really, really hate that we had to sneak away to do it. Besides, we both know he's going to be seriously pissed."

Mercy lifted a shoulder. "So I went against the king's order. Cannon will get over it."

"Will he? I'm not so sure. And we both know I wasn't talking about Cannon."

Mercy winced. Yes, Reaper was going to be seriously pissed off. Not only had she defied

Cannon and the Core – which included her consort, Reaper – but she'd snuck away from the pirates like a thief in the night, stealing a ship and putting herself in the path of their greatest enemies.

She took an extra-large swallow of the terrible ale, choking the vile stuff down where it sat in her stomach and burned like acid.

"If they'd only listened to reason, I wouldn't have had to steal a ship to be here. But none of them are exactly objective."

"That's true." Though she was speaking to Mercy, Atrea's attention was focused outward, on the room around them. She'd grown up working her father's ship as a smuggler, and after that spent several years in the Commonwealth Navy. Security was second nature to her. "But pissing off a Killer is probably a bad idea, even if he is your lover."

"Reaper would never hurt me."

Atrea cocked one blond brow. "You mean like you would never hurt him? You know, by lying to him and sneaking away to put yourself in the hands of the people who tried to kill you a few months ago?"

Mercy glared across the table at her. "I didn't lie to him. Not directly. And you know what I mean. He would never hurt me physically."

"Maybe. But there's still going to be hell to pay when we go back."

Mercy chose to ignore that statement. "Besides, Veritas can't hurt me anymore."

"Just because they can't directly kill you doesn't mean they can't get creative." Atrea tilted her head thoughtfully. "Although you are a lot safer now that you're their Queen. I suppose you could just force them to obey and we could all go home early."

Mercy shifted in her seat, nervous fingers adjusting her collar. She didn't like being reminded that claiming the Talented meant she could control them. She hated that aspect of her power.

"I'm not going to do that."

Atrea shrugged. "It was just a thought."

Having been tortured and almost killed by them herself, Atrea had no love for the organization of Talented who called themselves Veritas.

"You're my friend. Aren't you supposed to be supportive, instead of kicking my ass?"

"A real friend tells you the truth, even if it hurts."

Mercy couldn't argue with that, and her mood slid from anxious into dread. To say that the pirates were overprotective would be a massive understatement. Cannon, Dem, Treon, all of the members of their ruling body, the Core, and especially Reaper, dogged her steps even on board their flagship, *Nemesis*. The one visit she'd made to one of their colony worlds had turned into a ridiculous affair of armed guards and absolutely zero time to herself to enjoy or explore it.

Part of her understood. She was too valuable to lose. The pirates needed a queen, and she was the only one they had. The rest of her was beginning to suffocate under the constant supervision.

"I'm just saying," Atrea said with a shrug, "Veritas made the choices that got us all here. And when someone chooses conflict again and again, chances are it's going to be hard for them to choose peace without a really compelling reason."

"No one said this was going to be easy."

Descendants of psychically gifted soldiers, the pirates' ancestors were created to fight a war that ended more than a century ago. Once the war was over, the new government didn't know what to do with their army of psychically enhanced soldiers. In the end, they decided it was too dangerous to let them live. Most of the Talented fled Commonwealth space and gathered on the fringes, turning pirate to survive. Others scattered within the Commonwealth itself, going underground. They called themselves Veritas, and decades later, they had infiltrated the most successful corporations, and every facet of the Commonwealth government.

Some said they controlled the monarchy itself.

One would think the two factions of Talented would get along, but that wasn't the case. Veritas viewed the pirates as rivals, a dangerous threat to their power. They spent years trying to wipe out their brethren, nearly succeeding. Their history included everything from furious space battles to unleashing a deadly bio weapon.

The bad blood between the two groups ran deep.

"Come on, I'm sure it won't be that bad. Stop looking like you're about to cry into your beer." Atrea's voice reminded Mercy that this was not the time for dwelling on the past. She scowled at her drink.

"If I cry, it'll be because this stuff is so awful."

"We've had worse."

A smile tugged at Mercy's lips. "Sure. I think it was even when we came here. The old Wolf let us order drinks, and we were so damn proud, we choked the vile things down." She shook her head. "Nice to see they haven't improved over the years."

Atrea's face didn't soften, but Mercy could see the humor in her eyes. "Yeah. I'm sure Dad had a good laugh at our expense."

Wolfgang's parenting style had often involved self-inflicted consequences. Mercy winced, thinking of him now. He was going to be just as angry as everyone else about this. Maybe more. Things had been strained between Atrea and her father lately, and guilt snuck in as Mercy considered how this could impact them. It wasn't just her own relationships at stake here.

Well, in for a credit, out hard coin as the saying went. This wasn't a choice either of them had made lightly.

"Have you given any thought to what we're going to do if they don't show up?" Atrea finally voiced Mercy's biggest fear. That all of this would be for nothing.

"They'll show. They're the ones who wanted this summit."

Atrea cocked her head. "Do two people really count as a summit?"

"I'm Queen, right? I mean, Cannon's always after me to step up and really embrace the role."

"I'm pretty certain this isn't what he had in mind."

So was Mercy.

When Veritas requested a meeting to discuss peace and cooperation between the two groups of

Talented, none of the pirates had been willing to entertain the idea. They immediately assumed it was a trap of some kind. Over a decade ago, Veritas unleashed a bioweapon that nearly destroyed the pirates, killing eighty percent of the female population. In the process everyone lost someone they loved. Mothers, daughters, sisters, wives. Then, just a few months ago they tried to take control of the pirates with a queen of their own, an unstable young girl cloned from Mercy's own genetic material. They almost succeeded.

A queen controlled a population of Talented by claiming them as hers. It was a kind of psychic bond. Through it, the Talented gained a connection they needed in order to feel whole. The downside was, an unscrupulous queen could then rule them through mental influence, manipulation, or outright control. Mercy overrode Rani's bond with her own, claiming the pirates – and everyone else – as hers. Technically, the Talented members of Veritas were just as much her people as the pirates.

Not that the pirates wanted to admit to that.

But facts were facts. Mercy wasn't exactly a fan of Veritas, either. They'd held her captive for a time and forced her to hurt her best friend. They'd taken control of the pirates and tried to kill Mercy. But the man responsible for both of those actions, Willem Frain, was dead. Things had changed. Mercy couldn't explain how, but she just knew it. She'd been feeling a low but constant mental pull for weeks. She'd told Reaper about it, and then Cannon. Both of them had been pleased, thinking the bond between members of Veritas and Mercy would mean an automatic end to future hostilities. That was good enough, as far as they were concerned. They had no interest in negotiating any further terms. Everyone wanted Mercy to just ignore the pull she felt.

Which was pretty damn short sighted.

The door to the waystation bar opened, and Mercy went still. She felt it – the warm, golden presence of another Talented mind. Just one, which was odd. Surely, Veritas would send more than one representative.

Then she realized she knew the person that mind belonged to. The mental signature was familiar. Her stomach dropped and she sat up straight in her chair before he entered the bar.

"What?" Atrea was already turning her head, following Mercy's gaze as the man stepped into the room. "Aw, hell."

Cannon was many things: a friend, Mercy's cousin, and the current pirate king. He also fit right in with this crowd. Mercy had never seen him wear anything heavier than armored clothing, and usually he didn't even bother with that. Right now he was dressed more like a merc than a pirate. A chestplate was strapped over a skintight black shirt she was pretty sure was threaded with thin nanofilament armor. It clung to his muscular arms while the chestplate made him appear even bigger than usual. His pants were standard armored clothing, but he also wore a belt with a scabbard down one leg and a holster down the other. One held a vibroblade, and the other a P266 plasma pistol. Illegal in most systems.

The dark color of his clothing seemed to

swallow the usual brightness of his green eyes, making them hard and indeterminate in color. Or maybe that was just the bad lighting in this place, and the anger that Mercy could see in the set of his mouth. He'd pulled back his shoulder length dark hair, but a few strands framed the stubbled chisel of his jaw in a way that screamed "scoundrel".

As he crossed the room to their table, Mercy tried desperately to think of what to say. She should start with an apology, explain why she'd stolen a ship and snuck away, and her reasons for why this summit was so important. Calm. Reason. Logic.

Cannon dragged another chair to their table and sat, his arms folded across his chest. His mental shields were so tight she couldn't get a hint of what he might be thinking, and his expression was no help.

She took a deep breath, words tumbling around in her head. "Tell me you didn't bring *Nemesis*, and there isn't a stolen Commonwealth flagship sitting in orbit over this waystation."

Atrea glanced at her, a quick startled look. And no, that hadn't been an apology. Maybe Cannon wasn't the only one pissed off.

He smiled, a small, grim movement. "And what did you expect us to do? Our Queen went running off to meet our greatest enemies in what is most assuredly a trap. And you didn't bother taking a single guard with you."

"Hey." Atrea's brows drew together.

Cannon spared her a glance. "You can't even properly shield yet. At least you had the forethought to wear that." He pointed to the Talent inhibitor on Atrea's neck, the patch nullifying her gifts and shielding her from attacks by other Talented. Then he was back to looking at Mercy. It would have been a lot easier to be mad at him if he yelled, or glared, or did something to tell her just how angry he was. This unnatural calm was disturbing.

And it reminded her of someone else. Anxiety rolled through her stomach. She didn't sense any other minds, but she couldn't believe Cannon would come here alone.

"Is Reaper with you?"

Cannon relaxed back into his chair, the tension going out of his big frame as though it had never been there. His lips twitched into what might have been a genuine smile, and Mercy's heart gave a hard thud in her chest.

Reaper was definitely here somewhere. But so closed off she couldn't feel him. That was not a good sign. Not at all.

"Damn it." She held on to anger and defiance to push back the unease. "I'm not leaving."

"Did I say we were leaving?"

Why did that perfectly reasonable tone make her want to lash out?

"Well, you sure as hell didn't want me coming here."

"I did not. But now we *are* here. For better or worse."

Mercy relaxed. At least it wasn't going to be a fight. She was tired of fighting about it. That was what pushed her into doing something this reckless to begin with. When words proved ineffective, action was the only recourse she had left.

Cannon swept a hand over the table and a screen popped up with menu options. When it looked like he was going to order something, Mercy pushed her glass across to him.

"Here, you can have mine."

He eyed her, then it. Took a cautious drink. Like Mercy, he couldn't hide his grimace. "You know, I'd step down in a heartbeat if you asked. No need to poison me."

"Funny."

He pushed the glass back to her. "I'm serious."

"I don't want your job, Cannon."

Atrea huffed out a laugh, shaking her head. "The two of you. The ale isn't that bad. You're just spoiled by that Thalian stuff you have on *Nemesis*."

Cannon said something back, but Mercy didn't hear it. Her mind was awash with the bright, warm feeling of Talented minds. A dozen, at least. Like basking in the sun on a summer beach. Her whole body relaxed, tension draining away. She closed her eyes, pushing past the pleasant side-effect to study the new minds. Unfamiliar. She didn't know a single one.

She opened her eyes to find Cannon and Atrea staring at her, both of them silent. The new group of Talented moved closer. Cannon lifted a brow in unspoken question. Mercy gave a nod, pushing her chair back.

"They're here."

CHAPTER TWO

*C*annon might have fit in with the rest of Birn's crowd, but the people from Veritas did not. It wasn't just how they were dressed, though that played a role. Corporate business attire had no place in a waystation on the edge of Commonwealth space. Their dress, their attitude, the sleek weapons they carried. Everything about them screamed that they didn't belong.

Silence descended in the bar the moment they walked through the doors. The agents of Veritas wore authority like it was just another suit. At the table next to Mercy, a man in merc armor eased his hand onto the grip of an illegal sidearm. Chairs slid back as others made similar moves, creating space in anticipation of a fight. Those at the bar slid down to the far end, opening what Mercy suspected was a clean line of fire from the bartender to the door.

If someone so much as clinks a glass, Mercy thought, *this is going to go badly. Cannon?*

I'm already on it.

Cannon was an empath. He could influence

emotions. What he did was subtle, because the tension didn't leave the room, but that knife edge of violence faded. A few people even went back to their drinks, though with a certain wariness.

Thank you.

Of course, my Queen.

Mercy shot him a glare. He *knew* she hated that. He just smirked.

The bartender continued filling mugs of ale, but one handed. His other hand had disappeared beneath the bar, and Mercy would have bet money that he was gripping a weapon. Or calling spaceport security. At Birn, "security" officials were all bought and paid for by the black market coin that passed through the system.

Well, maybe this wasn't the best place for a peace summit. But it was the only one both sides had agreed to. She sighed.

Nine people filled the doorway, and in the lead was one of the most beautiful women Mercy had ever seen. It was the kind of perfection that didn't happen without body alteration or genetic tinkering. Her long dark hair was coiled at the nape of her neck, pulled back from a face that should have adorned holo vids across the galaxies. Her cosmetics were done with a light hand, meant to highlight the perfection of bone structure and creamy skin, rather than hide any flaws. She had eyes an unnatural shade of jade green. Bio tech. It made Mercy wonder what else the woman had altered. Surely not the color alone; if she could afford that kind of enhancement, she probably had cybernetics as well.

The woman looked around the room, and

smiled. It was an expression of such superiority and condescension that it reminded Mercy of Willem Frain. Also an agent of Veritas, Willem had once held Mercy and Atrea captive for several weeks. He'd worn that same smirk more than once. Filled with arrogance, it said more clearly than words that nothing in the room intimidated this woman.

Her gaze lingered briefly on Mercy and Cannon, then moved on to sweep the rest of the bar.

She looked - and acted - like a representative of the Commonwealth. Not a merchant, not security. A government official. The sort of trouble smugglers and pirates especially didn't like. In a place like Birn, someone like that could disappear. This far out on the fringes, anything could happen. And by the time the Commonwealth investigated, no trace would be left to find.

If she twitched wrong, someone was going to start shooting. The man beside Mercy eased his gun from its holster.

"Leave," the woman said. Talent swept out from her, accompanying the word, a ripple that washed through the room.

Chairs scraped as hardened mercs rose from their seats and quietly, efficiently exited the room. The man beside Mercy stood, his weapon held down at his side. He walked right past the woman without looking at her again.

Every null in the place got up and walked out, blank faced and silent as drones. Even the bartender left, a partially filled glass of ale quickly overflowing from the dispensary at the bar, to spill foamed alcohol onto the floor. The strong smell of beer mixed in with the rest of the reek permeating the room to create an even less appealing miasma.

The woman and her entourage stepped farther into the room, walking casually over to the tables nearest to Mercy and Cannon. There were nine altogether. Two stayed by the door. Others arrayed themselves at tables nearby, while the woman stopped and eyed them with one perfectly shaped brow arched.

"Confident, aren't they?" Atrea kept the words pitched low as the three of them stood.

"I was going to say arrogant." Mercy didn't trouble to keep her own voice low. Forcing nulls to leave the area was a flashy move, one meant to show their power. But nulls were far more susceptible to influence. Mercy wasn't impressed.

She glanced at Cannon, but his face was carefully blank. He said nothing. He kept his gaze focused on the new arrivals, so much so that Mercy wondered if he'd met them before. There was a stillness about him that reminded her once again of Reaper, a predatory feel she just wasn't used to from the man who portrayed himself as the affable pirate king.

It was a good reminder that one of Cannon's best tools was his ability to charm people into forgetting just how dangerous he could be. No one came to rule a powerful, violent people like the pirates without being ruthless.

Mercy swept a quick look over the Veritas group again. She didn't want to be taken by surprise. But they seemed to be waiting, like the woman who clearly led them. Mercy realized suddenly that there were more women than men in the group, and she wondered if it was a deliberate ploy to irritate the pirates. Not a good negotiation tactic, if so.

The woman took a single step forward, now that Mercy, Atrea, and Cannon were standing. It was close enough to Cannon that she was inside his personal space. Close enough to show she didn't consider him a threat. She barely spared him a glance before her gaze moved beyond him to Mercy.

It was a move that took serious guts, taking her attention away from him while standing well within range of whatever he might do, be it physical or mental. Mercy wasn't so sure she would have risked it.

"I am Feria Navarro, a member of the Veritas security council. We have come to negotiate terms." The woman spoke directly to Mercy.

"For what?" Cannon asked, and the woman's gaze moved with some reluctance back to him. There was an uncomfortable silence, marked with tension. Cannon's posture was casual, but for once it fooled no one. There was nothing casual about this meeting.

Finally, Feria sighed, an exhale of irritation. "So, you would have him speak in your stead? Very well."

"Surely, you have files on the most influential pirates." Mercy nodded to Cannon, where he'd leaned his big frame against the table, arms crossed. "I'm sure I don't need to introduce you to our King."

"An empty title." The woman's lips twitched, a

barely perceptible sneer. "You are a queen. Your will rules. Not his."

"Well now," Cannon drawled the words. He'd donned his indolent persona. "I think I take exception to that."

The four men and women at Feria's back shifted position, but stopped instantly at some unseen command from her. They were not as confident as they wished to appear. Nor as dismissive. Cannon was a threat, and they knew it.

Feria gave him a cold smile that Mercy could only call predatory. "We did a full sweep of the area when we docked. You don't think we've identified all of your people?"

Cannon laughed, a sound of genuine amusement. "Oh, I know you haven't. But you should be less worried about them, and more worried about us, right here in this room."

Feria made a show of looking the three of them over. "A queen is a dangerous force, I'll grant you that. But Mercy is inexperienced and largely untrained." She waved a hand at Atrea. "That one is little better than a null. And you?" She leaned forward, so close to Cannon it looked almost intimate. "What good is an empath here?"

Mercy fought not to show her surprise. Cannon didn't advertise his Talent for sensing emotions, preferring that people see him as a telepath and telekinetic, the two most common gifts among the Talented. But he'd used his empathy for years to help regulate the pirates' penchant for violence, keeping his people as balanced as possible without the influence of a queen. The fact that Feria knew about it meant Veritas was very well informed.

How does she know that? She sent Cannon the question on the tightest of threads. Her shields and his were completely locked down, but she and Cannon trusted one another. That trust made it possible for them to communicate through those shields.

I don't know. A spy. Someone close enough to know my secrets. His mental voice was grim. Mercy knew from previous conversations with him that a Veritas spy among them was a likely scenario. This just confirmed it, and brought it a lot closer to home than they'd expected.

"You're right." Cannon spread his hands in a gesture of acceptance. "I am an empath. Perhaps not the most ideal Talent for a combat situation, but certainly good for a negotiation. Isn't that why we are all here?"

Feria considered him. "Yes. Let us negotiate, then." She looked at Mercy. "We wish you to rescind your claiming."

Surprise, surprise. Cannon's mental voice lacked the thread of amusement Mercy might have expected. He sounded bitter. Angry, but controlled.

Cannon, I wouldn't even know how to take back the claiming.

I know. Don't worry, you won't need to. They don't want to be connected to you? My heart bleeds.

Out loud, he said, "And what will you offer in return?"

Feria tilted her head. "We would be willing to agree to a ten-year cease of all hostilities with you and the pirate territories. As a show of how serious we are, we have combed our ranks for volunteers, those willing to donate genetic material for your attempts at repopulation. In exchange, we want Mercy to rescind the claim – and you will release Rani back into our custody."

Electricity moved through Mercy, a flash of heat and alarm that was almost painful.

"No." The refusal was out before she knew she was going to speak. Rani was the broken teenage queen Willem Frain had used to try and take control of the pirates. She was created from Mercy's own genetic material. Currently, she resided in stasis, hidden away on Ardon, the pirates' primary colony world.

Everyone looked at Mercy, even Cannon.

"There is no way I'm releasing that girl back into your custody. Willem – maybe all of you – created her to be a tool, and treated her like one. Manipulated her. Abused her. I am not putting her back into your hands. Ever."

Mercy. Cannon sounded exasperated. *This isn't a good way to negotiate. You don't draw a hard line and tell the other side what you aren't willing to give up.*

I don't care. My answer won't change.

But they didn't need to know that yet.

She looked at him and shrugged. Cannon rolled his eyes at her before turning back to Feria. "It seems the girl is non-negotiable."

Feria's lips pressed into a thin line. "Then why are we even here? I was told you would negotiate in good faith."

"And so far, I haven't heard you offering anything worth considering. A cease fire? Genetic material? Please. Do you think we would trust any material you gave us? And we already have an end to hostilities, courtesy of your new allegiance to our Queen." Cannon made the word an official title, the emphasis clear as he favored Feria with a mocking smile.

Feria's face remained expressionless, but a spark of impatience and anger lit those brilliant eyes. "Without the girl, Mercy could reclaim us whenever she wished. We need our own queen to stand apart from you and yours."

"That does sound like a problem." Cannon stroked a hand over his jaw. "Not ours, though. So far, all I'm hearing is what *you* need. I'm not feeling all that inclined to continue this conversation."

Feria stared him down, clearly frustrated. Her gaze flickered beyond him to Mercy, as though expecting her to override him. "You don't even want to be bound to us. You think we can't feel how little regard you have for our people?"

Mercy stiffened, and Atrea's hand brushed against hers, a silent warning. She struggled to control the surge of anger that rose with Feria's words. Was she just supposed to forget everything Veritas had done?

"You can't be serious." Mercy stepped around the table to stand beside Cannon, and everyone in the room readjusted. Atrea moved to stand at her back, and the people arrayed with Feria tensed. Two of them stood from the chairs they'd occupied.

It was clear they considered Mercy the largest threat.

Which meant they weren't yet aware of

Reaper's presence. Mercy felt his approach like an imminent storm, the cold radiance of power unmistakable, even among the brilliant flames of other minds with him. His dogs. The unit of specially trained men who followed him. Mercy could feel them moving around the building, taking up positions just outside. No one but a queen could feel Talent like Mercy did.

Reaper...

He didn't answer her with words, but she felt the brush of his mind, the cold touch of the killer like a chill wind. The warmth of the man who shared her bed had disappeared completely beneath his Talent. Born with the ability to kill with a thought, Reaper looked at people and saw the most efficient way to kill them. He saw every hidden vulnerability, every possible outcome. He spent most of his life unable to emotionally connect with others, his own feelings turning to ice each time he invoked his Talent. He'd probably already evaluated how he would kill every Veritas agent here.

Most people had a healthy fear of killers like Reaper. But Mercy had never feared him. From the moment they met, when he could have killed her but chose not to, she'd trusted him. That trust had never been misplaced. Now they were lovers, and Mercy had chosen him as her consort, a formalized bond. For some, it was akin to a marriage. Mercy wasn't quite sure what it meant for them.

As much as she dreaded a conversation about her actions, Reaper's presence calmed her. That chill touch of his mind was a wash of relief that cooled her anger. When she and Atrea stole that ship and left *Nemesis,* some insecurity deep within Mercy made her fear she would never see him again. It was irrational, but she couldn't control it. However much they might disagree on certain issues, she loved Reaper, and part of her would always be terrified of losing him. Of losing everyone she cared about.

As she'd lost her mother.

Feeling him now centered her, allowed her to regain control of her emotions and stop the flood of angry words she's been about to impart. She took a breath and re-evaluated.

"You're right." She met Feria's eyes. "I didn't choose to claim you. But it happened, and you're also wrong. I do care about what happens to you and *all* of the Talented. Not just the pirates. If we're going to survive, we have to learn to work together. This fighting, it's doing the Commonwealth's work for them. We are unique in all of the universe. Our Talent makes us rare. Science may have created us, but we can't figure out how. The records of those early experiments were either destroyed, or they're in some top secret facility deep in the core worlds, locked away where they'll never be found again."

"*You* can recreate it." Feria looked pointedly at Atrea, and Mercy felt her anger surge again.

So, Willem's work was well known. Mercy had hoped he'd been acting on his own, a rogue element. But clearly, Veritas knew who Atrea was, and they knew what Willem had forced Mercy to do to her. Awakening Atrea's latent Talent had nearly killed her best friend. Mercy never wanted to do anything like it again.

She stepped forward, putting herself into Feria's personal space. "Listen, you—"

This time, it was Cannon's hand on her arm. *Don't. You risked a lot to get us here. Do you really want to let emotion cloud your purpose?*

No, she didn't, no matter how tempting it might be. But it was time to stop fucking around.

"Believe it or not, I'm here because I was worried about you. All of you." Mercy waved a hand to include all of the people Feria brought with her. "I can feel you. The claiming pulls at me, and it's getting stronger. My theory is, the more chaotic and volatile your emotions, the stronger the pull will be." She paused. "And the more you fight the claiming, the more chaotic everything gets. Something needs to change before it gets worse."

"Just what are you proposing?" Feria's body language was stiff, her tone bitter. "You think we should just accept you?" She laughed; a dark sound. "Give up everything we've built and run away to turn pirate?"

"No. But surely working together makes more sense than the last one hundred years."

"You don't even know why we hate them, do you?" Feria looked from Mercy to Cannon. "You didn't tell her?"

"She knows our history."

"Your side, you mean."

Cannon, what's she talking about?

Hell if I know.

Feria folded her arms. "He told you, what? About the decree from the monarchy outlawing Talent? The great exodus to flee civilization? Some story about how we've persecuted and hunted them ever since?"

"You have," said Cannon, his tone so unnaturally even and controlled that Mercy knew he had to be leashing a lot of emotion behind it.

"No." Feria shook her head. "We were content to ignore you, but you wouldn't leave well enough alone. Every day, every hour, my great-grandparents had to fight to remain free."

"I don't know what the hell you're talking about," Cannon said. "But no matter what happened more than a century into the past, it doesn't excuse the bioweapon you used against us eleven years ago."

Mercy didn't know how he managed to sound so calm. The virus, Matera-D, was a biological weapon Veritas had tricked the pirates into taking. From its original hosts, it quickly spread through the pirate colonies and fleet. It was fatal to Talented women, and killed thousands before the pirates managed to isolate it. Cannon lost his mother and sisters.

"The intention of the virus was never widespread death." Feria's voice was stiff, the tone of someone who felt guilt but wasn't going to admit to it. "It was engineered to attack the specific genome of a queen—"

"Funny." Cannon cut her off. "The woman who helped create it is one of us now, and she tells a different story."

Shock turned Feria's face pale. After a moment, she rallied. "Sanah is with you? And her sister, Nayla?"

Cannon waited a beat before answering. Mercy

thought he was deciding how much to tell them. "They are. They have been. And don't act like you didn't know."

"We didn't." Feria's face was so bloodless, her unnatural eyes almost appeared to glow, their color luminous. "They just disappeared. Their brother stole a ship and disappeared a day later. We never heard from them again. Our farseers couldn't get more than glimpses. Please—"

"Sanah and Nayla are fine." Cannon cut her off again. "Niall, on the other hand…" He was referring to Sanah's brother.

Why would their spy report that you're an empath, Mercy asked, *but not share that Sanah and her sister had defected to you?* Whatever else she might be lying about, Feria's shock seemed genuine. Sanah and her younger sister, Nayla, had defected to the pirates five years ago. They lived among them now. Sanah had a husband and daughter.

I have no idea, Cannon said.

"You killed Niall?" Feria asked, her tone accusing.

"Yes. He tried to take Nayla back against her will." Cannon didn't mention the people who died in Niall's effort. "We protect what's ours."

"Which is exactly the point I'm trying to make." Mercy put a hand on Cannon's arm, and felt the tension in the flex of muscle beneath her fingers. This conversation needed to get back on track. If they kept getting sidelined by everything that had ever happened between the pirates and Veritas, they'd never get anywhere. "I believe you should rethink—"

Cannon's arm went rigid beneath her hand half

a second before Feria's eyes widened and her people closed ranks around her. She sliced the air with an angry sweep of her hand.

"This negotiation is over."

"What—?" Mercy didn't finish the question as a ripple of Talent went out from one of Feria's people, and a telekinetic shield went up around the Veritas group. They were backing toward the door. Had they sensed Reaper?

Cannon, what the hell is going on?

Another ship just jumped in.

One of ours?

No. He looked at her. *A Monarch-class. Not Nemesis.*

The Commonwealth Navy was here.

CHAPTER THREE

An explosion of Talent blinded Mercy for an instant. She heard the scrape of the door open and the strangled sound of someone gasping for breath. Then came a pained grunt and the thud of a body hitting the ground.

Mercy knew what had happened before her vision cleared. She blinked against the spots dancing in front of her eyes, and the scene coalesced. The Veritas agents beside the door were down, and Feria and her people had rallied behind their telekinetic wall, weapons drawn, Talent a breath from being unleashed.

Reaper, we can't be the first to draw blood!

He never even glanced at her. But his voice, cold and detached, slid through her thoughts.

They're still breathing.

He stood in the doorway, backlit by the orange-gold light of Toth, the star that Birn orbited. It was approaching dusk. Toth was setting as Birn continued its daily rotation, bathing everything in a harsh glow. He stepped inside the room, and everyone took a collective step back.

Everyone except Cannon and Mercy.

Reaper wore only the lightest armored clothing, his black shirt a second skin like Cannon's, long sleeved, with nanofilament armor woven into the fabric. Lean and athletic, he moved with the consummate grace of a predator, radiating a barely leashed intensity that touched the primal part of the brain. People drew back from him instinctively, understanding on an instinctive level that a killer walked among them. His dark hair was cut short, his skin a tawny shade that only intensified the color of his eyes. And his eyes were ice; nearly colorless, an indication that his Talent was active.

Fear and tension swept the room, but Mercy felt only relief. And a slight annoyance.

This is a peace summit. We're supposed to be negotiating with these people.

Reaper met her eyes, the impact of his gaze hitting her like a physical blow. He said nothing, and the weight of his silence said more than any words he might have uttered. She sucked in a breath.

Yes, Reaper was angry with her.

Feria stepped forward, hands clenched into fists at her side. "You had no right!"

Reaper ignored her, his gaze still focused on Mercy. "You need to get out of here."

"We all do."

"Yes." Reaper stepped over the prone form at his feet, walking toward her with purpose. "But right this second, it's going to be you."

One of his dogs flanked him, Jaxon. He wore the uniform of the dog units, the black armored clothing with colored accents along the high collar and sleeves. Reaper's unit was blue. Jax had shaggy brown hair that always looked unruly, like a child had decided to hack at it. He watched Reaper's back, but it was less to protect his boss, and more to keep anyone else from dying.

She took a step back as they approached. "I'm not going anywhere without the rest of you."

Yes, you are. Reaper's mental voice was implacable. He'd used the same tone when telling her there would be no negotiation with Veritas. She glared at him, just as determined now as she'd been then.

Sleeping with me doesn't give you the right to order me around.

No. But I will protect you, whether you want me to or not.

That had been made clear many times in the course of their relationship. All of the pirates were on the overprotective side, having lost so many dear to them. Mercy tried to be reasonable, but it was difficult to reason with emotion.

Why can't we all leave together? We can take the same ship. She and Atrea had taken a Viking to get here, a dropship that could be returned to *Nemesis* with a preset slave sequence.

Too risky. You won't be leaving via ship.

Then how...?

A flash of Talent and suddenly Dem was standing in the room. Tall and imposing, he was impeccably dressed in a pale gray suit, the color stark against the darkness of his skin. Dem had the same blue eyes as his brother, but he and Reaper had different fathers. The eyes were the only physical similarity between them.

Feria's people reacted. A disruptor flash went off at the same time that Talent lashed out, both splashing harmlessly against a telekinetic shield that covered Dem from head to toe, vibrating only an inch from his powerful frame.

Reaper's brother was the security chief aboard *Nemesis*. He was also a formidable telekinetic and teleporter.

"A teleporter?" Feria's tone was bitter. "You really think the worst of us, don't you? We asked for this meeting. Did you really think we'd come here to attack you?"

That was a matter of some debate. The very fact that Mercy was a queen who had claimed them made an attack not just unlikely, but very nearly impossible. On the other hand, as Reaper had pointed out more than once, there was always a way.

Mercy shook her head, remaining silent. She had a feeling there was nothing she could say at this point that Feria would listen to. She ignored the other woman as Dem took a step toward her.

"No. No way." She looked around at each of them. Cannon, Atrea, Jaxon, and Reaper. "I'm not leaving you."

Cannon stepped forward. "Mercy. In minutes, the Commonwealth Navy will be landing dropships on this station. Even now they're bringing in a fleet to blockade the system. *Nemesis* needs to leave now, while they still can. You are our queen." He paused, and his tone softened. "You must go with them."

She stared at him, then at Reaper, standing close beside her. She put her hand on his arm, desperation making the grip harder than she intended. *Please don't make me leave you. You're only here because of me.*

Reaper pulled her into an unexpected embrace. Public displays of affection were a rarity for him, but he'd engaged in them more frequently in recent days. His arm was warm around her waist, the faint stubble on his cheek rough against her own. *I'll be fine. Better, knowing you are safe.* He paused. *Remember, we stand a higher chance of our own escape without you. With you here, we would all be focused on your safety. Possibly to our detriment.*

Are you just saying that to get me to leave?

I'm speaking the truth. You just don't want to hear it.

She'd said something similar to him days ago, about this peace summit. She looked up at him, amused. *Throwing my own words back at me?*

Is it working?

"We are going." Feria's voice drew attention back to her group. They were edging for the door once again, only to be blocked by more of Reaper's dogs. "Through you, if we have to."

"So you can meet up with your Commonwealth allies?" Cannon flicked a hand toward them. "I think not."

Mercy felt his Talent reach out, but she wasn't prepared for the response to it. The telekinetic shield around Feria and her group shattered. Feria screamed, falling to her knees. Two more people collapsed to the ground beside her, keening, curled around their weapons. The rest seemed frozen, unable to move. She thought at first that pain had distorted their features, and then she realized that no, it was raw terror.

Mercy stared at Cannon. He was smiling, grimly amused.

What did you do?

Everyone thinks empathy is so passive. They forget how powerful emotion is. How difficult it can be to overcome. I'm just reminding them. He looked at Feria and her people. *Primal ones work best. Fear, for instance.*

Mercy looked back at the group in wonder, powerfully Talented yet incapacitated in a moment. She made a mental note not to get on Cannon's bad side.

Reaper gave her arm a little shake. *Now. Please.*

She looked up at him. He'd never asked her for something like that before. Maybe she was weak, because that one word, *please,* broke through all of her defiance and determination.

"All right. I'll go."

Dem took a step toward her and Mercy held up a hand. "Wait."

"We need to leave," he said, impatience making him gruff.

"I know. Just give me a minute."

She turned to Atrea, and wordless, gave her friend a hard hug. Leaving Atrea behind went against every instinct she had. She was more than a friend. A sister in all but blood. But Dem, for all his power, could not manage to teleport with more than one other person.

"Don't worry about me," Atrea whispered, correctly guessing her thoughts. "Tell Dad I'll see him soon. He's not allowed to yell at you until he can yell at us both." Mercy just squeezed harder before letting go.

She turned to Cannon. "What should I do?"

He grimaced. *Without me, some among the Core may try to push their own agendas. Don't let them. You are in charge in my absence. As Queen, you have that authority by right, and no one can take it from you or argue that you don't.* He hesitated. *Vashti will be a good ally. As well as Griffin, Treon, Dem and Sebastian. But be careful. Especially in who you trust.* That was all he said, but she understood the message. They still didn't know who the spy was.

Mercy nodded, then turned to Reaper. He pulled her into a kiss before she could say anything. It was hard and quick, the kind of kiss that said he'd be seeing her again soon, and that he was still angry with her. Or maybe she was reading too much into it. When she pulled back, color had bled back into his eyes, emotion warming the cold of the killer back to the Reaper she loved.

"Be careful," she said. "Try not to kill anyone that will start a war."

His lips twitched. "I'll do my best."

Then Dem took hold of her arm. The bar and everyone in it faded from view. There was disorienting darkness and the sense of pressure, like being underwater. She realized she couldn't breathe, and panic was just starting to set it in when a chill shuddered through her, settling on the back of her neck. The familiar walls of *Nemesis* materialized around her, the decking solid under her feet. She slid sideways as dizziness swamped her, catching herself against a bulkhead and clinging there for a few seconds, sucking air into her lungs. Nausea swept up with no warning, and she doubled over, retching.

Dem waited politely at her back, giving her space.

It is difficult at first, he said, *but the discomfort should fade quickly.*

It did, the nausea vanishing as quickly as it had come. Her hands trembled, and she took a moment before cautiously stepping away from the bulkhead to stand up straight. No fresh dizziness greeted the movement, and Mercy decided she would live.

"How the hell does Tamari manage so easily?" she asked, referring to Dem's precocious four-year-old daughter. Tama could teleport herself, and often did, even without the adult supervision she was supposed to have.

Dem smiled faintly. "Children are eminently adaptable. The first time, even the second and third, frightened Tamari. But by her fourth teleportation, she accepted the sensations as normal. She was never sick."

"Lucky kid," Mercy muttered. She started to step down the hall when she felt the strange compression of time that seemed to suspend everything for an eternal moment, the feeling that marked a space jump.

Nemesis left the system.

She spun on Dem. "You told them to jump?" The words came out more accusing than she intended.

"No," said a voice behind them. "I made the call."

Mercy turned, realizing for the first time that

Dem had teleported them, not into some nameless room or corridor on *Nemesis*, but onto the command deck. She'd only been to the CIC a handful of times, but she recognized the man who'd come to stand at her back. Sebastian, Cannon's second in command, and the true Captain of *Nemesis* in all but name.

Cannon hated being called "King" or any other titles thereof, so everyone called him Captain, instead. It meant that Sebastian, who commanded the ship far more directly, did so without an official title. He was just…Sebastian.

He didn't look like a pirate. At least, not in the same way that Cannon, or Reaper did. More like Dem, who insisted on wearing suits and could have passed as some corporate board member of a megacorp, if not for the cold killer lurking behind his eyes.

Sebastian had something behind his eyes, as well. Not cold or threatening, but something else. It wasn't anything Mercy could quite identify, but whenever she met his gaze she found herself relaxing and smiling, as though seeing an old friend. It was as if she knew him well, even though she didn't.

She'd asked Cannon once if Sebastian was an empath, like him. He'd smiled and shook his head. "No," he said. "But he is good with people. Almost as good as he is with ships." A strange response, and one he'd evaded elaborating on.

Like most of the pirates, Sebastian kept himself in excellent physical shape. He was tall, almost as large as Dem, who was by far the most physically intimidating of the pirates Mercy had met. As a whole, the Talented were not given to relying solely on their psychic strength, and adopted an almost militaristic view toward physical fitness and combat prowess.

Sebastian's age was indeterminate at first glance. Physically, he could have been anywhere in his twenties, but there was a presence to him, a weight that told Mercy he was likely older.

He had smooth, fair skin, brown eyes shaped with a distinct curve, and angular features. His black hair was long and straight, tied back into a braid that fell nearly to his waist. He didn't wear armored clothing like so many of them, but instead opted for a navy collared shirt that looked as expensive as Dem's wardrobe, and casual pants with no armor at all. It was an unusual choice.

"*You* made the call?" Mercy shoved an angry finger into his chest. "You aren't the one in charge here."

Dem made a sound beside her. From anyone else, she'd have said it was a grunt of surprise, but she doubted that. Nothing seemed to perturb his icy demeanor. Around them, crew members kept their eyes focused intently on their tasks, but Mercy could feel their attention as she stepped into Sebastian's personal space.

Understanding warmed his eyes. He didn't back away from her.

"I know you're worried about them," he said. "So am I. But our first priority must be getting you, the rest of the crew, and the ship to safety." He paused, lowering his voice. "Cannon gave me that order before he left. Surely he told you."

There was nothing Mercy could say to that,

and her anger left her as abruptly as it had come. Part of her had held out hope that somehow, they'd be able to wait for the others. Now, she felt cut off from Reaper, separated from Atrea…alone.

She felt alone.

It was the most isolated feeling she'd experienced since coming aboard *Nemesis* months ago. Then, she'd been afraid, distrustful of the family that had spent so many years hunting for her. She and her mother, Pallas, had fled from the pirates when she was only three years old, fleeing ahead of her grandmother's promise to kill her.

Lilith had been a real bitch. But the virus Veritas unleashed killed her grandmother, along with most of the other women. The vendetta to kill Mercy had died with Lilith. Returning home was one of the most difficult things Mercy had ever done, but these last few months had shown her that family was more than just a word to be feared. She had people here she cared about. People she loved. And she'd just left most of them behind on a world being blockaded by the Commonwealth. The very people who outlawed Talent and made having it a death sentence.

"Do you need to see Doc?" Dem's words shook her free of the dark direction her thoughts had taken.

She stiffened. "What? No. I'm good." No way was she seeing the doctor and his oh-so-charming bedside manner. "Why would you ask that? You know I hate the infirmary."

Dem gestured, and she realized she'd wrapped her arms around her middle, an unconscious gesture reflecting how she felt the farther the ship moved from Reaper and the others. She forced her arms down to her sides, straightening.

"I'm fine," she repeated, emphasizing the last word. "Just worried about the others. Do you think they'll be all right?" She deliberately didn't look at Sebastian, still resentful of his role in this.

Asking for reassurance from a killer was probably not going to get her the results she was looking for. But Dem was married to Sanah, an empath, and he'd been learning to connect with others more over the last few years. He studied her for a moment before answering. His expression didn't change, his face didn't soften, but the blue of his eyes darkened.

"Reaper has his dogs, and between them they've done many impossible tasks. Cannon is perhaps the most strategic and cunning individual I have ever known. And Atrea seems capable. They'll survive."

Sebastian laughed, a low sound that startled her into looking back at him, however reluctantly.

He met her eyes, amusement in his own. "Cannon and Reaper working together? They complement one another's strengths and weaknesses very well. Enough that they will make a formidable team. Perhaps you should be more worried for the Navy."

Something relaxed inside Mercy. Sebastian's words, the casual, teasing tone of them, did more to reassure her than Dem's clinical breakdown of their skills.

She unbent enough to thank him. "That's exactly what I needed to hear. Thanks."

He inclined his head. It was, she thought, an

acknowledgement of more than just her words. In that exchange, she'd finally let go of her worry enough to drop the last of her anger as well. Somehow, Sebastian knew that, and he smiled. A warm sort of smile that felt more personal than Mercy wanted it to.

Uncomfortable, she turned back to Dem. "Now, what are we going to do to get our people back?"

"We should call an emergency meeting of the Core. They need to know that Cannon is, for now, gone."

Mercy's heartbeat sped up. "Now, wait—"

"What do you think is going to happen?" Dem asked. "Cannon and the others will magically reappear on the ship and order will be restored? No." He shook his head. "That is no longer possible. Without the king's presence, the Core is likely to sink into the chaos of personal agendas and power grabs. Some will see this as an opportunity; others, as a devastating loss. All of them are going to blame you."

"Dem is correct," said Sebastian.

Mercy stood there, their words sinking in. When she didn't move or speak, Dem shifted closer to her. It was the only visible sign of stress he gave.

"Reaper is not here, Mercy. Do you understand what that means?"

"Yes."

"Are you certain?"

People feared Reaper. And he had made very clear just a few months ago what his response would be to threats against her. She suddenly felt the cold of his absence as more than just missing the man in her life. Dem's fingers tightened on her arm.

"You must establish your will immediately, before they have time to plot and plan. You must enter that meeting with a strong force at your back, a show of power that any of them will hesitate to cross."

She swallowed, her throat dry. "You mean I need to be Queen."

"If you value our lives, yes."

She blew out a frustrated breath. "Damn."

Her mind raced. These were pirates. Ruthless, formidable men and women who thrived in a society built on the strongest among them holding power. She avoided meetings like the one Dem was talking about precisely *because* she didn't want to play their games. But now she had no choice.

"I need to see Vashti."

Dem let go of her arm, a small, rare smile crossing his lips. "Yes."

Mercy's great-aunt had grown up playing these games, had survived a sister who tried to kill her multiple times, and was possibly the most manipulative and dangerous person Mercy had ever known.

"There may be a problem with that," Sebastian said.

"What problem?" Dem asked.

All of the warmth had fled Sebastian's eyes. His expression turned solemn.

"Vashti is in the infirmary."

CHAPTER FOUR

Something inside Reaper eased the moment Dem and Mercy disappeared. Whatever else happened, she would be safe. He looked at Cannon, and the two shared a wordless moment of agreement and relief. Both of them happy to see Mercy safely away.

Reaper had not always gotten along with Cannon. The two shared a tumultuous childhood. Cannon grew up in Lilith's household, part of her family. Lilith saw Reaper's mother as a possible rival and threat to her power. It didn't make for easy friendships, even as children.

And, of course, Cannon was an empath, while Reaper was a Killer, arguably two of the most opposing Talents in the spectrum. Cannon had never quite understood where he and Dem were coming from. In fact, the way Reaper remembered it, Cannon and Dem had been friends as children, being closer in age than Reaper was to either of them. But at some point, something had changed. Dem had done or said something, and the two had never been as close after that.

Reaper still didn't know what it was, all these years later. Not that it mattered. Or had any bearing on their situation now.

He looked over at Feria. The rest of his dogs had come into the room as Mercy and Dem departed, retrieving the Veritas agents' weapons. Now Feria and her people sat in a disgruntled group, disarmed and angry. She was glaring, her rage a barely contained thing simmering beneath her beautiful face and perfectly coifed hair.

Knox, Reaper's explosives expert, glared right back. He was fingering his satchel, and Reaper had little doubt that he imagined blowing them all to pieces.

Knox had lost more than most to the Matera-D virus that wiped out so many of the pirates' female population. Both of his parents were women, and he'd been the youngest child of three. His grandmother, his parents and his sisters all succumbed, leaving him the last of his family.

To say he hated Veritas would be a massive understatement.

Knox. Reaper felt compelled to issue a warning. He'd found other people could often be overwhelmed by their emotions.

I'm good, boss.

Are you? Killing didn't bother Reaper. But killing someone who might still be useful was a poor tactical decision.

Knox didn't take his eyes away from Feria and her group. *Yeah.*

I'm on it, boss. Ghost's words were on a tight, personal link. He gave Reaper a barely perceptible nod from where he stood beside Knox. *Good.*

Reaper set the problem aside, confident his team had it handled.

Cannon rubbed at his forehead, his expression tight. It was a gesture Reaper had seen him make before, when the emotions of others were sharp enough to pain him.

"So much for peace, eh?" Atrea said.

Cannon let his hand fall to his side. "Peace was a long shot anyway."

Atrea grunted in disbelief. She looked at Cannon and Reaper like they were idiots.

"You didn't really try, did you? Has it never occurred to you that they actually have the one thing you guys need more than anything in the universe?"

"Of course it has." Cannon looked back at Feria, but kept his voice low so it wouldn't travel beyond Reaper and Atrea. "We tried kidnapping women once. It was a mistake. Disastrous, in fact."

Atrea's mouth dropped open. "Are you serious? Of course you are." She shook her head, muttering something about *pirates* under her breath. "I'm not talking about *abducting* them. I'm saying if you guys could actually stomach one another long enough to work together, relationships would happen naturally. As they do."

"I doubt it." Cannon gestured to Knox. "I think you underestimate the depths of their hatred."

"Yeah?" Atrea said. "Well, I think you underestimate the power of a common enemy. And a common interest."

"*They* are our enemy." Perhaps Atrea didn't understand the situation. "The Commonwealth outlawed us, but it was our own people who continued to hunt us, decades later."

Atrea raised her hands. "I'm not saying they aren't assholes who deserve every bit of enmity you throw at them. I'm just saying that most people make the mistake of not *listening* to each other. A lot of problems can be solved with listening."

"That's Wolfgang talking," said Cannon. "You're speaking the words, but they're his."

She shrugged. "Dad's usually right. Listening to other people kept us out of a lot of trouble. And helped us manage when trouble found us anyway."

"We tried listening." Cannon's gaze moved to Feria's group, then back to Atrea. "We didn't learn anything worth remembering."

"Didn't you? Because I was listening, too, and I learned a couple of things." Atrea lifted a hand and ticked off fingers as she spoke. "One, they want Rani back. Bad. Two, they don't want Mercy to be their queen. Three, as much as some of your people don't like queens, *Veritas* really, *really* doesn't like them. It sounds like the whole virus was designed to kill a queen - probably Lilith - but it didn't work out as planned."

"No," said Cannon. His voice was stiff and cold. "No, it did not. Assuming I even believe that was their true motivation. Which I don't."

"Look, I'm not saying they haven't done terrible things, or that your problems with them will vanish because you opened your mind for a moment. But doesn't it make you wonder, just a little bit? Did they really try to kill you all? Why are they so hell bent on not being bound to a queen?

Why did they even *make* Rani in the first place? Why do they want her back so badly?"

"No," said Reaper.

Atrea rolled her eyes. "You guys are hopeless. Mercy was right to sneak off and do this thing without you. On the other hand, I'm not sure it would've mattered. You're so ready to believe the worst you won't listen. You are completely closed off. Ironic, considering you're a bunch of nosy telepaths."

She turned and walked away, crossing over to the bar and hopping across it with an easy movement. Reaper and Cannon exchanged a look.

"What common interest do you think we have?" Reaper asked.

He was genuinely curious what her answer would be. Atrea was an outsider. Her mother had been Talented, but she herself had been born a null, the gene recessive. She'd been raised away from them, only returning with Mercy after Willem had forced the queen to awaken Atrea's latent gifts. She knew almost nothing of their culture, and only the history Mercy and others had shared with her in the past few months. Mercy often saw things from a fresh perspective as a result of her own time distant from the pirates, and now Atrea appeared to share this trait.

Not that she was right. But maybe there was a point in all of her rambling that was worthwhile.

"Survival." Atrea rummaged among the drawers behind the bar. She pulled a long, thin tool from one of them, examined it, and tucked it into one of the pockets lining her armor. "The

Commonwealth still sees you as a threat. All of you."

"Maybe," Cannon conceded. "But Veritas has their claws in all levels of government. Megacorporations, planetary representatives, even the Navy, I'm sure." This last was said with a look toward the ceiling, and the ships likely now orbiting the waystation. "I believe they *are* the Commonwealth these days. And they've proven that with decades of hostility."

Atrea hopped back over the counter, narrowly avoiding the messy puddle of beer rapidly expanding across the floor. She glanced over at Feria, who was obviously listening. "That true?"

"We don't control the entirety of the Commonwealth." The other woman held herself stiffly.

Atrea snorted. "Just some of it, I suppose."

"We have influence, but hardly the power you seem to think."

"Yeah, I bet the military is particularly free of you. The Navy would be the most dangerous place for you to put people. They have so many policies and tests designed to root out Talented people, and a bunch of the old guard remember. They might not have fought in the Ascension Wars, but their parents did. They lived through a lot of the propaganda after, when the Commonwealth was hunting down Talented people. They recognize when someone uses telepathy."

Feria looked away, refusing to respond. Atrea shook her head and dragged a chair over to the bar, hopping up onto it so she could reach the ceiling. Cannon and Reaper watched as she used the tool she'd stolen to pry at one of the tiles. It finally gave with a crack, and she dug something out of the resulting hole, tugging it loose with both the tool and her fingers.

"You could have used a knife." Reaper glanced at the sheathed weapons on her person as he spoke, and she sent him a disbelieving look.

"And ruin the blade? I'm good with getting my hands dirty."

"What are you doing?" Cannon asked.

She held up a small device. "Retrieving the alarm to this place. We're going to need a distraction."

"You think a distraction is going to allow us to get to our ships?" Reaper was disappointed. Mercy talked about Atrea like she was some kind of mastermind, always coming up with plans. Getting them new jobs, trying to find Mercy's mother, or just landing them into trouble. All of it seemed to tether back to Atrea.

"No." She pocketed the alarm, jumping down from the chair. "But we are going to need a ship if we're going to get off this rock. Unfortunately, one of ours would never make it out of the system."

"Neither will any of the mercenaries' or smugglers' ships here," Reaper pointed out.

"Nope." She smiled. "We're going to need a Navy ship. This is an N-class planet. Non-habitable except for the habitat enclosing the waystation. If they follow standard blockade procedure, they'll land four dropships. Enough to hold eight fire teams. Most of those will disembark to search and seize. That's fifty-six soldiers we'll need to avoid, plus the three per ship assigned to watch the dock. Then each dropship will have a pilot and co-pilot, both combat trained."

Everyone stared at her.

She blinked. "What?" She rubbed fingers over her cheek. "Did I get something disgusting on my face climbing over the bar?"

"They just forgot you used to be Commonwealth military," said Jaxon, silent until now.

"Ah, right." Atrea's fair skin washed faintly red. "I, ah, promise my loyalties are with you all now. I mean, I'm one of you. Sort of."

Cannon gave her arm a quick squeeze. "You *are* one of us, Atrea. There is no question."

She wouldn't quite meet his eyes. "Right. Anyway, this would be easier if I could get my hands on a uniform, but a nice distraction should work just as well." She jerked her head toward Feria. "You better figure out if we're taking them with us or leaving them here for the soldiers to find. Which seems like a bad idea if you want off this rock."

When no one said anything, she waited a beat, then continued, "Do you plan to kill them all, then? Losing the fire teams might trigger a more aggressive response from those capital ships. Unless you're confident you can do it without a single soldier getting off a distress call."

Reaper did a quick calculation. More than fifty people at once was stretching even his abilities. And if they knew they were looking for Talented, it was possible they'd have some form of artificial shields or blockers. Not impossible to get past, but time consuming. He shook his head.

"Good." Atrea walked over to Feria's group,

stopping directly in front of them. "You can use that ability again, the one where you push nulls to turn their attention a different direction."

Confident, isn't she? Cannon sounded amused. Reaper glanced at him. It was true, for a woman who'd lived as a null for her entire life, she was singularly unintimidated being surrounded by powerfully Talented people. Only occasional fractures in her confidence showed from time to time.

But Atrea did have proprietary knowledge of the Commonwealth Navy's procedures. Reaper was content to let her lead. For now.

Beyond where Cannon stood, something else caught his eye. Reaper moved to better see the floor behind him. The growing pool of beer had reached a floor panel, the puddle ending in an unnaturally straight line as though running into a barrier. Reaper moved closer, and realized it was falling through a seam in the floor.

"Cannon," he said, pointing to the oddly shaped puddle.

Cannon eyed it, rubbing his jaw. "Probably an underground passage for bringing in illegal supplies."

"Or an escape route."

"Either way, it can certainly serve as ours. If we can find the way to open it." Cannon paused. "Perhaps behind the bar."

Reaper shook his head. "I'm sure there's a way on the other side. Ghost." He didn't lift his head when he called over the dog. He didn't have to.

A spectral form of Mateo, known as Ghost to his friends, appeared beside them. He still stood on the other side of the room with Knox and the others. Ghost could project copies of himself, illusions that could walk through walls or go behind locked doors. Like most telepaths, he could project his thoughts as well, so that his own awareness accompanied the illusion. Where Ghost's Talent truly became unique, however, was in his ability to make the illusions real to some degree. He could be an invisible presence, or give the form so much reality and weight that it could physically affect the world around it.

Reaper used him as a scout frequently.

"Boss?" Ghost asked. Ghost often had a deceptively lazy look about him, but the opposite was actually true. He was always watching, analyzing, cataloging. His Talent wasn't the only reason he made an excellent scout.

Reaper nodded to the seam in the floor. He didn't have to say anything more. Ghost knew what was expected. He looked down for a moment, running a hand over his close cropped beard. Then the specter next to Reaper disappeared, and he knew it had gone down beneath the floor.

Atrea joined them.

"What was that?"

She'd never seen Ghost at work before. Reaper briefly explained what he could do, and she shook her head.

"Every time I think you guys can't surprise me with some new gift, you prove me wrong."

Reaper didn't think her comment required a reply, so he didn't make one. They waited, every second that ticked by another moment closer to the Navy's fire teams deploying to find them.

Finally, Ghost's voice cut through Reaper's mind.

Gonna be tight quarters, boss. It's a pretty rough tunnel. I think they must have hand dug it about a hundred years ago.

But it will work?

Yeah. Goes all the way to a warehouse just outside the spaceport. They probably use it as their smuggling hole. The tunnel gets pretty narrow in the middle. We'll have to go single file, and some of the bigger guys will be a tight squeeze. But it will do.

Reaper looked over at Knox, and then tilted his head toward Feria and her crew. *Get them up. Jaxon, Titus, you help him. Jax, get a good strong signature on all of them.*

Jaxon was a Hunter. He could track a psychic signature across galaxies. Tracking them across the station would be child's play, if anyone tried to run.

Cannon?

I can keep them contained. Too emotionally scrambled to try anything, at least for a time.

Good enough. Reaper turned back to the seam in the floor.

Ghost, can you open it?

Sure thing, Boss. There's a lever built into the tunnel wall.

A moment later the hatch slid open, sour smelling beer spilling down into the darkness beneath it.

Cannon smiled. "Time to go steal a ship."

The last place Mercy wanted to go was the infirmary. Unfortunately, that's exactly where she ended up.

On the way there, she sent a quick message to Wolfgang's datapad, letting him know she was back, and Atrea was safe with Reaper and Cannon. Safe being perhaps an exaggeration, but only a small one. Mercy had confidence that between the three of them and Reaper's dogs, the group was as safe as they could be. For now.

Given that the planet was being blockaded by the Commonwealth Navy, it was a situation that could deteriorate fast.

She winced.

It was a cowardly way to handle things, but she didn't want to give the old Wolf that news. She amended the message to say that she would be tied up dealing with pirates and politics for a few hours, but perhaps they could meet for dinner later.

Yes, because that was going to be a fun meal.

But she hoped to have a plan by then, some way of getting everyone back.

Of course, Atrea was always the one with the plans.

Mercy fired off the message just as she and Dem reached the lift that would take them down a deck. It was occupied and already moving, so they stood and waited for a few minutes. Until Dem made an impatient noise beside her. Before Mercy could ask what was happening, he'd grabbed her arm and they'd taken another dizzying journey through darkness and pressure that left her doubled over and retching.

I thought you couldn't teleport again so soon?

Not over the kind of distance between Birn and our ship. But teleporting short jumps is much easier.

Great, just great. *A little warning next time?* Dry heaving was *so* much fun.

Why? Would it improve the experience?

Probably not. But it would improve her reaction to it. Maybe.

Once she'd recovered enough to straighten, she saw where they were. The infirmary. Vashti lay on one of the beds.

She was so still, an unnaturally grey pallor leeching color from her normally bronze skin. In her seventies, Mercy's great-Aunt still had several decades of life ahead of her, yet she often wore the appearance of age and frailty like a cloak, drawing it around her so that when people looked at her, they saw an ailing old woman instead of a powerful scion of the queen's line.

Mercy had seen her hobbling around with her cane many times. This was the first time she'd seen her truly look old. The hollows around her eyes were so dark they appeared bruised. Her cheeks looked sunken, and the wrinkles around her mouth and eyes were deep and pronounced. Only days ago, Mercy had sat in her quarters sipping tea, laughing as she listened to Vashti's stories about her parent's courtship.

What could have happened since that time?

Doc stood nearby, his expression even more grim than his customary scowl. His lab coat was, as ever, starkly white and wrinkle-free. He kept a rigid, immaculate appearance, every black hair neatly in place, his face clean shaven and smoothly expressionless. It gave him an ageless appearance.

He served as the leading physician on *Nemesis*, but Mercy knew there was much more to Hikaru Jiro than that. For one, he was also a member of the Core, the ruling council that served as a counterbalance to the King or Queen, made up of the most powerful Talented among the pirates.

His bedside manner left a lot to be desired, but Mercy didn't think it was just his usual gruff nature this time. His dark eyes were bright with emotion. Normally she would have said it was irritation, but today she thought it looked softer. More like worry.

"What happened?" she asked.

Doc shook his head. "We don't know. I received an alert early this morning. She was found in her quarters, unresponsive. It looked as though she collapsed too quickly to call for help."

Given that calling for help on this ship meant reaching out with a near-instant telepathic hail, that was alarming.

Mercy and Dem exchanged a look.

"Who found her?" asked Dem.

"Griffin."

Griffin and Cage were two of Vashti's nephews, both of them Mercy's cousins. They often accompanied Vashti wherever she went, silent guardians always at her back, and powerfully Talented in their own right.

Doc jerked his head toward the hallway. "I made them wait outside. I don't need people cluttering up my infirmary while I work." His tone was pointed as he eyed them. He was obviously not happy that Dem and Mercy had teleported in, and Mercy couldn't really blame him. Having two people suddenly appear in front of you was a startling experience. Doc had said a string of things in his native language that Mercy's translator couldn't process. She was pretty sure she understood the gist, anyway.

The trip wasn't exactly fun for her, either. Teleporting twice in such a short period of time had left her stomach with a sickly unsettled feeling that wasn't going away as it had before.

"Have her quarters been searched?" Dem asked.

"Griffin found nothing out of place."

Dem's mouth tightened.

Mercy had become good at reading micro expressions in Reaper. Dem was remarkably similar in his reactions.

You suspect an attack? She sent the question telepathically, on a tight thread, in case he didn't want to voice his suspicions aloud.

With Cannon and Reaper gone, Vashti is your most powerful ally. The timing is too convenient.

Do you trust Griffin?

I trust him with Vashti's life.

An interesting quantification, Mercy thought. *Do you trust Doc?*

A look toward the physician. *Yes.*

Then go do what you have to. I'll stay put.

Dem sent her an unreadable look. A nod followed, and he vanished.

"Chikushou!" Mercy didn't need a translator to know Doc was swearing.

He muttered something about putting up shielding to block teleportation, but Mercy smiled. No matter how irritated he became with Dem's comings and goings, she knew Doc would never actually block him, because doing so would also block Tamari, Dem's young daughter. Everyone on the ship had a soft spot for the tiny teleporter. Even Doc.

"How is she?" Mercy nodded to Vashti. She was surprised at the depth of concern she felt. Her relationship with her aunt was complicated. Vashti told Mercy only the things she wanted her to know, and kept her own counsel about everything else. In their first real interaction, she'd neatly maneuvered Mercy into intervening in a situation that had been part personal problem, part political gambit. No matter how much she enjoyed Vashti's stories or sharing tea with her, Mercy never forgot that their goals and agendas might not always be aligned.

Doc flicked a hand and a holographic screen appeared above Vashti. "Scans indicate bruising, likely from when she fell, an elevated heart rate, low body temperature and dangerously low blood pressure. Whatever else might have happened, I can tell you one thing: she's in shock."

"Shock? From what?"

Doc shook his head, the movement sharp and irritated. "*Shirimasen.* We can only guess. She bears no physical injuries and doesn't show signs of burn out. We can only presume that whatever happened was mental, possibly Talent-related. An attack, or perhaps something she saw."

"Saw?"

Doc gave her a penetrating look. "You didn't know."

It wasn't a question.

Mercy wasn't sure how to respond to that, so she crossed her arms and waited.

Doc gestured to Vashti, lying deathly still on the bed. "She has strong secondary gifts in telepathy and telekinesis. But her primary gift is precognition. She never told you."

"No." Mercy couldn't say she was surprised; Vashti was a woman of many secrets.

Doc grunted, a noise that indicated he was also unsurprised.

Mercy remembered a conversation she'd had once with Reaper about Vashti. How he'd grown up learning from her. He'd told her once that his own Talent was based in the cognition family of gifts, seeing everyone's vulnerabilities, the most efficient ways to kill at any given moment. Suddenly it made sense why Vashti would have been one of his mentors.

"Vashti sees the future."

"No." Doc eyed her. "Has no one explained to you how cognition works?"

She gave him a look and he huffed, a sound of profound impatience.

"The past is set." His voice was clipped and hard. "Those with postcognition get fixed visions of what has come before. There can be some variation, depending on the Talent in question. Some are more emotion based, others more sensory. But what has happened does not change, because it has already occurred. It is stable. A fixed point in history. The future..." He shook his head. "Precognition is a difficult gift. Vashti does not see the future. She sees probabilities."

Mercy stared down at her aunt. "Do people often collapse when they see these probabilities?"

"No." Doc was not a man who showed much emotion beyond irritation. But something flashed in the depths of his dark eyes, and a shadow briefly crossed his face. "I have only seen it once before."

"And?"

He avoided her gaze, becoming engrossed in adjusting Vashti's scanner. Alarm coursed through Mercy. Doc wasn't someone who avoided things. In fact, he was one of the most confrontational people she had ever met.

"What caused it? Did you treat that person?"

He hesitated. "No."

"But you know something." Something bad, she thought.

Doc stopped fiddling with things and sighed, turning to face her.

"When most people collapse due to Talent, it is because they've overextended themselves. Their brain shuts down all ancillary activity as it attempts to accommodate the trauma and deal with it."

Mercy fought impatience. She already knew this, but snapping at him would probably shut him up instead of moving him forward. Doc was rarely in a conversational mood. She didn't want to say anything that might remind him of that.

"Burn out," she said, keeping her voice even.

"Yes. Going into shock is quite common in those circumstances. However, Vashti shows no signs of burn out, which means her Talent wasn't overextended." His eyes took on a faraway look. "Cognition is a sensory Talent. You see things, hear them, and sometimes you feel them as well. It varies from person to person. It can often be… overwhelming. Sometimes it is difficult for the person to distinguish between a vision induced by Talent, and reality."

"That doesn't make sense," Mercy muttered without thinking.

Doc shot her a look. "No? Why not?"

She gestured to her aunt, at a momentary loss of what to say. "She's…Vashti."

A rare smile graced Doc's lips. "You think because she is strong that she is unassailable?"

"Well…yes."

He shook his head. "No. Everyone has limits. Me. You. Vashti. Even Reaper."

She gave him an incredulous look and his smile faded.

"I have seen the strongest of us brought low. Once, Lilith was thought to be invincible." He paused. "She died choking on her own blood as it filled her lungs, lying in her own piss and shit."

Mercy flinched away from the image. In her memory, her grandmother was an impossible force of will. Towering and indomitable.

"In the end, there were too many sick. We could barely treat those with a chance of living. We couldn't keep the dying comfortable or clean. Not even the Queen."

For the first time, real fear pricked at Mercy. She looked from Vashti to Doc. "You don't think the virus…"

"What? No." He waved a hand. "No. Everyone's been inoculated now. Matera-D can no longer harm her or anyone else on this ship."

Mercy let out a shuddering breath. One near-genocide was enough.

"No, I've gotten off track," Doc muttered. "Whatever she saw overwhelmed Vashti. It was either too intense, or too traumatic. Perhaps both."

"What could do that?"

"I couldn't begin to guess."

Mercy stared at Vashti. "How long before she wakes?"

"Again, I cannot predict. It depends greatly on what she saw, and how it affected her. If, indeed, that is the cause of her condition. It could be minutes, or hours. Even days."

"Well, what did the other precog see? The one you said collapsed before."

"That was over a decade ago." Doc busied himself with the scanner he'd been using on Vashti. "A few months before Matera-D wiped out half our population."

"So they saw all of those people dying?"

He slipped the scanner into his lab coat pocket.

"No. As I said, the future is probabilities. That precog saw *everyone* dying."

"But, the virus only attacked the female half of the population."

"That is true."

"So how could everyone die?"

Doc made a noise in his throat. "Enough." As quickly as it had come, his conversational mood vanished. "I've wasted enough time on useless talk. I have work to do. If you want to know more, look up the prophecies in the library archives."

"We have archives?"

He rolled his eyes. "*Baka dayo.* Of course we have archives. We have history. Science. Medicine. Even works of fiction." His tone was as acerbic as it had ever been. "You've been here for months, yet have not opened a single file?"

It was on the tip of her tongue to tell him where he could shove his sanctimonious attitude, but she'd promised Dem she'd stay here until he returned, and she didn't feel like explaining to the security chief how she'd ended up either storming out of the infirmary, or involved in a physical altercation with the good doctor.

It wouldn't be the first time. And she doubted very much that Dem would be understanding.

Besides, Vashti was the important one here. Doc needed his energies focused on her.

So Mercy modulated her tone and asked with icy politeness whether she could access the archives from her data pad.

"Of course," snapped Doc. He showed her how with ill grace, and left her to her own devices immediately after.

Mercy forgot him soon enough, losing herself in the bottomless library of information now at her disposal.

She didn't know what to search first. Her fingers itched to look up more about the prophecies Doc had referenced, but she had more immediate problems. Like an imminent meeting with the Core, and no Vashti to turn to for advice.

She reached out to Dem. *Find anything?*

No. Her quarters are clean, and Griffin spoke with her less than thirty minutes prior to finding her. She seemed fine.

A dead end. That was distinctly unhelpful. *Are you coming back?*

Soon. The Core is demanding a meeting, as I knew they would. They will be gathering shortly, and I will come to collect you.

Won't that just be fun? Like a dock inspection was fun. She grimaced.

She passed the next hour searching through dry documents of Law and Rule laid down regarding the Queen's powers and the Core's, and what happened when the two clashed. There were variations of circumstance, amendments and rights based on what was good for the pirate colonies as a whole. It was obviously inspired by the Commonwealth Charter, and the powers given to the Planetary Representatives and the Monarchy.

But the pirates' body of government differed in one particularly salient way. In theory, the Core could overrule the Queen via a unanimous vote. But as with all disputes, the Queen could still overrule this vote in one single stroke: a challenge.

The pirates respected power above all else, and no Talent was more powerful than a queen's.

Most challenges ended up in the arena, a fighting circle where disputes were settled, usually violently. Not long ago, these altercations had often been to the death, but Mercy had recently put a stop to that. Their population was struggling; they couldn't afford to lose numbers to every disagreement.

Still, the pirates leaned to violence. Fighting continued to be the preferred method of settling conflict. The problem with challenging a queen, however, was immediately apparent to Mercy.

The very nature of her bond to them prevented the pirates from directly harming her. And she could use her own gifts to influence them, applying a kind of mental pressure for them to see things her way and agree to her wishes.

Assuming she even could. It wasn't as though she'd practiced it. Mercy had been meeting regularly with Vashti since the claiming, learning what she could about her abilities as queen from someone who'd grown up with one. But it wasn't the same as real training. Secondhand information wasn't enough.

Besides, she hated that particular gift. It smacked a bit too much of slavery.

She remembered all too well what it was like when Rani had taken control of everyone aboard ship. The mindless way they had followed her will and ignored everything else. Rani had forced people to do terrible things. Mercy never wanted to be associated with that.

She tapped a finger on her datapad, thinking.

According to Cannon, the Core would almost certainly attempt to overrule her. They would test her. Some of them hated what she was and would go to any lengths to avoid another queen ruling over them. Until now, Cannon's presence and role as King had kept the equilibrium. Everyone had been able to almost ignore Mercy's presence, and the fact that she'd claimed everyone here as hers.

They wouldn't be able to ignore it any longer.

When the challengers came at her, she couldn't - *wouldn't* -control them. She couldn't meet them in the arena because everyone would know the fight wouldn't be fair. She was going to have to stop things before they got that far.

She had no idea how to do that. And no idea how much time she had before Dem was coming to collect her.

She'd barely had the thought when a burst of Talent went off beside her and he was standing there. She stared at him, dismayed.

"So, not long at all, then."

"What?" Dem frowned at her.

"Nothing," she muttered, closing her datapad's holoscreen and rising to her feet. Her stomach had finally recovered from the double teleporting, but now dread rolled through it.

"Are you ready?" Dem eyed her, but his tone was dubious.

"Do I have a choice?"

His gaze moved to Vashti, then back to Mercy. "No."

"Great, thanks. You're a real comfort. Any advice?"

His frown deepened. "My idea of playing politics is to hit harder and faster than anyone else." He shrugged his broad shoulders. "It usually works well for me."

It would. If only Cannon were here. But he wasn't. Mercy was going to have to do this on her own. She squared her shoulders. *Hit harder and faster than anyone else. All right, then.*

"Let's do this."

CHAPTER SIX

The room the Core used for meetings was, Mercy imagined, what would have been the officer's mess on *Nemesis*, had the ship fulfilled its original purpose and served in the Commonwealth Navy. Pirates being pirates, it had become the ship's bar, instead. For meetings like this, it was cleared out of anyone who didn't serve on the Core, the pirates' version of a Council of Sovereign Planets.

Mercy had asked Cannon once why the pirates styled their ruling body off of the Commonwealth that betrayed them. He'd shrugged, and said it just worked out that way. Those who commanded ships in the first pirate fleet became the original Core members, answering only to their Queen - Mercy's great-great grandmother, Amestris. As colonies were established, the pirate government grew from there.

With *Nemesis* serving as the Queen's - or King's - base of operations more often than not, the bar turned into a council chamber for meetings. Tables were moved into a rough circle, and the doors were shut. It wasn't necessary to lock them. Everyone on the ship knew better than to try and enter when the most powerful pirates were gathered in one place.

Drinks were poured, bottles provided by Valko, the bartender. He was a telepath rumored to have a small, secondary gift in precognition. Pirates said he always knew what someone was going to order before they asked. Mercy knew there had to be more to him than serving drinks, however. Not only did he provide the alcohol for meetings, but he sat on the Core himself. He had to be powerful to have earned one of the twenty-one seats.

She wondered if the Council of Sovereign Planets served alcohol at their meetings. Probably wine. Something expensive and refined, likely in amounts small enough to savor, but not so large as to dull anyone's senses or scramble their thoughts.

The pirates served Bennethan rum, a beverage best described as liquid fire. They didn't bother with tiny cups, either, but knocked back as many glasses and bottles as Val would supply.

She'd been to exactly one meeting before. Cannon and Reaper convinced her to go, but she hadn't felt comfortable. She might be a queen, but Cannon was the true leader of the pirates. No one knew what to make of her. Half of them were wary, thinking she was just going to be another Lilith. The other half eyed her with ill-disguised hunger, calculating how best to manipulate and use her. For most of them, that meant trying to maneuver themselves into her bed, and being chosen as her next consort.

That was something she wasn't exactly eager to do anytime soon. Consorts as a whole were something she'd never considered before coming here, and while multiple partners were a common and ingrained part of the pirate culture, it wasn't something Mercy was looking to jump into. Certainly never with someone only looking to boost his own political or psychic power base, and especially not with Reaper as her first. They were still figuring out their relationship together. Adding another person to that, even one she had sincere feelings for, felt dangerous.

She stopped outside of the closed doors. Beside her, Dem waited, as silent and patient as a statue, while she stood and thought about what she was about to do. The small of her back felt hot, and nausea made her swallow. Damn, she didn't want to walk into that room. If Cannon were here, she'd have felt much better about this.

But then, if Cannon were here, she wouldn't need to do it at all.

Are any of them empaths? She sent the words to Dem telepathically, not willing to risk speaking them aloud.

No.

Well, she had that going for her, at least.

They may try to penetrate your shields, however. To test you.

Her brows drew down as a kernel of anger started to burn inside of her. She held onto it, preferring that over the butterflies of uncertainty and dread.

And what will happen if they penetrate my shields?

Dem's eyes chilled, cold seeping through the blue. *They will not.*

Wait. Mercy stared at him. Gingerly, she probed outside of her shields and felt another barrier, a solid wall of Talent. *No. You can't protect me.*

Dem's eyebrows rose. *Mercy—*

No, Dem. These are vicious, violent men and women who are just waiting for me to slip up, for an opportunity to prove I'm either not strong enough to be Queen, or not trustworthy enough. I can't walk into that room with you shielding me from whatever they might throw my way.

Very well. The barrier vanished. Mercy couldn't be sure, but she thought the corner of his mouth might have twitched before he caught it. Dem's version of almost smiling.

For fuck's sake. She rolled her eyes. *I don't need you testing me, too.*

She turned and strode forward, using her telekinesis to throw open the doors.

The last time she'd been to a meeting, the atmosphere had been focused and intent. Although emotions had run high in the wake of Mercy's claiming, the Core remained in control. They'd asked questions, discussed, even argued, but everyone had stayed seated and the meeting progressed under Cannon's guidance. His influence kept tempers from boiling over, and his calm acceptance soothed a lot of rough edges.

More so than Mercy had realized at the time. Because his absence was obvious the moment she strode into the room.

Practically no one was sitting. Instead, they stood around the circle of tables and chairs, body language universally stiff and angry. The air was heavy with tension. Glasses of alcohol weren't even touched - probably a good thing, under the circumstances.

Mercy recognized everyone here, though many she knew only in passing. Others, she'd spent more time with. Bruzer, the pirate in charge of the flight deck and hangar bay stood beside Valko. Griffin was here, and Sebastian. While some were physically in the room and present, others stood as holo-projections from whatever colony or ship they were currently on. Doc attended via holo as well, since he'd opted to stay in the infirmary to monitor Vashti, who normally would have been in one of these chairs herself.

Treon was the only one sitting, languidly kicked back with his feet propped onto a table as though the whole thing bored him.

His eyebrow went up as she strode into the room, and she squelched the automatic surge of irritation he inspired. She hadn't figured out yet how much of Treon's arrogance was real, but she knew many of his actions were a manipulation.

He wasn't the only one to note her entrance. As the doors flung wide, people turned to direct their ire and outrage at whoever dared disrupt a Core meeting.

A pirate she'd met a handful of times before stepped forward, his lip curled into a sneer.

"You have no place here." He gestured to Dem. "Shouldn't you be escorting her to the brig?"

So, that was the way they were playing it.

She studied him. He wore his dark hair long and pulled back from a square face that might have been handsome, if not for the arrogant sneer he wore. He was older than Cannon or Dem, perhaps in his mid-forties, and she had the impression that he sometimes felt he should be the one leading as king. His instant dislike of Mercy had been clear from the first moment they met.

"Wick, isn't it?" she said, her tone cool. He commanded a dreadnought and several corvettes, she remembered. Quick to anger, but able to put temper aside and see reason as well. Usually.

He eyed her with open derision. "You think remembering my name wins you something? You've refused a place at this council on multiple occasions. You don't get to claim one now because you suddenly find it convenient."

"I don't find it convenient at all."

His eyes narrowed. "Because of you, our king is gone. Perhaps lost forever." He paused, sweeping his gaze over the rest of the Core. "It has been suggested, that may have been your goal all along."

Mercy smiled. It felt grim, even to her. She looked around the room. She was pretty sure she knew who had made that 'suggestion'.

"Is that what you all think? That I snuck off to lure Cannon away? And Reaper? Did I plan to ditch him as well? I suppose you think *I* tipped off the Navy?"

"Your friend was a Navy officer," said another man she barely knew. She searched her memory for his name, finally settled on Xavier. Younger than most of the people here, he looked barely into his second decade. Young and handsome in an almost pretty way, with smooth golden skin and fair hair he wore in a tousled fashion that had to be deliberate. His Talent must have been something hugely powerful to get him on the Core at such a young age.

Mercy was only a handful of years older, but sometimes she felt ancient.

Xavier propositioned her once, and caught her so by surprise that she'd laughed in his face. It was right after she'd chosen Reaper as her consort, and the bold suggestion from another man so soon had shocked her. She made the mistake of assuming he was joking. He wasn't.

He was still angry about that laugh, if the look in his eyes was any indication.

She nodded to him, keeping her expression cool and distant. "Yes, Atrea was. And what reason would I have for doing this? For getting rid of Cannon and Reaper? For betraying them to the Commonwealth?"

"Why, to clear your path to taking command, of course," drawled Treon from where he sat, still looking bored. "Cannon, as King, stands in your way, and Reaper...well. Choosing him as your first Consort had to be a calculated move. Maybe you had second thoughts. Realized just how dangerous he really is." He gave a shrug, and she wanted to smack that indolent look off his face. "Too dangerous to keep close, no matter how much protection he gives you. How else could you safely remove a Killer?"

Mercy held Treon's gaze with her own long enough to see the anger in his eyes. She noted the tension in his jaw, belying his casual posture. He was, she realized, so coldly furious that he was barely holding it together. She had a sudden sense of the sheer storm of Talent being held back by a thin thread of control, and nearly gasped.

In the time she'd known him, she'd seen Treon in many moods. She'd never seen him like this. What else had they been saying in this room? And what would happen if that thread snapped? She made sure he saw the anger in her own eyes before she looked away.

This is what they believe? She sent Treon the question on a tight personal thread, the kind reserved for close friends and family. Which, as Reaper's youngest brother, he was.

It is the nonsense they've been discussing for the last while, yes. Even his mental tone was clipped and hard.

She made sure to look at each Core member. She marked each of them with her gaze. Some looked smug, others thoughtful. Doc looked irritated, but that was his usual expression. Griffin likewise wore a look of frustration. Not everyone believed this load of crap.

"Let's be absolutely clear: are you accusing me of something?"

Wick's jaw set. No one said anything. Accusing her would be seen as a direct challenge. And no one wanted to challenge a queen, even an untrained one like Mercy. Though she could swear she saw Wick contemplate it for a moment.

She waited out the silence. When it became clear no one was going to speak, she gave a nod. "Very well. Until someone is ready to make an accusation, I don't want to hear about this again."

"You can't just table the discussion," someone

protested. She didn't recognize the voice, didn't see who spoke.

Mercy made a show of looking at Dem. "Was I unclear? Did I stutter?"

She thought his mouth might have twitched again. "You did not."

She was just opening her mouth to say something else sarcastic when another voice rang through the room.

"Cannon *did* name Mercy as his successor." Sebastian stepped forward from where he stood between Griffin and Doc. "In this very room. You all bore witness."

Wick gave a dismissive wave of one hand. "In the case of his death, yes. But Cannon is not dead." Unspoken, but hanging in the room was the word *yet*.

Sebastian angled his head. "Are you arguing against Cannon's wishes? Rule and Law make the line of succession clear: in the absence of a legitimate queen to take leadership, the acting king or queen may name a successor. As Cannon has both named a successor *and* Mercy is a legitimate queen, the law is absolute: Mercy is Queen."

"*If* Cannon is dead. Given that his absence is temporary and Mercy has made her own feelings plain by all but abdicating her role—"

"Do not speak for me." Mercy took a deliberate step forward. "I'm right here. In the room. Or were you planning on continuing to put words in my mouth?"

Wick gave her a nasty look. "Have you not said, in this very room, that you wanted nothing to do with being queen?"

"I don't believe those were my exact words, no."

"They weren't," Sebastian said. With a flick of his wrist, a holo-screen shimmered into being in the center of the room. Words scrawled across it and Mercy's own voice filled the room, echoing them.

"...so long as Cannon rules as King, I see no reason to disrupt what is clearly already working. You already have a ruler."

That's right. Cannon had mentioned that all meetings of the Core were recorded. Mercy remembered saying that, during that first meeting he'd all but dragged her to.

Sebastian gave another wave of his hand, and the recording stopped. "But Cannon is no longer here. Mercy is. The King's wishes are clear, as is the Law. Mercy has *not* officially abdicated, and she *is* a queen. These are the facts. I call for a vote."

Is a vote necessary? Mercy had never reached out to Sebastian mentally before. His mind had a unique feel. Warm, but oddly distant.

Technically, no. But it will pass, and the arguing will be put to rest. It is a strategic move that gives them the illusion of choice.

Aloud, he said: "All in favor of ratifying her claim to the throne?"

"Until Cannon returns," Mercy said quickly. Sebastian met her gaze with a smile.

"As regent, then. Until Cannon's return."

Another holoscreen appeared, and each of the pirates made a notation on a datapad. The tally, in the end, was twelve to seven, in favor of Mercy's regency. Both Vashti's and Reaper's votes remained uncast.

How did you know it would pass, she asked Sebastian.

He gave her a nearly imperceptible shrug from across the room, and her eyes narrowed. She wasn't going to let him brush aside her question quite that easily. She made a mental note to corner him later when he couldn't dissemble.

It's done, said Dem in Mercy's mind.

She let out a long breath. Sixty percent of the vote wasn't exactly a confidence booster, but then she herself wasn't so sure this was a great idea. Several of the Core wore sour expressions, including Wick and Xavier. Doc looked pleased, or as pleased as he ever managed. And Treon was smiling. It was a sharp sort of smile. He was still angry. But she had no doubt he'd voted for her.

Of course I voted for you. Don't be ridiculous. You are, after all, my sister now. Family sticks together.

Get out of my head, Treon.

Treon was a powerful telepath. Perhaps the most powerful alive. He picked up on thoughts as easily as breathing, often whether someone was shielded or not. It was one of the more irritating things about him.

As you wish, Your Majesty.

He *knew* she hated being called that.

Mercy walked forward and took a seat in the empty chair where Cannon normally would have been.

"Great," she said. "Now let's discuss getting our people back."

"Cannon's order—"

"Cannon isn't here. And as we've just established, I'm now Queen. And I'm *not* abandoning them." Mercy leaned forward and swept the room with a steady look. "I understand we can't risk *Nemesis*. So let's talk strategies. How do we recover them?"

Sebastian took his seat, and others began sitting as well. Some of the tension drained from the room.

"There are, at our last scans, three capital ships over Birn, including one Monarch-class," Sebastian said. "Several smaller corvettes, as well. This was not some Navy vessel stumbling upon our meeting. It's a blockade. There is no way to get in or out of the system now without being noticed."

He lifted a hand, and a holoscreen projected in the center of the room, showing Birn, with several angry red dots pinpointing the Navy fleet's position around it.

"And, there's something else. Treon?"

Reaper's brother sat up, putting his feet down. "Oh, are we finally discussing the only interesting part of this meeting?"

"Treon," said Mercy with a sigh. It was exactly the tone she'd heard Cannon use with him more than once. He sent her an irritated look, and she just raised one eyebrow in return.

"It has been our belief that Veritas tipped off the Commonwealth to our presence," he said.

Mercy relaxed fractionally.

Treon was powerful enough that he could create problems for her. If he chose to defy her, others might see that as weakness on her part.

Fortunately, he seemed to realize that and was sticking to business.

"I'm not so certain that's true," Mercy said, frowning. "Their own people seemed shocked when the Navy jumped in. It felt like a genuine reaction."

Treon waved a hand. "An argument could be made that those they sent to parlay had not been included in the plan. However, I'm now inclined to agree with you."

Mercy was surprised. She'd expected this to be the argument people would most resist. Believing the worst of Veritas came naturally to all of the pirates.

"How could the Commonwealth have known?" demanded Wick. "We knew. And Veritas knew. It wasn't us, so it had to be them." He gave Mercy a disgusted look. "It was always going to be a trap."

"I believe Treon had the floor," she said, her tone cool.

Wick subsided with a scowl, but many around the tables were nodding in agreement with him.

"At Sebastian's request," Treon continued, "I scanned the system before we jumped out. And found Talented minds."

"Veritas was there, so that makes sense," said Griffin from where he sat next to Treon.

"Yes, but these were very specific minds." Treon steepled his hands in front him.

"I thought only queens could sense Talent," Mercy said.

"That is normally true. I'm told you feel it rather like a beacon, yes?"

"Sort of," said Mercy, thinking of the warm

glow radiating from each person in this room. Dem's, like Reaper's, was the only aberration - a cold flame. Killers seemed to register differently from other Talented.

"But you aren't in their minds, past their shields, correct? You just know when in someone's presence whether they are Talented. You feel it."

"Yes," said Mercy.

"What I do is different. Most telepaths can make an educated guess on whether or not someone is a null based on their shields. Nulls don't learn to shield properly, so their minds often project their thoughts unconsciously."

Mercy knew that. She'd had to shield her entire life, even living in hiding among nulls, just to keep other people's thoughts out of her head. She nodded to Treon to show she was following him.

"I don't have to guess. Talented *think* differently from nulls. We guard our thoughts. Create different pathways in the mind, which creates a sort of...psychic pattern. Each one is unique. This begins even in the womb, though it isn't always detectible until the child is older. I've identified the Talent of every child born aboard this ship in the past decade, for example. I can tell you when someone is a precog, or a telekinetic. If I get past their shields, I can tell you even more."

"Is this normal for telepaths?"

"No."

So, he was unique. That actually explained a lot about Treon.

"I believe it to be a previously uncategorized sub-Talent of telepathy," said Doc. "But it is difficult to say without a wider pool of data."

In other words, until someone else was born with the same ability, Doc couldn't be sure.

"Interesting. So, you can identify Talented minds."

"Yes."

"And what was so unusual about the minds you found at Birn?"

"Not *at* Birn. *Above* Birn. Amongst the Commonwealth fleet." Treon touched the holoscreen with a hand, spinning it his direction and expanding it. He highlighted an area in the middle of the fleet.

Mercy leaned forward, frowning. "It looks like empty space."

"Yes, it does. But it isn't." Treon pointed to the dark patch that appeared to have no ships or any other markers. "*That* is where I discovered these Talented minds."

"In empty space." Wick sounded skeptical, and Mercy couldn't blame him.

"So it would seem," said Treon.

"Could they be using some kind of Talent to mask their presence? An…illusion?"

"An illusion so complete it fools mechanical sensors? Perhaps." Treon shrugged. "Or perhaps they have some kind of cloaking device."

The Commonwealth had been trying to develop the ability to cloak ships for decades. To Mercy's knowledge, they'd never succeeded. However, that didn't mean it was impossible. Odds were good that if they ever did succeed, they wouldn't be announcing it to the general public.

"And why would a Commonwealth ship, in the

middle of a Commonwealth fleet, feel the need to be hidden?" asked Griffin. It was a good question.

Treon shrugged. Mercy studied him. His eyes were bright, his handsome jaw still tight with tension. Anger still simmered below the surface, and for the first time she thought it might not have anything to do with anything that happened in this room.

"There's more," she said. "What?"

"The minds I felt. One of them was a killer."

Around the table, there were startled intakes of breath and a handful of expletives. Veritas had never, to their knowledge, had a killer in their ranks. That particular Talent had always been exclusive to the pirates, and was a distinct advantage.

"Not a mind I recognized," Treon continued. "And I've made a point of becoming familiar with *all* of the killers." He fidgeted, the fingers of his right hand clenching and releasing. Treon didn't fidget. Ever.

"And..." he hesitated. "There were two others. One of them was like nothing I've felt before. I didn't - *couldn't* - pinpoint its pattern."

That was certainly worrisome.

"You have no idea what sort of Talented it might have been?" Mercy asked.

"No. The pattern felt almost like it was fluid, changing at any given moment. I couldn't seem to lock onto it."

Everyone was silent for a moment. Even Wick looked thoughtful. Mercy could see Doc's holo projection taking furious notes on a datapad.

"And the third?" she asked, turning back to Treon.

Treon met her eyes. "The third was a queen."

Everyone froze.

"That's impossible," said Dem. He'd been so silent until now that Mercy had forgotten he was next to her.

"Apparently not," said Treon.

Dem leaned forward. "We spent years searching for a queen. Searching for Mercy."

"Yes, and Reaper ended up stumbling across her on some space station when he wasn't even looking." Treon spread his hands. "Who is to say there aren't more out there? In hiding, perhaps? They are rare, yes, but do we really know how rare? It's even possible there are unstable versions, clones like Rani."

Mercy held up a hand. "Wait. In their negotiations, Veritas were desperate to get Rani back. It was the thing they wanted more than anything else. Feria said they needed her in order to be autonomous from us, to remove my claiming. If they had another queen, they wouldn't need Rani for that."

"These people I sensed were not with Veritas," said Treon.

"How can you be certain?" asked Dem. "Just because Veritas has never had a killer before..."

"No, that's not why. I..." Treon hesitated. "When I was scanning them, *something* felt me. A presence unlike anything I've encountered before. Separate from their minds, but connected. It... blocked me. It shoved me back into my own mind."

Doc whispered a quiet oath from his end of the table. An uneasy murmur rose as others reacted. What was powerful enough to not only block Treon, but to move him when he didn't want to be moved?

Mercy had heard many jokes at Treon's expense since coming here. Comments about his unmatched power. But truth was a common thread that lay beneath all of them. Doc had a system he'd tried to develop, for measuring the level of one's Talent. He'd given it up because, in his words, "Treon shattered the curve".

Treon's mouth twisted like he was tasting something he didn't like. "It hit me hard enough that I don't recall the first few minutes after it occurred."

"You blacked out." Dem's voice was even, but he'd gone tense beside Mercy.

"If you must call it that," said Treon bitterly.

Horror crept through Mercy. "And this thing, whatever it is, it's hovering over the planet where Reaper and Atrea are. Where Cannon is. Where our people are trapped."

Treon looked at her, his face grim. "Yes."

The discussion went on for hours, but went nowhere. All they had in the end were guesses with no hard facts, and no plan. Taking any ship back into the system was deemed too risky without more information.

"Surely, we can at least get word to them. Treon, can you reach Reaper?" Mercy asked. Telepathy between family members often had a greater range.

"Unfortunately, no. My Talent is…strained, at the moment. In a few hours, perhaps." His hand clenched into a fist. How much had it cost him to admit that?

"Dem?" She looked to Reaper's oldest brother.

He shook his head. "I have already tried. We are too far. I can feel his mind, but the connection is not strong enough for words." He gave her a long stare. "*You* could try."

She bit her lip. She'd come a long way in her time with the pirates, but she was still mastering her Talent.

"After the meeting," she said. She would need

as much focus as possible. "If I don't succeed, Treon, you'll try in a few hours."

"Of course."

"We need information." She drummed her fingers on the table. "Our priority has to be warning our people, and then getting them out of there. We don't even know if this weird presence Treon discovered will try and interfere."

"We don't know it won't, either. Clearly, they are there for a purpose," said Sebastian. "They might even have brought the Commonwealth to Birn."

"Why? What do they hope to gain?" Mercy asked.

No one answered. What answer could there be? They didn't know enough to play at guessing.

Mercy drew in a breath. "Sebastian. Jump to new coordinates. Not into Birn's system, but as close as we can comfortably dare. Close enough that we can reach Reaper mentally. Dem. You will put together a scout team. Talents such as farsight, and make sure someone is excellent at shielding. I trust your judgment."

"Yes, my Queen."

Mercy frowned at him, but Dem just smiled faintly. Her eyes narrowed. *You're enjoying this.*

Cannon said you'd be good at it. He was right.

Please. I've been Queen for five minutes. I could be terrible. You don't know.

You won't be.

Mercy's jaw clenched. "We'll reconvene when we have more information."

Reluctantly, the meeting broke up. Mercy wanted a word with Treon, but he was the first to leave. His mind was completely closed off and he wore a such a dark scowl that people scurried out of his path.

Damn, she told Dem. *I wanted to ask him more about what he experienced, and what this other queen felt like.*

I would give time for his ego to recover, Dem said dryly. *I'll run him down tonight and let you know.*

Thanks.

Dem nodded and headed for the door, presumably to put together the team she'd asked for.

Wick approached her. "Mercy, a word."

He was the last person Mercy expected to speak to her. She turned, feeling herself tense. Dem stopped, tilting his head in an unspoken question.

The bar was almost empty. Valko had disappeared into a back storage room. People attending via holo projection had already flickered out. Only Griffin and Sebastian were still in the room. The two of them paused at the door when Wick spoke.

"Please," he scoffed, eyeing how everyone had frozen. "What is it you think I'm going to do? I would just like a private word with our new Queen, should she see fit to grant it to me."

Mercy? It was Dem who was asking, but she felt the attention from all of them, waiting for her decision. She almost sighed.

Wick was right, much as she hated to admit it. What exactly did they think he would try? Her bond with the pirates kept her pretty safe as a queen to begin with. The bomb that had nearly blown her to pieces six months ago notwithstanding, there was little harm that most Talented could do to a queen directly. It took a killer's Talent, or a sneaky sort of sideways attack like a bomb or a sickness to murder a queen.

Just because he can't kill you, noted Dem, *doesn't mean he can't hurt you.*

"I'll be fine," she said aloud, for Sebastian and Griffin's benefit as well as Dem's. "Go on."

After a moment's hesitation, the three of them left, leaving Wick and Mercy alone.

She fought the urge to cross her arms, knowing the posture to be a defensive one. "What do you want?" she asked, facing him.

He smiled. It didn't reach his eyes. But at least he wasn't sneering at her anymore.

Wick closed the distance between them, his posture unassuming, his hands spread as if to show that he was harmless. "Now that you're Queen - temporarily - you should think about who you would like to ally yourself to."

She quirked an eyebrow. "Like you, you mean?"

"I have been on the Core longer than most. I have many connections, and I am notably among the most powerful telepaths." He leaned inside her personal space, and she had to resist the urge to back away. "You could do worse."

She found she wasn't interested in playing politics or bantering with pretty words.

"Treon has informed me that he and I are family now," she said, "so I am already allied with *the* most powerful telepath."

Wick's smile slipped. "Treon's loyalty will only remain so long as Reaper is your Consort. There is no guarantee that Cannon and the others will return from Birn." Wick put a hand on her arm, and

Mercy almost flinched. "You should prepare your-self for the worst."

There was something so false, so oily about him, that she didn't want him to touch her. Added to that was the small fact that Talent could be enhanced through physical touch, and Wick had just admitted to being a powerful telepath.

She took a deliberate step back, pulling her arm away. "Thanks, but I'm not writing them off just yet."

"Of course, of course." He was all smiles again. "Just think about it. I could be a powerful ally. And you will need someone strong to take Reaper's place by your side, should the worst come to pass."

Mercy had been turning to go when he spoke. Now she stopped dead, her head angling back in shock. Surely, she hadn't heard him correctly. "Are you propositioning me?"

"I thought that was obvious." He couldn't quite keep the condescension out of his voice. The implied *even to you* hung in the air between them, and Mercy wanted to rip that smug look off of his face. She curled her hand into a fist so she wouldn't give in the urge to lash out.

"If you think I would *ever* take you as a consort, you are completely out of touch with reality."

She had the satisfaction of seeing his smugness sour, the oily smile fading into a scowl.

"It would be a mistake to discount me. Only a fool chooses consorts based on emotion, Mercy. You might be many things, but you never struck me as foolish."

Liar. Every interaction she'd had with him had given her that exact impression. That he saw her as a foolish girl at best, and a threat to his own power base at worst.

She kept her expression neutral, her words completely without inflection. "I'll take that under advisement."

"Good, good." He inclined his head. "I'll bid you good day, then."

She stood for a moment, marveling at his sheer arrogance. Wick might have been handsome enough, but everything about him irritated her. At his worst, he made her skin crawl.

"Not if you were the last pirate in the universe," she murmured to the room. She took a deep breath, and reminded herself that soon, Reaper would be back. And fools like Wick wouldn't dare to approach her.

She wasn't surprised to see Sebastian and Griffin waiting when she stepped outside. She cast a look around, but Dem was nowhere to be seen.

"Ah, Tama has wandered off from school again," Griffin said. One of Mercy's many cousins, he had the trademark coloring of the family. Bronze skin, dark hair, green eyes that could be bright with laughter, or dark and stormy with anger. "We told him we'd stay and make sure you were all right."

Tamari, Dem's precocious daughter, had a habit of wandering off whenever something more interesting than her schooling presented itself. A teleporter, she was often able to dodge her teachers' best efforts to contain her. Mercy herself had tracked Tama down more than once. But with Dem on it, she wouldn't be needed this time.

"Thanks," she said. "I'm good." *Just a little*

creeped out. She thought of Wick's smug smile. *Maybe a lot creeped out.*

"You want to get something to eat?" Griffin asked.

Mercy made a face. His friendly offer, so soon on the heels of Wick's proposal, hit her wrong. "Um, no. I'm actually meeting with someone for dinner." She hoped, anyway. She hadn't checked her messages yet to see if Wolfgang had responded.

Griffin's face fell. "Sure," he said. But Mercy could sense his disappointment. "I need to check in on Vashti anyway." He hesitated, then walked away.

Mercy let out a breath as she watched him go. Griffin's mother had been one of Lilith's daughters, a half-sister to Mercy's own mother, Pallas. He was, effectively, her cousin. Like Cannon. Surely, he hadn't been asking her out romantically?

"Mercy, a moment of your time?"

Really? Mercy kept the thought to herself as she turned to face Sebastian.

"You better not be about to proposition me or ask me to dinner," she said.

He smiled faintly. "No." Then his smile vanished. "Wait, is that what Wick did?"

She waved a hand. "It doesn't matter. What did you need?"

Sebastian narrowed his eyes like he might pursue the matter for a moment, but to her relief, he let it go.

"I have something for you. A…gift."

"Oh." Mercy instantly felt awkward. She hardly

knew Sebastian. Certainly not well enough to be trading gifts. "Um...I'm not sure what to say."

He smiled, a kind sort of smile that said he understood her. He tilted his head, the long braid of his hair falling over his shoulder. "It's not that kind of gift. More of an inheritance, you might say."

"Oh." Her brow furrowed. "From who?"

"Lilith."

Shock washed through her. She'd been thinking vaguely of something her mother might have left behind, or perhaps her father, before his death. Her grandmother had never crossed her mind. Largely because Lilith had spent most of Mercy's childhood wanting her dead.

"That's, um, interesting." She stopped, unsure what to say. She didn't *want* anything from Lilith. "Maybe later? I should really be meeting Wolfgang."

Sebastian looked at her, his dark eyes patient. "You've only heard one side of Lilith's story. I think it's important that you get a complete picture of her. Especially since you are a queen, and she was not just your grandmother. She was the last queen we had."

"A complete picture? I'm not sure I understand."

"It's not quite the dinner hour yet. I'm sure Wolfgang isn't expecting you this early. If you wouldn't mind accompanying me briefly? I would prefer not to have this conversation standing in the corridor, but I would like the opportunity to explain."

Put like that, Mercy couldn't think of a polite

way to refuse. A laugh bubbled up suddenly and she grinned at him.

"What?" he asked, surprised.

"Cannon said you were good with people. He just failed to mention how good. Or the fact that you apparently have diplomacy down to a science." She shook her head, and moved to join him.

Sebastian smiled as they walked. "I'm no diplomat. I'm just good at listening."

"Uh-huh."

"It's true. You'd be surprised how little most people actually pay attention to what others are saying."

She noticed that he shortened his stride so she could easily keep up. Mercy was tall. When she walked beside Reaper, their strides matched. They were close in height. But Sebastian towered over her, and his long legs could have easily outpaced her. Instead, he walked beside her as naturally as if they did it every day.

Walking through *Nemesis* with him was an interesting experience. Doors opened before they reached them. The lift was waiting for them when they got to the end of the deck, and after they entered it, the doors slid shut and the lift began to move seemingly of its own volition. She hadn't seen Sebastian select a destination, and she certainly hadn't done so.

"How does that work?" she asked, curious. "Your Talent. Are you always connected to the ship?"

"Yes. The longer I'm connected to something, the easier it is to maintain the link. I've been aboard *Nemesis* for a long time." There was affection in his voice, as though he spoke of a treasured friend and not a hunk of metal and nanograph traveling through space.

"How much of the ship are you connected to?"

"All of it." He smiled at her. "You're going to ask me what that means." He leaned back against the wall, splaying a hand over it. "It means with little effort, I can control any system on this ship at any given time. Open any door, program any computer, calculate a jump, or lock down any area I want."

"Are you…aware of the people aboard? Do you know, for example, who else is in a lift right now, on another deck?"

"If I focus on that area, yes. But I try to give people their privacy as much as I can."

"But you could spy on everyone if you wanted to."

"It would be a little difficult to filter if I tried to see everything at once. But yes, if it happens aboard ship, I will know it." He paused. "If I want to. Some things should remain private. I can remove myself from an area as well."

Mercy was intrigued to see him flush. It was the first time she'd seen a pirate react with any sort of embarrassment.

Charmed, she grinned at him. "You mean you're not a voyeur?"

"No. I certainly try not to be."

Which meant he hadn't always succeeded. If she knew him better, she might tease him about that.

The lift stopped, and he stepped out, not quite looking at her.

It occurred to Mercy there might be a very specific reason for his discomfort.

"You haven't ever…um…accidentally spied on Reaper…with me?"

"No!" His eyes went wide and he held up his hands. "No, definitely not. That would be more than embarrassing. Reaper would not react well, I think. I like my life. I'd prefer to keep it."

She laughed. "Fair enough.

She realized the moment she followed him off the lift that they were in an area of the ship she'd never ventured before. A short hallway opened up into a huge room, the nanograph walls giving way to clear plasteel panels that arched into a dome overhead.

In the center of the room, a hexagonal shape surrounded something that thrummed with power. She could feel it beating against her skin, the rhythmic pulse of it almost like the beat of drums. Not unpleasant, but a little odd.

"What is this place?" she asked, turning in a circle as she took it all in. A padded bench lined the walls in front of the plasteel, as though people could come here and sit and relax, or even sleep.

Sebastian's gaze followed her as she moved around the room. "The heart of *Nemesis*."

"I thought the engine room was the heart."

"No. That's where the propulsion engines are. But after the incident last year with the bomb, I moved the jump drive."

"You…moved the drive?" Mercy stared at him, incredulous. "How?"

"Nanograph can do almost anything, reshape itself endlessly. My connection with her makes

Nemesis more adaptable than any other ship out there." He nodded to the hexagonal compartment. "If those idiots had managed to blow themselves up in the engine room, they'd have destroyed the entire ship. No one else manages the jump drive anyway. Just me. So I moved it. If something happens, and the propulsion engines go down—"

"—or get blown up?"

"Yes, or some idiot puts a bomb in the engine room again, I can close off that part of the ship and save most of the crew, salvaging *Nemesis* in the process." He shrugged. "No one else can get here; the lift will only go to this room with a special key, or my Talent. No one but Cannon and the Core even know where the jump drive is now."

"Wow." Mercy walked a circle around the drive. "It's safe?"

"Yes. As long as no one's trying to blow it up. The compartment has special shielding that keeps the drive and any energy it gives off contained."

"I can feel it," Mercy said, rubbing at her arms.

"If you stayed here long enough, you'd stop noticing. Monarch-class vessels boast the most powerful drives in existence. This one alone could power a small planet." Sebastian came to stand beside her. "It's breathtaking."

His voice was soft, and Mercy realized this place was special to him. Looking around, she noticed a doorway at the far end, and she glimpsed a room beyond it not very different from her own quarters.

"You live here?" she guessed.

"Yes." He spread his hands. "Welcome to my home. Where I feel closest to *Nemesis*. The accommodations are a little spare, but the room is large, and the view is fantastic."

She couldn't argue with that. Right now, looking up, she could see nothing but blackness and stars, but if *Nemesis* were closer to any celestial bodies, it would be spectacular.

"Wow. This is impressive."

"Now that you know - and you're Queen - I'll have a key made for you. So you can use the lift to come here whenever you'd like." He glanced down at her. "You should come up next time we pass near a nebula."

"I just might. The observation deck has nothing on this place."

He laughed, a low, melodic sound. "Being connected to the ship does have some perks."

"You brought me here to show me this?"

"Yes. And to talk with you in private." Sebastian crossed over to the bench, taking a seat and gesturing for her to do the same. "People don't always react predictably when Lilith comes up in conversation. I didn't think talking about her out in public would be wise. Especially right now, while everyone's still adjusting."

"You mean to me. Being Queen." Mercy took a seat a few feet from him. The cushion gave slightly, reshaping itself to fit her exactly. It didn't look it, but the bench was surprisingly comfortable.

He inclined his head. "Unfortunately, yes. That's not a reflection on you. But people are going to be volatile for awhile. They're worried about Cannon."

"So am I! I want him back as bad as anyone. I want them all back."

"Yes. But Cannon saved us in the wake of Lilith's death. People like to complain, some even imagine they could do the job better, but deep down, they know they're wrong. Everyone trusts Cannon, even those who don't like him."

"And they don't trust me." Even to her own ears, Mercy's voice sounded glum. None of this was a revelation. Hell, she didn't exactly trust all of the pirates yet herself. But it was surprisingly disheartening to begin as Queen knowing that no one had much faith in her.

"Give them time. They just need to get to know you." Sebastian paused, choosing his words with care. "Lilith made mistakes."

"Oh, really? Is that what you're calling it?"

Sebastian sighed. "Mercy, you have to understand, she wasn't always a bad Queen." He was silent for a moment. He seemed to be thinking deeply, his thoughts turned inward. Finally, he said, "Did you know I wasn't born here?"

"No, I didn't."

He looked away, out into the darkness. "I don't remember much of my early childhood. Just flashes. Places and vague faces I can't quite recall. But I spent a number of the following years as a slave. I'm not sure how long. My last master was a mercenary. He chained me to his ship and used my Talent to win battles."

"I'm so sorry." Mercy started to reach out, to touch his hand where it gripped the edge of the bench beside him. But she stopped, unsure if that sort of comfort would be welcome.

"You must know that though many Talented escaped the Commonwealth, there is a thriving black market in human trafficking. Everything from nulls to illegal clones, to Talented like us. We fetch a premium price, of course. We're rare. And powerful." For someone who'd experienced this so personally, his voice was surprisingly calm and free of bitterness.

"Doesn't that make you angry?"

He turned and met her eyes. "Of course. I've spent my entire life being angry. But I can't let my emotions rule me if I want to put a stop to it. For that, I need a clear head, time, and resources. This issue extends across the entire Commonwealth. Slaves are taken on one world, and shipped like cargo to others. As many as we've tracked and freed, there are millions, maybe billions more out there. The network is so vast, and so pervasive it's a galaxy-wide problem. It has backers in the highest levels of Commonwealth government. In the richest megacorporations. With so many credits and hard coin to be made, many aspects of the slave trade are protected and financed by those in power. Cut off one supplier, and a dozen more spring up in its place."

Mercy didn't know what to say. Everything felt inadequate. It was a reality of the universe, she knew, but she'd never come across it firsthand before. The closest brush had come back in her smuggling days.

She cleared her throat. "I knew it happened, but I had no idea it was so extensive. We avoided smugglers who dealt in black cargo when I was working with Wolfgang. I remember once, he found out an old contact was shipping illegal clones. The authorities caught and arrested him right after we left the system. I never asked, but I'm pretty sure the old Wolf tipped them off."

"Traditional smugglers are only a small part of the network. Most of the high end merchandise is shipped via licensed merchants working for mega-corporations. You'd be surprised how many there are. The manifests list something different, of course, but the cargo is often human, kept in stasis pods and hidden among regular cargo crates to avoid detection by port authorities."

"And you track these merchants and try to disrupt them?"

"That's why I'm telling you this." He turned on the bench so he was facing her. "Not only did Lilith give me my freedom, but she helped me track and free thousands more. She backed all of my efforts without question, even during the worst of her madness."

"Madness?"

He hesitated. "Yes. When I first knew her, the signs were small. Infrequent. Most of the time, she was a powerful queen with a strong personality, but not cruel. The cracks were less visible then."

Mercy struggled to reconcile what he was saying. "She murdered my father when I was three," she said.

"I didn't say the signs weren't there, just that they were less frequent. From what I've put together, Lilith began her reign as a strong queen. Respected, even. As the years went on, she became paranoid, erratic, more quick to anger."

Mercy's heart pounded. This sounded like

something progressive. Like an illness or a disease. Something hereditary? As much as she'd worried about becoming like Lilith, those fears had been vague. Now she wondered if she had to worry about something more specific.

"What do you think happened?" she asked.

"Lilith was the strongest person I'd ever met. Bold, commanding, but also uncompromising when it came to protecting her people. She was magnificent." His voice rang with admiration, and something deeper.

"You…loved her?" Mercy asked gently.

"Of course. She was the mother I never had. She took me in, treated me as her own son, gave me a life I'd never dreamed possible. And the means to give that life to others with the same unfortunate circumstances as myself."

"I see."

"I don't think you do. Yet." His dark eyes were steady. "I know you've heard all of the stories. As time passed, the Lilith I knew changed. Her paranoia grew more rampant. She saw betrayal everywhere she looked, and she was deeply, deeply afraid of something."

"Afraid." Mercy drew back. In all of the descriptions she'd heard of her grandmother, fear had never been among them. "What did she have to fear?"

"I don't know. But whatever caused it, the emotion grew to dominate her life. She wasn't afraid for herself. I know people think everything she did was self-serving, but they would be wrong. The thing that terrified Lilith most was losing her people."

Mercy's first instinct was to think that Sebastian was clearly biased. That he owed Lilith his life and his freedom, and consequently he didn't see her with clear eyes. After all, Mercy had a lifetime of tales that told a vastly different story. Her grandmother had assassinated people. She'd killed Mercy's father. Hunted Mercy and Pallas. Incited the pirates to a knife's edge of temper and violence.

Her nickname was the Bitch Queen.

What Sebastian was saying seemed like an excuse for all of that simply by giving it a reason. Whether caused by a physical or mental illness, it didn't matter, ultimately, that Lilith's actions had been rooted in fear.

She'd still done terrible things. Terrible, awful things.

"I'm sorry, Sebastian. I understand that she saved you. And you loved her. But she was the nightmare that haunted my childhood. Her specter chased us through every spaceport, every new life my mother and I tried to establish. My grandmother might have been the key to your freedom, but she robbed me of mine."

Instead of looking disappointed, Sebastian nodded. "I understand. Still, I wanted you to know there was more to her than what you've heard. That she could be giving, even kind." He stood up as he spoke, and knelt beside the bench.

A drawer opened where none had existed a moment before. He reached inside and pulled something out. Mercy caught the glint of something dark and metallic in his hand as he regained his feet.

"I have something for you. It was hers, but it was also her mother's, and her mother's before that. I'm not sure how many Queens wielded it in total, but I do know that it goes back at least as far as Amestris."

Amestris had been Mercy's great-great grandmother. She was the Queen who first established the pirate colonies. The one who united them in the wake of the Commonwealth's edict against Talent. Intrigued now, she found herself leaning forward as he extended his hand.

In his palm lay a wide circular band made of some metal Mercy had never seen before. So dark it was almost black, with a filigree pattern made of delicate links, almost like a fantastical chain or web. The room's lights glinted off the intricate swirls and interconnected strands.

"Is that a bracelet?" Mercy had never been one to wear jewelry. She and her mother had always traveled too light to worry about anything of value. And there wasn't much cause for playing dress up when you lived as a smuggler. But she felt a sudden, unexpected yearning for the beautiful piece.

It was a connection that went all the way back to her ancestors, the first pirate queens. Even if Lilith had worn it, this was more than just a treasured object of her grandmother's.

"Yes," said Sebastian. "And no."

Mercy stopped reaching or it when he said those words. "What does that mean?"

"It's a bracelet, and more."

"More?"

"In the Ascension Wars, Talented had more

than just their mental gifts to fight with. Weapons were designed just for us, special blades and guns which could be triggered and powered with the use of Talent. This is one such relic. Here."

He held it out to her, smiling when she still hesitated. "It won't bite you, Mercy. In fact, this could be a distinct advantage. Only a few of these old weapons are left. The Commonwealth destroyed as many as they could."

Gingerly she took it. It felt cool and smooth. She had to resist the urge to run her fingers over it. A small sliver of doubt crept in. She didn't know Sebastian well. At the same time, Cannon had specifically mentioned that she could trust him. Even Reaper seemed to trust him, and that could only be said for a handful of people.

And she didn't sense anything deceitful. He seemed genuine in everything he'd told her.

She turned the cuff over in her hands, looking for a clasp. She didn't find one.

"You should be able to slip it on."

It seemed too small for that, but when she slid it over her hand, sure enough, it glided on smoothly, then seemed to shrink so it fit snug and comfortably against her wrist.

"Now what?"

"Focus your Talent on it. As you do when you connect with someone else's mind."

Mercy took a deep breath, and settled her mind. Then she stretched out her thoughts, brushing against Sebastian's shields, but ignoring them as she sought something else. It was odd. When she'd first looked at the bracelet, it seemed inert. A hunk of pretty metal. But now it glowed with Talent. Warm and golden.

Mercy felt it the moment she connected, like something clicking into place. There was a flash of Talent and she felt as though something engulfed her wrist and hand. It wasn't painful.

When she looked at her arm, the bracelet had vanished. Instead, she saw a brilliant light emanating around her hand and fingers, focused into a point, like a flame. Or a blade. She moved her fingers and the blade moved with them, extending and separating to move with her. Like individual knives connected to her fingers. She closed her hand into a fist, and it gelled into a single blade.

"Will this...cut someone?"

"Not in a physical sense. It's like a psychic weapon. A blade that attacks the mind. Cut someone with it, and you can cripple or kill them. They will feel pain, but there will be no visible wound."

"How do I...?"

"Break the connection."

It took some effort to pull her mind away from it, but when she did the glow vanished. The bracelet did not return.

Mercy frowned. "Didn't that work?"

"Look closer," said Sebastian. She did, holding her arm carefully up near her face. The filigree pattern was still there, like faint markings on her skin. The bracelet had become a part of her.

"Whoa. Can I take it off?"

"Of course. It will respond to your commands. If you reconnect, just imagine very clearly taking it off. I believe even during the wars these weapons were rare and valuable. This was a security feature to avoid losing them."

Mercy stared at her arm for a few moments more. Carefully, she rubbed a hand over her wrist. She could barely feel a faint pattern where the filigree lay.

"Every Queen we've had has worn it," said Sebastian. "It's right that you should have it now."

"Thank you, Sebastian." Mercy meant it. It felt like she was connected to her past now. She might not have grown up here, but she was one of them. A pirate. And now she had something that went back to the very beginnings of their history. "I'll treasure it."

"If you ever want to know more about Lilith, you have only to ask."

That part Mercy was more uncertain of. She wasn't sure she wanted to know all of the details of her grandmother's life. When Vashti woke, she'd ask for her thoughts on it. Her aunt had been trying for months now to teach Mercy what she knew or remembered about being a queen. Out of everyone, Vashti had the most knowledge on the subject. Daughter to one queen and sister to another, she was the closest Mercy had to a true mentor for her specialized Talent. It was possible that something in Lilith's past could prove valuable.

"I'll think about it."

The tunnel was dark, seemingly endless, and so narrow in places that Cannon had to remove the chestplate he wore to squeeze through the gap. At irregular intervals, lights would flicker overhead, alleviating the utter darkness with a faint glow.

Reaper had the impression no one had used this tunnel in a long time. Perhaps the bar and its patrons no longer remembered it was there. Because whenever the light did spill from above to illuminate their path, however briefly, a thick layer of dust coated the floor beneath their feet.

On the last dregs of their power, the lights struggled against the darkness, a losing battle. Much of the trip was made in pitch blackness. The group had to feel their way along the walls.

Reaper stretched out his senses. It was difficult to focus with so many other lives around him. He kept seeing the various ways he could end them on an infinite loop. He pushed past the instincts of the killer and instead sought out the twisting path of the tunnel. Far ahead, he could sense the mental presence of Ghost's spectral form, and Zion's. They were scouting. Reaper used their location to pinpoint the direction he needed to go.

In a way, it was the proverbial light guiding him forward. He was first, after the scouts. Atrea was behind him, her presence an uncomfortable prickle of heat up his spine. Having someone at his back like that brought out the killer in him, especially someone as skilled as Atrea. But he'd placed her there deliberately. Mercy would never forgive him if he let something happen to her sister. For though they called one another friends, it was clear to him that they were family in all ways but blood.

Behind her came Cannon, and behind him, Reaper's dogs, with Feria and her people sandwiched between them. Knox brought up the rear. He'd placed a few strategic explosives along their back trail. If anyone tried following them down the tunnel, they would be in for a nasty surprise.

Tension in the group was high. Reaper felt more than heard a disturbance not too long after they began their trek into the dark.

Report, he sent back to his dogs.

No problems, boss, said Titus. *One of Feria's people doesn't like tight spaces. Had a bit of a panic. We're all moving again now.*

No one stays behind.

Everyone accounted for. No one stays, Titus confirmed. That didn't mean they were happy about it. Feria had argued up top, before going into the tunnel. Now, she remained silent, concentrating on feeling her way forward. Like the rest of them.

The longer they walked, the more restless the

minds around him became. Everyone was ready to get out of this place and back into the open air. Even if the port was crawling with Navy fire teams.

Boss, Zion's mental voice sounded grim. *We have a problem.*

What is it?

The Mother-damned Navy decided to set up their command station in one of the empty warehouses. Guess which one?

Reaper didn't like guessing. But he understood the gist of Zion's meaning.

He stopped, cursing beneath his breath.

"What's wrong?" Atrea's voice sounded unnaturally loud, echoing down the tunnel even though she spoke the words softly. Reaper's muscles flexed and released as he had to resist the urge to silence her. If she hadn't been wearing a dampener, he could have spoken with her telepathically. He still could, but forcing his way past the device could cause more problems than it solved. If it stopped working, and Atrea's Talent became an issue, it would complicate things.

"Our exit opens next to the Navy command center," he said, his voice barely above a whisper.

"Fuck me."

Reaper didn't think that required a response.

"Weren't we taking this tunnel to avoid a fight?" she asked.

"That no longer appears to be an option."

Wait, Cannon said. Reaper could tell from the feel of the link that Cannon had included multiple people in his telepathic conversation. *Perhaps there is another way.*

This is a tunnel, Cannon. One way back, one way forward. There are no turns.

Maybe not. But our direction doesn't matter. We just need to avoid detection.

"The don't-look-at-me trick," said Atrea. "Mercy does it. So does one of the Veritas people."

For a moment, Reaper thought Cannon must have included her in the telepathic link. Then he realized her mind had just been working along the same lines, trying to solve the problem.

Titus, ordered Reaper. *Find out who among Feria's people can hide our presence with Talent. Ghost, Zion - how many personnel do we need to avoid?*

Maybe twenty.

Reaper did rapid calculations in his head. The bar had held at least that many nulls before Feria's people forced them out. It was doable.

A few moments later Titus was back. *They can do it, once we're closer. We have to be careful, though. Apparently this is a more subtle, difficult trick than just telling nulls to leave. They have to distract everyone from noticing us without significantly changing their behavior. We don't want to call attention in any way.*

Reaper thought about the chaos that would reign if this failed. Fireteams called to their position. If things went poorly, the Navy could always call in an orbital strike. Even a killer would be hard pressed to overcome that.

Impress upon them the consequences of failure, he sent back to Titus.

Already done, boss.

They began moving again, faster now that the end was near. Unfortunately, no lights flickered on at the exit. Reaper practically ran into the iron rungs of the ladder that led up and out. He felt around carefully until he found the same sort of lever the entrance had, but did not trigger it.

Reaching out with his Talent, he confirmed for himself the number of Navy personnel. Closer to two dozen minds. Nulls that were on their guard. Oddly, they didn't seem afraid.

Even more odd, Reaper had a tough time connecting with them. He couldn't seem to penetrate their shields, even though they felt like the same instinctive barriers nulls always had.

He could *see* the holes and vulnerabilities, but he could not reach past them. At least, not without the sort of effort that might be noticed, even by a null.

Cannon, do you see anything odd about their shields? The nulls.

Moments dragged past. Reaper could sense the others shifting restlessly in the line behind him. The air in here felt heavy and close. Everyone wanted out.

Strange, Cannon said finally. *I can't get a sense of their emotions. Like everything is locked up tight behind a full shield.*

But their shields are not complete, Reaper said. *I can see the weaknesses. But I can't get past them.*

Nor can I. Titus, find out if shields prevent our friend's Talent from properly distracting them.

More seconds ticked past, until even Reaper felt a building pressure to move. The longer they stayed here, the more the trap tightened around them. Birn was not a large spaceport. It wouldn't take the fire teams long to search the entire waystation.

All right, boss, said Titus at last. *They think they can do it. But not a distraction. They have to get inside shields for that. Instead, it'll be more of a directive. A pressure not to look at us, and not to see us when they do. It's more difficult to pull off. There's a chance it won't work.*

How big of a chance?

Twenty percent. Maybe twenty-five.

Not great odds. But better than staying here. They had to do something. Still, Reaper said nothing. Something felt wrong, the feeling so acute he stood still and thought through their situation again from the beginning, going slowly through every moment since the Commonwealth jumped into the system.

Reaper, Cannon pressed.

Nulls shouldn't have shields like that. In fact, they don't. So why can't we reach them? I don't like it, Cannon.

Neither do I. But we don't have a lot of options here.

No, they didn't. Which meant they might very well be doing exactly what someone wanted them to do.

Zion, Ghost. I want you in flanking positions. Their spectral forms could move invisibly, but still act and effect the physical world if necessary.

He reached back to Titus. *Now.*

Reaper's hands tightened on the lever. An eternal minute passed before Titus came back. *Go, boss.*

He pulled the lever, opening the hatch. Bright light spilled down, throwing back the darkness. It blinded him temporarily. Ignoring the tearing of his eyes, he felt for the iron rungs and pulled himself up and out. They couldn't afford to waste time.

He kept his focus on the Navy men and women as he moved. Waiting for any sign that they'd noticed the hatch flinging open or the hole that had opened up in the floor next to them.

Reaper froze. A man stood so close to the hatch that he could have reached out and touched him without taking a step. He was part of a group, armed and armored, and far too close for comfort.

Wait, he sent back to Cannon.

The warehouse was huge. A few empty cargo crates lined the far wall, stacked haphazardly. There were three entry points: the huge cargo door open on the other side of the Navy command station, and two smaller doors closed and locked on either side of the room. Sealed with tech binders that would make opening them noisy, at best.

The cargo door would have to be their exit. Unfortunately, that meant moving past all of the Navy personnel.

The group beside him wore shock troop armor, and they were armed with plasma rifles and disruptors. It was clearly one of the fire teams reporting to the mobile command station, situated just beyond them and guarded by more armored troops. Officers with datapads coordinated with holo projections from the ships in orbit.

Reaper remained still, but not a single head turned towards him. He continued his climb until he was free of the tunnel. When no one noted his presence, he sent Cannon an all clear. He positioned himself between Atrea and the fire team as she climbed out behind him.

Those odd shields bothered him. If the worst happened, he wanted to be close enough not to rely on his Talent to kill them. He felt the others moving behind him, but didn't take his gaze off of the soldiers.

Cannon would get the others out. Reaper didn't need to check in to know that. He felt Atrea move up beside him, and irritation flashed through him. He wanted to tell her to go, but he couldn't risk speaking. That twenty-five percent margin for error was just too big to take risks.

The man standing nearest him shifted. It was a restless sort of movement. None of this group had the casual air of men waiting for orders. Instead, tension held them still. Normally, Reaper could have picked up easily on their thoughts, but right now he had to guess at the reason for their unease. It was dangerous for nulls to hunt Talented. Even highly trained and armed nulls. It could be as simple as that.

But even as Reaper thought that, another man's head turned. He swept the room with a searching gaze, his eyes passing right over Reaper and Atrea without pause. Cold rose within Reaper, icing his veins with a familiar readiness. These men sensed something, even if they didn't yet know what.

This whole thing could fall apart in an instant.

The nearest man stood an arm's length from Reaper. Close enough for blades.

He closed his hands into fists. He rarely felt the need to access the weapons he'd inherited from his father. Worn about his neck, the two pieces of ancient tech connected to form a torque that rested against his collarbone and usually lay dormant. It vanished into his flesh so completely that only someone who knew what to look for would notice anything odd, a barely raised pattern in his skin.

A moment's concentration was all it took to flare the tech to life. Heat warmed his skin, a sharp contrast to the ice filling him with cold darkness. It flowed over his shoulders and down his arms until he held blades in his hands.

Beside him, Atrea inhaled sharply. She was too much the professional to react more, but the sudden appearance of a weapon in Reaper's hand had startled her. It wasn't solid, like a real knife or sword would have been, but a shimmering, reflective shape, barely perceptible to normal eyes.

Atrea was clearly a highly observant individual. Reaper noted it dispassionately, adding it to his growing catalog of her skills. Slowly, she eased one of her guns free, the movement carefully smooth and incremental. Once the weapon cleared its holster, she gripped it in both hands, and like him, waited.

A small part of Reaper's mind was aware of the people moving behind him. Crawling out of the tunnel. Moving quickly and quietly past the fire team, past the command station, and out the cargo door. The rest of his mind was focused, his awareness expanded to include all two dozen of the soldiers in this room.

He waited, suspended in the cold dark. He was aware of Cannon stopping at the door, ushering others through.

Go, he sent.

I don't take orders from you, Reaper. In case you've forgotten. Tension made Cannon's mental voice harsh. It wasn't his usual relaxed drawl.

Reaper was unfazed.

You are King. You are more necessary than I.

And we have a Queen now. Cannon paused. *I'm not leaving until the last of us are out.*

One of the men in the fire team paced away from the rest of his unit. Only three steps, but enough to have tension spiking through Reaper. The man stopped. He was facing the cargo doors, a frown marring his face. Though his gaze wasn't focused on any one spot, he stood directly across from Cannon.

Mercy is still learning, Reaper said. *If something happens to me, she'll need you.* He paused. *Cannon. No one else can do this.*

Beside him, Atrea sighted her gun on the man watching the cargo door. Reaper approved of the move. It left him free to deal with the rest of the fire team.

Still, Cannon hesitated.

Imagine Treon teaching her, supporting her. Or Griffin. Even Vashti, without another voice to balance their agendas.

Fuck. Reaper heard capitulation in Cannon's tone. *I'm going. Don't fucking die.*

Reaper didn't answer. Survival was the obvious goal.

Cannon stepped outside, disappearing from view. The soldier stayed still, his eyes moving over the entire doorway, looking for whatever had sparked his interest. A moment passed, and he turned and walked back to his unit.

Reaper didn't relax. Half of the Veritas group were still moving towards the exit. Knox was the last to climb out of the hatch. He eased it closed.

Every time one of the soldiers in the room moved or spoke, it grabbed Reaper's attention until it was clear they weren't taking notice of any of the Talented in their midst.

One of the women walking with Feria was too pale, her face tight with strain. The other woman had an arm looped through hers, supportive. Reaper realized that must be the source of the Talent helping them stay hidden.

Titus...

On it, boss. His dog grabbed the woman's other arm, and he and Feria half carried her as they moved towards the cargo door.

Once they were through, Reaper felt them stop on the other side. Likely to keep the young woman in range for Reaper and the others. Only four more remained, not counting Reaper and Atrea, still a silent presence beside him.

Knox and the rest moved quickly, efficiently. No one took notice of them. One, two three…and then it was only Reaper and Atrea.

He glanced at her, a flick of his head telling her to go. She didn't hesitate, moving quickly, angling the gun down at her side, but still ready if she needed it.

Only once she was out did Reaper move. He kept his gate even, his blades ready as he stepped around the fire team and walked to the door. At last, he stepped outside and around the corner, where the rest of their group waited.

Ghost, Zion. Spectral forms appeared beside

him. *Scout,* he said. They weren't out of danger yet. Now they were at the most risk of discovery, out in the open. And the Veritas woman was spent, her face pinched and the hollows around her eyes telling Reaper that she was dangerously close to burnout. They needed new cover.

This warehouse was positioned right beside the docks. Their next move needed to be gaining a ship. But that would require dodging more Navy troops, and the same trick wasn't going to work twice. Even as he watched, the woman sagged against Feria, shaking her head. Reaper knew without being told that she'd let go of her Talent. Anyone looking at them now would see them.

And he still didn't like that oddness with their shields. Nulls did not have barriers like that. Not without help.

What now? He sent the question to Cannon. *We can't stay here.*

Cannon cast a look around. *There are empty docking spaces. We head for one of them, as close as we dare to a Navy dropship.*

Another fire team could be along at any moment. Reaper looked at Ghost.

Teams are moving in a standard grid pattern, boss. I think they've already searched the docking spaces. They'll circle back around soon. We need to move now.

Reaper glanced at the woman Feria was holding up. It was clear she wouldn't be moving under her own power.

Titus, carry her.

Feria tensed and looked like she wanted to argue when the dog stepped forward to take the young woman from her. But none of them dared start an argument. They might hate each other, but both groups were now in a situation of mutual survival.

Reaper ignored her glare, just as Titus did. The man was probably the most even tempered of all of Reaper's dogs. Like the rest of them, he was young and fit. His white blond hair was cut short, his dark eyes a startling contrast to his fair coloring. He easily lifted the young woman. He was an object reader, part of the precognition family of gifts. But he also had a blunt form of telekinesis, an odd pairing as the two Talents were so completely different. Titus couldn't manipulate small items, but he could use his Talent like a crude shield or a battering ram if they ran into trouble. He was also the medic on the team, which made him the best choice to deal with someone on the edge of burnout.

Let's move. Reaper took the lead once again. They kept to the same order they had in the tunnels, with Zion and Ghost keeping an eye on the locations of the various fire teams searching for them.

For just a moment, thoughts of Mercy distracted him. He felt an unusual flash of discomfort as he wondered about her situation on *Nemesis.* He knew she and Dem had made it back to the ship, and he knew the ship had safely jumped from the system. But that didn't mean she was safe.

As a rule, outside concerns didn't intrude when he was on a mission. The stray thought caught him off guard. He pushed it away, unwilling to be distracted when he could least afford it. Mercy would be fine. She had Dem and Treon as allies.

Vashti as well. Others, like Sebastian and Griffin would also help keep her safe.

Right now, he needed to stay focused. Something was very wrong about this entire situation. The Navy's presence in this system, so outside their normal patrol routes, was telling enough. But the strange barrier protecting the nulls was something else entirely.

He couldn't worry about Mercy, when he needed to be concerned with his own survival. Something told him the most dangerous threat was yet to come.

Mercy eventually lost the battle of trying to dodge Wolfgang, as she'd known she would. He was waiting outside her quarters after she left Sebastian's, and without a word, he pulled her into a hug. As always, he smelled of old leather and burnt metal. His battered old jacket was responsible for the former, and the latter was the odd scent spaceships collected on their travels through the dark.

Tonight, the smell of whisky wreathed him as well. Mercy stiffened in his arms.

"Who told you?" she asked, the words muffled against him.

A hand stroked her hair. "It's all over the ship, girl. Everyone knows who was left behind."

She went to pull away, and he let her, but only so he could look her in the eye.

He looked good. His gray hair was newly cut. He'd never quite left behind keeping it military short. A faint stubble covered his jawline. She always knew things were really bad when he forgot to shave. This was just growth since the morning, though. Nothing to worry about, yet.

His blue eyes, framed by age lines, saw too much. "Are you all right?" he asked.

Mercy blinked back tears. Because she wasn't all right, not really. Some of the most important people in her life were marooned on that planet.

But she refused to cry. Silent, she shook her head without saying anything. As usual, Wolfgang didn't need to be Talented to read her.

"Don't worry about Atrea," he said with a smile. "I raised my girls to be smart. She'll be all right."

Guilt had Mercy fidgeting, running her fingers over the cuff that now marked her wrist. Wolfgang might think he knew the full story, but he didn't.

He didn't know that some malevolent, powerful presence was hovering over Birn, perhaps with bad intentions toward the pirates hiding there. She swallowed, considering whether to tell him.

He frowned at her. "We aren't doing this again, are we?"

"Doing what?"

"That thing you do, where Atrea ends up in trouble and you blame yourself." He crossed his arms. "You lived with us for fifteen years. Been through thick and thin together. And you *still* don't understand that Atrea gets into trouble all on her own?"

Mercy looked down. "But she wouldn't even be on Birn if —"

"Mercy."

She stopped talking, and Wolfgang gave her shoulders a squeeze.

"You have to stop feeling guilty for being loved." He sighed. "Do you remember when you were fifteen? And Atrea decided she was old enough to take jobs on her own?"

Mercy remembered, all right. Things had gone sour on a contract, and rather than take on a new, less than favorable option, Wolfgang meant to jump the line and leave the system early. Except when he went to do it, his daughter was missing.

Atrea was sure she could negotiate better terms. And she might have, but it turned out the supplier had a nice side business selling illegal clones. And he thought Atrea was pretty and young enough to make a great Prime. Primes were the source material cloning companies used when making their product.

She'd nearly gotten herself kidnapped, and instead of jumping out of the system before trouble could start, Wolfgang had to storm the supplier's warehouse to get his daughter back. Mercy, having played lookout for her friend, was caught in the middle. She was the one who made the call to tell Wolfgang. On the one hand, getting Atrea into trouble with her father. But on the other, saving her life.

"I remember," she said.

"Atrea is too smart for her own good. My girl is brilliant. She comes up with amazing ideas and plans, and she's been responsible more than once for filling our coffers with hard coin or getting us out of trouble. The problem is, she's just as responsible for getting us *into* trouble. She's overconfident and stubborn, and she barrels ahead without always thinking everything through." He shook his head. "Atrea is going to do what she thinks is best. Nothing I say has ever stopped her. Don't think *you* can stop her, either."

That was all true. "But—"

"Let me ask you something, Mercy. Whose idea was it to set up the meeting with Veritas?"

"Mine."

"Are you certain of that?"

Mercy thought back. She'd decided to do it while talking with Atrea, that much was true. Well, drinking with her would be more accurate.

The conversation was not entirely clear in her memory, truth be told. The plan had just sort of evolved, starting when Mercy had said something like "I should just negotiate with Veritas anyway. None of *them* are going to do it." And ending when they decided to steal a ship and send a message to set up a meet.

"I mean, we came up with it together, I guess," she said.

"Exactly. Atrea wasn't just dragged into it by you, Mercy. She was an active participant. Likely an enthusiastic one."

Well, Mercy couldn't argue with that. She might not remember everything about that night, but she had a sudden, vivid memory of Atrea sitting bolt upright, bottle of Bennethan Run in hand, and saying "I've got it! We're going to steal a ship."

"You have a habit of doing this," Wolfgang said. "It's not healthy."

"What do you mean?"

"Whenever someone does something to help you, or protect you, or just because we love you, it terrifies you. You find reasons for anything negative to be your fault."

She scowled. "I don't do that."

He held up a hand. "I could go all the way back to your childhood, but for the sake of brevity lets stick with recent events." He ticked off fingers for each thing he said. "When you and Atrea were kidnapped, you blamed yourself. When Willem Frain took over this ship, you blamed yourself. When that bomb went off and almost blew us both to hell and back, you blamed yourself. Now here we are again, and you're blaming yourself for the decisions others made." He lowered his hands. "That's a lot of guilt to be shouldering."

"That's not what I'm doing."

"Isn't it? Were you not just taking all of the blame for Atrea's current situation? For Reaper? And Cannon? They *chose* to go to Birn, every one of them."

"Only for me." How could he not see that? Irritated, she glared at him.

"Oh, I see." He crossed his arms over his chest. "My mistake. Clearly, the universe revolves around you."

"That's not what I'm saying, and you know it." Flickers of anger made her voice sharp.

"It is exactly what you are saying. Did it ever occur to you that, for better or worse, Atrea's place is with these people now? That her future is impacted every bit as much as yours by however things go with Veritas? That just maybe, she has a vested, *personal* interest in ending these hostilities that has *nothing* to do with you?"

She opened her mouth, but nothing came out.

Wolfgang, damn him, just stood there. All of Mercy's anger drained away.

"Am I really that selfish and arrogant?" she asked in a small voice.

"Mercy," Wolfgang said gently. "It's not arrogance. Yes, guilt can be a selfish emotion. But it's rooted in something else."

"What?"

"Fear. Judgement."

"You think I'm afraid of others judging me?"

He stared at her for a long moment. Then he said, "Have you ever forgiven yourself for Pallas?"

Mercy sucked in a breath, stunned. If he'd reached out and slapped her, she wouldn't have been more shocked. "What?"

"You've always blamed yourself for her disappearance, Mercy. For her death. That's a hell of a thing for a child to carry."

It felt like her face had gone numb. She stared at him for a beat, but his words still hung there in the air between them. She couldn't come up with a reply. Words tumbled around in her head and she couldn't make sense of them. After a small eternity, she fumbled open the door to her quarters.

"I don't...I'm not all that hungry." She turned to step inside.

"Mercy."

Wolfgang reached for her, but she'd already moved away.

"No," she said. "Maybe tomorrow. I'm tired." She shut the door before he could protest, only feeling a little bad that she'd essentially closed it in his face.

She stood for a moment with her back against

the door. Processing. Was she selfish? Did she take on guilt and blame for things that weren't hers to shoulder?

Did she blame herself for her mother's disappearance?

She couldn't stop the questions. Her emotions seemed to be spiraling between fear, worry, anxiety, and guilt. And now there was another layer of uncertainty beneath all of that.

The truth was, she wasn't hungry. Instead, Mercy indulged in something she rarely used: the bath tub in her quarters. Using water to bathe on a ship could be dangerous. If the gravity generators stopped working, for example, she could find herself free-floating in a bubble of water. But with telekinesis as one of her Talents, the danger was minimal. Moving the water wouldn't be hard.

She slid aside the panel that normally hid the nanograph tub, shaped to look like white marble. It was large, much bigger than anything she'd expected on a ship, but the pirates had rebuilt much of *Nemesis* to suit their needs, and many of them enjoyed luxury. She filled it with warm water and sudsy oils that would soften her skin and fill the tub with frothy bubbles she could disappear into.

Disappearing for awhile sounded amazing.

The bubbles formed in a rainbow of colors that swirled into glittery spirals in the water, pooling and flowing around her when she stepped over the edge of the tub and sank beneath the water.

She submerged completely, allowing the water to block out the world. Silence closed around her, and she lay with her eyes closed, feeling her muscles relax and the worries of the universe retreat. For a little while, at least.

Well, for a few seconds. The problem with all of that silence was that it gave her mind time to focus and think.

Do I blame myself for Mom? Even now, all these years later, Mercy couldn't bring herself to think the word *dead*. She knew in her heart that Pallas was gone, that she'd probably been gone for years. But some part of her would never stop yearning for the possibility that one day, her mother would just show up, alive, with some explanation for where she'd been.

The problem was, her mother had told Mercy since she was three years old that they had to run and keep running, because grandmother wanted her dead. Wanted *Mercy* dead.

Her entire childhood had been constant moving and running to keep Mercy safe. Then her mother vanished, and Mercy was on her own, until she found herself drawn into Wolfgang and Atrea's little family. They'd accepted her and given her a home when she desperately needed one, and refused to let her keep running.

She came up out of the water when she couldn't hold her breath any longer. The air was scented from the oils, vanilla and lavender, for relaxation. But no matter how hard she tried, Mercy couldn't completely relax. Wolfgang's words kept tumbling around in her head.

Do I blame myself for Mom? Do I blame myself for everything negative that happens to the people I love?

A brush against her mind startled her. It was

the polite equivalent of a knock at her door, and she recognized the mental signature.

Sebastian?

I thought you'd want to know, we've completed the last jump. We're now as close as we can safely get to Birn. You can try contacting Reaper.

Thank you.

Pushing aside her earlier thoughts, Mercy took a deep breath and closed her eyes, settling her mind. She'd never tried to reach someone over this kind of distance.

She thought of Reaper, his distinctive mental presence. The cool wash of his Talent and mind. Focused on just that, she didn't think about how far away he was.

A familiar whisper barely on the edge of her consciousness brushed against her shields, so faint it might have been a snowflake landing on a window. Cold and then gone, melted away.

Reaper.

She reached again, straining.

There. She tried to grab it, but it disappeared just as fast.

Damn it. Frustration would only interfere. She concentrated on breathing and staying calm. He wasn't going anywhere. Neither was she.

A few minutes later, settled again, she reached once more for that cold hint of snow and ice.

Reaper. Nikolos.

*Mercy...*the sound of her name was so faint she thought for a moment she might have imagined it. Then it came again. *Mercy.*

Unsure how long she could keep the connection, she spoke quickly. *There's something in the system with you, not the Commonwealth Navy and not Veritas. Talented. They're in some kind of cloaked ship, and they're powerful enough to throw Treon back into his own mind.*

She waited, heart in her throat. His reply didn't come back with words. It was more of a feeling. A grim sort of acknowledgement. Relief made her light headed.

At least they knew, now.

Be careful. Come back to me.

Just that whisper brush of his mind told her he was still there, still listening.

I love you.

That hint of cold started to fade, and she panicked, sitting up in the tub so fast that water sloshed over the side. She couldn't lose the connection yet! There was still so much he needed to know.

Reaper, they have a killer, and we think one of them is a queen. We don't know what the others are, but they're powerful. Treon couldn't even identify one of them. You don't know if your Talent will work.

She waited again, but this time there was nothing. She had no idea if he'd heard. She ran frustrated hands through the wet tangle of her hair. Why had she wasted time with emotion when she should have just focused on the information he needed? What if he got himself killed?

A second later, cold brushed her skin like a feather light kiss, and she froze. She'd felt that exact thing before. It was one of Reaper's ways of showing affection that didn't require words or public displays.

Her whole body went limp, tension draining

away. He'd heard. Her face scrunched up as she tried to make contact again. A headache crept into the edges of her mind, forcing her to give up.

The tub heated, keeping the water warm. The bubbles faded. Her skin wrinkled with the moisture, and still she stayed. The pattern on her arm was more visible in the water, the glittery colors seeming to outline where the bracelet lay on her wrist.

Finally, her stomach growled. No matter how much she wanted to skip dinner, she knew she needed to eat. The last thing she'd eaten had consisted of some greasy fried tubers and that terrible sour ale on Birn, so many hours ago she gave up trying to do the math. She forced herself to leave the cocoon of scented water behind, drying off in an instant with a small ripple of telekinesis that sluiced the moisture from her skin.

Her hair remained damp, and she twisted it into a knot at the nape of her neck and dressed in some comfortable cotton sleepwear.

She might have needed to eat, but her stomach wasn't entirely settled. Worry and stress had it tied into knots. The headache only made it worse. She ordered a bowl of noodles and broth from the galley and ate it slowly. Dutifully, she poured herself a glass of *mnemosa*, the green drink filled with some sort of nutrients and vitamins that replenished the mind's energy. The pirates drank it routinely to boost Talent.

Mercy couldn't quite learn to like the stuff. Faintly sweet, it wasn't an unpleasant taste, but Willem Frain had given it to her during her captivity. Pair it with a nutritional bar, and she'd probably throw up. As it was, she forced herself to sip it while eating her dinner, only so that if Reaper tried to make contact again, she'd be ready.

She contact Sebastian and left a message for Treon, detailing what she'd told Reaper - or at least what she hoped he'd gotten out of the conversation. Then she made herself go to bed., but rest didn't come easy.

Her thoughts tumbled around in her head until she finally resorted to a mental exercise Vashti had taught her. Similar to meditation, it followed a pattern that tricked the mind into relaxing. Or at least, that's how Mercy thought of it.

Her mind drifted, and before long, faded into sleep.

Or into dreams.

It had been months since she'd dreamt of her mother. But even after all these years, she recognized the figure standing before a wall of books, antique shelves full of vintage paper and printed words. The long fall of dark hair down to her hips was so much like Mercy's own. The petite frame and rigid stance, her hands clasped lightly behind her back, was also familiar.

The last time she'd seen Pallas in a dream, her mother had been disappointed that Mercy continued to search for her. Frozen in time, she hadn't aged a day since the last time Mercy saw her.

Seeing her now, Mercy felt such a sad longing it closed her throat. She desperately wanted her mother to turn around and pull her into a hug. To tell her everything would be all right. No lectures, no disappointment. Just love and support. But it never went the way Mercy wanted it.

Always, memories intruded, turning the dreams into warnings rather than wishes.

Not this time. This was her dream, she was going to control it.

She cleared her throat, stepping towards her mother. This place didn't look like anywhere they'd ever been. Mercy couldn't recall visiting any museums or archives with old books, certainly no place with rows of shelves filled with them.

There was a chair, too. Something old and antique, with comfortable looking cushions covered in burgundy fabric and white flowers. A brick fireplace burned to one side, the flames providing the only light by which to see. The light flickered over Pallas's hair, catching the strands of auburn and lighter gold that threaded through the dark length of it.

Mercy took a breath, and reminded herself that she was the one in control here. "Mama?" she said, heart pounding. Just this once, it was going to be perfect.

"No." And the voice that spoke didn't belong to Pallas.

The woman turned around. Mercy felt all of the blood drain from her face. Bronze skin shone on the firelight. Green eyes flecked with amber, so like her own, so like her mother's. But not. Mercy's eyes held no amber flecks.

She might not remember knowing her, but Mercy had seen enough holos and pictures to recognize the woman standing before her.

Her cruel lips curved into a smile. "Hello, Mercy," said Lilith. "At last, we meet."

ercy stared at her grandmother, the villain who had haunted her nightmares as a child. Funny, in those dreams, Lilith had been a towering, terrifying figure. Her hands had reached for Mercy like the talons of some monster. Her face had been a visage of rage and hate that woke Mercy from a dead sleep and had her crawling into her mother's bed for comfort.

She'd never imagined Lilith like this. Petite. Normal. Her face was more striking than beautiful, all hard angles and sharp intelligence. She wore armored clothing, her hair falling over one shoulder in a long braid. A belt hung around her hips, holding a holster that was strapped to her leg. The armored vest hugged her frame, emphasizing her small waist. It tapered into armored pants and boots that reached up to her knees. Gold and black and red, with white accents flashing at her throat, sleeves, and waist.

She looked like a pirate queen. Far more than Mercy ever had.

Clearly, her subconscious was thinking harder about what Sebastian had said than she'd realized.

What the hell? She'd play along. "You're shorter than I remember," she said. The Lilith of her nightmares would never accept anything that smacked of criticism, especially not from an upstart granddaughter she'd never wanted.

Dream Lilith smiled and her eyes sparkled with humor. "Am I? Well, I imagine you were also much shorter when last we met. I'm surprised you remember me at all."

"I don't. But you were the monster chasing us for much of my childhood. Mother showed me holos, so I'd know what you looked like."

"Did she? And how is Pallas these days?" There was an almost wistful note when Lilith said her daughter's name. The firelight flickering shadows over her face tricked the eye with an illusion of longing.

Mercy didn't know how to respond to that. As a figment of her imagination, shouldn't Lilith know everything Mercy did? Then again, dreams could be tricky.

"She's...gone. Dead." The word fell heavily from her lips and hung in the air like a weight between them.

Lilith's eyes narrowed. "Don't lie to me, granddaughter."

"I'm not." Mercy frowned. "Mom disappeared off some backwater world when I was thirteen. She never would have left me willingly, which means she was taken by someone. Or killed. Or taken and *then* killed. Whatever happened, it's been almost sixteen years, and she's not coming back." She almost added *you heartless bitch*. If they'd never had to run, her mother might still be alive.

Lilith jerked back, reacting as though Mercy had slapped her. "Taken," she said. Her brow furrowed. "No." She'd gone pale, the warm tones of her skin going cold.

Confusion filled Mercy. What kind of messed up dream was this?

And why was she always dreaming of her dead mother – and now grandmother? Couldn't she have a fun dream involving Reaper for once? Something sexy?

"The concern is touching, but a little too late," she said dryly.

Lilith didn't seem to hear her. She paced in front of the fire, whispering to herself. "No, no, no, no...this wasn't supposed to happen. Not to Pallas." She dug fingers into her hair, yanking at it and mussing her braid.

Mercy regarded her with a wary eye, as one would a wild animal. Lilith in any incarnation was unpredictable, at best. But this Lilith seemed truly distraught, stopping her pacing to lean against the arm of the ridiculous chair taking up half the room.

"Oh, my sweet girl. What you must have suffered." The sorrow in her grandmother's voice sounded real. Her bottom lip even quivered.

Anger rose in Mercy. How dare she act like Pallas meant anything to her? Like she had never hunted them? Sent Killers after them? Was this some kind of proprietary fixation? *I can kill you, but no one else can?* Fuck that.

"This is touching, really." Mercy said. "But just a couple of decades too late."

Lilith's gaze focused on her once again, and seemed to sharpen. She straightened, her demeanor changing back to regal in an instant. Not even the hair pulled from her braid and hanging loose around her face could detract from her presence.

"My time is short." Lilith's words were hard and clipped. "We need to make use of it. What's done is done, and we can't change it now."

"How practical of you." Mercy couldn't decide what made her angrier: Lilith's emotional response to Pallas's death, or her easy ability to shove it aside in the next instant.

"Practical is necessary for survival. It's astonishing you've lived this long without Pallas to protect and teach you." Lilith eyed her. "What do you know of your abilities?"

"Are you fucking kidding me?" Mercy crossed her arms. "This is some messed up dream. I'm not talking about Mom with you, and I'm not chatting about my Talent, either. Whatever this is, we're done."

Lilith's head tilted. "I see you have my temper."

Mercy ignored her, pacing away in the small confines of the room and attempting to focus her will on waking up. With the dreams of her mother, she'd never wanted to wake, hoping to drag out every last second. But this was entirely different. She closed her eyes and thought as hard as she could about waking. Finally, she bit the inside of her cheek until she tasted blood, sharp and metallic. It filled her senses with an element of reality, washed away the warmth of the fire and the cozy feel of the room. Coldness swept her, and she relaxed.

She opened her eyes, expecting to see her room, the walls and furnishings shrouded in darkness.

Instead, she saw endless black. Stars dotted the distance, bright pinpricks of light glimmering faintly. A slow, rhythmic clapping sound had her turning sharply to see Lilith still standing there. The bright beauty of a nebula wrapped around them, casting where they stood in shades of blue and gold and green.

Lilith stood in the middle of it all, clapping as though she was applauding Mercy. One elegant eyebrow raised. "I see you are every bit as powerful as I'd hoped. And feared."

Confused, Mercy cast another look around. The dream should have ended. Instead, it just appeared to have shifted locations. There were no shelves of books, no floor beneath their feet, no chairs, no fire. Just the two of them, standing together in what appeared to be deep space.

Impossible. But then, dreams often were.

"This is no dream," said Lilith, seeming to read her thoughts. Mercy tested her shields, but they felt solid. She scowled as Lilith waved a dismissive hand. "Oh, don't look at me like that. I don't need to read your mind to know what you're thinking. You show everything you feel on your face. You're going to have to work on that, if you expect to last long as Queen."

"So you're giving me advice now? No thanks."

Lilith sighed. "Difficult child. I should have expected that."

"I'm not a child."

A low laugh. "You are to me. A child with no real training. You've managed to survive so far due to *what*, I can't imagine. Luck, I suppose? But luck runs out."

"Wow, so not only were you a crazy tyrant, but you're also really condescending. Great reunion, Grandma."

"Hiding behind sarcasm. You are a great deal like your mother, you know. Pallas always had a sharp tongue as well."

"Don't talk about my mother." Painful shards dug into Mercy's chest each time her mother's name passed Lilith's lips. "You don't get to talk about her."

"Child, she was my true daughter. I will talk of Pallas as much as I please. Not to mention, this whole thing is going to prove impossible if we don't at least cover what she taught you."

What whole thing? What the fuck was this, and how did Mercy end it? She tried once again to focus on waking up, closing her eyes and narrowing her thoughts.

"That won't work, I'm afraid. I allowed it the first time only because I wanted an idea of your raw strength. Which is considerable. But without focus and training, strength has limits." Lilith gave her a thin smile. "This is my creation. You won't break free unless I allow it."

Mercy grit her teeth. No figment in a dream was going to dictate to her. She pushed harder.

Lilith's smile faded. "Granddaughter you might

be, but I will only warn you once. Don't push me, Mercy."

"Fuck you." There was something hugely liberating about looking the architect of all her terrors in the eye and telling her to fuck off. Feeling reckless, Mercy closed her eyes and focused everything she had, every ounce of will, every drop of Talent. Dreams were just a construct of the sleeping mind. That meant they could be controlled and even changed with conscious thought. Hell, she might even be able to blow this nightmare to pieces with her Talent.

Lilith was a star burning in her mind's eye, her Talent the brightest Mercy had ever seen. It hurt to look at, like staring into the center of a sun. She took her gathered will and arrowed it straight at the heart of that glowing orb, a spear thrown with all of her might.

The explosion blinded her, surging through her in a wave of impossible heat, burning so hot it hit with a tingling numbness. It was the sensory aura before pain washed up, eclipsing everything with its intensity. Nothing she'd ever felt had prepared her for this. Everything was pain. Her entire world. All of her awareness. There was nothing else.

Just agony so bright and sharp, she would do anything to end it.

Even die.

Mercy burst into a million pieces, her thoughts scattering, her sense of self thrown in a cascade of showering sparks into the nothingness around her. Desperately, she scrambled for the pieces of her soul, but they slipped past her like grains of sand falling through her fingers. With every piece gone, she lost more of her hold on who she was, on her very existence.

Until the last piece slipped away and she had only the fading sound of grandmother's voice as an anchor in the storm. Then, it, too, was gone.

"I warned you. When you are ready to listen, I'll be waiting."

Mercy's last moment was the storm ripping that awareness from her. Then there was nothing.

*M*ercy.

The voice came from far away, reaching through the emptiness to whisper to her. At first, it sounded like Reaper. Disorienting thoughts jumbled together. Reaper wasn't here. Or was he? Where was here?

Was she on Birn? On Verath 6, looking for transport? On a space station floating in ceaseless cold? In her bed, huddled and terrified of the monster who bore her grandmother's face?

Mercy.

The voice coalesced. Not Reaper. There was too much urgency to it, layers of emotion his lacked, even at moments of deep feeling. She hid away, not ready to face whoever it might be, cushioned by the layers of numbness around her. Friend or foe, it didn't matter. Outside the safety of her sheltering cocoon, a universe of pain awaited her. She burrowed deeper into the emptiness.

Mercy! A *zap* accompanied her name this time, sharp and unexpected. It jolted through her, not painful, exactly, but sharp enough to prick through the numb cocoon around her. The first tendrils of the agony awaiting her slipped through, and she groaned.

No. She cringed away, but it was too late. That tiny glimpse of sensation was all it took to drag her consciousness awake, kicking and screaming.

Her head felt like it was going to explode. *Again.* Pain hammered the inside of her skull, reverberating down through her body in aching echoes that made even the thin sheet wrapped around her a grating torture. She groaned again and refused to open her eyes. Afraid that even the slightest hint of light might blind her.

"Mercy, thank the Mother." The voice was familiar, the relief in it palpable. *Sebastian. What was Sebastian doing in her room?*

Because he *was* in her room. She recognized the bed beneath her, the sheet draped over her, the familiar feel of the place even with her eyes closed.

"Please, I know you're awake. The lights are off. Please open your eyes. I need to know you're all right."

There was something in his voice. Fear? It resonated deeply enough that she cracked her eyes open. True to his word, the room was dark. The hammers in her head didn't beat any worse for the tiny movement.

Sebastian was sitting on the bed beside her, the dark fall of his hair loose around a face pinched with anxiety, a white blur in the darkness. He leaned closer when her eyes opened, examining her with furrowed brows.

"No signs of burnout," he said. "But we should probably have Doc check you out, just to be safe."

"No!" Mercy tried to sit upright and immediately regretted it. The world spun, and her stomach lurched as the pain in her head increased tenfold.

She heaved over the side of the bed, unable to stop her stomach from emptying its contents all over the floor. At least she'd missed the bed. And Sebastian's shoes.

He held her, keeping her hair out of her face, his arm a warm, supporting presence around her shoulders. He waved a hand and the mess on the floor disappeared, absorbed into the monograph and, she presumed, shuffled off to the ship's recyclers. After a minute, he eased her back into bed, propping the pillows behind her so she was at least partially sitting up.

"I think you experienced a starburst. A single overload of Talent that doesn't, in and of itself, lead to burn out. Usually." A quick frown flitted over his features before a glass floated to his hand. He held it out for her to drink, and she didn't even wrinkle her nose at the sight of the green mnemosa that filled it. Dutifully, she sipped at it. When the first few swallows went down and stayed down, she drank more.

Her stomach settled a little.

"No Doc," she said firmly, looking Sebastian in the eye. His face had become clearer in the darkness now, as her eyes either adjusted or her brain woke more fully. "No infirmary."

Looking worried, he said nothing.

"I mean it, Sebastian."

"Can you tell me what happened?" he asked, evading her command.

"I should ask you that. Why are you here?"

He froze, the glass between them.

Mercy's brain was still sluggish, but not *that* sluggish. Her room was coded to her and Reaper and no one else. But Sebastian was the one person who could go anywhere on the ship he pleased. "Have you been spying on me?"

She couldn't be sure in the dark, but she thought a flush might have darkened his face.

"Not exactly. Just…it was thought it might be a good idea to keep a thread of awareness tied to you. While Reaper and his dogs are away."

"Really. Who, exactly, decided this? You?"

"Among others."

Her eyes narrowed. "Who?"

"It wasn't spying," he insisted. "I just keep my subconscious connected to whatever part of the ship you're in, so if anything unusual happens, it will trigger my conscious self to react."

"Hmm. And some might still consider that an invasion of privacy. What *unusual* things constitute a trigger?"

"Violence. Weapons fire. Screams of pain or fear."

Mercy thought about that. "Sometimes things that are…aggressive, physically, aren't violent in the sense of a threat," she said. She was still not the least bit mollified. "And how exactly do you differentiate screams of fear or pain from screams of a different sort?"

It might have been embarrassing, talking about this, but she was too disoriented and overwhelmed with other emotions to give shame a place. Besides, there was nothing shameful about enjoying sex.

"Well…" He cleared his throat. "…Let's just say someone added an emotional filter to the triggers for me."

An emotional filter. So, an empath. Mercy couldn't imagine Sanah helping with something like this. At least, not without telling Mercy what was going on.

She glared at Sebastian. "You mean Cannon helped you. So this has been going on for a lot longer than the short time Reaper's been gone. How long?"

"Since the bomb."

The bomb someone had engineered to have planted in a lift Mercy frequently used. Whoever had masterminded the event had telepathically erased all memory associated with it from the minds of the perpetrators. Reaper had killed those responsible…save for that one.

"So, this was Reaper's idea?"

"Not exactly," he said, hedging. "Let's call it a group decision."

"Was this the entire Core, or just a certain few? Let me guess: Reaper, Cannon, Dem, Treon, you, and Vashti."

Sebastian said nothing.

"Enough of this. Lights, half." The room brightened, but not so much that it hurt her eyes.

Mercy threw back the sheet, not even caring that she wore thin cotton nightwear, shorts and a camisole that did little for modesty. It was her damn room. She swung her legs over the side, forcing him to stand up and step back, or get hit in the process. The movement caused her head to spin, the headache spiking down the back of her neck and behind her eyes. She breathed shallowly and waited for the rush of fresh nausea to pass.

Coffee. Coffee would help. Jaw clenched, she stood, ignoring Sebastian's protest and forcing her legs to move, one in front of the other, until she'd crossed from the bed alcove to her small kitchen. She grabbed the counter like a lifeline and clung there, waiting for the pain in her head to recede enough to function.

To his credit, Sebastian kept his distance and said nothing after his initial protest. She ignored him, though she knew he watched her, ready to spring in if she collapsed. *Not going to happen.*

It took longer than she might have liked before she felt safe enough to move again. Cautiously, she eased around the counter until she could reach the auto-galley. Normally, she made her own coffee from the stash Cannon kept her supplied with. But right now she couldn't face the steps necessary to do it. She called up the holoscreen, selected the tabs for coffee, hot and dark. A few seconds later, the galley portal dispensed a steaming thermal cup filled with her fragrant vice of choice.

She took the cup in both hands and sipped. It hit her mouth, dark and nutty with notes of caramel and blackberry. Maybe it was her imagination, but she swore the pain receded more.

"You'd be better off drinking more mnemosa."

She didn't even look at him. "Choosing that green stuff over coffee? No."

"We should talk about what happened."

She took another sip, and decided she could risk moving again, at least far enough to get to one of her chairs. Carefully, she maneuvered the few feet it took to reach one, careful to move her head as little as possible. The worst part was the actual movement of sitting. But once she settled into the chair and it formed around her, supportive and cushioning, she relaxed and close her eyes.

She'd taken three more sips of coffee before Sebastian's continued silence began to irritate her as much as if he'd spoken.

"You have the patience of a priest," she said, cracking her eyes back open. He'd taken a seat in the other chair in the room, and didn't look like he planned to move anytime soon.

"I'm not leaving until you talk to me about what happened."

Irritation bloomed brighter. "You want to talk? Let's talk about everyone making decisions for my protection without consulting me."

He looked down, his hands folded in his lap. "That was not my first choice. However, there were some who thought you might not agree to it. And it was important that we protect our Queen."

"One, I wasn't Queen yet. Two, if you knew I wouldn't agree, that makes it even worse."

He looked up, meeting her eyes. "You have always been our Queen. Whether you choose to bear the title or not, you can't change what you are, Mercy." His voice had lost the warmth it usually held. Now it was edged like a blade, sharp and hard. "You are the only queen we have. We were dying before you came. Killing each other slowly. How can you fail to see how important you are?"

"I'm still a person, with a right to my privacy."

"Yes. And I have given it to you, as much as I can."

"As much as you can," she scoffed. "How generous of you."

He leaned forward, and now his eyes sparked with a temper she hadn't known he possessed. "Do you understand that you are *essential* to the survival of everyone on this ship? To our very race? That *without you*, we die."

She contemplated him, some of her irritation fading. She did understand that. What she didn't quite know was how to convince him - and Cannon, and Reaper, and everyone else on this damn ship - that she also needed to feel free, not suffocated by their need to keep her safe.

Sebastian leaned back when she didn't say anything. "What I did was a passive connection. An awareness linked through the ship to where you are at any given time. I have no idea what you are doing and I'm not spying on you. In fact, I'm aware of *everyone* on this ship, always. It's a side effect of my Talent, of being connected to *Nemesis* so deeply. I can't *not* be. As I told you before, I do my best not to actively watch anyone. However, the triggers were added for you, specifically, so that if someone decided to plant another bomb, I could isolate you the moment something happened and keep you alive. Hopefully." He paused, some of the edge leaving his voice. "Even if I had to rip apart the walls of the ship to do it."

For long minutes, silence fell between them. Mercy drank more of her coffee, and Sebastian sat stiffly. Temper flexed the line of his jaw.

"I see it, now," she said.

His gaze flicked up to hers. "What?"

"Well, you're so…kind. Warm." She struggled to find the words. "You didn't seem as hard as the rest of the pirates I've known. I couldn't fathom how someone like you could survive in Lilith's family."

"Kindness does not equate a lack of strength."

"No, you're right. It doesn't." She looked down into her nearly empty cup and thought about Wolfgang's gruff demeanor, and the kindness he'd shown to a frightened child with nowhere to go. And more, the place in his life he'd given to a runaway Talented girl with powerful enemies hunting her. "I should know that better than anyone."

"I'm sorry for not telling you, Mercy. I should have, regardless of what the others thought. But I can't regret what we did."

"No. I don't suppose you can."

The silence stretched, even as the tension bled from the room. "Now," said Sebastian a few moments later. "Can we talk about what happened here tonight?"

She didn't want to talk about Lilith. Her jaw clenched "I had a nightmare. It was nothing."

He lifted a brow. "A nightmare caused you to lash out so hard with your Talent that you overloaded into a starburst? What kind of nightmare?"

"An ugly one."

"Could you be more specific?"

"No."

Thinking about it now, Mercy felt foolish. She'd dreamt of her grandmother and reacted like a child afraid of the monster in the dark. Used real

Talent in a stupid dream, and hurt no one but herself.

"I can't force you to talk about it," Sebastian said, studying her. "But you probably should. Any nightmare that powerful could be a symptom of some deeply held emotions or past trauma. Things it might be wise for you to deal with during waking hours."

"Mmm," she muttered, noncommittal.

A ping on the room's console came as a welcome distraction. Usually people on this ship communicated telepathically, but sometimes, as in the middle of the night, they traded more traditional messages. If she'd been sleeping, she'd have woken to find the message waiting for her. But since she wasn't, she pulled a holoscreen up from the arm of her chair and checked it.

She sighed, setting aside her empty cup. "It looks like I'll be visiting the infirmary after all. Vashti's awake."

ercy's presence faded, leaving an odd feeling in its wake. It wasn't like anything Reaper had experienced before. A sense of loss. An odd twinge that was almost a phantom pain in his chest. Whatever it was, he found it distracting. He allowed the cold to rise up just enough to numb the strange sensation. The effort it required surprised him.

What is it? Cannon sounded strained.

Reaper realized his Talent was more active than he'd intended. The tension in the group rose to a corresponding level. *Nothing.*

Doesn't feel like nothing.

Reaper told him about Mercy's warning, and the other Talented in the system. Cannon's face turned grim. He cast a look over at the Veritas group, huddled together under the watchful eyes of Reaper's dogs. Reaper knew what he was thinking.

Mercy says they are not with Veritas, he added.

How does she know? Cannon glanced back at

Reaper. *She doesn't know them as we do. I'm afraid our Queen does not truly understand them.*

Perhaps. Reaper scratched his chin. *If they already have another queen, however, they wouldn't need to get Rani back to gain their freedom from Mercy. And they have never had a killer in their ranks, to our knowledge.*

Cannon didn't answer right away. Finally, he gave a grudging nod. *A fair point. I suppose it would be conceit to think that we are the* only *Talented in the entire universe. We know there are more of us scattered throughout the Commonwealth. Not just in Veritas, but individuals struggling to survive on their own. And slaves, of course. But...a queen? A killer? And whatever that other presence was that Treon couldn't identify? When is the last time your brother failed at something?*

Reaper shrugged. *We have a more immediate concern at the moment.*

Emotion warred on Cannon's face, but finally he gave a nod. *For now. But these new Talented add an unknown element that could be more dangerous than any army the Commonwealth might throw at us.*

A problem we can deal with once we have escaped.

Cannon let out a frustrated breath. *Agreed. We need to get out of here.* He cast a look around at the cavernous space they occupied. It was meant to hold ships.

The docking bay was empty, but that didn't make it safe. Commonwealth soldiers guarded the berths to either side, and the Navy ships that occupied them. Reaper's dogs had distracted one set of soldiers so the group could slip into the empty bay. Now, they waited inside, separated from the ship they desperately needed by a wall, armed soldiers, and the crew left on board.

The wall was their most immediate problem.

Search crews would eventually be back this way. They couldn't stay here indefinitely.

"Ghost, Zion," Reaper said aloud. He jerked his head toward the wall, and the two spectral forms moved through it.

"That's a useful Talent," Feria said, from where she sat with the rest of the Veritas group. Her hair had lost its perfectly coifed luster, disheveled strands escaping and the entire mass leaning precariously to one side. She was holding one of her people, the young woman who had covered their escape from the tunnel, across her lap. Though dressed in corporate business attire like the rest of them, the sleeping woman looked little more than a child now, her face unnaturally pale and impossibly young. Exhaustion was etched into her features.

Titus said she'd come perilously close to burnout, something they had neither the time nor the resources to deal with. Reaper hoped she would wake when the time came. Hauling around an unconscious body was going to make an already complicated situation more difficult.

When he didn't respond to Feria, irritation flashed over her face. "So, you're just going to ignore us?"

"No." Atrea stepped forward, giving Reaper a look he could only describe as reproving. He hid a smile. Despite all expectations to the contrary, he found he rather liked Mercy's friend. She feared him more than Mercy did, of course, but Atrea didn't let fear get in her way. She treated Reaper much like she did everyone else, and he found he was oddly grateful for that.

Atrea knelt beside Feria. "Until we escape, we're all in this together."

"Together." The other woman's lips twisted into a sardonic smile. "It feels a lot like we're prisoners."

"I think trust is difficult for now." Atrea sent Cannon and Reaper a sideways look.

"We didn't call in the Navy," Feria insisted. "Our ship left the system just as yours did. Do you think they planned to abandon us here?"

"They wouldn't have any reason to fear if you were working with the Commonwealth military," Cannon pointed out.

"But we aren't."

"We have only your word for that." Cannon walked over and stood beside Atrea, looking down at Feria. "What do you know about another ship in the system? Possibly cloaked."

Confusion filled her face. "Another ship? Cloaked? We don't have that technology. No one does."

Cannon said nothing. Feria's gaze moved from his face to Atrea's. Her brow furrowed as confusion gave way to anger. "You can't be serious. Our scientists and engineers are at the top of their fields. The kind of tech you're talking about simply doesn't exist."

Cannon glanced back at Reaper. "She's telling the truth."

"Of course I am." Feria glared at him. "Whatever game you think you're playing, we want safely out of this system as badly as you do. Clearly, this peace summit was a terrible plan. And an utter failure."

Ignoring her, Cannon walked back to Reaper. Atrea stood, wearing a frown. "What's going on?" she asked.

"There is a ship," Reaper said. "Cloaked. It carries Talented like us."

"Well," Cannon said, "sort of. They are not just any Talented. We aren't sure how many, exactly. But Treon sensed the presence of a Killer and a queen. As well as some form of Talent he's never encountered before."

Atrea looked at Reaper. "I thought Killers were unique to the pirates."

Reaper said nothing. They were. Or, he'd always thought that to be true. But being a Killer was dangerous. There had been several times in the last century when names had been lost, missions failed or never returned from. Men and women who were presumed dead. Killers were a valuable resource. The pirates had used Hunters whenever possible to try and confirm deaths. To try and track the missing.

But Killers didn't like being tracked. Some went to great lengths to keep their psychic signatures out of Hunter minds. There were those long gone who had gone unaccounted for. It was possible they'd lived. Even possible they'd had children. Or been captured and cloned. Cloning was an imperfect way of making new Talented. They tended to be unstable, both in gifts and in mind. That didn't mean it was never attempted.

Boss. Ghost's mental voice came to him. He

heard Cannon saying something to Atrea, but focused his own attention back on the problem at hand. As he'd told Cannon, the presence of this ship and these other Talented, while worrisome, wasn't their most immediate difficulty.

Yes? He could tell by Ghost's tone that he wasn't going to like what he was about to hear.

The ship should be fairly straightforward to get to. A pair of guards at the front of the berth, a pilot and two crew members on board. They're all armed, and they all have that shield around their minds.

Reaper thought about the Talented they'd just been discussing. It was possible they were working with the Commonwealth. That they were responsible for shielding these nulls. But if that was the case, why not simply come down to the surface to hunt them personally? Surely, they'd be more effective than nulls.

He dismissed the thought. They didn't have the time for random speculation right now.

Five null minds, even shielded, wouldn't be that hard. They'd have to strike swiftly and move quickly, before reinforcements descended.

I think I know how they're shielding, boss.

Reaper frowned. *What do you mean?*

Ghost didn't yet know of the discussions they'd just had amongst the group. His attention and conscious mind had been with his spectral form.

He means, Zion said, *that the Navy isn't alone.*

An image came to Reaper. A form slumped in a chair, bedraggled hair obscuring a face tilted down. He could see it was female, dressed in inexpensive synth-cotton, ill-fitting and shapeless. The hair was long and an indeterminate brown, tangled and limp as though unwashed for a long period of time. The chair was fitted with a gravitational field device, similar to the one that had once held Mercy captive.

Who is she?

Near as we can tell, a slave. Zion's mental voice was sharp and bitter.

We heard the crew talking, added Ghost. *She's Talented. They called her a freak. Speculated about whether or not she's worth the money they paid. Whether she can keep their minds safe from 'the other freaks'.*

A slave complicated things. Frustration rose briefly in Reaper, but he let it go almost immediately. Giving in to emotion wasn't going to help them. The situation continued to change, and they needed to alter their plans with it.

There was no way Cannon would agree to leaving a slave behind. So, wasn't it a good thing that they'd already been planning to take this particular ship? Unless...

Reaper cursed to himself. *You'd better check the other berths. We need to know if she's the only one.*

He hoped to the Mother that she was. Freeing multiple slaves could take this escape plan from difficult to impossible.

"What is it?" Cannon's voice interrupted his thoughts. Reaper realized his emotions must have tipped him off to their new situation.

Sometimes, he missed the days before Mercy, when he lived in a place without emotion most of the time. Now, he found himself relying on the cold less and less. He'd realized through her that the numbness that made him an efficient killer was not always an advantage.

"We have a complication." Briefly, he told Cannon and the others what Ghost and Zion had found.

Cannon cursed. He looked at Atrea. "The Navy's using slaves now? I thought the Commonwealth had laws against slavery."

"We do. I mean, they do." She hesitated. "But technically, the Talented are under a kill order, considered weapons of mass destruction. They don't have the same rights ordinary citizens do. But I never saw them being used as slaves during my time in the Navy. This must be something new."

"What do *you* know about this?" Cannon directed the question at Feria.

Anger glittered in her eyes, her mouth pressed into a thin line. "Don't be naive. Illegal or not, slavery is a huge industry in the Commonwealth. *Especially* for clones and Talented."

"Clones aren't considered people, either," Atrea muttered. She shrugged when everyone looked at her. "I'm not saying I agree. I'm just pointing out, neither Talented nor clones are actually protected under Commonwealth law. This makes them not only high reward merchandise, but low risk."

"That's not news," said Cannon. "We've been quietly freeing slaves for a long time. But the Navy? An entity of the government, using slaves? That is news to us."

"To me, too," Atrea said.

"Don't look at us," Feria added. "You might think we control the government, but you would be wrong. If we actually controlled the monarchy, Talent would no longer be outlawed."

Boss, Ghost's mental voice came to Reaper. He opened his mind to Cannon, including him in the update. *There aren't any others. Just her.*

Reaper and Cannon exchanged a look. *If we remove her from the equation, their minds will lose that shield,* Cannon said. He lifted a shoulder. *Theoretically.*

Reaper spoke aloud for the benefit of everyone else. "So, we free the woman, steal the ship, and get out of here."

"Damn right," Cannon said. "The nulls will be much easier to deal with once those shields drop."

"Shift change should be in about thirty minutes." Atrea tapped fingers against her holstered sidearm, her head cocked. "Provided they're following standard op, anyway. These men will go join the search, trade out with whichever teams are coming in."

"Guards tend to be less alert at end of shift," Reaper said.

She nodded. "They do."

Ghost, Zion. Can you do it?

The answer was a long time in coming. *I have to physically manifest to remove her restraint, boss. And there are three crew members in line of sight. If they didn't have those shields, it would be no problem. But even with Zion, this could go sideways. What if she doesn't drop the shield right away? Slaves are often indoctrinated to be subservient. Afraid. She's likely to be unwilling to listen. At least initially.*

Reaper weighed the situation. Three crew. Two

guards. Those shields. No way to do this without raising an alarm.

Can you get into the cockpit? Lock yourselves in?

Yeah. Ghost sounded confident. *Shouldn't be a problem. Pilot's sitting in the crew compartment, chatting with his friends.*

Do it. When I give the word, get the ship ready for flight. We're going to need to jump the moment we're free of the atmosphere.

He flexed his hands. Heat washed across his collarbone, down his arms, even as cold rose up from within. He looked at Cannon.

"No choice. We go in. Fast. Lethal. Maybe we can keep them from calling for help." The guards from the other berths would be first on scene, then would come the rest of the fire teams. And those ships in orbit would be waiting for them.

No choice.

"Zion and Ghost can unlock the docking restraints, prep for takeoff while we get everyone on board." He shook his head. He liked efficiency. Smooth operations. This was going to be the opposite.

"What if we could jam their communications?" Atrea said suddenly.

"What?" Cannon asked.

"I know their frequencies. I might be able to isolate the one they're using. Send some interference. They'll trace it pretty quickly, clear it up or switch to a new channel. But it might buy us the time we need."

Reaper nodded. "Do it."

Maybe this had a chance in hell after all. But Reaper was sure of one thing. Once they escaped

Birn, that other ship would be waiting for them. The one with the queen, and the Killer. Not to mention the Commonwealth fleet with them. Military vessels with full armament. And they would be flying a dropship with limited jump capabilities.

Once they escaped Birn, the real trouble would begin.

CHAPTER THIRTEEN

Shielding so strong that he couldn't break through it was something Reaper rarely encountered. His Talent was good at finding flaws. It was, essentially, the very core of his gift. Find a weak point, and exploit it.

But the shields surrounding the nulls were shockingly without flaw. Given enough time, he could force his way past. He was sure of that. But time was something they didn't have.

Plasma rifles and disrupters were too loud. They needed something silent. He triggered the weapon that was always a part of him. Knives filled his hands, a shimmer that was barely visible. The heat that spilled down his arms died away, snuffed out by cold as the Killer rose up within and dominated all else.

He might not be able to penetrate their shields, but his Talent worked in other ways. The most efficient methods of killing the guards flowed through his mind, one after another.

Standard issue armor for Navy fire teams would only partially deflect the full brunt of a plasma rifle hit. Such an attack would stagger them at the very least, and depending on range, might still incapacitate. But it was too loud, and they couldn't trust that it would work.

The armor would also deflect most blades. But Reaper's were not like a normal blade. They attacked the mind. They could cripple or kill, but there would be no blood. And while shields might guard against a telepathic attack, these weapons had been designed as a specific counter to shields.

He looked at Atrea, who had been fiddling with the alarm unit she'd stolen from the bar for the past several minutes. Her face was screwed up in concentration, her brow furrowed. At last, she let out a sigh and sat back.

"I think that'll work. Won't know for sure until they try to use their coms. This thing was designed to work on a wide frequency, not across an encrypted signal. So…I'm about eighty percent sure."

"I guess that's the best we've got," Cannon said. He looked at Reaper. "Do it."

Knox. Titus. Distract. Both men had telekinesis at a great enough range to do as he asked.

The dogs moved forward until they stood with Reaper just inside the mouth of the docking bay. An overhang spanned the length of the opening, providing shade when workers were offloading goods, or security when the great doors needed to close. Right now, it provided a well of shadow that kept them hidden from immediate view.

Each bay was large enough to house freighters ten times the size of the dropships the Navy had used. The guards to either side of this one stood so far apart that there was barely a line of sight between them.

Titus, his white blond hair a pale smudge in the shadows, focused on the set of guards to the left. Knox, the set to the right.

Reaper waited, his gaze on the two guards to the right. He heard as though from a great distance voices speaking softly behind them, a low murmur barely on the edge of his consciousness. The rumble of Cannon's drawl. Atrea's higher pitched questioning. An acerbic, clipped tone he'd come to associate with Feria.

None of that mattered. He knew Cannon would have them ready to move. Shift change was a short time away, perhaps less than ten minutes. The guards had begun to fidget, anticipating the end of their long vigil.

Knox, Titus. You will take the left. Now, he said.

Knox and Titus acted as one. In the distance, something small would move in each of the guards' direction. Fuel lines might come loose, or a canister might fall from one of the cargo shelves lining the docking bay walls. It didn't matter what it was, as long as it captured the attention of each set of guards.

Reaper felt their notice shift away from where he stood. He moved in that moment, covering the distance quickly, as silently as he could. This set of guards consisted of one man and one woman. Both held their weapons in a ready position, but they were facing the wrong direction, away from the danger. Reaper's clothing created a rustle of sound.The man started to turn, but by then it was too late.

Another pirate might have hesitated to kill a woman, even a null. The female gender was so treasured and rare, it was deeply ingrained in their culture not to harm one. Reaper didn't hesitate.

He aimed for the base of the skull, striking at each of the guards simultaneously. He dropped low and surged up with two quick cuts, severing their mind's connection to the body. It had the same effect as severing a spinal cord.

They dropped like stones, but Reaper caught them with his telekinesis, dragging the bodies quickly into the mouth of the docking bay to drop them into the shadows. He trusted Titus and Knox to be doing the same with the other pair of guards.

Ghost. Zion. Go.

On it, boss.

A moment later, the dropship engines spooled up, power flickering on across the ship.

Reaper sent a pulse to Cannon, and moved to the dropship, knowing the rest of the group would be right behind him. If Atrea's jamming had worked, the crew inside the ship would be trying to signal a problem, but the message wouldn't get out. They'd have only moments before the jamming either failed, or the crew switched to a new frequency.

Or until reinforcements arrived, if Atrea's rigged signal failed.

The airlock door was locked. Then Knox was beside him, kneeling down and placing a small charge on the seal.

Reaper backed up, and found Titus standing back, waiting.

"Any problems?" he asked.

"No, boss." Titus shook his head. "Not yet."

Knox set the charge and backed up. A moment later a small concussion blasted out, and the seal on the airlock popped.

The ship was nanograph. It would self-repair, and in the meantime safety doors would keep the inside of the ship safe from the vacuum of space.

But they had their entry.

They moved with the precision of a unit long accustomed to working together. The crew inside was prepared, having heard the blast. Knox and Titus entered first, throwing up telekinetic shields. Plasma bolts splashed harmlessly off them. Jaxon joined Reaper and they jogged up the ramp together.

Reaper allowed his knives to vanish. A brief telekinetic choke made each of the three crew, two men and a woman, fall limp and unconscious. They might even live. Their deaths were of no use one way or the other, as they would have no impact on the mission's success.

"Dump them outside," Reaper told his dogs. *Ghost, Zion, time?*

Launch ready in under two minutes, boss.

"Everyone get strapped in."

While everyone else found a seat and prepared for launch, Reaper approached the restrained woman Ghost and Zion had shown him earlier. She appeared unconscious at first glance, but that couldn't be right; Talent didn't continue to function when its user wasn't controlling it. At best, it would cease to work. At worst, depending on the Talent and the user's mastery, gifts could go rogue, causing damage of unimaginable proportions.

Her hair hung in a long tangle, obscuring her face. A stink wafted to him from where she sat; her cheap synth cotton clothing looked old and frayed, it's mending abilities long exhausted. Dirt scuffed the sleeves and hem, smudging the places on her body where her skin was visible. It was impossible to tell what color her hair might be, beneath the layers of grime.

Her age was also difficult to determine. She might have been a girl or a woman of several decades. Though her posture was one of sleep, her body was actually rigid, tense against her bonds.

This woman had been imprisoned for a long time, and for so valuable a slave, no one had taken even basic care with her.

Reaper eased back the tangle of her hair, and though her head was slumped forward, he saw that he'd been correct. She was not asleep or unconscious, but her focus was turned completely inward, where her Talent lay. He doubted she was even aware of the physical world around her.

"Titus," he said softly, calling the medic on his team over. "We need her out."

His dog knelt beside the chair, ripping open a pouch along his arm and pulling out a capsulet. He pushed back a sleeve and depressed it into her arm. The tension left her body on a soft sigh. Reaper felt it the moment her shields went down. The minds of the nulls blazed open for him. Easy, now, to reach out if he wanted.

They had realized something was wrong. Multiple fireteams stormed in their direction. They knew something was wrong. The moment this ship went airborne, they would be contacting those capital ships in orbit.

He needed to delay that possibility for as long as possible.

Reaper strapped himself into a crew seat, closing his eyes. Methodically, he selected the nearest minds. Eight of them. It was child's play to slip past their instinctive, merely human shields, and find the flaws, the vulnerabilities, in their minds.

Eight bodies dropped to the deck, their light going dark.

"Reaper." Cannon was sitting beside him.

He opened his eyes.

"How many?" Cannon asked.

"Too many. I cannot kill them all, and eventually they will get a message through."

Cannon's hands tightened on the safety straps around him. Reaper knew what he was thinking. This dropship had a single light turret. It was meant for cover fire while landing troops, not space battles.

Those capital ships could destroy them without even trying. And the dropship's jump capabilities were limited. These Vikings were meant for short range jumping, not jumping through multiple systems. It could be done, but they would burn through fuel quickly. They might not get far enough away. Assuming they even escaped Birn, the Commonwealth would make educated guesses on their jump path.

Thrusters engaged, lifting the dropship from the dock. It didn't matter how many troops Reaper killed now. They couldn't hide a ship taking off. And they couldn't jump until they broke free of the atmosphere. That would be their most vulnerable moment.

Tension in the crew compartment was palpable. No one spoke. There was nothing to do now but wait.

Reaper wasn't used to feeling powerless. None of them were. Talent was a gift, a power that they each carried within them, a weapon no one could take away. But in some situations, Talent wasn't enough.

Oddly, Reaper thought of Mercy. He had the strangest urge to reach out to her, to try and span the distance between them. In case the worst happened, he wanted his last moments to be with her. But that would also mean her last memory of him would be feeling his death, and while the Killer in him had no frame of reference to understand what that would do to a normal person, he understood that he could not put Mercy through that.

The pull of Birn's gravity tried to hold on to them, while the force of their lift pressed Reaper back into his seat. When the ship crossed the barrier of the atmosphere, there was a moment between losing the influence of the planet's gravity, and the gravity generators of the ship kicking in. Only the straps holding fast kept them all from floating, weightless. Then this passed, and the seconds ticked on, eternally slow.

Reaper expected at any moment for the small dropship to be rocked by a burst of fire from those capital ships. He didn't dare ask Ghost or Zion for an update. It wasn't worth the risk of distracting them for those few seconds. The ship would either jump in time, or it wouldn't.

Atrea sat across from him. Her eyes were squeezed shut. Cannon turned and looked at Reaper, meeting his gaze. This was taking too long. Both of them had the same thought: *we're not going to make it.*

Reaper felt the vibration of the deck beneath his feet a second before the jump drive opened otherspace and took them through. The odd feeling of a space jump slid through him, twisting his belly as formless pressure seemed to bear down on him.

And then they were out, in regular space again.

It took a lot to surprise Reaper, but he found himself shocked, gripping the safety straps too tightly. It had all taken too long. Those capital ships should have fired.

Ghost, Zion, report. With a shudder, Zion appeared to wake from where his body had been strapped into a seat. He'd let the projection go and returned to his own mind.

"We made it, boss," he said hoarsely. "No sign of nearby jump activity."

Reaper and Cannon exchanged a look.

"What?" asked Atrea.

"It took us too long to jump," Cannon said. "We should be dead. There is no reality in which the Navy did not notice an unauthorized flight of one of their dropships leaving Birn. What is the Commonwealth's policy on government property, ships in particular?"

"Better to be destroyed than fall into unauthorized hands," Atrea said. "You're right, they should have shot us down."

"So why didn't they?"

No one spoke. No one had any answers. Reaper thought about those Talented Treon had sensed, but he said nothing.

"Let's get a signal sent to *Nemesis*," Cannon finally said. "We can figure out this mystery later. For now, let's go home."

Boss, we have a problem. Ghost said from the cockpit.

What is it? But even as he asked, he realized what was wrong. The vibration beneath his feet died. Light faded to dim as reserves kicked on.

We just lost power. We can't send a signal. And we can't jump.

They were dead in space.

CHAPTER FOURTEEN

*V*ashti poured the tea with careful precision. Steam rose from the fragrant liquid, a blend of black tea, spices, and citrus that Vashti favored. Because she was watching closely, Mercy saw the faint tremor in her hand. But Vashti had insisted on serving the tea herself.

She'd said very little since being released from the infirmary. Doc had grumbled, but Vashti stood firm. She was fine, and she could sit or lie down in her own quarters more comfortably than in the infirmary. By the time Mercy and Sebastian had arrived, Vashti was leaving; though she did hold Griffin's arm perhaps more firmly than usual. Like Mercy, Griffin was family. He seemed to play a role that was part bodyguard, part aid, though he was a Core member and powerful in his own right.

Mercy would much rather she'd waited before going to see Vashti. She could have avoided both the infirmary, and the significant looks Griffin kept shooting in Sebastian's direction.

It was a long walk back to Vashti's quarters.

One taken slowly, with little conversation. Vashti might have claimed to feel fine to Doc, but it was clear to Mercy that for once, at least, the older woman's fatigue and weakness was not an act. Her long hair, streaked heavily with white, hung lackluster around a face lined with weariness. Griffin was extremely solicitous, shortening his strides to match hers without making it obvious he was doing so.

Mercy hid a smile, but Griffin caught the expression just as she turned her head, and gave Sebastian a glare.

What is his problem? She finally asked Sebastian the question as the four of them took seats around Vashti's table. Griffin was scowling at Sebastian again. What the hell could have happened since the meeting the day before?

We arrived together. Sebastian's mouth twitched, like he was trying not to smile. *During sleep cycle.*

You and I? So what? That's no business of his. And people are up at all hours. It's a Mother-damned spaceship.

Vashti poured the tea into four cups, passing one to Griffin.

He believes we slept together. I think, said Sebastian, *perhaps he has some aspirations in that direction.*

Mercy stared at him. It took her brain a moment to comprehend.

For me? Like...romantically?

Is that so shocking? Sebastian took the cup Vashti offered him, not looking at Mercy. She didn't know what to say to that. She was silent long enough that Sebastian spoke again.

People do expect you to choose another Consort. You know this, right?

But, Griffin — he's my cousin!

There has never been a law against cousins romantically pairing. And since the virus, there is even less reason to avoid such things.

Mercy smiled automatically at Vashti as she took the proffered cup. *Well, I have a law against it.* She thought back, her tone sharp. *A personal one.*

Perhaps you should make that clear. You have rather a lot of relatives, you know. Some fairly distant.

Uncomfortable with the entire conversation, Mercy took a sip of tea without waiting for it to properly cool. She immediately regretted it. The hot liquid spilled over her tongue, burning it and the roof of her mouth. She hissed in a breath in a futile attempt to cool it.

"Careful, dear. It's hot," Vashti said.

"Thanks," Mercy muttered.

"Perhaps if you didn't try holding a mental conversation while you drank, you'd save yourself from such mistakes." Vashti's tone was dry. Her comment prompted another glare from Griffin.

Mercy slammed her fist onto the table, jostling the teapot and cups.

"Stop it," she told him. "I'm not dating Sebastian, but even if I was, it wouldn't matter."

Griffin's eyes widened. He looked like so many members of Lilith's family. The same bronze skin, green eyes, and dark hair.

"I don't care what passes as acceptable here," she continued. "I'm not dating family." *Ever,* she added silently. Because there was a whole host of reasons why that would never be happening.

Starting with trust issues and ending with blood relatives.

Griffin couldn't have looked more surprised if she'd stood up and thrown her tea on him. But better to be truthful with him now than allow this to continue.

She looked at Vashti. "Can we talk about how you ended up the infirmary, now?"

"As you like, dear." Vashti held her cup in two hands, blowing gently on the surface. "What would you like to know?"

Mercy sighed. The past few months training with her aunt had given her a pretty good handle on Vashti's methods. "Can we skip the part where you make me ask a bunch of questions while you dance around not answering them? We both know you're a precog, and you had some kind of traumatic vision. I'd like to know what it was."

"As you wish." Vashti's gaze cut to Griffin. "Leave us."

By the way he stiffened, the order surprised him. He glanced at Sebastian. "And he gets to stay?"

Vashti simply raised an eyebrow, and Griffin subsided, still looking disgruntled. Without another word, he stood and left, the chair clattering against the table from the hard push he gave it.

"He's a good man," said Vashti after the door to her quarters slid shut. "But like many among the Core, a little too used to getting his way. He resents being challenged. Even by me."

"Then this must be a difficult day for him," Mercy said.

Vashti smiled at her. "Indeed." She took a drink of tea, then set the cup down in a decisive motion.

"You want to know what my vision entailed. The short version: an end to our way of life. Something is coming. It will make the conflicts we have experienced in the past feel like a child's game of war."

Discouraged, Mercy felt her shoulders slump. "Damn. Then my peace summit with Veritas really was meaningless."

"I did not say this war would be with them. In fact," Vashti sipped her tea, "I see them fighting beside us, not against us. For the short time in which we fight at all."

"But you just said—"

"Yes, dear. I said our way of life would end. I did not say it would take long to happen."

"If not Veritas, then who do we fight?" Mercy asked. "The Commonwealth?"

"No." Vashti hunched over her tea, as though cold. She closed her eyes, remaining like that for so long that Mercy became concerned. She exchanged a look with Sebastian.

Vashti was many things. Weak was not one of them. Then again, who knew what sort of fatigue might plague her after her recent experience?

"It's time," her aunt said at last, opening her eyes. She straightened, squaring her shoulders and throwing off frailty as though it were a coat she could shrug aside. "We thought – hoped – we would have more time, but that is not to be."

Mercy glanced sideways at Sebastian, but he was looking down, as though his tea had become thoroughly fascinating. She looked back at Vashti, confused.

"Time for what?" she asked.

"For your real training to begin."

"But I've *been* training. For months, now. With Reaper. With you."

"I can only teach you so much. I am not a queen. And I can't prepare you for what is coming."

"There isn't a queen to teach me. And you still haven't said *what* is coming."

"Destruction on a massive scale. Mass extinction of multiple worlds. The Commonwealth thrown into chaos."

Mercy stared at her. "What? What do you mean mass extinction?"

"I don't know all of the details, but based on what I have seen, I would hazard to guess a supernova."

That could be millions, if not billions of lives. Mercy couldn't begin to comprehend that level of destruction. Her mouth was dry. "Where?"

"Somewhere in the Commonwealth. More than that, I don't know."

"But that's millions of star systems." Mercy's heart sank. "We have to try and find out where. Evacuate the inhabited worlds. How can this be? The Commonwealth has tens of thousands of satellites and stations monitoring the galaxy, looking for cataclysmic events."

"Perhaps. But they can't monitor every corner of the galaxy."

Mercy closed her eyes, thinking. Supernovas were destructive, yes, but relatively rare. Rare enough that they didn't often occur near inhabited space; certainly not often enough to be a worry. So, why was this one an issue? Wouldn't the more inhabited systems be monitored the most? And why did this event make Vashti want to increase her training? What could any of this have to do with her?

"This is horrifying. If it's truly going to happen, it's a nightmare." She opened her eyes. "But what do I have to do with it? What is it you think I can do?"

"Once this event happens, as I said, it will throw the Commonwealth into chaos. The monarchy will be gone. The government as it currently exists will be gone. A power vacuum will exist. Fights will break out, wars over resources and territory. Over the throne itself. It will be a return to the Ascension Wars which created us." Vashti took a breath. "All of that is bad enough. But something else will happen. I can't— I can't see it clearly. But something—*someone*—is coming. We will be gathered like wheat left to ripen in the fields, formed into an army. To take the Commonwealth, or what will remain of it." She gave Mercy a level look. "Only a queen can protect us."

"I don't understand. How could someone take control? The Commonwealth and Veritas have been trying for decades. How is it that someone could just show up and shape us back into an army?" She thought about it. "Only a queen could do that. But I've already claimed everyone. Even if another queen came, she would have to..." She trailed off. Suddenly Vashti's focus on her training made sense. "You think another queen is coming. The one Treon sensed?"

"Possibly." Vashti shook her head. "I don't know. I just know she will be more powerful, more dangerous to us than any threat we have ever faced."

"Worse than Lilith?" Mercy laughed, but no one laughed with her. She looked at Sebastian. He was tense and pale. Vashti's lips pressed together, and it took Mercy a moment to identify the emotion that flashed across her face. Because it was something she had never before associated with the woman who had survived the deaths of three consorts and her sister's reign.

Fear.

"You both know something I don't. Wait." Mercy pointed at Sebastian. "How could *you* know? Vashti *just* woke up. Unless…this isn't the first time you've had this vision."

"No." Vashti looked down, her hair falling forward to hide her face. "Nor the second."

"How many?" Mercy asked.

"I've lost count."

"How long ago did they start?"

"When I was a girl. The first time was right before my mother's death. I was nineteen years old." She let out a long breath. "They've gained in intensity over the years. The closer the event gets, the worse the visions become."

"Your mother's death…" Mercy mused. "She was Queen before Lilith. Some believe Lilith had her killed to assume the throne."

A smile ghosted across Vashti's face. "A fiction we encouraged."

"We?"

Vashti ignored her question. "Our mother *was* murdered, but Lilith and I thought it best not to panic everyone with the circumstances. No one could prove how she died, in any case."

"I don't think I'm following. You're saying you and *Lilith* covered up how Kiana died? *Together?*"

"Yes."

"Why? How did she really die?"

"I had the first vision that night," Vashti said, her gaze distant. "It woke me. This nightmare of destruction and death. We were at our family home on Ardon. I woke my sister and we ran to mother's chamber. We found her awake, but not conscious. Unaware of the physical world. Her mind was engaged in conversation, or so we thought. This was not unusual, you understand. My mother was Queen. She was often distant, mentally, speaking with Core members, Captains, allies and the like. But I knew something was wrong. We tried to rouse her. I couldn't penetrate her shields, but Lilith — another queen — could." A faint smile. "My sister was powerful even at a young age. But the moment Lilith connected with her, mother threw her out of her mind with such a towering rush of strength, it knocked my sister across the room.

"We knew then, this was no normal conversation, but a deadly combat our mother was engaged in." Weary sorrow filled Vashti's face. "She lost."

Mercy struggled to make sense of what she was hearing. "Why would it be better for everyone to believe Lilith murdered her own mother?"

"Someone went into a queen's mind, attacked

her, and killed her. On the same night when a powerful young precog — the queen's own daughter — dreamt of worlds being destroyed and a galaxy at war. With *us* serving as soldiers."

"I see your point." Queens were so hard to kill, it was considered impossible for anyone but a Killer...or another queen. Mercy might not have known them long, but she did know the pirates would rather die than go back to a life of servitude, living as soldiers in someone else's war.

"At first," Vashti said, "only Lilith and I knew of my vision. There was a lot happening at the time. The pirates needed a Queen, and my sister had to take my mother's place. A daunting task for a seventeen-year-old girl, one who had just witnessed her own mother's murder. Lilith had to prove herself as both a ruler, and a suspect. I helped her as much as I could. But the vision came again. And again. We talked about it. Realized we had to take steps, to prepare. To try and stop this future from coming." Vashti shook her head. "We were young, and perhaps foolish in trying to handle it ourselves. We were trying to stave off a panic. Instead, we forged ahead alone, and my sister began to slip away into paranoia. As the years passed, it grew worse. Until she didn't even trust me."

"You're saying everything Lilith did, all of her tyranny, was a result of that night?"

"Any girl who experienced what she did would have been affected by it. Look at what losing your mother did to you. Add the pressure of ruling a powerful and violent people, many of whom don't trust you, and yes. The pressure was too much. Lilith grew obsessed with building her power base. With protecting herself. She believed that she was the only one who could save us from what was coming."

Mercy was quiet. She went to take a drink of tea, an automatic action without thought, then realized it had gone cold. She set the cup aside.

"How often are these sorts of visions wrong?"

Vashti gave a short, bitter laugh. "A single vision might change before it manifests. But this one has remained true for over fifty years. The chances of it changing are quite unlikely."

"But it *could*." Mercy wanted desperately to believe it. "If we found the star, if we evacuated the worlds within range, if—"

"And the queen?" Vashti interrupted. "What do we do about her? Lilith and I spent decades searching for her. We've never found more than rumors. And most of those are so vague it's impossible to tell what they really refer to."

"Maybe we've already found her. Maybe Treon sensed her at Birn."

"Perhaps. But what if that *was* her? The queen who will take control of the Talented and wield them like a sword. What does that mean for those we left behind?"

Fear rose within Mercy. She thought of Reaper, of Atrea, of Cannon. She tried not to think about the fact that nearly a full day and night had passed, with no real word from them. Her brief contact with Reaper hadn't been substantial enough for her to feel certain he'd received her warning. And even if he had, what good would it do if this queen really was so powerful?

She could take Reaper away. As Rani had. And

a trained queen would make it impossible for Mercy to win him back. Sickness crawled through her, twisting her belly. *Don't panic,* she told herself. *Nothing has happened yet.*

"How do I fight someone like that?"

Vashti reached across the table and took Mercy's hand. "Now, my dear, you see why you need training. As a queen."

"And where will I get that?" Mercy pulled her hand away. "You know more about being a queen than anyone alive — at least, anyone alive and *here.*"

"True. But there is someone who can teach you. I believe you've already been in contact with her."

For one confused moment, Mercy thought she meant Rani, the only other queen she'd ever met. But it couldn't be. Rani was a clone, unstable and poorly trained. Not a suitable mentor in any sense. Then, a whisper of thought came to her.

"No," she said aloud. "It's not possible."

"Isn't it?"

"She's dead."

"In our world, dead doesn't always mean gone."

"You're saying the dream I had last night wasn't really a dream. That I was seeing, and speaking with, my grandmother."

"A piece of her, perhaps." Vashti gave Mercy a sad smile. "Just as some of us can travel mentally over great distances, and others can take control of minds, there are those who can transfer at least a part of one's consciousness."

"Transfer. Into what?"

"A vessel," Sebastian said. "Something capable

of holding the complexity of human consciousness. Another mind is an obvious choice. But not the only one."

She stared at him. "None of this surprises you. You *knew* about it already."

He didn't deny it.

"Sebastian," Vashti said, "is one of the few who know all of this. Lilith and I told him shortly before her death. His Talent is one of the few capable of helping to preserve that small piece of her."

"You—you helped Lilith to survive?"

"Part of her," he said. He spread his hands. "It was the only way to ensure she could help you."

"*Help* me. She wanted to *kill* me."

"There was a time," Vashti said, "when my sister became consumed with paranoia and fear. When she was dangerous, even to me. But not at the end, after she grew sick. It was like the old Lilith returned. Sebastian was with her. He stayed by her bedside when I could not. One of us had to survive, you see, so I went away with those being quarantined."

"She was calm and lucid," Sebastian continued. "She cried and apologized over and over. She said she'd ruined everything. Destroyed our chances of survival. In her attempts at building power, she had all but insured Vashti's vision would come to pass. I was the one who told her there might still be a way to stop it."

"You suggested transferring her consciousness," Mercy said, both fascinated and appalled. What did that mean? Had Lilith's soul gone on to the Mother? Or had what they'd done trapped it here, somehow, in the physical world?

Was she actually dead?

"I did. Not into a person. That is an abomination. Murder, at the least. But into an object. Similar to how my mind occupies *Nemesis* sometimes. The brain of a ship is complicated enough to hold a human mind."

"You put her into a ship?"

"No."

Mercy knew before his gaze dropped down to her wrist. Her hand covered the filigree pattern woven over her skin. It was no coincidence that she'd dreamt of her grandmother the night that Sebastian gave her this weapon.

Lilith wasn't dead. Mercy was wearing her.

CHAPTER FIFTEEN

"I thought you'd be angry." Sebastian's voice was subdued. It was just the two of them. Fortifying tea had not been enough, and weariness finally drove Vashti to rest. Mercy and Sebastian left her quarters, and shared a silent walk back to Mercy's room. He finally spoke as they approached the door. "I was certain of it."

Mercy glanced down at her wrist. "Because you gave me a wearable piece of my grandmother's mind? The grandmother who tried to kill me. Oh, and apparently she can now invade my dreams, or pull me into hers, or something like that." She looked over at him. "And give me a headache so strong I throw up. Yeah. I thought I'd be mad, too. But I'm not."

She gave a shrug, passing her palm over the door lock. It slid open. "I think maybe the whole end-of-the-universe-as-we-know-it vibe might have displaced my anger."

His mouth twitched. "It's a lot to process."

That was an understatement. Mercy was about to step inside when something prickled at her awareness. A sound, out of place. She stopped, listening. Sebastian went still beside her.

Sounds aboard ship could travel in odd, unexpected ways. It was often the layout, the way one corridor fed into another. Or the way air circulated. Sometimes, a sound from one deck could echo on another.

Of course, the last time she'd felt something out of place, a bomb had nearly killed her.

But Sebastian merely cocked his head, his posture relaxed.

"This way," he said.

He moved quickly down the corridor, all the way to the end, where it split into two directions. He stopped beside a panel she'd never noticed before. The seams were practically invisible, a thin, barely perceptible line in the wall. It slid open, seemingly of its own accord, but she realized Sebastian must have triggered it via the ship's own commands.

The sound became much more distinct. Weeping, quickly muffled. Sebastian cocked his head, looking at Mercy. *A girl,* he said in her mind. *One of the Veritas agents you absorbed with Rani's defeat. The youngest of the lot. Seventeen. The teleporter.*

Octavia, Mercy told him. *Her name is Octavia.*

Well, Octavia is huddled inside one of our maintenance tunnels, usually utilized only by maintenance drones and bots. He paused. *I don't believe she is hurt. At least physically.*

The sound of crying had stopped, the silence now so complete that Mercy wondered if the girl was holding her breath.

Or, given that Octavia was a teleporter, she might have simply left.

She is still inside, Sebastian said. *There are nanites in every part of this ship. Even if she teleports, I will be able to track her.*

Mercy stuck her head inside the opening. "Hello?"

She'd had a handful of conversations with the Veritas agents who had stayed after Willem Frain's death. Enough to tell them they were as much her people as the pirates, to encourage them to embrace their new lives, and to offer to listen if any of them wanted to talk further.

There was an understandable amount of resentment. They didn't choose to be here. But then, they *had* helped Willem and Rani take the ship, and participated in events which resulted in at least one death and could have been much worse. They weren't prisoners, exactly, but they also weren't permitted to go back to Veritas. At least, not yet. Not now, while relations between the two groups were still strained, even openly hostile.

Mercy had advised them all to accept their new situations and circumstances. Life among the pirates might be different, but they could make real lives here. And perhaps, she thought privately, realize that the pirates weren't the monsters they'd been led to believe.

Sanah – a former employee of Veritas, herself – had spoken with them at some length as well. Not only had she made a place for herself among the pirates, but having lived among both groups, she had unique insights to offer. And as an empath, she could do so in a way that helped bridge decades of hostility.

None of that meant it was going smoothly, or that any of them had actually accepted their new way of life yet. As the youngest, Octavia should have had the easiest time. In theory. Mercy knew a little about her background. Octavia had no family; at least none she knew of. She'd been found and recruited by Veritas as a child, an orphan living on her own, moving constantly from one spaceport to another, working as free labor in exchange for passage on less reputable ships. Had she stayed in that life, it was likely some slaver would have eventually picked her up. Veritas had saved her, become her family. They raised her and trained her in her Talent.

Willem had taken a particular interest, something that made Mercy's skin crawl. She couldn't imagine a worse mentor.

"Octavia? It's Mercy. I just want to make sure you aren't hurt. Is it all right if I do that?"

There was a scuff of fabric on metal and a snuffling sound, but no more. Well, it wasn't a refusal.

"Octavia? I'm coming in." She grabbed the sides of the open panel and hoisted herself up, crawling inside a space designed more for drones than human workers.

Mercy wasn't normally claustrophobic, but the walls of this tunnel were so close she couldn't move without brushing against them. It was a tight fit. Reaper couldn't have done it. Nor could Sebastian, though she supposed he could direct the nanograph to reshape itself and create a larger space.

Ambient light shone from the walls, a soft glow that lit the tunnel well enough to see the honeycomb pattern that ran the length of the ship, providing nanites and power throughout.

Octavia huddled at the end of the tunnel, where it turned a corner, providing a slightly wider space that allowed her to sit with her knees drawn up to her chest. Her head was down, the many small braids of her black hair falling forward around it, a curtain hiding her face.

"Octavia, please tell me if you're hurt," Mercy said. She already knew from Sebastian that she wasn't, of course. But that wasn't the point. She needed to get Octavia talking.

"N—no." The reply was so soft, Mercy almost didn't hear it.

"No, you're not hurt? Or no, you're refusing to answer?"

Another long silence. Mercy lay stretched out in the tunnel. Unlike Octavia, there wasn't enough space in this section for her to sit upright. She had to stay on her stomach, and she could only inch forward or go back. Slowly, she inched forward.

"Octavia?" she pressed.

"I'm not hurt," Octavia said. Her voice was muffled, her forehead pressed against her knees. She was wearing rather nice clothing. Not the utilitarian flight suits so many of the young wore as they went about their assigned duties on the ship, but a tailored looking pair of pants made from high quality self-cleaning denim, and boots that looked like they were real leather. Mercy couldn't begin to calculate the cost of that, and Octavia certainly hadn't been wearing them the last time she saw her.

Why does she look like she just went shopping? Mercy directed the thought on a private thread to Sebastian. *She's seventeen. Tell me the men on this ship aren't trying to buy her affection.* One of the ways the pirates courted or showed their favor was through expensive gifts.

She has no official protector. It is certainly likely, especially given her Talent, that there are those who are attempting to woo her.

Damn it, I asked Max to keep an eye on her.

Max was sworn to Mercy. She provided him with opportunities and training he would otherwise not be able to access, and in return he worked for her. Except she'd been fairly terrible at coming up with things for him to do. Looking out for Octavia was one of the first things she'd ever really asked of him.

Max is sixteen, Sebastian pointed out reasonably. *There is not much he could do to interfere if more powerful men are paying court to the girl. Also, he is not a teleporter. Asking him to keep track of Octavia is akin to asking him to keep track of Tamari.*

I see your point. Tamari went pretty much wherever she wanted on the ship because no one could stop her. As a precocious four-year-old, even her parents' strict demands that she have supervision whenever she teleported were difficult to enforce one hundred percent of the time.

Octavia was older, and had a lot more training with her Talent. Chances were good that if she didn't want to be found, she wouldn't be. At least, not by Max. Sebastian was a different story. His connection to the ship gave him a definite advantage.

Apparently, Mercy had asked the wrong person to keep an eye on her. She'd been going with the idea that Max and Octavia were close to the same age, would be attending some of the same classes, and so on. But she eyed those boots the girl was wearing, and knew she'd put Max in way over his head.

"I'm just going to stay here for a bit," she said to Octavia. "All right? If you feel like talking, I'm here." At least the surface was nice and flat. It wasn't too bad.

She let the silence stretch for a bit. Octavia had stopped crying. And if she wanted to leave, she certainly could. There was nothing Mercy could do to stop her. She took the fact that Octavia stayed as an encouraging sign.

"I should have checked in with you more often." Mercy made a note to check on *all* of the former Veritas people. "I didn't, and I should have. I let myself get distracted. And I let myself think that Sanah would be enough of a resource. But the truth is, I'm responsible for all of you. I'm the one who decided you should stay." *I'm your Queen,* she thought, but didn't say. She wasn't sure how comfortable any of them were with the idea. She certainly wasn't.

Octavia didn't say anything, but Mercy could tell she was listening. Her posture had changed slightly, her legs relaxing, her head lifting, though she still looked down.

"I should have asked if you were all right. I

want you to feel free to come to me with anything. I care about you. About all of you."

"I heard you met with Veritas." Octavia's voice was so low Mercy had to strain to hear it. "To negotiate peace. Is that true?"

"I did." Mercy's mouth twisted. "It didn't go exactly as planned. But I think it's time for peace. Past time." Especially if what Vashti had told her came true.

"If it happens, can I go home?"

"Why don't we talk about that. What was home like?" Mercy really wished they could be having this conversation somewhere else. The floor of the shaft, smooth though it was, pressed uncomfortably hard against her ribs and hip. But she didn't want to suggest it and risk Octavia shutting down. Now that she had her talking, she wanted to keep it going.

"I lived on Abanel. At the Starside building."

Abanel was the home of the monarchy in the Commonwealth, one of the most densely populated worlds. Mercy wracked her mind for what she knew. Starside sounded vaguely familiar. She thought it was owned by a mega-corp, and it housed a school, didn't it? For disadvantaged youth. Some corporate write off, if memory served.

"You lived in a dormitory?"

Octavia's head moved in the dim light, and Mercy realized she was nodding.

Well, it was nice to know Veritas hadn't neglected her education. Of course, they'd probably had some long term plans for Octavia.

"You liked it there?"

A barely perceptible twitch. "It was okay."

"Do you miss your friends?"

Another nod.

"I'm sorry you can't go back right now." She sighed. "Look, I don't know how much you knew about what Willem was doing. About what he did to me, and to Atrea, and even to Rani."

I don't know what to say. She sent the thought to Sebastian. *I don't know how to deal with kids.*

She's seventeen. Certainly old enough to make her own choices.

Mercy shifted, trying to ease the pressure against her ribs.

"Look, Willem was not a nice guy. You were there, on the space station, and here when he threatened to kill everyone, when he tried to kill me. I'm sure you witnessed a lot worse." She paused. "Until we can reach some kind of agreement with Veritas, sending you home would just be putting you back into the hands of someone else like him. I'm not willing to do that."

Octavia turned her head away, mumbling something Mercy didn't quite catch.

"What was that?"

Octavia shrugged, not answering.

She said 'it's not like here is any better', Sebastian told her.

"Here isn't any better? Can you tell me why?" Mercy asked gently. "Because I'd really like to know. If someone is treating you badly, or scaring you, or pressuring you, I want to know. That isn't supposed to be how things are."

"It's always how things are." The sheer cynicism in the girl's voice broke Mercy's heart. She might have *been* this girl, if she hadn't run into Wolfgang and Atrea first.

"Not if I have anything to say about it," Mercy promised. "Please, tell me."

There was a moment, when Octavia looked up. She met Mercy's eyes for the first time, and Mercy thought she had her. Then she said, "There's nothing you can do. Nothing *anyone* can do." And then she was gone, a rush of air filling the space she'd occupied.

"Mother damn it. Sebastian?"

It will take me a moment to find her. It's a large ship.

Mercy used the time to back out of the tunnel. She sent her own thoughts questing for a familiar mind.

Max. My quarters. Now.

Am I in trouble? She had the vague impression of a room filled with students, and realized he was in class. She sent a quick message to the teacher excusing him.

I don't know yet. Get here.

On my way.

Mercy felt relief as she emerged back into the openness of the corridor, wincing as she stretched. Her ribs were definitely bruised.

"She is with Tamari," said Sebastian. "In one of the empty holds, *not* where either of them is supposed to be. However, I've notified Dem and he'll keep an eye on them."

Dem was not only Tamari's father, but the only other teleporter on the ship. Mercy relaxed.

"I am getting to the bottom of this." She strode back down the hall to her quarters. "I don't know what is going on, but I'm going to find out."

Sebastian accompanied her, saying nothing. She didn't protest when he followed her into her quarters. Sebastian sat down, while Mercy paced the length of the main cabin.

When the tentative mental knock came, Mercy was already opening the door to let Max in.

He'd grown in the past six months, and now he was tall enough to look her in the eye. He'd begun to fill out, but was still lean and gangly. His shoulders were a little broader, his feet not quite so big for his frame anymore. His hair had grown. It was long enough now that he'd tied it in a messy, dark knot at the back of his head. If he started sporting a stubble, she was going to think he was emulating Cannon.

Well, there were worse role models.

"What's going on?" he asked as she stepped aside to allow him entry.

"That's what I want to know. What's going on with Octavia?"

From the way his shoulders suddenly hunched, she knew she'd struck a nerve.

She crossed her arms. "I asked you to watch out for her."

"I have been." His nervous gaze went to Sebastian, seated in one of the chairs with his hands folded before him, and back to Mercy. "I tried to make friends, but she wasn't interested. So, I do the best I can. It's just hard when she can teleport at any moment to wherever she wants."

"Why didn't you tell me you were having difficulties?"

He shrugged, not meeting her gaze. "I've been handling it," he mumbled.

"How?"

"I asked Tamari and Rasa to keep watch." He gave a quick smile, the kind Mercy hadn't seen from him much since Kator's death. Both boys had been put in danger when Willem Frain invaded *Nemesis*. One had survived. The other had not.

Mercy arched an eyebrow. "You asked a four-year-old and a telepathic cat to keep an eye on her?"

"Well, Tama can go anywhere Octavia can." He grinned. "Plus, she's cute. Octavia was comfortable being her friend."

Well, Mercy couldn't argue with that. Most people were comfortable around Tamari. That child could charm anyone. And the giant, telepathic cat that was her constant companion kept her safe, even when her parents didn't know what she was up to.

But there were some things a child and a *kith*, however intelligent, might not pick up on.

"Who's been bothering Octavia?" she asked.

"Bothering?" Max looked cautious, like he wasn't sure what qualified.

"She's wearing expensive boots. We found her hiding where no one would look, crying. She doesn't trust me enough to share whatever is going on, and I don't blame her. But I need to know what it is, so we can stop it."

"Well." Max looked thoughtful. "You know how we all have areas of training we're assigned based on our history and our Talent?"

Mercy nodded. It had been the root of the animosity that had once existed between Max and Kator, before the two became friends. Max had access to the pilot training Kator wanted.

"But Octavia is an outsider. Her family history is Veritas." He lifted a shoulder. "Her Talent is really rare and powerful. She can teleport with another person already! Dem says he didn't learn how to do that until he was older than she is."

"That *is* impressive," Sebastian said.

"So a lot of people are trying to get her to sign a contract," Max said.

"A contract?" Mercy asked. She looked from Max to Sebastian.

"Like what the dogs do," Sebastian said. "But instead of working as a soldier, you serve in other ways. The more rare the Talent, the more in demand you might be. Normally, this is an equitable, good relationship, where the benefactor provides you with opportunities and payment commiserate with your abilities. Similar to the relationship you have with Max. But it is quite possible some have been trying to pressure Octavia into a bad bargain." Sebastian shook his head. "We should have foreseen this and provided her with a specific protector. When Nayla came aboard, Doc took her in immediately to prevent something like this. Being young, female, powerful, and without family, Octavia is especially vulnerable." His eyes sparked with anger and self-disgust. "We allowed ourselves to be blinded by where she came from."

Mercy looked back at Max. "Who is pressuring her?"

He hesitated, and Mercy gave him a look.

"A bunch of people. But the worst, I think, are Wick, Xavier, and Griffin."

"Griffin?" Mercy was surprised. "What makes them the worst?" she asked Max.

He fidgeted.

"Max?"

"Well. They aren't just pressing for a service contract. They're courting her."

"Courting."

"You know." He looked embarrassed.

Yes, she did know.

Griffin and Xavier were at least within five or six years of Octavia in age, but Wick was more than old enough to be her father.

"Have any of them touched her?"

"Uh…"

"Come on, Max. How far has this gone?"

"I'm not…sure. I mean, I saw Wick put his hand on her arm once. And one time I found her talking to Xavier, but the way he was standing she couldn't get by him in the hallway. He was leaning in, and I don't know what happened, but the next thing I saw, she was at the other end of the hallway and he was pissed about it. She seemed fine, though."

Mercy closed her eyes, taking a moment to control her anger. It wasn't Max's fault that she hadn't been more explicit in her instructions, or that she herself had failed to check on Octavia.

"Let me be clear," she said, opening her eyes. "From now on, if anyone appears to be making Octavia uncomfortable, I want to know about it. I am hereby placing her under *my* protection." She looked at Sebastian. "I can do that, right?"

"You can."

"Good." She probably needed to do that for all of the former Veritas people. Establish once and for all that they were as much hers as the pirates.

"But, it would be better if someone else did it." Sebastian stood up. His eyes were narrowed thoughtfully. "Politically speaking. If Reaper was here, I would suggest him."

"Why?"

"One, many already consider you a Veritas sympathizer. There are those who use your push for peace as evidence that you shouldn't be Queen."

Of course there were. Mercy really hated politics sometimes.

"Two, you *are* Queen. Taking someone under your protection now also removes their choices. When Lilith did this, the person in question wasn't just protected by her, they were considered hers. They worked for her."

The last thing Mercy wanted to do was make Octavia feel like she had even fewer choices.

"Why Reaper?"

Sebastian smiled. "Frankly, because he's scary enough, people would leave her alone. As they did for you when you came aboard. But he's not here. Nor is Cannon. And if Dem extends his protection, that is also limiting her choices. People will assume he's chosen her for dog training." He shrugged. "Which wouldn't be a bad choice, *if* it's what she wants."

"What about you?" Mercy asked.

"Me?" His eyes widened.

"You're a Core member. You're in charge of

this entire ship, to a degree that basically means you *are* the ship. And honestly, if people aren't afraid of you and what you can do with that kind of control, they're stupid."

"All right." Slowly, Sebastian smiled. "Politically speaking, it isn't a bad solution."

"And you *can* protect her." It wasn't really a question. Mercy didn't doubt it for a moment.

"Yes, I can."

"Then let's make it clear that you are. First, we'll have a conversation with Octavia." She smiled. "Then, feel free to make your protection known in whatever kind of display you'd like. The more overt, the better."

Sebastian met her eyes. His were bright with amusement, though she could still detect anger in the tension of his jaw. "Scare them into backing down?"

"Damn right."

"That's what Lilith would have done, you know."

Not long ago, those words would have been a slap in the face. With some regret, Mercy forced herself to accept them. Maybe Lilith had been a tyrant. But maybe she'd been trying to save her people from certain death, and lost herself in the process. Mercy was going to have to try and do the same thing, without the same consequences.

She forced a smile. "Well, maybe I'm not as different from my grandmother as I once thought."

She ran her fingers over the pattern on her wrist. Hopefully, she would be different enough.

CHAPTER SIXTEEN

*M*ercy couldn't sleep. She lay in bed, staring into the darkness. She'd tried contacting Reaper before bed and failed. It worried her. Why couldn't she reach him? She'd even tried reaching out to Atrea, but that had been a failure as well. What was happening to them? A parade of worst case scenarios played out in her mind. They'd been captured. Killed. Taken deeper into Commonwealth space, beyond her ability to reach. The possibilities made her sick to her stomach.

She needed to go to sleep if she wanted to meet with Lilith again. That was the plan: meet this ghost of her grandmother and find out more about what she wanted. Learn what she could from her.

She brushed her fingers over the pattern on her wrist, tracing it over and over. The bracelet that held Lilith.

But beneath that pattern lay the lemniscate tattoo she and Atrea shared, each of them carrying the symbol on their bodies. It was more than just ink indelibly painted into her skin; it held low level tracking nanites. But their range was too short to be useful. It had been more symbolic, anyway: the idea was that they would always be connected, even if they weren't sisters by blood. If she and Atrea stood in the same city, on the same planet, *maybe* Mercy could have used it to track her. But not now.

She tossed and turned, trying to force her mind away from her friends and loved ones. Wherever they were, she felt powerless to help them, and that was part of the problem. She hated feeling helpless.

Doc could give her something to sleep, but Mercy hated the idea of that even more. She should just be able to *will* herself to sleep. What was the point of having fantastic powers of the mind if insomnia could still defeat her?

Mercy.

A powerful voice boomed through her head. She sat bolt upright as her heart tried to beat its way free of her chest. Seconds later, she realized the voice was familiar.

Treon, she thought, scowling. *What do you want? I was sleeping.*

No, you weren't.

She clenched her teeth, reminding herself that Reaper's brother was at least as useful as he was obnoxious, and that his heart was *sometimes* in the right place.

I was trying to. Thanks for ruining that.

This is more important.

She sighed, flopping back in her bed. The quicker this conversation finished, the quicker she could sleep. In theory, anyway. *What do you want?*

Have you been able to reach Reaper recently?

Not tonight. She grimaced. *Why?*

It might be nothing. There was a long silence. *It's probably nothing.*

If she'd been worried before, it was nothing to the alarm she felt now. Treon loved his family. She never doubted that. But he had a tendency to self-absorption that bordered on narcissism. If he was this worried, it didn't bode well.

She sat up and flung the covers aside, swinging her legs over the side of the bed. Lilith would just have to wait.

What are you talking about? she asked.

Mercy went to push out of bed, and found herself stepping into an impossible dream. Instead of the nanograph floor of a ship, her bare feet moved across wood floors, the different grains beautiful and vibrant in a way that nanograph couldn't imitate. She looked down and noted that she was still wearing the loose cotton clothes she'd put on for sleep.

She had a moment of disorientation. Was she asleep? Was this a dream, or one of Treon's famous telepathic landscapes? She glanced around.

Huge double windows set into the wall opened on a stunning vista. Mountains rose in the distance, and a forest of trees filled the space in between, standing like tall sentinels amidst fields of golden grass. Some of the trees had green needles, others a silvery, nearly purple color that caught the light of the setting sun and seemed to glow.

One of the windows was cracked open, a light,

cool breeze brushing delicate fingers across Mercy's face, ruffling her hair. Wherever this was, it was a home, a structure on a planet. Not aboard a ship.

She turned away from the window to look around.

The walls were a pale, neutral color, almost white, with holoscreens set into them. The screens rotated through a variety of family portraits. A beautiful young woman with a baby cradled in her arms, two young boys at her feet. One of the boys had dark skin and the other fair, but both had icy blue eyes that were unmistakable. The boys sat completely, unnaturally still, neither of them so much as fidgeting. The baby fussed and cried, and the young woman murmured softly to the child, her voice musical and soothing.

As Mercy stared at the holo, it faded to another, the same young woman standing with a man. He held her in his arms, stiff and awkward as though such an intimate pose was unnatural to him. Mercy sucked in a breath, shocked. He looked like a slightly older, more remote version of Reaper. His face was so expressionless it might have been carved from stone. His blue eyes were devoid of any warmth.

But the young woman had her face turned up toward his, caramel colored hair spilling over her shoulders in a loose wave. She smiled up at the man, her lips moving as she said something to him. Her eyes were a golden brown, sparkling with laughter. She was so vibrant in the holo that she might have been real. As Mercy watched, she lifted a hand and cupped the man's face. In that moment, he glanced down at her and his expression softened.

"Beautiful, isn't she?"

Mercy had expected Treon the moment she realized where she was, and who she was looking at. But it wasn't his voice behind her.

"She is," Mercy said as Lilith came to stand beside her. Unwilling to tear her eyes away from Reaper's parents, she didn't look at her grandmother. She realized she'd never seen holos or pictures of his family before.

Here, in this place, her worries from moments ago felt distant, like dreams from a time long past. She frowned. This wasn't right. The holo she was watching changed again, but she forced herself to turn away from it.

"I can't be here," she said to Lilith.

Her grandmother looked much as she had before. A warrior queen. Younger than she should have been, with expressive green eyes and a vibrancy far more fitting to a living woman than a spirit...or whatever she was.

"We have a lot of work to do, Mercy," Lilith said. She waved a hand at their surroundings. "Here is exactly where you need to be. I thought perhaps this setting might be of interest to you."

The implications of that statement were alarming. Was this ghost or consciousness, whatever it was that remained of Lilith, aware of the world as it existed around her? How else could she know that Reaper's family would matter to Mercy?

"Why?" Mercy asked, her tone guarded. "Why bring me here? Why now? And how did you do it? I wasn't asleep."

Her grandmother contemplated her with narrowed eyes. It was a penetrating look, the sort that said she was looking inside Mercy and weighing what she found.

"We have limited time," Lilith said. "Are you certain you want to waste it on questions like these?"

Mercy frowned at her. "According to Treon, a telepathic construct works like dreams you control. All aspects can be built, altered, or changed. A short time can pass, or months, even years. An eternity. We have as much time as we need."

A smile banished the hard lines of Lilith's face. "Very good. At least you've learned something."

"Answer my question."

Lilith turned away, pacing toward the window. She stood and looked out, while frustration built within Mercy. She was sure her grandmother was being deliberately evasive.

"He was a good choice," Lilith said, just as Mercy opened her mouth to say something scathing and angry.

"What?"

"Reaper. He was an excellent choice for your first Consort." Lilith glanced over her shoulder at her. "You'll need to be just as strategic in choosing the rest."

"I didn't choose Reaper out of some strategy."

"No? A pity." Lilith's mouth turned down in disappointment. "It would have given me some small measure of hope for your future."

"I've been here five minutes, and it's already been too long," Mercy said, striding over to the window. "I'm going back."

"Are you?"

"I am. So you made a construct. That doesn't mean it has to stay in your control."

Amusement flitted across Lilith's face. She tilted her head, watching Mercy. "Fighting me didn't go well for you last time. I suggest you think again."

"I don't have time for this bullshit. Reaper is in trouble. I have to go back. We can do…whatever this is later."

Lilith sat in a chair that hadn't been behind her a moment before. It looked antique, the wooden frame ornate and detailed. She sat on the cushioned seat as though occupying a throne.

"I thought we'd established that time here has no meaning." Lilith folded her hands together, her elbows supported by the arms of her chair.

"That doesn't mean I have to stay."

A matching chair appeared behind Mercy, the cushion's edge hitting her in the back of the legs.

"Sit. Down." Lilith's voice lost whatever conversational quality it had possessed. The aura of command that cloaked her permeated the room, and Mercy found herself obeying before she consciously thought about it.

Her teeth ground together. This was not at all how she'd intended this to go.

"Enough of whatever petty concerns you have back in the real world. For now, you are here. With me." Lilith leaned forward, her eyes and tone equally intent. "Make use of me, you foolish girl. I am the *only* queen you have. And trust me when I say, even if you could find them, the others won't have any interest in training you."

"Others?" Surely, she didn't mean Rani. But no. There was also the queen Treon had sensed. The one in the cloaked ship, near Reaper, Atrea, and Cannon. Suddenly much more interested in this conversation, Mercy found herself leaning forward in a way that mirrored Lilith. "What others?"

Eyeing her, it was a moment before Lilith responded. Mercy had the distinct impression that her grandmother was deciding how much to tell her. Really, how was it that a mere echo of the woman had such a heavy weight of realism? If she didn't know better, Mercy would think this *was* Lilith, all of her. That the two of them sat in a real room together, and that her grandmother was still alive.

Which, thank the Mother, couldn't be true.

"The other queens," Lilith said. "The reason you should be far more concerned about training with me than whatever pulls you back to the physical world. They all answer to *her*. She is no doubt already aware of you, and you are..." Lilith's gaze traveled over Mercy in an evaluating fashion. "... no match for the least among them."

"Her? You mean the queen who killed your mother, Kiana," Mercy said, remembering the story Vashti told her. An emotion crossed Lilith's face, fleeting and lost to shadow as she tilted her head down and away from the window. It looked like sorrow. Loss.

When she lifted her head again, Lilith was perfectly composed. Only a glint of anger in her eyes betrayed her feelings.

"Yes. The murderous bitch. Vashti and I call her

the Alpha." Lilith hesitated. "We believe she was the first queen ever created."

"That's impossible. The first queen was created during the Ascension Wars. She would have lived hundreds of years ago."

"Yes."

"Even with the best anti-aging treatments available, she could only live to maybe one hundred and fifty."

"She's not using anti-aging treatments." Lilith grimaced. "I have a theory."

"What theory?"

Lilith stood, crossing to one of the holos. It showed a teenage Reaper and Dem with a much younger boy, the three of them standing close together. The young Treon kept casting anxious looks up at his brothers, then turning back to smile at someone unseen, probably his mother.

The boy who was Reaper looked particularly uncomfortable. While Treon appeared nervous, and Dem stared stoically straight ahead, the young Reaper looked away. He stared down at his feet, and there was something in his posture that said he wished he was anywhere else. He shot one quick glance up in the direction where Mercy assumed his mother stood, recording the holo. There was a longing in those eyes, an uncertainty that tugged at her heart. As if the boy wanted to share an easy smile with her, as Treon did, but didn't quite know how. Mercy moved to touch the portrait, but Lilith beat her to it.

Her grandmother's fingers touched the holo and it wavered, ripples moving across it. The three boys vanished. Mercy's arm fell back to her side.

A new scene formed, a shadowed figure sitting on a throne, a long fall of silvery hair obscuring her face. The hands that clutched the arms of the throne were old, wizened and wrinkled.

Around the figure dozens of women appeared, one by one. They ranged in age from young girls to grown women, but none of them had reached middle age. They, too, stood obscured in shadow.

"I don't understand," Mercy said after a moment. She stared at the new holo but couldn't fathom what Lilith wanted her to perceive.

"Look closer," Lilith said. "Tell me what you see."

"A woman," Mercy said with some reluctance. It chafed at her to be playing Lilith's game, even a little. "Old, and powerful." She nodded to the throne. "A Queen."

"And?"

She shook her head, gesturing to the rest of the women. "People? Women? I don't know. Are they her subjects?"

"In a way."

Mercy rolled her eyes. "Just tell me whatever it is you want me to know."

"I want to see how you think," Lilith countered. "How your mind works. That knowledge will be integral to our training together. What else?"

With a frustrated breath, Mercy took a step back, attempting to get a wider angle on the holo. The women moved, but only slightly, barely shifting in place. The woman on the throne sat with her head held high, her posture an imperious one, though Mercy could see nothing of her face through the shadows.

Every time one of the girls moved, the woman on the throne would shift or twitch, her movement barely perceptible.

"It's like she's a spider in a web," Mercy found herself saying. "And each of the girls is connected to her by the web's strings. When they move, she feels it — no, that's wrong." She thought for a moment, trying to identify what it was that had caught her attention, giving her the feeling that she was jumping to the wrong conclusion. Lilith, for once, said nothing, merely waiting. Mercy's eyes narrowed. Something about the way the figure moved...

"She's controlling them," Mercy said. "She moves first, then they do."

"Very good," Lilith said, sounding pleased. "That is exactly what I believe is happening."

Mercy looked at her. "But how does that explain how she's remained alive all this time?"

Lilith gave her a long look. "Think about it, Mercy. How am I still alive?"

Mercy wasn't convinced Lilith was still anything, but she kept that thought to herself; clearly, this echo of Lilith believed it, and that was what mattered in this context. She brushed fingers over her wrist, where the bracelet sat against her flesh in the real world.

"You're saying she possesses them? That her consciousness transfers to a younger body?"

Lilith gave a genuine smile. "Yes, exactly."

"But what about the women?" Mercy looked back at the holo. "What happens to them once she...takes over?"

"We know from studying many powerful

telepaths over the years, that no two minds can occupy the same space for long. A physical body isn't meant to house multiple consciousnesses." Lilith paused. "Not without going mad."

As Mercy watched, one by one the young girls and women vanished from the holo, fading into the shadows. Until the only one left was the queen on her throne. Her silvery hair brightened to gold. The wrinkles on her hands melted to smooth skin. Light slanted across what was now a portrait of one single woman, chasing shadows from half her face. The suggestion of a striking, powerful young woman stared outward, as though looking straight at Mercy.

"She kills them," Mercy said. "And takes over their bodies."

"I believe so."

"How many times can she do this?"

"As many as she wants." Lilith looked grave. "I believe she has achieved a sort of macabre immortality."

Mercy glanced sideways at her. "And this is the woman you and Vashti think will come and destroy us?"

"Yes and no. She'll come to *control* us. To sweep us up into her army as she crashes over the galaxy like a wave, powerful and unstoppable."

Mercy didn't know what to say.

Lilith contemplated the holo. "Once, I thought I would be our chance at stopping her. I did everything in my power to prepare. Gathered the most powerful of our people around me. I focused on nothing else but gaining the strength I would need to face her. Unfortunately, I was so blinded by my goal that I became my own worst enemy. I was ruthless in my pursuit, removing anything or anyone I saw as an obstacle or a threat. *I* was the galaxy's salvation, you see. Nothing else mattered." Her voice dropped to nearly a whisper. "I failed."

It was a moment before Mercy could speak. She couldn't seem to tear her eyes away from the woman in the portrait.

"And now?" she asked finally.

Lilith faced her. "And now, *you* are our last hope." Lilith offered a hand, holding it out like an offer of truce, or even more disturbing, friendship. Mercy froze. It was the last thing she expected from her grandmother. "Now, granddaughter. Are you ready to begin your training?"

CHAPTER SEVENTEEN

*T*reon did not consider himself someone prone to impetuous action. When the connection to Mercy's mind vanished, he didn't jump to conclusions or panic. If anything, he became irritated. He needed her emotional link to Reaper, damn it.

He reached for her again, but while he could sense the presence he knew distinctly as *Mercy*, it was in a distant, removed fashion. He could not reach her. Without missing a beat, he called for his brother.

Dem.

Treon, I am busy. I have asked you repeatedly—

I can't reach Mercy. Her mind is closed to me.

Silence answered him. It stretched, but Treon waited patiently. He knew both of his brothers better than they had ever understood him, and he knew exactly what Dem was doing: teleporting to Mercy's quarters and physically checking on her.

To pass the time, he crossed to the cabinet in his own quarters where most people would have kept liquor. He took out a bottle, one among dozens identical to it, and opened it, pouring himself a tall glass of green liquid. Without Mercy's aid, he was going to need as much *mnemosa* as he could drink. The boost would be a temporary one, but it might be enough.

She is asleep, but unresponsive.

Asleep? Impossible. I was just speaking with her.

Perhaps your wit is not as engaging as you imagine.

Treon paused with the glass halfway to his mouth, momentarily nonplussed. Dem's attempts at humor had become a regular occurrence in recent years, but it still surprised him every time. Dem had always been the stoic one, unable to even pretend emotions as Reaper always had. Marriage to Sanah and fatherhood to Tamari had changed him.

We were speaking of Reaper's situation, he said, making an attempt to keep his mental voice free of irritation. *I find it highly doubtful that she would drop off to sleep in the midst of our conversation.*

As she is unresponsive to both physical and mental stimuli, I agree with you.

Yes, we are both agreed that something is wrong. What is it?

I don't know.

Treon drank down half his glass, his mind was working as he did so. Reaching out, he casually pulled Sebastian into the conversation.

Treon? Sebastian sounded sleep fogged.

You were supposed to be monitoring Mercy.

I have been.

Then why is she unconscious in her quarters?

Silence answered him, but Treon was far less patient with the delays of others who were *not* his brothers. *Well? Your safeguards were obviously not triggered, as you were sleeping.*

No, Sebastian said slowly. *Because nothing is harming her. She is not in distress.*

Not in distress! We cannot wake her. Clearly there is something wrong.

No. She is...training.

Training? For the first time since Sebastian joined them, Dem spoke. *What kind of training?*

The queen kind. If you want to know more, you'll have to ask Vashti. But it was arranged, approved, and agreed upon by Mercy herself. She is not in any danger, and will wake on her own, likely in a few hours.

A few hours. Treon's irritation bloomed into frustration. *I need her now, not in a few hours.*

Unfortunately, once begun the training cannot be easily interrupted.

Treon cursed. Well, he'd already half-resigned himself. Now he had to commit to the action.

Very well. I will handle this without her.

Treon? Dem sounded *concerned.* Since when was his unflappable brother prone to worry? *You said this was about Reaper. What is going on?*

I'm not certain yet. That's why I needed Mercy's help. It may be nothing.

The foreboding deep within Treon argued against that, but there was no need to worry everyone until he knew for sure. For now, he was only certain of one thing: until a short time ago, he'd been able to sense a faint echo of Reaper's presence. Too far to reach telepathically, but distinct. Now, he could not.

While his own connection to Reaper was deep, as brothers, Treon had observed that Dem's connection to Sanah ran even deeper. Though her own telepathic gifts were weak, Dem could still connect with his wife at great distances. He had hoped to use Mercy's emotional bond with Reaper in a similar fashion, boosting her telepathy with his own to reach his brother. But now that was no longer possible.

It left him with only one alternative. It was one he wasn't altogether comfortable with.

You just keep our Queen safe, he told Dem and Sebastian. *Let me worry about Reaper and the others.*

Treon—

Do not argue with me, Dem. My mind is quite made up. None of you can help me. Only Mercy could have, but as she is unavailable, I will manage. I do need uninterrupted quiet to do so, however.

Of course you do. There was a sense of irony to Dem's tone that Treon chose to ignore.

He downed the rest of his glass of *mnemosa,* then refilled it to the brim. This would, he suspected, take everything he had. He locked the door to his quarters and activated the mental shields he'd placed on them and renewed with frequency. No one could interrupt him now, even if they wanted to. To be certain, however, he needed one more precaution.

He drank down the second glass of *mnemosa.* He could feel the surge of strength that rose through him as the mental stimulant hit his system. Once it wore off, he would crash, likely into an extended deep sleep. But for now, he would take every drop of boost he could get.

The first bottle empty, he grabbed a new one and walked into the sleeping chambers of his quarters. He placed the bottle and empty glass on the shelf set into the alcove beside his bed, and then stretched out on top of the covers. If the worst happened and he burnt out, he didn't need to fall and compound matters by hitting his head.

Settled, he clasped his hands over his chest, closed his eyes, and moved seamlessly from the physical world into the vast mental landscape he'd spent years familiarizing himself with. He'd created his own place within it, a personal piece of the overall framework. It was, in many ways, more comfortable to him than the physical world. He'd built every corner of it, every room, every detail. It was like a universe that belonged to him, and only him. He could manipulate it to anything he wished. Unlike the quick landscapes he brought others to when he wished to hold an unchallenged advantage over them, this was his alone. He never brought anyone here. It was his sanctuary.

In it, he stood in a room that mirrored his quarters on *Nemesis*. This was his most frequent crossover point, a sort of mental airlock into the world that existed entirely outside of physical reality. From here, he could step beyond the mirror, and it would expand into impossible places. Gorgeous vistas he'd created from bits and pieces he'd seen or imagined.

But he wasn't here to visit any of those places today. He needed to stay in this mirror image of the real universe, because that was where he would find his brother.

He took a moment, breathing slowly and deeply, centering himself for the task ahead. Here, his entire being became his mind, his mental abilities. It was as though he left the distraction of his physical form completely behind, and could act with a clarity and precision beyond anything he was capable of in the physical world.

Doubt, an unwelcome and strange emotion for him, pricked at his awareness, and he ruthlessly shoved it down. There could be no room for uncertainty here.

He closed his eyes, picturing his brother, Reaper. Feeling him, the distinctive mental presence that was Nikolos. He concentrated on it until that was all he felt or sensed.

Treon imagined that Hunters did something similar when tracking someone, but he couldn't be sure, of course. What he did was not the same. It was his own ritual, his own pattern. He'd studied the matter, and even among powerful telepaths, he felt certain that no one else had even attempted something like this.

He gave another moment for Nik's presence to fill his mind, and then he let go. He exploded outward, his mind traveling across light years in an instant. He knew where he'd last sensed Reaper, but he did not want to focus solely on that point.

Anything could have happened. A teleporter could have taken his brother somewhere else. A ship could have jumped him deep into the Commonwealth, or in any direction. He could be dead. It was important not to let speculation distract him or lead him in the wrong direction.

What Treon was doing now was largely passive. After the initial burst of energy, he used very little to maintain his search. His mind simply drifted, waiting like a spider sending out tendrils of ever-expanding web for something to cross into it. That *something* would be Reaper's presence.

Even so, that first step had used a huge amount of energy, not only a good chunk of his own, but most of the boost he'd gained from the *mnemosa*. Had he not chosen to fortify himself, he might have found Reaper, only to have no reserves left. This way, he hoped to have something. Enough to find out what had happened, and perhaps even to help his brother if he needed it.

And he had not forgotten that presence, that overwhelming force that had flung him from Birn's system back into his physical self with such strength.

He drifted for what seemed hours, but in this mental place, it might have been minutes or even seconds. When the faintest trace of Reaper came, he almost missed it. It was merely a feeling at first, a brush of something familiar that made him hesitate without quite knowing why.

He waited, and it came again. Cautiously, he drifted closer. He didn't want to go too far down this path if it proved false. But the closer he drew, the more certain he became. The sense remained faint, but it was distinct, and definitely Reaper.

Killers were often so coldly flat. Their minds could be difficult to differentiate without close examination. But Reaper, like Dem, was only half Killer. The influence of their mother made them unique among their kind.

Treon sped up, stars passing in a blur as he moved. At last he came to a dropship, drifting and dead, as though left behind and forgotten by whatever capital ship it belonged to. Commonwealth

Naval markings decorated its sides. Here on the mental plane, it was a mere outline that housed the minds within it, a shell barely perceptible. But in the real world it would be solid and real.

He didn't wonder why his brother was in a Navy ship. He merely dropped his mind inside to see for himself.

In the cockpit, two forms slumped in the pilot and copilot's seats. He knew them. Ghost and Zion, two of his brother's dogs. He felt the pulse of their minds, faint but there, and knew they were alive. Alive, but not consciously aware. Asleep? No, something deeper, more dangerous. Not unlike the condition he had left Mercy in.

Treon frowned at the comparison. Once Sebastian had mentioned training, he'd strongly suspected what had happened to Mercy. *Someone* had pulled her into a mental construct, a landscape not unlike his own. He had his own suspicions as to who and why, but that was a situation to confront later.

The question was, had the same sort of thing happened here? And if so, who was responsible? Pulling a Killer like Reaper into such a place was both smart and dangerous. In a telepathic construct, the creator was in control. Reaper would not be able to use his Talent to kill them. But the transition would be incredibly dangerous. To pull someone into such a place required a mental connection, a link of minds. In that moment, Reaper could kill in an instant. It was one of the reasons Treon had never taken either of his brothers across without their permission and approval. Such a move against their will would constitute an attack, one they would respond to instinctively.

Treon found himself struck with an overpowering sense of curiosity. He looked around, looking for the smallest clue to either support or refute his theory.

The cockpit itself was dark. Not unusual, in the mental plane. Physical things did not have the same presence here that they did in the physical world, unless someone put the energy into them to make them more real.

He drifted beyond the cockpit into the crew compartment, and here the minds crowded close together. Some he knew, others he didn't. He went first to Reaper's, his brother's presence stronger here, but still subdued. Near him were Atrea and Cannon. All of their mental sparks felt faint and distant, as though muffled in some way. None of them, then, were conscious in the real world.

From here he examined each of the other occupants of the compartment, those he knew, and those he didn't. Titus, Knox, and Jaxon, the group he knew to be agents of Veritas - those who had met with Mercy to negotiate a truce. He spent a long time examining each of them, looking for anything that might be different about their condition, but they were exactly like all of the rest.

There was another person here as well, a woman he did not know, and who clearly did not belong with the well-dressed group from Veritas. She was too thin, in the way of someone who regularly did not get enough to eat, and dressed in cheap, ill-fitting synth cotton that had long ago lost its cleaning and mending abilities, if it had ever possessed them. It was filthy, and so was she. Her hair was a long mess of tangles and filth that made him loath to touch her, even here where the touch would purely be mental.

But she was the only anomaly in the group, an unexpected, unknown, extra person for which he had no explanation. A slave? She certainly looked the part. But looks, Treon knew, could be deceptive.

Carefully, he brushed her mind with his. Like the others, she wasn't conscious. Unlike them, she was not so distant and faint. She had not been drawn into whatever construct the rest of them were a part of. He tilted his head, considering. Too insignificant? Or was she, in actuality, the construct's architect?

He could sense the flavor of her Talent, and she was a telepath of moderate strength, one gifted in shielding. That did not lend itself to the idea that she could be the mastermind behind this. That would require someone extremely powerful.

Treon wasn't even sure he could have done it, not with so many minds all at once.

Still, he sensed something…something odd beneath the surface. He almost delved more deeply into her mind, but reminded himself that personal curiosity was less important than the mission at hand. If she was not the architect behind whatever had happened here, her secrets could wait.

He left the mysterious young woman and looked around at the ship.

All around the compartment, anything not tied, bolted, strapped, or magnetized floated. They had no power, and no gravity. It was dark, but faint light emanated from emergency glows which floated amongst the rest of the flotsam. Probably deployed by Reaper and his dogs before whatever had happened to them took place.

He would not be able to determine what knocked out the power from this side of things. But it did concern him, because without power, they would soon run out air. If they didn't freeze first.

Space was an incredibly cold place.

He had two choices. Rush back to *Nemesis* and get a rescue ship dispatched, hoping it could reach them in time, if he even had their location correct. There was nothing nearby to use as a frame of reference, no handy planet or station. They were effectively adrift in the empty space of no man's land. That made things difficult.

His other choice was to attempt to wake one of them. They might be able to tell him their last known coordinates. They might be able to get the ship up and running again.

They might be able to tell him who had done this.

Reaper was the obvious choice, but waking a Killer, even his brother, could prove exceedingly dangerous. With that in mind, Treon chose Cannon.

Carefully, he brushed Cannon's mind. Like the others, it felt distant, faint. Treon needed to be careful, or he'd end up being pulled wherever Cannon's awareness was, instead of waking him to this place.

Experimentally, he gave a light *push*. He felt a

ripple like a stone thrown into a pond, but then the ripples settled, and nothing had changed.

Of course, it would not be so easy.

He poured strength into his shields, then reached out with his surface thoughts to connect with the lightest of touches to Cannon's mind. This was the part that had made him choose Cannon over Reaper.

Once connected, he gave a tug. Slowly, he increased pressure until he was pulling Cannon's awareness back from wherever it had gone.

Except, he wasn't. Cannon stayed stubbornly *elsewhere*. Treon frowned. He would just have to pull harder. He poured more of himself into the effort. Still, Cannon's spark didn't move. Treon was starting to feel the strain, so far from his own body and having already expended so much of himself.

"That's not going to work."

Treon spun toward the voice, and was shocked to see one of the Veritas people standing, awake and aware. The woman looked as though she'd been through some difficult times. Her clothes were wrinkled and askew. Her hair, once pulled neatly back, hung bedraggled around a face that was startling in its youth.

This woman was barely more than a girl. He was surprised that Veritas would bring someone so young on such a seemingly important mission. But then, perhaps her Talent made her essential.

Speaking of her Talent, dark circles surrounded her eyes, and her skin was unnaturally pale. If Treon didn't know better, he'd say she looked as though she was suffering from burn out.

His eyes narrowed. How, then, was she awake and speaking to him?

More than that, how was she here at all, on the mental plane? Victims of burn out couldn't access their Talent without extreme discomfort. Not to mention the risk of death.

"Hello," he said. "And who might you be?"

"That's not important." She waved a hand, dismissing the question. She took a couple of steps, circling the compartment, studying him in a way that felt *wrong*. "You're interesting, though. A true planewalker. Do you know how rare that is?"

He watched her, turning to keep her in his line of sight as she moved. It struck him all at once what was so wrong about her. She carried herself and spoke with a confidence that felt far older than this woman looked.

"Is it?" he said. "I know plenty of telepaths who walk the mental plane."

"Do you?" She stopped, hands on her hips. "And how many of them can cross so great a distance, as you have done? How many could bend the plane to their will? How many could make it their own?" She leaned forward, power practically rolling off her, piercing him with a knowing gaze. "How many others are there like you?"

Certain now, that he was dealing with a mind much more powerful than the girl's true self, he smiled. It was tinged with only a shadow of his usual arrogance. "There is no one like me."

"There used to be, once."

"No."

She laughed, a sound that sent chills through

him. "Oh, I like you." She grinned at him. "You have no idea what you are. Do you?"

Torn between affront and a warning instinct that buzzed at him to be cautious, Treon said nothing.

But she nodded slowly, a knowing glint in her eyes. "No. I don't think you do. How delightful. You've barely scratched the surface of your power." She looked around and grimaced, her gaze settling on Reaper. "Such a waste. So many of you have no idea what your true potential is. You play at it like children."

That pricked at Treon's pride, but he didn't let it show. It took an effort to hold his silence.

She tilted her head, looking back at him. "I think you will join me, planewalker."

Now, he spoke. "No."

She arched a brow. "No? Would you not trade yourself for all of them?" The sweep of her hand encompassed the entire compartment. Reaper, and everyone else.

"No," he repeated.

He'd expected some sort of negative response. Displeasure, or anger at his refusal. Instead, she laughed again.

"Selfish, are you?" she said. "I can work with that."

A drop of blood fell from her nose, dripping down her chin. She scowled, wiping it away with her fingers. It wasn't real, of course, not here. It was merely a warning, like pain. A manifestation of the strain being placed on the young woman's body and mind.

"What's the matter?" he asked. "That body and

mind not powerful enough to make a suitable host?"

She glared at him. "It is no matter," she said. "There are plenty more where this one came from."

"Or you could come yourself, speak to me *as* yourself."

"Oh, you are a tricky one." She shook a blood-smeared finger at him. "But I know better than to face a planewalker here."

"Am I so frightening? Come, you are clearly a queen. What match am I for that? Surely, you would be more comfortable in a form that could actually hold your power."

"You're right. My next choice will have to be much stronger." As she spoke, the drip of blood became a gush, and the girl's eyes rolled back into her head. She collapsed. As she did, the spark of her mind went dull, and then faded to nothing.

She was gone.

Treon felt a flash of regret, almost grief. So young a life, snuffed out for nothing but a few moments of conversation. It confirmed his worst fears: he had found the mind behind whatever had happened here. And she was more powerful than he could have imagined. With a realization that he was, perhaps for the first time in his life, completely out of his depth, Treon felt the first hint of fear.

In moments, she would return, housed in fresh body. Perhaps one of the Veritas people. Perhaps one of the pirates. Perhaps even Reaper.

Indecision held him immobile as precious seconds ticked by. What was the best course of action? What could he do? It was unsettling to feel such uncertainty.

But the simple truth was, Treon was no longer sure he could save Reaper. He didn't even know if he could save himself.

CHAPTER EIGHTEEN

The young boy stared up at Mercy, the hope in his eyes overshadowed with wariness. He was painfully thin, wearing a ragged tunic five times too large for his small frame. His hair appeared as dark speckles of uneven lengths on a roughly shorn scalp. His nails were bitten to the quick, a heavy chain hanging from one thin wrist. It dangled, free of the bulkhead it had once connected to.

She stood holding out her hand to him, playing out a series of events that had happened many years ago.

Lilith had been taking Mercy through experiences like this one for the past several hours. She didn't just *show* Mercy what happened, somehow, she shared the memories as though they belonged to Mercy. As though she *was* Lilith. This was the fifth such event, and by now, it no longer felt odd.

Hope finally eclipsed wariness, and the young boy lurched forward and took Mercy's hand. As he did, she felt something snap into place, a familiar link that bound them together. A feeling of comfort and *rightness* filled her. He was hers, now.

By the time she mouthed the boy's new name, she'd already figured out this was Sebastian. She remembered the story he'd told her, how Lilith had freed him, and she recognized the shape of his face, the dark color of his eyes. Her heart gave a pang for the boy he'd been, and for the first time, she saw Lilith through the lens of his experience. To him, her grandmother would never be the heartless ruler many had described her as. She would always and forever be the woman who saved him, the woman who gave him a real name, the woman who showed him what it meant to be free.

The scene faded, and Mercy was once again standing in the house with its picturesque windows and holoscreens of family portraits.

"Explain to me what the claiming is," Lilith said, not for the first time. She had yet to be satisfied with Mercy's answer. Each time, she would shake her head and show Mercy something new.

"I don't know what you want me to say. When I claimed everyone, I *felt* them. All I have to do is think about someone, and I know roughly where they are if they're using Talent. Sometimes I get a sense of their mood. They're..." She struggled. She'd already tried words like *linked, connected, joined,* and even *following*. None of those had been good enough for Lilith.

Mercy threw her hands in the air. "They're part of me now. I feel them all of the damn time, and most of the time I wish I didn't."

Lilith studied her. "Being Queen is not easy.

You are the one linked to *them*. *You* are *theirs*, not the other way around."

Mercy stared at her. Those weren't at all words she'd expected Lilith to say. The tyrant everyone feared, the woman who had made the pirates so afraid of a new queen.

Her grandmother sighed. "I lost sight of that, when I was building my power base. I thought any sacrifice was worth the cost if it meant we would survive what was coming. I didn't realize my mistake until the end, when it was too late, and I was beyond recovery." She looked pensive. "You must be stronger than I was."

Mercy didn't know how to answer that.

"The claiming is a promise," Lilith said. Apparently, she was done showing Mercy scenes.

Lilith strode to one of the chairs and sat. They'd been at this long enough that the sun was setting over the mountains in the distance, filling the sky with a purple glow that faded to a brilliant sea green.

"The first generation of Talented were too independent. Too frightening for the nulls who created them. They changed the shape of the war." Lilith turned away from the beautiful scene out the window to look at Mercy. "How much do you know about the Ascension Wars?"

"I've read about them." Mercy shrugged, taking a seat in the other chair. She stared at that sunset, worried. How long had she been here? How much longer must she stay? A worry that wouldn't quite leave her burned at the back of her mind. *Reaper.*

"Do you know how long they lasted?"

It took Mercy a moment to answer. But Wolfgang had been thorough in his demands for education. History had been one of the big ones.

"Several hundred years," she said. "I think three hundred?"

Lilith shook her head. "That's what the history holos say, but it was closer to a thousand years. Everyone likes to focus on the last part of the war, when the battles intensified, and the myriad little empires and warlords were either wiped out or joined a side. The Ascension Wars were much more than just the era of the Ashir Empire against the Challa Collective. They began a long, long time before that last bloody campaign."

Mercy remembered reading something about smaller conflicts, but they were vague and non-specific. As Lilith said, history focused on the larger war.

"There is a reason" Lilith continued, "that ship technology stagnated for so long, why ships from the era of the wars are all but gone now. They were the most valuable weapon for hundreds of years. All too often, whoever had the largest fleet won. Systems cobbled together their own shipyards. Mines for material to make ships were coveted, fought over, and guarded like precious jewels. Ships were churned out fast, and often cheaply. Corners were cut, and the quality of ships being produced in that era was significantly less than what we have now. Systems that couldn't produce ships fast enough had to find other ways to victory. That's when heavy research and development started going into technologies like cloning, bioweapons, and biotech."

"How do you know all of this?"

Lilith smiled. "I did a lot of research. There are very old documents in our archives, hand written journals by generals who served in the war, or scientists who helped create us. You should read them."

Against one wall, a bookshelf appeared. Mercy recognized it from her first "dream" with Lilith. So, that hadn't been some randomly chosen setting. Her grandmother had intended her to study.

Unease filled her. The shelf stood floor to ceiling, and it was full of books. Just how long did Lilith intend her to stay here?

"What does this have to do with the claiming?" Mercy asked, hoping her grandmother didn't mean her to read those texts *now*.

"The first generation of Talented had no Queen, no need for one. They were autonomous, soldiers of unbelievable power, created with no thought for what that power would mean to the rest of humanity. Records from this era are largely nonexistent, but from what little I found, they eventually turned on their masters. I'm unclear on the details, but I believe this took place on Arcadius V."

Mercy thought of the star charts Wolfgang had insisted she and Atrea commit to memory. "Arcadius is a dead world," she said.

"Exactly."

"You mean it wasn't, always?"

"Five hundred years ago, it was a thriving technological mecca. A center of scientific discovery and development." Lilith gestured, and one of the books floated free of the shelf and over to her hand. Mercy gave a start.

"I thought Talent didn't work in mental land-scapes." She immediately felt stupid for saying it. Clearly, Lilith has already been using Talent, when she'd shown Mercy all those memories.

Lilith smiled. "This is not the mental plane as you know it, Mercy. This is my home. The bottle I occupy, if you will, and like the djinn of legend, I can shape it as I wish. Which includes using Talent." She flipped the book open and passed it across to Mercy.

It looked like a journal, notes jotted down in a sort of shorthand that made them difficult to decipher. But clearly labeled among them were the words "Arcadius Institute of Applied Genomic Engineering".

"That is but one such journal. There are others, from other locations on the planet. It seems many of the scientists there were working on secret or classified projects which they didn't trust to save in a digital environment. Many of them kept journals like this one, though this is the only one I've found that seems to specifically reference what we are."

Lilith looked back out the window. "Whatever happened on the surface of the planet, nothing survived. It is lifeless now, and the handful of artifacts in anyone managed to salvage give few clues as to its fate."

"You think the Talented did this?"

"Shortly after the last records we have of Arcadius V, an order was issued. Arcadius V was part of the Knara Cluster. They were three systems allied together. They dispatched their combined fleets to one of their own military stations and destroyed it. They took heavy casualties, and this seemingly insane assault on their own army effectively removed them from the Ascension Wars. They never recovered, and the Cluster was absorbed into the Ashir Empire."

Mercy drummed her fingers on the surface of the book in her lap. "So, you think the Talented turned on their creators, and were in turn destroyed by the army they served."

Lilith inclined her head. "There is no mention of them again for nearly two hundred years. Instead, biotech and clones became the superior soldiers in the war. When the Talented again appeared as soldiers in the war, this time they were connected to a queen. A failsafe."

"But it's only a failsafe if the nulls control the queen."

"True. Which begs the question of how, of course, but my research has yet to reveal the answer. However, without that connection the Talented are designed to kill one another. Their link to a queen provides stability, a clarity of mind that otherwise falls to instinct and violence."

"But I thought—" Mercy choked back the words before she finished the sentence.

Her grandmother smiled at her, a sharp expression devoid of humor. "You thought I made the pirates that way? That my influence drove them to violence?" She shrugged. "I encouraged a certain amount. I wanted our army sharp when the fight came to us. But no, the infighting you saw when you joined them was far more a result of having *no* queen for over a decade, than it was anything I did. Our creators were afraid of what we could do. They wanted a guarantee of control, and a built-in model for self-extinction if they needed it."

"Kill the queen, and the Talented destroy themselves."

"Something like that."

Mercy stared down at the book in her hands. "So, without being claimed by a queen, the Talented…"

"…become violent, unpredictable, and self-destructive? Yes."

How long, Mercy wondered, had Veritas gone without a queen? It could explain a lot of the past several decades, the unceasing hostility they seemed to harbor for their brethren, the pirates.

"By the time Talented were reintroduced to the Ascension Wars, clones and soldiers altered with biotech were the best soldiers money could buy. Cloning allowed a near limitless supply of numbers, and of course they produced only top of the line, military grade models. Biotech took a normal soldier and elevated him to the most dangerous adversary on the field. Then, the Talented came. They strode onto the field like gods. The others became little more than children playing at war."

Lilith fell silent. Unsure if she was meant to respond, Mercy spoke cautiously. "The wars ended shortly after that?"

"No. They continued for another two hundred years. First, all of the other factions united into the Challa Collective in an attempt to counter the Ashir's new super soldiers. But they soon found it didn't matter how many clones they put onto the field, or how powerful the biotech they implanted in their soldiers. The Talented still won, again and again. You must remember, the Ascension Wars sprawled across the entire galaxy. Even with gods walking the battlefield, it takes time to occupy system after system, negotiating surrenders and swearing allegiances as you go. The galaxy is an enormous place, and the new Ashir monarchy wasn't about to stop until every last system and world had sworn to the new Commonwealth."

Mercy thought about this. Something occurred to her which she had never before considered. The timeline Lilith had just laid out snapped into sharp focus in her mind.

She knew of the royal family, of course. Everyone did. The Commonwealth was still young, less than three hundred years old. But the last system had joined it a hundred years ago. The timeline of the Commonwealth's creation followed the timeline of the Talented nearly exactly.

"Did the House of Ashir create us?" she asked, naming the royal family.

Lilith gave her a look of approval. "Yes. They financed it, at any rate. They controlled us. And I have no doubt they led the vote that exiled us after the wars."

That was ancient history. King Adahn, the architect of that vote, had been dead for nearly forty years. His son Adriyen had taken the throne, but died sixteen years later, killed in a space jump tragedy that took not only his life, but those of his wife, son, and infant daughter. Not to mention the entire crew of the ship they were on.

It sent the Commonwealth into a brief period of instability. But no one wanted a return to the wars that had plagued them for so long. Within days, Adriyen's cousin, Sereya, was crowned King. The line of Ashir continued, and the Commonwealth breathed a collective sigh of relief.

Well, the nulls did. The Talented were rather less enamored with the ruling government of the Commonwealth, including the royal family. Mercy could see why.

Still, she shook her head, bursting with all of this information, none of which she could relate to training as a queen. "I don't see what this history lesson has to do with anything."

Lilith gazed at her. "It's important that you understand where we came from. Especially when and why queens were created. You must have foundational knowledge if you are truly to understand our abilities, and what they were meant for."

"I suppose," Mercy said. But she couldn't help feeling this had been a giant waste of time. She closed the book she held. "Look, this has been interesting, but I can't stay. I've been gone too long already. I have to get back." *To Reaper.*

Lilith gave her a look devoid of sympathy. "You will stay until we are finished, however long that takes. Which, I'm afraid will be quite some time."

"I can't." A thread of panic moved through her. "I have people counting on me. I can come visit for a few hours at a time, but then I have to go back."

Lilith stood, everything of warmth and humor leeched from her. Her eyes were intense, her bearing commanding. Anxiety spiked inside of Mercy; this was the grandmother who had callously ordered her death.

"Did you fail, somehow, to understand what is

at stake? *You cannot leave.* You think you have people counting on you? The *galaxy* is counting on you. All of our people are counting on you. If you fail, they will *all* be lost, not just the few you worry about now."

Mercy had to resist the urge to try and disappear beneath Lilith's gaze. Somehow, this version of Lilith sent her straight back to childhood. She gritted her teeth. *Screw that.* She was not a child anymore, and her grandmother needed to accept that. She stood and met Lilith's gaze without flinching.

"I am committed to this plan."

"Are you?" Lilith looked incredulous. "If you're so committed, why are you trying to leave?"

"Because Reaper, Cannon, and Atrea are in trouble. I *need* them. If I'm going to succeed, I need them every bit as much as I need training with you. I need people around me I know I can trust when this goes down." Surely, Lilith could understand that.

"You are correct, you do. But you will have to wait and trust they will be there when we are finished. This piecemeal training you describe, a bit at a time, is ridiculous. You speak of time when we already have none. We might be too late, even now. Vashti's visions have increased in frequency and intensity." Worry flashed across Lilith's face. "This is always a sign that a vision is soon to become reality."

"How did you know—" Mercy stopped her own question. "Sebastian."

Lilith smiled. "Your instincts are good, but no. I did not need Sebastian to tell me."

"Then how?"

"My sister and I have no need for an intermediary to communicate." Something, some complicated emotion, moved over Lilith's face like a shadow. "At least, we haven't until very recently."

It took her a moment, but then understanding washed through Mercy. Her hand moved to cover her own wrist. "Your bracelet. Vashti used to wear it."

Lilith inclined her head. "Until we decided it should be passed to you, so I could train you properly."

A sudden thought struck Mercy. "Is this how Vashti remained free of Rani's influence? Because she was connected to you?"

Lilith made a noise, derisive. "*That* girl. She had no chance to influence my sister. Not while *I* remained connected to Vashti."

Mercy cocked her head. "But you're dead. How could you have remained Vashti's Queen?"

Lilith smiled tightly. "Because, my dear. It was vital that she and I remain in contact while we waited and prepared for you. The bracelet was the most expedient way of doing so."

"And now that I have it…"

"Yes. Now we must move on. You will claim Vashti and she will have a new Queen. Finally." Lilith looked back out the window. "It's time. *Past* time, truthfully. I should have been training you from the moment you arrived, but Vashti convinced me to wait. You would not have been open to learning from me, in the beginning."

That was an understatement. Mercy still marveled that she was open to learning from Lilith *now*.

She let out a breath. The idea of staying here while Reaper, Cannon, and Atrea were in trouble scared her to her bones. "How long do you think this will take?" she asked.

"Time is a construct of the physical world. In fact, it is a human construct that doesn't precisely exist, but that is a different discussion. The point is, here, we have no need of it."

Mercy frowned. "You're saying time doesn't pass here?"

"Not as such, no. It will pass in the physical world to some degree while you are here, but that has more to do with how your mind processes what you experience. If you see it as a dream, you will wake up within a few hours, no matter how long you spend here. If you instead interpret it as *real*, you could wake up days or even weeks later."

"So, I need to think of this as a dream."

"That would be best."

A dream. She could do that. "All right. What's next?"

Lilith held out her hand. "Let me show you, granddaughter."

*T*reon did not relax. The time for caution had passed. He reached out and connected with his brother's mind, trusting in their years of familiarity to keep him safe. And if not, well...he didn't let himself consider that possibility.

Attempting to free Cannon had failed, so Treon didn't even try that. He delved past the surface thoughts, past Reaper's shields, deeper than he had ever dared intrude before. He had seconds, maybe less.

He found Reaper imprisoned. Oh, it wasn't the sort of prison he could fight to free himself from. No. She was too clever for that. Reaper was in a dream. And though he was alone, separated from the others, he was not *alone*.

REAPER KNEW he wasn't in any normal dream. One did not grow up in a house with Treon without learning the signs of a mental landscape. The vague feeling of unrest was the first warning. He knew then to look around with careful attention to detail. Sometimes, small things would give it away. No visible scuff marks on the floors or walls, for example. No breeze or drafts of moving air. But Treon had learned to emulate even those details, so Reaper learned to look beyond them.

Like the fact that he was certain he didn't know this place. He'd never been here before. That was a mistake if someone meant him to believe this was real. People dreamt of the familiar: childhood homes, ships they'd spent years serving aboard, favorite vacation spots. But this place held no familiarity for him.

He didn't know how he'd come to be here, instead of conscious and aware on the dropship. He had no memory of the transition. One moment, he was there, troubleshooting how to get power back with Cannon and the rest, and the next he was here.

Here was a huge, cavernous room. He felt a faint vibration beneath his feet. He stood on the deck of an extremely large capital ship. That vibration was the only part of this room that said *ship*. The rest had the regal look of some ruling government's castle.

The floor he stood on was some form of polished stone. Pale grey, with flecks of blue and veins of bronze. Intricately carved columns stood at equidistant points around the room, dividing the walls into sections from which hung flowing banners he didn't recognize. Each was emblazoned with a different symbol or swept with different colors. One had a roaring cat not unlike Tamari's

Rasalas, except instead of copper rosettes against pale fur, the cat was sleekly black. The background of that banner was white, the contrast striking. The next was entirely different: this banner was cut in two, one side deepest black, the other a brilliant white gold that almost hurt to look at. The white gold bled into the black as he watched, forming a half-moon shape with tendrils of fire. A star, he realized. The next banner was a brilliant crimson with a shield and sword featured prominently. It went on like that, each banner unique, each showcasing colors and symbols that seemed to stand for something. Military units? Family arms?

In the center of the room was a long, ornate table. At the far end stood a chair that could only be described as a throne, even more beautifully carved than the columns, and half again larger than any of the other chairs situated around the table. It also stood on a raised platform, so that whoever sat in that chair would be above everyone else in the room, an unsubtle declaration of power.

He turned sharply, moving before he consciously realized he'd sensed something. A woman stood with her arms crossed, leaning against one of the columns. She was young, maybe twenty, with black, straight hair and fair skin. She wore armored clothing that was fitted to her athletic frame, in a stark black that emphasized her pale skin and the unsettling blue of her eyes.

A Killer.

As a rule, most Killers did not possess Talents of overwhelming power in other areas. His bother

Dem's telekinesis was the exception, not the norm. So, this woman should not have been strong enough a telepath to create this place and pull him to it.

The woman pushed away from the pillar, walking with a smooth, easy gait to the table. She didn't even glance at him as she passed. He watched her, watched the way she moved, trying to identify strengths and weaknesses, even if his Talent wouldn't function here. She smiled, but still did not turn to look at him.

That was when he realized someone else had joined them. A man this time. Older, and also a Killer. He had the same black hair and pale skin as the girl. A relative, perhaps. He moved to join her, but unlike her, he watched Reaper carefully. As one predator does when entering the territory of another.

The man gave Reaper a shallow nod, a simple acknowledgment between equals. Reaper did nothing as the man claimed a chair across from the woman. Even as he did so, a third person joined them. This one was a young girl, barely more than a child herself. She had long dark hair and green eyes that reminded him of Mercy, but her skin was much paler, and she bore no other resemblance to her. He could not tell what her Talent was, but was willing to bet she had one. Especially when she took a chair close to the Killers, and they both moved just slightly. The woman gave a twitch, instantly stilled, and the man shifted fractionally in his chair, his attention moving from Reaper to the girl.

Interesting. The girl was dangerous. Reaper gave her a second, longer look.

More people arrived. No one spoke. Neither did Reaper. He'd learned that speaking first in situations like this one only gave your opponent the upper hand. If he remained silent, instead, forcing them to come to him, to speak first, he would be in a stronger position.

He catalogued each person that arrived. An older man in an expensive suit. A boy not even a teenager yet. A set of women he initially took for identical triplets, but almost immediately realized were clones. Another man, this one his own age, cloaked in an arrogance that reminded Reaper of his brother, Treon.

They kept coming, one after another. He tried to see how they were getting here, but the room had no windows or doors, and all of them seemed to appear out of thin air.

At last, all of the chairs at the table were full, save for two. The throne at the head, and the chair directly to his left remained empty. He waited, but no one else came. He wondered if the remaining chair at the table was meant for him.

He had no intention of taking it. He stood and waited, making the decision not to move until he had to. This was a construct, not the physical world. It wasn't like he would get tired.

"Stubborn," said a feminine voice from behind him. He turned slowly. He hadn't felt her arrive, but he wasn't surprised. This gathering was happening for a reason.

The woman who stood there was roughly his age. More striking than beautiful, she had a strong face with sharp cheekbones and a long, narrow nose. Her angular features were softened by a fall of golden hair that tumbled over her shoulders and spilled down her back. Treon would have said she looked like the Valkyries of legend, warrior women who rode the battlefield collecting the souls of the fallen. Reaper practically heard his brother's voice in his head, poetic.

But Reaper looked at her and saw not the woman, but the power that rolled off of her like a wave, filling the room with her presence. Power he shouldn't have felt in a mental landscape, but did. The pressure of it beat at him like the sun on a hot day.

Those seated at the table straightened in their seats. Reaper just looked back at her, returning her intense stare. She smiled, moving past him and straight to the throne. She sat down, then looked at the empty space and back to him, her expectation clear. Reaper didn't move.

"Nikolos, isn't it?" It didn't alarm him that she knew his name. To bring him here, she had to have connected with his mind on some level. "You should sit. It only gets harder from here."

That decided him: he would fight every person in this room before sitting in that chair.

"That would be a mistake," she said.

Cold washed down his spine, and it wasn't the cold he was used to from his Talent. Was she still somehow connected to his mind, reading his thoughts? Or was she just that good at reading him? Neither possibility was good.

"I brought you here to give you a chance," she

said. "Join me now, here, and I will let the rest of your people go."

"No," he said.

"Think carefully. Your Talent is strategic by nature. You're used to making decisions that are the most expediently available in the moment. You should apply that thinking here."

He said nothing. Irritation flashed across her face briefly. He guessed *no* was not something she was accustomed to hearing.

"You are already mine." That power he felt intensified. It prickled against his skin like hundreds of needles. "Sit."

Reaper didn't move. The needles sharpened, digging deeper, pain arching through his body. He drew in a sharp breath. His teeth clenched.

He knew if he stepped forward and did as she asked, the pressure and pain would end. He stood still and focused entirely on her. On how he could kill her.

Here, in a place she manifestly controlled, it would be next to impossible. He couldn't use his Talent, but she clearly had access to abilities he did not. Additionally, at least forty people were in this room, each of them loyal to her.

There was also the fact that she was definitely a queen. He knew beyond a doubt that if he took that seat she was offering, he would be allowing her to claim him. He would never let that happen.

The pain and pressure built in intensity. His vision wavered. Everything in him screamed to take those steps, to sit in the chair.

His knees hit the stone floor, his legs giving way as he refused to take a step. He leaned forward, his forehead making contact with the cool stone. His breathing became ragged, his entire being nothing but pain. Darkness crowded his vision, and he knew with a sudden clarity that she could crush him, that he would die here.

He thought of Mercy. Knowing he would never see her again was a torment that welled up from within, eclipsing everything else. Thinking of how vulnerable she would be once he was gone filled him with rare emotion. His heart raced, his mouth going dry. His hands clenched into fists as sweat slicked his body.

If he took the chair being offered, he could live to see Mercy again. He could fight his way back to her. For the first time, he wavered. He found himself staring at the legs of that chair with no memory of crossing the floor to reach it. He must have crawled on his hands and knees.

No. The voice was his own. It came from a cold place inside him, untouched by the pressure, pain, or fear he was feeling. *If you sit in that chair, your bond to Mercy will sever. You will belong to another queen. An enemy. She could use you against Mercy.* Memory flooded his mind, the feeling of Rani controlling him, forcing him to do her will. He remembered holding Mercy, imprisoning her.

She had woken him from that terrible place, claiming him for her own. But if Rani had ordered him to kill her? If this queen did?

He would not be used against Mercy. He refused.

He reached out and wrapped a hand around the chair's leg. He used it to pull himself up to his knees. He stood, the effort required to reach his feet leaving him shaking. He reached out and gripped the back of the chair with both hands.

The queen smiled on her throne.

Reaper ripped the chair away from the table, putting his entire body into the movement, throwing it as far as he could. It tumbled across the stone floor, sliding several body lengths away.

The queen's smile vanished, and Reaper knew she would kill him now. That was fine. If he died, he couldn't be used against Mercy. He found that an acceptable trade.

"That was foolish," the queen said. Her head tilted as she studied him. "But interesting."

All at once, the pressure and pain left him. He staggered, nearly catching himself against the table. He reeled away from it, afraid that even occupying that space would be too close to acceptance.

Catching his balance, he righted himself and readjusted. He was standing close to the throne now. Less than three steps away. He looked at the table. All eyes were on him. He knew the next few moments might be his only chance.

Talent wasn't the only way to kill. Killing her here would not kill her in the real world. He knew that from experience. But it would end her control over this place, over him.

He looked at the pair of Killers seated at the table. He needed an opening, an advantage. Even the barest hint of one. "You don't need me to join you," he said. "You already have Killers."

"Killers," she scoffed. "That's not what you are. Once, your kind served as Generals on the battlefield."

"I am no General."

"But you are." She swept an arm toward the others. "You all are. You don't just see vulnerabilities in people. You look over the whole battle. You see what needs to happen, and have the ability to make decisions unbiased by sentiment and emotion."

Reaper said nothing.

"But even so, *you* are different."

"We are all the same."

"No." Her lips thinned. "You are—"

He moved, leaping across the distance that separated them. He could not manifest weapons here, but he needed none. His hands grasped her head as he landed on the dais, practically on top of her. She grasped at him, fingers digging painfully into his arms, but it was too late. He jerked sharply, putting his entire body into the movement. Her neck cracked. Her arms went limp.

He'd expected the Killers to be on him by this time, so it was something of a shock to turn and see that no one had moved. Her body slumped in the throne beside him, then slowly faded. The mental landscape should have begun to fade with it, but nothing happened.

Everything remained sharp and clear.

A chair scraped the stone floor as it was pushed back from the table. The girl with green eyes stood up.

"As I was saying," she said, "you are different. Your connection to *her* makes you different."

He stared at her. She felt as innocuous as she looked. No roll of power. But those seated at the table moved subtly with her. There was a deference there he had missed.

It was her the whole time. The woman on the throne was a feint, an illusion. And he fell for it.

She smiled. "The time for games is over, Nikolos." She snapped her fingers. The chair he'd thrown appeared behind him, striking his legs so hard he fell into it. He immediately rolled over the arm and onto the floor, landing hard enough to knock the wind from him.

Or he would have, if breathing here had been necessary.

He went to rise and suddenly there was a hand on his arm, pulling him to his feet. He turned, catching sight of his brother's face just in time to stop the fist he'd been driving toward his stomach.

Treon. Here? How? Then again, it was Treon. Better not to ask.

"Time to go, brother," Treon said.

The girl stepped forward, her eyes wide. "It is a mistake to interfere, planewalker."

"And yet, here I am, Your Majesty." The way Treon said the words, they were mocking.

She contemplated him. "You risk much. For what? For him?"

"He *is* my brother." As he spoke, Treon was walking backwards, slowly pulling Reaper with him.

Surprisingly, she smiled. "I told you, you're special. Do you know how many Talented could come into my creation and control it? How many could take something if I didn't wish them to?" She lifted her chin. "Try. Try to take him from this place. Let's see how powerful you are, planewalker."

Reaper felt something tug at him. A pull that

seemed to anchor him here, his feet sticking to the floor. He tried to lift one, and couldn't. Treon cursed.

He felt his brother shift, adjusting his stance. Treon leaned forward, his head close to Reaper's. "This is going to hurt, I'm afraid."

"Just do it."

Treon's voice was grim. "Oh, I am. We have no choice." His hands gripped Reaper harder. "Ready. And *now*."

It felt like something was ripping Reaper in two. Fiery pain streaked down his spine. He could feel the two forces pulling at him, one like gravity pressing him down, the other like the engines of a great ship, exploding into takeoff. Someone screamed. He realized with a shock that the sound came from his own throat.

It seemed to last for eternity. He wanted to kill his brother. If he'd had his Talent, he would have, purely on instinct. At last, the pain crested. His vision flashed red, then white. He felt himself falling.

The next moment, the pain was gone. But he felt every breath like a jagged knife through his lungs, the air cold enough to hurt as he pulled it in and exhaled it out.

Air.

Cold.

He was back in the real world. Back on the ship. He opened his eyes to darkness illuminated by the ambient glow of the sticks his dogs had lit right before everything changed. One floated nearby, illuminating Cannon's slumbering face.

"Can you get them up?" he asked Treon. His

voice sounded hoarse. There was no answer. He looked around, but saw no one.

Treon?

He could feel his brother's presence, but could not hear him.

Reaper let the cold of his Talent take him. It was comforting to slide into the numbed familiarity of it. He examined Cannon carefully. "I think I can sever the connection." He spoke both aloud and with Talent, unsure if Treon could hear him. "It will either wake him or kill him." His gifts were more blunt than his brother's.

His gaze moved across the cabin to the Veritas agents. Best to try with one of them, first. Cannon was too valuable to risk.

He simply had to trust that Treon was all right.

TREON WOKE with the mother of all headaches. If the inside of his head exploded, it couldn't possibly feel worse than the agony throbbing through him in time with his pulse. Every heartbeat hammered at the inside of his head in a sickening, unrelenting rhythm. He tried to move, but his vision swam to black. He groaned.

Pulling Reaper out of that place had used up everything he had. The backlash had very nearly killed him. But *she* was still out there, still somewhere too close to his brother, Cannon, and the others. She might be feeling the effects of backlash as well. Treon had felt the landscape collapse when he forced it to let go of Reaper. That had to have incapacitated her, at least temporarily.

But he couldn't count on that.

He had to get them help. Their ship was still dead. He started to reach out mentally, on instinct, and pain blinded him. He blinked back the involuntary tears that burned his eyes.

Mother damn it, he hadn't skimmed this close to burn out in…ever. He couldn't remember ever feeling this horrible.

So, using his Talent was out. If he tried, he'd pass out for sure, and who knew when he'd wake up again?

Treon flung a hand out, groping blindly. He managed to knock down the glass he'd set beside his bed earlier, and then his fingers brushed the bottle beside it. He grasped at it, dragging it from the shelf to the bed. Every movement drove a fresh wave of nauseating pain through his head, but he kept going. It took him three tries to get the cap off the bottle, and then he splashed cold *mnemosa* over half his bed, his shirt, and himself getting the bottle to his lips.

He swallowed some, and immediately, it tried to come back up. He choked it back grimly, refusing to give in. Vomiting would surely push him over into unconsciousness, not to mention wasting more *mnemosa*. He waited, breathing shallowly, counting his heartbeats, for the bit he'd drank to take effect.

Finally, the headache receded slightly. Cautiously, he lifted his head. The pain increased, but his vision remained clear. He slowly moved into a sitting position, sipping more from the bottle.

He just needed to be able to move. That was all.

He couldn't pass out without letting someone know where Reaper and the others were.

Ten horrible minutes later, he thought he could stand. He tried it, slipping over the side of the bed and onto his feet. He almost fell. He had to hold onto the bed for balance.

Not good.

Moving like a drunkard, he made his way across the room to his doorway. It opened onto an empty corridor, and he held onto the hatch opening for dear life, sure if he let go, he'd fall.

He managed three steps before his legs simply gave out and he slid down the wall.

He winced. "Damn it." His voice was hoarse and weak, and speaking hurt.

Since when did speaking aloud hurt? This was patently ridiculous. Someone was going to come and find him sprawled on the floor in the middle of the hallway. It was humiliating.

Please, someone. Come find me. It was the only chance Reaper and the others had. Treon would not be able to go back on the mental plane for hours. Perhaps days. Desperation clawed at him.

Just then, he had a horrible realization. He had a comm in his quarters. He could have triggered it, contacted Dem. Contacted *anyone*. But no, he was so fucking dependent on his telepathic prowess, the idea had simply slipped right past him. He was the worst kind of idiot, and now his brother might die because of it.

Or worse.

He put a hand to his forehead, closing his eyes. He cursed himself, wishing he could scream his frustration.

Something brushed against his leg. He opened his eyes. Had that been fur?

A giggle sounded near his ear. It *had* been fur. Relief swamped him. His idiocy wouldn't get Reaper killed after all. *Tamari.*

He looked around, but didn't see anything. Where was she? Perhaps the imp was playing hide and seek, and using Rasa's invisibility again. Too bad he had no time for games.

"Tamari," he said, croaking out his niece's name. "This is very important. Uncle Treon needs to talk to you."

He felt that softness of fur again, and Rasalas became visible. The great cat was sitting next to Treon, his tail wrapped around himself. He kept swishing it, and every swish brushed against Treon.

The damn thing seemed bigger every time he saw it. The *kith* watched him with slitted, green-gold eyes. Down at this level, Treon couldn't help but feel as though the cat had him at a disadvantage. The thing came up to his waist when he was standing.

As he watched, Rasalas stretched, arching his back. Muscle rippled and flexed beneath silvery fur patterned with copper rosettes. Talons that were frankly a frightening length scraped at the floor. Then he purred and bumped his head against Treon's foot. Checking to see if his prey was sufficiently incapacitated? Treon was never quite sure how the *kith* viewed humans who weren't Tamari.

"Good kitty," Treon said. The cat continued rubbing his head on Treon's foot. As long as it was just his head and not those claws, everything would be fine. Wherever Rasa was, Tama was nearby. The cat never left her side.

"Tamari, please. I need your help, *halla.*" The name was an endearment Hunters used. It meant something like beloved daughter, beloved clan-child. Treon wasn't precisely sure. Dem used it, and he'd picked up the habit.

Finally, the little girl materialized next to him. She was crouched down so she could peer directly into his face, so close to him he could feel her breath. It smelled of candy. She'd been to see Doc. The irascible doctor didn't think anyone knew how he gave Tamari sweets every time she came to the infirmary. It was the worst kept secret on the whole ship.

Treon smiled.

Tamari's hair was in pig tails today, little round puffs of dark curls that stuck up on either side of her head. Her eyes stared into his, big and blue and beautiful.

Treon grinned. If he'd felt even slightly better, he'd have tweaked her nose, the scamp.

She was wearing the space suit he'd made for her. It was functioning, because why not make it real if he was going to do it? The real advantage to this was that the nanograph grew with her, adjusting for her increased size. It was her favorite outfit.

"Uncle Treon," she whispered. "Why are you on the floor?"

"Uncle Treon isn't feeling very well, *halla.* I need you to get your father, please. As soon as possible."

Her eyes rounded. She bit her lip. "Papa will be mad."

That just meant she was wandering when she should have been somewhere else. Again. "Not today, he won't," Treon said. "Please, Tama. It's very important."

She studied him for a moment, then straightened. "Okay," she said, and promptly disappeared.

Treon looked at the cat, who hadn't moved. Apparently, he was staying with Treon.

"That's good, right?" he asked. "That means she's coming back."

Rasalas blinked at him, saying nothing. Treon closed his eyes. Yes, Tama would be back soon, and Dem would be with her. Everything was going to be all right.

He wasn't given to praying often, but Treon spent some prayers then. *Mother, please let it be all right.*

 ilith's idea of training meant reliving pivotal moments in her life as a queen, including the training she received under her mother, Kiana. As Lilith, Mercy learned how to claim people, and how to subtly influence them. Kiana used this most often to calm disputes or violence before it started. Unlike Lilith, she'd been on a mission to take the war out of her people. Kiana wanted a self-reliant society that did not resort to fighting and plundering to survive. She encouraged farming and industry.

Her efforts were largely responsible for the pirate colonies becoming truly self-sustaining. The Core was formed at her insistence on a functioning government, and it was also her idea to create their own system of money. This was based largely on the Commonwealth's economic system, since the pirates were still very much tied to it. They often sold goods back to the Commonwealth through a black market that added a high markup.

Mercy was impressed. Kiana could have used her abilities as Queen to force compliance with her goals, but instead, she took a far more delicate approach. Lilith explained that she wasn't changing anyone's way of thinking, merely making them open to listening to other possibilities.

This had the effect of not taking control away from people.

"That was my mistake," Lilith said frankly. "I didn't allow people enough control to make their own choices. I forced things too much. This led to more resistance and resentment, slowing results. Ultimately, it didn't help me as much as I thought it would at the time."

There were also other lessons, like strengthening her shields. Mercy was unhappy with this at first. Reaper had already trained her in shielding. But Lilith thought they could improve even more. In fact, queens could strengthen not only their shields, but their followers' shields through the link of the claiming. It was similar, Lilith explained, to when a queen used the link to *borrow* Talent.

Mercy had experienced this once, right after she claimed everyone and took them from Rani. She'd borrowed Reaper's Talent and killed Willem Frain. She'd borrowed Nayla's gift for healing and saved Wolfgang. But she hadn't been able to do anything remotely like that since. It didn't matter how many times Lilith described how it worked, she couldn't seem to grasp it.

With a sigh, Lilith left her to read - there was *so much* reading to be done - and promised to return to the idea later.

Mercy read about the history and deployment

of the Talented. This book was difficult to go through. It was a gathering of redacted documents and shorthand notes that required manual translation of each line. This was a slow and arduous task. It had never been read completely, according to Lilith, who had herself only managed a few pages before her death. Mercy struggled with it for what felt like months. It was fascinating.

The Talented were organized into military units. Complimentary powers would be paired together. Sometimes, a unit of Talented would be dropped into a planetary war zone, and the entire battle would end, almost overnight. They had that great of an impact.

The Queen never went into battle. Too valuable, she was kept with the fleet. They would move her from ship to ship, often laying false trails regarding which ship she might be on to keep her safe. From there, she would coordinate attacks and entire battles, serving as the communication hub for all of the Talented units in the field. The fleet would move her where they felt she was most necessary.

Early on, there was mention of one unit that went rogue. A powerful telepath who refused an order. There were no details on what that order entailed, only that he refused, and the Queen got involved. Her influence made him obedient.

Mercy found several places that detailed events like this. Times when the Queen was called upon to make certain orders were followed. One account toward the end of the wars was particularly chilling. It was during the transition of the Ashir Empire into the Commonwealth of Sovereign

Planets. An Admiral refused to hand over his fleet. From what Mercy pieced together, several Talented ships had been decommissioned at this point, their crews and spec ops units disbanded. But these men and women were never heard from again. So when the order came down for Admiral Mori Shinjo to stand down and bring in his fleet for decommissioning, he refused. He demanded proof that the Captains who came before him were still alive and the missing Talented crews had not been betrayed by their government. Instead, the newly formed monarchy and Council of Sovereign Planets brought in the Queen. Mori Shinjo and his entire crew inexplicably committed mass suicide. At the same time. On holo recording.

The footage was used to prove an imminent threat to public safety. Talent was officially outlawed.

Mercy had seen the footage dozens of times. She'd spent years wondering if her Talent made her unstable. Learning that the incident had been manufactured and forced was a huge relief, but one that also made her angry. That propaganda was almost entirely responsible for the fear and mistrust with which nulls viewed Talented to this day. And it was completely untrue.

When Mercy wasn't reading, Lilith taught her greater uses for her telepathy. She learned how to move her mind into the mental plane, how to create and control her own landscapes, and how to take other minds there.

"This is what Treon does," she said, delighted.

"Yes," Lilith agreed. "Treon has a tendency for more complexity than he needs. He likes to show off. You don't need to do that. Keep it simple. It's a useful technique for communicating on a more intimate level over long distances, or for questioning people."

"Questioning...?" Mercy had a sinking feeling. "Do you mean torture?"

Lilith shrugged. "I didn't often need that. You can learn a lot from people by recreating memories or dreams. Especially when they don't realize they aren't real at all."

Okay, that was creepy. Mercy couldn't help a shiver. Sometimes, Lilith would remind her of her mother, and Mercy would forget for a little while who exactly she had been. Then her grandmother said something like that, and brought it all rushing back.

Right. Scary, nightmare Queen. Tyrant. Murderer. Whatever her reasons, Lilith had not been a nice person. In point of fact, there was one subject Mercy had yet to broach with her. Mercy's father.

Her mother had always said that Lilith killed him. Was that true? Mercy wasn't sure she wanted to know the answer. Not yet.

So, she kept training. Her telekinesis and telepathy were improving. Her shields had never felt stronger. She felt more confident than ever about the claiming. Surely, she was approaching a time when she could leave this place.

But no. Every day, Lilith broached something new or retread old ground.

"You've made a good start on your Consorts, but we should talk about your strategy going forward," Lilith said. She sat down across from Mercy, interrupting her morning reading at the kitchen table. Mercy had taken it over as her research station. It was covered in books, paper, and pens. For whatever reason, technology didn't reliably work in this place, which was why all of the reading was in ancient book form, and all of Mercy's notes had to be hand written on archaic paper.

Not this again. "I don't have a strategy," she said, not bothering to look up. "I don't even know if I'm going to *have* multiple consorts."

"Don't be ridiculous. Of course you will."

Mercy bit back a sigh. She hated it when Lilith dictated to her in that authoritarian way. Sometimes, her grandmother forgot which of them was dead, and who was the real queen. Reluctantly, she looked up.

"Fine." She said. "For the sake of argument, let's say I do have multiple consorts. I'm certainly not going to pick them based on strategy."

Lilith laughed. "Surely, you don't plan to use sentiment to make your choice?"

"Yes," said Mercy. "Sentiment, love. Whatever you want to call it."

"Mercy, this will be your power base. You cannot afford to let sentiment guide you. You got lucky with Nikolos, but you really must learn to be practical."

Mercy leaned back, putting down her book and her pen. "Like you? Because that worked out really well."

Lilith's eyes narrowed. "Where will sentiment get you when half the galaxy is destroyed, and your people are ripped from you? Even your consorts."

"The whole goal is to stop that from happening."

"Yes. And your best chance to do that is to prepare. Obviously, I took it too far. But that doesn't mean you should disdain every decision I made."

Mercy wasn't so sure about that. Besides, she didn't believe that all of Lilith's choices had been purely practical.

"You can't tell me you chose your consorts based solely on their power. You had children with these men. You had to feel *something* for them."

For the first time since they'd started this, Lilith looked uncomfortable. At first, satisfaction filled Mercy at finally getting the upper hand in a conversation with her grandmother.

Lilith's lips thinned as she pressed them tightly together. "Children are a different matter. Of course, I cared for them."

Something in her body language bothered Mercy. She was being truthful, but there was more here than Lilith was saying. "What?" she asked. "What are you not telling me?"

Lilith fidgeted in her chair. *Fidgeted!* Something was definitely going on.

"We should talk about children as well, I suppose," Lilith said.

"What about them?" Mercy asked, wary.

"You should be careful about getting pregnant. About the possibility of birthing another queen."

What? That made no sense. "I think children are an expectation, both as a queen and a consort. Remember, the pirates have a population problem."

Lilith leaned forward. She reached across the table and took one of Mercy's hands in a hard grip. "Listen to me, as your mother did not. Having a child queen makes you vulnerable. It would make the perfect vessel for that parasite."

"Excuse me?"

"Do you think your mother took you and ran all those years ago just to escape me?"

Mercy raised an eyebrow. "Yes."

Lilith looked surprised at the vehemence of her reply. "Don't be foolish. I *told* Pallas if she bore you it would put us all at risk. I told her she needed to terminate the pregnancy. She refused."

"My mother refused to kill me. Not surprising." Nor was it surprising that Lilith had ordered her to do it.

Disappointing, perhaps. Mercy kept wanting to excuse all of her grandmother's behavior as a response to a galaxy-ending vision of the future.

It needed to stop. Lilith was helping her, yes. Training her, yes. And it was true that her grandmother had believed the things she did were necessary evils. She'd even managed a few good deeds in her life, such as freeing slaves like Sebastian. But that didn't absolve her of the horrible things she'd done. Mercy couldn't afford to forget that.

"Sentiment stopped her," said Lilith. "She put us all at terrible risk."

"That's why you wanted to kill me. Because I was a risk?"

Lilith's gaze was unflinching. "You have no idea what it was like. What *she* is like."

"She," said Mercy. "You mean the queen Vashti

saw. Other than Vashti's visions, what do you know about her?"

"It will be better if I show you."

Before Mercy could protest, she was falling into another of Lilith's memories.

✦

HARD FINGERS SHAKE ME AWAKE. "Lily, wake up!" My sister, Vashti. She holds my shoulders in a bruising grip. Moonlight streams into the room, glistening off the tears that streak her face. She is frantic. "Lily, you must come! Something is wrong with *Maman*."

Groggy with sleep, I fumble to shove back my covers. Vashti must have come in through the courtyard entrance. The curtains float on the breeze, the doors standing open. I'd closed them before going to bed. Now, the light from Ardon's three moons shines into my bedroom like daylight, slanting past the curtains and making me blink against the brightness. If all three moons have risen, we are in the early hours of morning.

Our estate is built more or less like a star. The central courtyard holds elaborate gardens, with the main house formed around it. Our rooms are positioned like spires, each one in a different direction. Vashti's is on the opposite side from my own. We always take the far quicker route through the courtyard to see one another, rather than the much longer path of the hallways that spiral around the estate.

"What is it? What's happened?" I ask, finally disentangling my legs from my sheets. Vashti and I are the only ones home, besides our mother. Our fathers, sister and brothers are all away, most of them representing *Maman* in various parts of the fleet, or on other colonies.

"I don't know." My sister, usually so collected and calm, is wringing her hands. This sends a spike of alarm through me. "I…I had a dream, Lily. A bad one. I went to *Maman*, but—" Vashti's words break on a sob. Her hair is a dark tangle around her face, her robe askew over her nightgown, and in the moonlight, my sister looks impossibly young. Though she is two years older than me, right now her tears and her terror make her look less like the nineteen-year-old young woman I know her to be, and more like a child, afraid and alone.

This is bad. I slip my feet into slippers, grabbing the silk robe I left pooled on the floor the night before.

My sister's dreams come true all too often. She's had them since childhood, and she has grown so accustomed to the things she sees that very little phases her. Last year, she dreamt of an earthquake that swallowed half the spaceport. She'd calmly informed us over breakfast, as though reporting on the monthly accounting. Six weeks later, when the earthquake came, the spaceport was empty. Our ships were all in orbit or docked elsewhere, because *Maman* knows better than to discount anything Vashti sees.

So do I.

Maman? No one answers my telepathic call. If my mother hears, she is silent.

I run across the courtyard as fast as I can, ignoring the cold that raises goosebumps on my legs. The *accoi* flowers have bloomed with the moons' rise. Their fragrance blankets the gardens in a cloying sweetness. Normally, I find them enchanting. Not tonight. Fear is a living, ugly thing inside of me. It sickens my stomach and the flowers' scent sticks in the back of my throat.

The doors to *Maman's* room stand open, I assume from Vashti's previous visit. I can hear my sister's running feet behind me, her breathless sobs following me as I run straight through the doorway without pausing.

Maman is lying in her bed, but she isn't sleeping. Her eyes are open wide and staring, and for a moment my heart stops. *I* stop, frozen, standing there in the moonlight, trembling. But then she thrashes, and hot relief floods me. My mother is alive.

But something is definitely not right.

I kneel beside her, the sleeve of my robe pooling at my wrist as I reach out to touch her.

"Lily, be careful. I think—" My sister's words are lost to me the moment my hand connects with *Maman's*. A vortex pulls me in, sucking me right past her shields into a spiral I can't pull out of.

I fall into her thoughts, into her mind. This isn't the first time I've been in my mother's mind, and I know what to expect. Like me, she is a queen. We are unique among the Talented. Born to be the connection that holds us all together. It is a great responsibility, my mother is fond of saying. A duty only we can fulfill. We are born to it, as surely as any monarch born to a throne.

A queen's mind is an overwhelming place.

When I connect with my mother, I have to try hard to hold on to my sense of self. The mental presence of a queen burns bright, a welcoming, comforting power that draws people in and makes them want to be a part of it. It feels like finding a piece of yourself that has always been missing. I long to sink into that brilliant glow and feel whole.

But for another queen, like me, that would be disastrous. Queens do not claim other queens. *Maman* is vehement about this. She says if I try, I might die. *Maman* thinks we were designed to only exist one at a time.

I have been in my mother's thoughts many times in the past. It is her favorite teaching technique. But this time is different. That brilliant, comforting warmth has dimmed. Another presence overshadows it. Just as bright, but sharp and jagged, the heat uncomfortable.

Another queen. I thought I knew what it felt like, to be in the presence of one of us. But I've never experienced anything like this. It can be overwhelming, yes, but also beautiful. My mother's strength and power has always been a source of pride. Something for me to aspire to.

This presence feels brutal, the power like a fist pummeling everything in its path. It beats against me, burning hot against my mind. Even so, I feel something shielding me from the worst of it. I realize my mother stands between me and this other presence. *Maman* is fighting for her life, for *our* lives now. She is losing.

My mother, the most powerful person I have ever known, *is losing*. I stare, horrified, frozen, my face burning hot with the conflict before me. I have to help her. I don't know how, but fear and desperation drive me to try. I move. Just a small, abortive jolt forward. It is enough to draw attention.

I feel it, the moment the other queen turns her focus on me. That malevolence is unmistakable. She draws away from my mother, her radiance with its sharp edges following her like a cloak.

Maman.

No. Lily! My mother's voice is weaker than I have ever heard it. Feeble. *Leave. Go!*

Who have we here? This voice is nothing like *Maman's.* It slides over me like an oil slick, pervasive and suffocating. *Your daughter?*

The presence circles me, examining, weighing. My terror increases, some instinct within warning me that this is the most danger I have ever faced in my life. I feel myself tremble. *Maman...*

Lily, do as I say. Go now! My mother has never sounded so desperate, so fearful.

A queen, says the oil slick voice. *She is young. The young are so malleable. I will take her.* The presence comes for me in a great rush. No warning. Pain like nothing I have ever felt spears me, burning me from the inside out. Her brightness is a hungry flame consuming me.

I scream.

LILY! My mother's light flares, a blinding brilliance that eclipses the malevolent radiance and my own, tearing us apart. A shockwave hits, catching me on a titanic explosion of energy that throws me out of my mother's mind, back into my body. I scream as my mother dies, sacrificing herself to save me. I scream my fear and pain and denial so loudly, my voice gives out.

Then the brightness and warmth is gone, and my world goes dark.

* * *

LILITH SQUEEZED Mercy's hand hard enough to hurt. She blinked, the transition from the memory difficult. Shaking, she pulled her hand from Lilith's, clasping it to herself.

The memories she'd seen thus far had all been fairly pleasant, the emotions easy to deal with. This was...

This was not that. Mercy deeply regretted the fact that food was unnecessary here. She could have used the settling effects of alcohol right about now.

"That was..." *Terrifying. Horrible. Traumatic.* Mercy couldn't settle on a word to describe what she'd just seen.

Lilith raised an eyebrow. "I promise you, actually living it did not improve the experience."

Mercy took a few moments to gather her thoughts. "What happened —it's why you wanted me dead. Why you think I shouldn't have children."

Intellectually, Mercy could almost understand it. It *had* been terrifying, and Lilith was barely more than a child herself when it happened. Her mother died. Her world changed forever. Something like that left its mark on a person. Mercy ought to know. She still wasn't over the loss of her own mother after almost sixteen years.

But emotionally, it was hard to reconcile your grandmother trying to kill you, no matter her reasons.

"Besides," Mercy continued, "it's not like you didn't take risks yourself. Kind of hypocritical, don't you think?"

Lilith frowned at her. "What do you mean?"

"I mean here you are, telling me not to have children, and you had four daughters. And however many grandchildren." She waved a hand. "Every one of them could have been a queen."

Lilith stared at her with a strange expression. She wore it for so long that Mercy began to wonder if something was really wrong.

"They weren't mine," she said at last.

The words hit Mercy like a slap. "What?"

Lilith looked away. "Except for Pallas, and she was a mistake. The other girls weren't mine. Not of my body."

Lilith's words made no sense. Dizziness tilted the world sideways. Mercy gripped the table's edge. "No. That's not possible. My mother had sisters. She showed me holos. They all looked like you. Their children look like us. All green-eyed and dusky skinned. Cannon is King because he is your grandson."

"Please." Lilith gave her a pitying look. "A strong Queen has heirs. I wasn't going to advertise the fact that mine were adopted. I chose my girls carefully, and what didn't fit, I changed. You should do the same. There are plenty of powerful children out there, orphaned by circumstance." She paused. "And Cannon is King on his own merits. He was always a smart boy, wise beyond his years. His empathy held them together when they had no Queen."

Mercy held up a hand. She had to take a moment before speaking. She realized she was done. Just done with the secrets and half-truths, the high-handed dictation of what *she* should do. "Do *not* tell me what you think I should do with my body and my future family. It is *none* of your business. I don't even know if I believe you."

"Why shouldn't you?" Lilith's eyes widened. "Why would I lie?"

"Because you are a manipulative bitch who would say anything to get me to agree to your way of doing things."

"Don't presume, Mercy. I have told you nothing but the truth."

Furious, Mercy glared at her grandmother. "Why did you have my mother?"

"What?"

"You wanted her to kill me, right? So why not follow your own advice? If Mom was the only true child you had, why did you have her at all?"

Lilith stood up. Anger radiated from her. But Mercy was long past letting her grandmother's temper intimidate her.

"What, no answer?" she asked.

"Don't push me, Mercy."

"No. I am done with this bullshit." Mercy shoved away from the table, standing up. "If I'm your only hope to save us all from this alpha queen of yours, you have to be honest with me. And honesty doesn't just mean telling the truth. It means telling the *whole* truth. Even the inconvenient parts." She stared her grandmother down.

"Either tell me everything, or let me go the hell home."

"I *am* telling you everything."

"Are you? Why is my father dead?"

Lilith stared at her. Her lips pressed into a thin line of disapproval.

"No answer? Nothing to say? I don't remember him at all. I was too young when he died. But Mom showed me holos of him. I know what he looked like. She told me stories. I know what type of person he was. A good man. A man who loved his wife, who loved me. Why is he dead?"

"Mercy—"

"The truth."

With a sigh, more irritated than yielding, Lilith scowled. "She wouldn't listen to me."

"Excuse me?"

"Pallas had always been a good daughter. Obedient. And then *he* came along, and suddenly she wouldn't listen anymore. She married him against my wishes. She had you against my advice. He needed to go. I was sure if your father was gone, she would stop defying me."

The silence stretched between them. Mercy had no idea how long she stood there, the blood rushing in her ears, the dizziness she'd felt overwhelmed by a haze of rage. Finally, she turned on her heel and walked away.

There was nothing more to say.

ercy left the house. She didn't know how far the illusion stretched, but she intended to find out. Not because she thought it was a way out, but because if she didn't work off some of her anger, she couldn't think calmly.

And she needed to be calm and clear when she decided to leave this place. She couldn't afford to let her emotions rule.

The wind blew through her hair, cold against her face. The tall grass lashed at her legs. She could feel the press of it through the fabric of her clothing. Mercy had to admit, Lilith had done a fine job creating Ardon, if this was what the pirate colony world really looked like. The reality and the detail of it. It felt unbelievable that she, too, might one day create illusions so complete that no one could tell the difference.

She stopped, drinking in the view of the mountains in the distance. Snow covered the peaks, white against a sky that was a deepening rose color. Beautiful. And not real.

Taking long, deep breaths of cold mountain air,

Mercy closed her eyes. Her face felt hot and tremors ran through her body. Funny, how angry she was over the death of a man she'd never known. In all the ways that mattered, she *had* a father. Alive and well, back on *Nemesis*. Wolfgang Hades was her father.

And Lilith was the reason for that. She would probably argue that no, this alpha queen was the reason. The reason why Kiana died so young, leaving Lilith to take control as Queen. The reason for every bad decision she'd made throughout her rule. Except Lilith wouldn't call them bad decisions. She'd say they were necessary. Hard choices. Oh, she admitted that some of them crossed a line. That she'd gone too far. But deep down, Mercy thought her grandmother truly believed that most of what she'd done was necessary.

She was wrong. Mercy refused to accept that the only way to survive what was coming involved making heartless decisions. Choosing consorts for what they could do, refusing to have children because of what they might become. Killing anyone who got in her way.

There had to be a better way.

She heard footsteps behind her, the brush of the grass against cloth, and tensed. She was not ready to face Lilith again. Not yet.

But it wasn't her grandmother who came to stand beside her. It was Sebastian.

He said nothing. He held a piece of grass in his hands, slowly stripping it of its layers, letting the pieces flutter away on the wind. His long black hair, usually braided, was loose around his face. Strands floated around him, rippling in the air.

"Did she bring you here?" Mercy asked. Her voice sounded cold. Hard.

"Yes."

"Why?"

He sighed, tossing the strand of grass aside. "She wanted my help. She thinks she's failing with you."

"Failing." She looked at him. "I can't see her using that word."

His mouth twitched, not quite smiling. "No. She's frustrated. I believe the word she used was *unreasonable.*"

"And not to describe herself, I'm sure."

He laughed. "No. Of course not."

Mercy plowed her fingers through her hair. "I can't just forget everything she's done, Sebastian. I've tried. And I can't do it." The wind stung her eyes. "But I still need her help. How do I reconcile that?"

"I don't know." His expression was serious. "I wish I did."

"I know to you, she was something more. That you care for her." Mercy shook her head. "But that's never going to be my relationship with her."

"I know." Reaching out, he took her hand in his. "Mercy, if there is one thing that is clear to me, it's that people are complicated. My relationship with Lilith doesn't have to inform yours. Just like your relationship with Reaper doesn't have to inform ours."

Her stomach did a funny little flip. He squeezed her hand lightly and then let it go. She could still feel his touch, the warmth where his fingers had pressed against her skin. She didn't know how to respond, her emotions clouded.

"The important thing is," he continued as though nothing had happened, "can you learn from her?"

Mercy took her time responding. Her face was cool now, her hands steady. The anger had faded. "I have," she said. "I am."

The wind whipped his hair across his face, and he brushed it back. "Then maybe that's all you need. Maybe that's enough."

"Maybe."

They stood together for a long time, until finally, Mercy lowered herself to the ground, laying back in the grass. After a moment, Sebastian joined her. They stared up at the rose-colored sky.

"What's happening on the ship?" Mercy asked. The question had been burning in the back of her mind since Sebastian appeared, but she'd been too afraid of the answer to voice it. "Have you heard from them? From Reaper and the others?"

"We're jumping to them now."

"*What?*" She sat bolt upright, her heart racing. Then she remembered the way time worked here. "Are they all right? How long, before we reach them?"

"Treon has had contact with Reaper. He believes he has the correct coordinates to reach them. We won't know for sure until we finish the jump." He paused. "They were alive when Treon spoke with Reaper."

Mercy squeezed her eyes shut. She wanted so badly to leave, to shatter this peaceful place and go back to the real world. In her mind, she'd been here so long already. It felt like months stretched back in the time she'd spent training with Lilith.

But that would be the rash decision. The one Mercy would have made two years ago. The person she was now couldn't afford to be rash. She reached down through the grass and dug her fingers into the earth.

"I hate being responsible."

"I'm sure they're fine," Sebastian said. But worry threaded through his voice.

She glanced at him. "What aren't you saying?"

He sighed heavily. "We didn't get much out of Treon before he collapsed."

"Collapsed. Treon?"

"He used too much *mnemosa*, pushed his gifts too hard. Doc says he'll be out for the next twelve hours, at least. But apparently the ship the others are on is dead in space, and even if they could get power back, it's a dropship. It won't have enough fuel for another jump from its current position."

Her stomach clenched. "So, if we don't reach them…"

"But we will." His hand brushed hers, and she gripped it, hard. "Even if Treon's coordinates are off, we'll be close. Dem will be able to reach Reaper, and we can find them."

"I hate this," she whispered.

"I know," he said.

Reaper. Atrea. Cannon. Reaper's dogs. All people in danger because she insisted on a peace summit that had proven to be a disaster. Wolfgang would berate her for believing it was her fault. But she didn't see any other way to look at it. Not now.

Gently, Sebastian tugged her down beside him, putting his arm around her. She let him. It didn't feel like an overture. Just someone who cared about her, offering comfort when she needed it.

She took it, lying with her head against his shoulder, feeling the silk of his hair on her face. She told herself he was right; they would be all right. They had to be.

Reaper was coming back to her.

EVENTUALLY, they had to return to the house. To Lilith. Mercy steeled herself. But to her relief, Lilith didn't pick up their previous conversation. Instead, her grandmother decided to use Sebastian as a training tool.

She returned to the idea of shielding others, and of borrowing gifts. Sebastian got to be the practice dummy, more or less. And having him there did help Mercy connect with what Lilith was trying to show her.

She couldn't borrow his gift, of course. Not here. But she felt how it might be done, and Lilith seemed satisfied with that progress.

Mercy found it increasingly difficult to focus, however. The more time that appeared to pass in this place, the more time she felt must be passing in the real world. And she wanted to be in the real world when they caught up with Reaper and the others.

She found she could no longer lose herself in reading the books Lilith assigned her. The lessons, too, soon lost their appeal. She felt as though she's gained a fundamental understanding now that would just require time and practice. She could do that in the real world.

The more the idea took hold, the more she itched to return to reality.

Finally, Lilith's patience snapped.

"If you're not going to apply yourself, why are you here?" her grandmother demanded.

Mercy didn't take the comment well. "I *am*." Hadn't she dutifully been practicing all this time? Hadn't she put aside her feelings to learn everything she could? What more could she do?

Lilith eyed her. "You're distracted. This is what comes of choosing consorts based on sentiment."

"We are *not* having this conversation again." Or ever, if Mercy had anything to say about it.

Lilith crossed her arms. "You may as well go." She flicked one hand in dismissal. "You're useless as it is."

"Of the two of us, I'm not the dead one."

"Well, that can always change."

Mercy's eyes widened. Outrage left her breathless. "Are you threatening me? *Again?*"

She wasn't sure whether he was being brave or stupid when Sebastian stepped between them, hands raised.

"I think," he said, "that everyone could use a break. Mercy's been on the mental plane for quite a long time. It's not good to remain parted from the physical mind for so long."

Lilith, far from being offended by his words, seemed to take them as her own idea. "Yes," she said, eyeing Mercy critically. "I do think you could use a break. But you need to come back soon. You have much more to learn."

Mercy grit her teeth and didn't respond. Sebastian kissed Lilith on the cheek, then turned and took Mercy's hand.

"You should be able to feel a connection to your physical self. A tether," he said. "Just think about it, and you'll feel it sort of tugging at you."

Mercy nodded, and concentrated. There. Once she felt it, she wondered how she'd ever not known it was there. It was not unlike the connection she felt to the Talented she'd claimed.

"I've got it," she told him.

"Good. Follow it, and it will pull you right out of this place. You'll wake up."

Lilith watched them. "You could do worse," she said, looking at Mercy and then pointedly at Sebastian. "For your second consort."

Sebastian leveled a look at her.

"What?" she asked, sounding almost defensive. "It's true."

Sebastian shook his head. He let go of Mercy's hand and stepped away. "I'll see you on the other side," he said, and vanished.

"Good bye, grandmother," Mercy said. It hurt to admit it, but Lilith deserved some acknowledgment. "Thank you for training me. But stay out of my personal life."

She grabbed at the tether, hoping to leave before Lilith could respond. She felt it begin to pull her away. Of course, her grandmother had to get in the last word.

"Queens don't have personal lives, Mercy. We have responsibilities and duty. Remember that."

As though she could ever forget it. The weight of the galaxy rode on her shoulders. The dream spun away in a dizzying spiral. Mercy woke with a gasp.

She was in her quarters. The lights were dim, but it wasn't dark. Someone stirred beside her, and she blinked to clear her vision. Sebastian. He looked a though he'd been sleeping in one of her chairs.

"You're here," she said, surprised.

"I check on you from time to time," he admitted, stretching his neck and wincing. "I was here when Lilith called to me."

"How does she do that, exactly?" she asked, sitting up. She looked down as the covers slipped down her body, but thankfully she was fully clothed in the same pajamas she'd worn when she went to bed.

Sebastian lifted a shoulder, rubbing at it. The chair had apparently not been the most comfortable bed. "I put her into the bracelet. I can feel it when she wants my attention. It's hard to explain."

"I bet. How long…?"

"About half a standard day."

Half a day? That was all? It had felt so much longer.

"More importantly, though," he continued, "we've arrived. Dem is overseeing the recovery of the dropship, and you'll be happy to know all of our people are safe."

Relief and joy had her leaping out of the bed and hugging him before he'd finished speaking.

"They're all right? They're alive?"

"They are," Sebastian said on a laugh. He

stepped back, letting her go. "I imagine you'll want to dress in something a little more formal." He bowed his head in a gesture that was almost formal. "I'll leave you to it."

He left, the door to her quarters sliding shut behind him. Mercy barely noticed. She was already reaching out mentally.

Reaper?

She felt the connection snap into place, his response instant.

Mercy. We're home.

CHAPTER TWENTY-TWO

As it turned out, the dropship was already on board. Mercy pulled on real clothes and was flying out her door when she stopped dead. Emotion swamped her, too myriad and too fast to process. It overwhelmed her ability to speak, the words caught in her throat as unexpected tears rushed her eyes.

Reaper was standing in the hall, his hand poised at the door. She gaped at him. Somehow, seeing him standing physically before her was even more emotional than hearing his voice.

You're alive. You're here. She thought the words because she knew if she spoke them aloud she would break and cry.

In the next moment, she was in his arms, and he was crushing her to him. If she'd had any doubt of how Reaper felt in this moment, the strength with which he held her erased them. His arms locked around her so hard, her ribs hurt and her breath constricted. Seeming to realize it, he loosened his grip.

Not that she was complaining. Her own arms

were wrapped around his neck. She held tightly, then pulled back so she could look into his eyes. They were pale blue, but not the icy cold of the Killer. Instead, a familiar warmth sparked in them.

She kissed him, her mouth crushing his so that it was more painful than exciting. The scruff of beard he'd grown over the last few days was rough against her skin. She didn't care.

I'm so glad you're back. She whispered the words in his mind.

So am I. He said nothing more, but she could feel the tension in his body, hear in his mental voice the relief he felt.

The tears she'd held back streaked down her face. She couldn't stop them, and she didn't want to try. It didn't seem like two days since he'd been gone. It felt like weeks. Months. Years.

Damn Lilith and her training.

They needed to have a hundred conversations. But right now, she didn't care about any of that. She pulled back, still holding tight to his arms because she couldn't quite bear to let him go. Her gaze roamed over him, cataloging the scruff she'd already felt, the weariness etched into his face, and the dirt and grime he'd picked up in whatever trials he'd suffered.

"Here," she said aloud, her voice shaking a little. "When was the last time you ate?" She pulled him to the kitchen area, ordering up a dish she knew was a favorite of his. Red meat in a hearty, savory wine sauce, over thin pasta so delicate it was almost transparent. She started to order up a glass of wine and then stopped. She ordered water, then pulled two tumblers down and poured two glasses of whiskey.

The occasion seemed to call for something stronger than wine.

"The others - they're back and safe? Cannon, and Atrea?" She knew they must be, or Reaper would have told her by now. But she had to ask. To *know*.

"Yes. They're here. They're safe."

She let out a breath, tension leaving her with it. "Good."

Instead of saying any of the other words crowding her mind, she put them aside as she worked on his plate. Questions could wait. News could wait. She had a sudden longing to just be with him. To ignore the rest of the world and just be together.

When she placed the plate in front of him, along with one glass of water and another of whiskey, he just stood looking at her. His hair, always so military straight, was mussed in a way that closed her throat again.

Mercy. He didn't say anything else, just her name.

"We're not very good at this," she said, a laugh bubbling up her throat. "Being apart. Not very good at all."

"No," he agreed. He looked down at the plate, blinking like he was just now seeing it. She wondered if the savory smell of the food had finally reached him. He picked up a forkful and ate it, chewing slowly. His eyes half-closed in pleasure.

"When was the last time you ate?" she asked.

"Before leaving *Nemesis*," he said, after swallowing.

She stared. "That was more than three days ago."

"Yes." He shoveled another forkful into his mouth, swallowing quickly and chasing it with water. He drank the whole glass down, so she took it and refilled it while he ate more. She mentally reached out delicately, felt at the strands that linked her to Cannon and Atrea. Just a hint, like Lilith taught her. They were fine, if exhausted and hungry, like Reaper.

She had no doubt that Wolfgang would take care of Atrea. But who would look after Cannon? Worried, she glanced at Reaper. "Does Cannon… have someone?"

He paused, fork halfway to his mouth. "Someone?"

"You know, someone to take care of him now that he's back. Make sure he eats."

He stared at her. "He's hardly a child."

"Right. Of course." Embarrassed, she let it drop.

But men *were* sort of children, right? When it came to taking care of themselves? Wolfgang had always pushed it when he was sick or exhausted, insisting he could do just a little bit more, when he should have been resting.

Cannon was King. She knew he'd dive right back into catching up on work, instead of taking care of himself.

She reached out, brushed against his shields.

Mercy? Surprise colored his mental tone. *I know you're with Reaper. We can debrief tomorrow.*

Sure, she said. *Just as long as you put down whatever work you're reading right now, and go get yourself something to eat.*

Silence answered her. Then his voice came, sounding like he couldn't decide between shock and irritation. *Excuse me?*

You heard me. Consider it an order from your Queen. Go. Eat. Rest. No work. She accompanied the words with a subtle pressure. As Kiana would have done. The choice was still Cannon's, but doing what she asked would feel right, something he would recognize instinctively.

Her heart began to pound. This was the first time she was trying this in the real world. What if it didn't work? What if he knew what she was doing and it pissed him off?

Finally, his voice came again. *As you wish, Your Majesty.*

Relief flooded her. She smiled and didn't even admonish him for the title. *Good night, Cannon.*

Good night, Mercy.

She looked up to find Reaper watching her, an odd look on his face.

"What?"

He swallowed the last bite of his meal. "Nothing," he said, picking up the tumbler of whiskey for the first time. "You just seem very comfortable with your abilities."

She found herself tucking her hair behind her ear, a habit from childhood whenever she felt anxious or self-conscious. She stopped, dropping her hand back to the counter. She wrapped it around her own glass of whiskey.

"I've been working on them a lot," she said,

hoping he would leave it at that for now. She didn't want to open that box yet, sidetracking them into everything that had happened. He took a drink, watching her.

Then he set the glass down and said, "We should talk."

"Not yet." She reached for him, taking his hand in hers, linking their fingers. "Soon." She wanted to shut out the world. Just for a little while.

Stepping back, she began backing away from the kitchen, a step at time. He followed without questioning her, allowing his fingers to stay loosely hooked with hers. She changed the lighting, using her telekinesis to flip the dial. Light dimmed further, and then glows appeared along the walls like sconces, flickering to imitate the look of flames. She'd only discovered the different settings herself a few weeks ago. They were meant to create the illusion of being planetside. There were settings for the seasons: warm summer days, a fireside winter night, even one for storms with the relevant rumble of thunder and flashes of lightning. She could set the wall to show any scene she liked, as well, adding to the ambience, but she ignored that for now.

Reaper laughed. "Your control is much improved."

She smiled at him and decided to show off a little.

Reaching out with telekinesis, she used her new control to turn on the bath in the bathing room, to add a hint of oils and scents into the water. Not too many. She wasn't sure how Reaper would feel about a tub filled with rainbow water and scented bubbles. She stopped just outside the door, allowing the tub time to fill.

She kicked off her boots. Reaper watched as she floated them across the room and put them away. Slowly, she reached up and stripped off her shirt. Without taking her eyes from him, she shimmied out of her pants.

Nik didn't move. His gaze followed her every move, but he stood completely still.

That would never do. Feeling mischievous, and just maybe wanting to prove something, she reached out with telekinesis again. This was much harder, more precise work. She formed her Talent into a blade, then cut down the length of his shirt, from neck to waist. She had to be slow and careful to avoid nicking his skin.

The garment flared open, exposing his naked chest.

"You can't bathe in your clothes," she said, admiring the play of light across his muscular torso.

"Is that what I'm going to do?" he asked with a low laugh.

"Among other things."

He reached out to snag her to him, and she danced out of the way. He could have grabbed her, but he let her get away. She pointed a finger at him. "Bath, first."

She turned and sauntered into the bathing chamber, making sure to put a little extra sway into her walk. Seduction play was *so* not her thing, but she enjoyed seeing Reaper's responses, knowing that he liked it, even if he didn't say so. So much of communicating with Reaper involved reading non-verbal cues. She thought she was starting to get rather good at it.

He followed her in, and she finished stripping off her clothes before stepping into the hot water of the bath. It was almost too warm, but she sucked in a breath and kept going. She finger combed her hair. Thank the Mother for nanites that kept it smooth and silky, so her fingers didn't get caught, and it didn't tangle hopelessly every time she moved. She glanced over her shoulder.

"We forgot the whiskey. Grab it, will you?"

Mercy sank into the bath, holding her breath as she gave her skin a moment to get used to the heat. Her hair floated around her, long, dark strands made heavy by the water. Then she lay with her head agains the tub's ledge, thankful she'd rated one big enough for two.

Reaper removed his ruined shirt, stripping off the rest of his clothing. The glasses floated in a moment later, and he caught them, placing them on a shelf beside the tub. Her body had sunk below the water line, and a froth of bubbles covered the surface of the bath. But Reaper watched her as intently as if he saw every curve her body had to offer.

She realized a moment later that the frothy bubbles were moving, parting to the sides of the tub, leaving the water clear and her body visible. She laughed.

"Are you getting in?" she asked, when he just stood, drinking her in.

"In a minute." He sat beside the tub, his gaze moving to her face. He looked so serious that she sat up in the water.

"What is it?"

"I know you don't want to talk about it yet, but I have to. There was a moment. A time, while I was gone, when I wasn't sure I'd be making it back to you." His voice held no inflection. "I knew I was going to die."

"Nik." She slid through the water until she was close enough to take his hand between her own. She wasn't sure if he needed the comfort, because his face was emotionless. But she needed it.

"I worried about you," he said. "About what might happen to you, with me gone."

Her heart tripped in her chest. About to die, and he'd thought only of her. Of course, he had.

"I was afraid." He said the words so softly, they almost vanished beneath the sound of the water still filling the tub. She shut it off.

"Of what?" She knew Reaper didn't fear death. Until a moment ago, she'd have said he didn't fear anything.

"Of your future. If I die, I'm just another Killer. No one will mourn."

"Don't be stupid."

He smiled faintly. "No one but you."

There were others, but she let it go for now. This was a side of Reaper she'd never seen before. She didn't want to shut him down because she argued with him.

His smile faded. "But you're different. Mercy, if I'm gone, you're vulnerable. I know you don't want to talk about it. You don't want to consider it. But you need to."

"Consider what?"

"Other consorts."

She looked away, and he reached out, his fingers taking her chin, tilting her face back toward his.

"I'm serious," he said.

She bit her lip. This was *so* not the time she'd have picked to discuss this. "I know. I've been thinking about it a lot." She took a deep breath. "I think I am. Open to it, I mean. Maybe."

He held her gaze. She felt her face heat and knew he noticed her embarrassment.

"Who?" he asked. His voice was calm. Only a slight lifting of his eyebrows betrayed his surprise.

She didn't pretend to misunderstand him. "Sebastian," she said, barely speaking the name, she said it so softly. "We've grown closer, recently. It's early days, but...there's something there." She looked down, playing with some of the bubbles, chasing them in circles with her fingers. "We're becoming friends, but I think he has feelings for me that go beyond that, and I'm...I'm not indifferent to them, or to him."

Her heart pounded. Of all of the things she had to tell Reaper, this one troubled her the most. She'd barely begin to accept it herself. Reaper had said from the beginning that consorts were an accepted part of pirate culture, that she should have more than one. But saying that and accepting the reality were two very different things. She was afraid to look up and see his reaction, but she had to know. She forced her head up, her gaze taking in his face.

"Nothing's happened yet," she said quickly. "But it could. If I wanted it to. If he did."

Reaper brushed her cheek with his thumb,

smiling. "Sebastian is a good choice. He's a good man, powerful, and he and I get along well. If he is your choice, I approve."

"You do?" She still couldn't quite believe that Reaper was all right with this. That a man as dominant as he was, with his gifts, could accept sharing her with another man.

He leaned down and took her mouth, kissing her. Her lips parted in surprise and his tongue swept inside.

I guess we're done talking, she thought.

We are.

Reaper slid into the tub, sending the water sluicing around them. He kissed her again, pulling her against him, stretching full out in the water so that his body covered hers. They lay with Mercy's head against the cushioned backboard that ran along one end of the tub, Reaper above her. Her breasts pressed against his chest, her hands roaming over his shoulders, down his back, trailing through the water.

Heat made her body as liquid as the bathwater around them. She let her legs fall open, and he settled between them, the hard length of his erection pressed against her.

His mouth left hers to trail her jaw, down to her throat. He pressed kisses to her skin, almost feverish, his teeth scraping her flesh and drawing a moan from her throat.

She'd intended to play when she drew him here. To tease him, using her newly won control over her Talents. But she felt an urgency in him that woke a matching need in her. She wanted him with a fierceness that staggered her. Maybe it was the separation, so much longer that she'd antici-pated. Maybe it was the talk of Consorts, creating a need to reaffirm that they belonged to one an-other. Maybe it was his near-death.

Or perhaps it was just him. Nikolos, and the effect he had on her. A look, a touch was some-times all it took.

She gasped when she felt her nipples pinched to hardness, invisible vises tightening on them like clamps. She squirmed, while he flicked his tongue over her throat, working his way down her collar-bone. The vises loosened, the blood flowing back in a rush that speared heat straight to her core. It was on the knife edge of painful, but he took one nipple into his mouth, swirling it with his tongue until the sharpness eased to a burning warmth that drew lines of fire from one breast to the other, arrowing down to her clit. Then he moved to the other nipple, doing the same. She had trouble breathing, feeling like she was on the cusp of orgasm and he hadn't even touched her yet. Not really.

He thrust a finger inside of her with no warn-ing, pressing his thumb to her clit and moving it in small circles as he worked her in a fast, implacable rhythm. The orgasm hit so fast, so sudden that it shocked her. Her nails dug into his shoulders as she arched, trembling.

That told her just how hurried Reaper was. Normally, he liked to take his time while he made her crazy. Not today.

Mercy took a shuddering breath, her heart beating fast and hard. Reaper needed something from her. She intended to give it to him.

Languid with release, she moved her body against his, enjoying the friction as he slid against her. The oils in the water made them both slick.

Her control was tenuous, so she only used telekinesis to push him back, to help as she rolled him over until he lay back and she straddled him. His hands went to her waist. It pleased her to see that his breathing was fast and uneven. His eyes were dark, half lidded as she lowered herself over him, slowly and deliberately. She was still too sensitive. She had to bite back a moan as he slid inside her.

She kissed him, the scruff along his jaw just adding another layer of sensation as she started to move. He let her set the pace, thrusting up to meet her rhythm. But it wasn't enough, and she could see the restraint in his eyes, in the faint tremble of his arms.

Restraint wasn't what Reaper needed. Experimentally, she reached for the connection between them, the bond between a Queen and her claimed. Mercy touched it lightly, sending a vibration through it, a wave of intent and desire meant to shake his control. He shuddered, his entire body going tense beneath her. She did it again. He groaned.

Then his control snapped.

His hands tightened on her hips, and though she was the one riding him, he took control. He held her still while he thrust up, hard and fast and relentless. The heat built quickly, sensation coiling so tightly, she whimpered. It crested, and she cried out, his rhythm drawing the orgasm out until she thought she couldn't stand it anymore, the pleasure too much, her body too sensitive. Finally, he tensed, arching up as he came, warm seed spilling into her. He pulled her close, holding her tightly as his orgasm played out, as tightly as he had when he'd first seen her.

As though he never intended to let her go.

They lay together, wrapped around one another, still connected. The water was still warm, and a pleasant weariness washed through Mercy. She had no intention of moving until he did.

After a time, Reaper relaxed. He drew her off of him, down beside him in the water. Lazily, he traced circles on her back with one hand. She waited, but he said nothing. His eyes were closed, and she could see the weariness weighing on him. Whatever he'd been through over the past few days had been hard.

Eventually, Mercy wondered if he'd fallen asleep, but then he stirred, the water rippling around them as he shifted and sat up. Wordlessly, he held his hand out to her, and she took it. Reaper pulled her to her feet, and together they stepped out of the bath. Telekinesis sluiced the water from their skin.

"You said you nearly died," she said. "Want to talk about that?"

The Core meeting was called before Reaper had time to rest beyond the little he and Mercy had already managed. They'd spent most of their time together talking, trading stories. He was still pale with exhaustion.

Cannon, likewise, looked tired. His stubble bordered on a full beard and dark circles hollowed around his eyes. Mercy wondered if he, too, had suffered an experience like Reaper's. She hadn't seen Atrea yet, but Wolfgang sent her a message. Her best friend was sleeping, so at least one of them was smart enough to rest. Mercy hadn't seen any of Reaper's dogs either, so she assumed they were doing the same.

Before Cannon had even taken his seat, Doc bore down on him, looking furious. A heated exchange took place. Well, the heat was largely on Doc's side. Cannon remained calm and immovable.

Mercy could guess the conversation. Doc took the crew's health seriously. He'd have wanted to examine everyone when they returned. Guessing by his irate gestures toward Cannon, and then Reaper, she was pretty sure they'd both dodged his attentions.

Did you forget to check in at the infirmary, she asked Reaper, amused.

Forget? No.

Cannon finally put a hand on the doctor's arm, saying something low that seemed to calm Doc. The doctor gave a grudging nod, but still looked pissed as he made his way back to his seat.

Looking at Cannon, Mercy realized all over again that he was not related to Lilith by blood, no matter his appearance. She looked at the other Core members as they entered the room and took up their places. If they knew, would it upset his position as King? Would they rebel against his leadership based solely on his bloodline?

Sebastian came in and nodded to her as he passed. His gaze collided with Reaper's and held for so long that Mercy wondered if they were having a private conversation. But then he turned away and took his seat near Doc. Vashti sat on his other side, and Griffin next to her.

Mercy frowned, looking at her aunt. Something was wrong. Vashti leaned into her chair as though it was the only thing holding her up. Beneath the dusky color of her skin, her face was wan. She looked old. Worse than when she'd left the infirmary, not better. Had she had another vision?

Reluctantly, she reached out to Griffin. *What's wrong with Vashti?*

How would I know? She doesn't tell me shit.

Taken aback, Mercy withdrew. Someone was

certainly bitter. She turned to Vashti, knowing before she asked that she wouldn't get a straight answer.

Are you all right?

Fine, dear. Just tired. Vashti met her eyes from across the room and managed a weary smile. Mercy suppressed a sigh. Why was nothing ever straightforward with her family? She resolved to corner her aunt after the meeting.

About half the Core members were attending via holo. Most of them were Captains of other ships. *Nemesis* had jumped back to pirate controlled space immediately after retrieving the dropship, and now, quietly, the fleet had been gathering. Just in the last hour, several ships had jumped in. Mercy felt it each time it happened, souls she'd claimed moving closer to her, their connection strengthening. Cannon must have issued an order, but thus far Mercy hadn't heard the reason behind the fleet's movement.

Perhaps he was preparing for war. With the alpha queen making her presence known so openly, Vashti's vision felt closer than ever. Reaper said the others had all experienced visions similar to his, so Cannon knew about the alpha queen now.

There was none of the usual chatter today. The general tone of the room was subdued and serious. Even the alcohol was missing. Valko was serving what looked like water and bottles of *mnemosa*. The tone was so vastly different from the last Core meeting she'd attended, that Wick didn't even sneer as she and and Reaper passed.

Or maybe he was just that scared of Reaper.

Once everyone had arrived, the doors closed. Only Treon's chair was empty, his absence an unease in the room. People kept glancing to that empty space. Treon might annoy people with his arrogance, but no one could deny that his extreme self-confidence was, at least in part, earned. They were now realizing that he was vulnerable, which only made them more aware of their own vulnerabilities.

Mercy sat beside Cannon, Reaper taking the chair to her other side.

Do you know something I don't? she asked Cannon. Up close, she could see how haggard he was. But his eyes glinted with something hard beneath the harsh lights in the room.

It seems a lot of people have been keeping secrets, he said. He cast a look down the tables at Vashti. *It stops today.*

He was furious, she realized. It burned beneath that weary exterior, tension obvious in the line of his shoulders, and in the taut muscle of his arms where they rested on the table.

Uncomfortable, she shifted in her seat. It occurred to her abruptly that she too, was keeping secrets from him. Her training with Lilith. What she'd learned there. Did Cannon even know he wasn't really her cousin? That Lilith wasn't his grandmother?

Now wasn't the time to bring it up, that was for sure.

What is it? Reaper asked, clearly picking up on her sudden unease.

Nothing. She hadn't had a chance to tell him

everything about her time with Lilith, yet. She would, but it would have to wait.

Around them, conversations buzzed throughout the room, some telepathic, some low-voiced as holo projections spoke with the live people beside them. From the bits Mercy could pick up, rumor was running wild. But most people had no idea what had truly happened. Veritas was mentioned more than once, with undercurrents of suspicion and dislike.

Where are the Veritas people? she asked Reaper. In the excitement of getting back him and the others, she'd forgotten to ask.

Safe, he said. *Once* Nemesis *jumped to retrieve us, people started speculating about what happened. Veritas featured heavily. Dem has them in custody for their own safety right now.*

That's not right. Worried, Mercy looked around for Dem. He was standing by the doors, arms crossed over his chest. Formidable, as always. *They should be here.*

Here? Reaper looked surprised. *This is a Core meeting, Mercy. We don't even allow other pirates to attend.*

This threat exists for all of us. They should be part of these discussions.

Reaper was silent. He swept the room with a look, then returned his gaze to her. *You think they'll accept that?*

Cannon stood before she could reply, and the room hushed.

"I'm going to start," he said, "by saying something that should be self-evident. I am King here. The Commonwealth might be a constitutional monarchy, but we are not." He looked at each Core member. "Debate as much as you like, but at the end of the day, my rule stands. Unless one of you would like to challenge me?"

No one said a word.

"Because I will take that challenge, here and now. Get it out of the fucking way, or shut the fuck up."

What is going on? Mercy asked Reaper on a tight thread.

I don't know.

"No one?" Cannon said. "Are you certain? Because someone here is colluding with our enemies. Someone in this room is a traitor and a spy."

Cannon, Mercy started to say.

Not now. His terse comment cut her off, and he shut her out completely. He was reading the room, she realized. She could see the flair of Talent from him, a radiance that seemed to glow from within.

"We have been wrong," he continued. "So wrong. For decades, someone kept a secret from us. Because of that silence, we have looked in the wrong direction for our enemy. We are now woefully unprepared for what is coming." He spent the next few minutes outlining Vashti's vision.

"I spoke with the precog who has experienced this vision at length prior to this meeting." He did not name Vashti, only described the vision and its frequency. He held up a hand when questions and comments filled the room. "I'm not done."

When they didn't quiet fast enough, he slammed a fist onto the table in front of him. *"I am not done."* A wave of Talent swept out from him.

Everyone fell silent under a blanket of unnatural calm.

"We have spent decades fighting Veritas. Warring with the wrong people. Meanwhile, our true enemy has had plenty of time to prepare, to gather intelligence on us, and to place her spies." Cannon looked around the room. "I've met her, the queen who is coming. She makes Lilith seem like a pleasant dream." He went on to describe how he, Reaper, and the others had been pulled into telepathic interactions with her. How Treon's interference had interrupted that.

Mercy gave Reaper a questioning look.

Apparently, when Treon pulled me from the landscape, it disrupted all of them.

"There is no doubt in my mind that we got lucky," Cannon continued. "I have no idea where I would be right now without Treon's efforts. Where Reaper would be."

He swept a hand to the side, gesturing to Mercy. "Mercy is our Queen. Since apparently there is some resistance to that, let me be clear: Mercy. Is. *Queen.* And she is all the protection we have right now. Her claiming is the *only* thing that helped me in that place."

No pressure, thought Mercy. Reaper's hand brushed hers beneath the table.

Pale faces looked back at Cannon as he sat down.

"Now, questions?"

Instead of erupting into pandemonium, silence ruled the room. People looked at one another, looked at Mercy, at Cannon. The unnatural calm Cannon had imposed still covered them.

"Veritas is not our enemy?" Xavier asked doubtfully.

"We have both been manipulated against each other," Cannon said.

"So, we are to forget everything they have done?" Wick said.

"Of course not. That isn't realistic. However, we must put aside our past, or risk being divided and vulnerable when *she* comes for us. And she *will* come."

"What does Veritas say?" one of the holo figures asked. Mercy couldn't remember his name.

Mason, Reaper told her.

"We don't know." Cannon shook his head, weary. "Several of their people did not survive our encounter. The handful who remain are not recovering as fast as we would like. I haven't been able to speak with them, but I believe their encounter with the queen differed from ours in some way. Perhaps because they have not accepted Mercy's claim, they were more vulnerable." He sighed. "Even if they recover, I don't know that we can trust them. I've reached out to our own people in their territory, and have yet to hear back."

"What of this spy you mentioned?" Dem asked, his voice a low rumble.

A murmur of discontent swept the room.

"He will reveal himself in time," Cannon said. "I have no doubt of that."

"And until then?"

"Until then, we prepare as best we can. I've called in the fleet. I'm asking each of you to be vigilant, and remember what is at stake when we speak with Veritas. Peace is now a necessity."

"There are many ways for a vision to be interpreted," Wick said thoughtfully.

Cannon looked at him. "Yes, you have a theory?"

He spread his hands. "I'm merely saying that it would be wrong to jump to conclusions. Historically, visions are difficult to interpret. They carry symbolism. One thing which may appear obvious might actually mean something completely different. This destructive harbinger, for example. You theorize a supernova, because the visions showed the mass extinction of worlds, and a supernova is one thing capable of such wreckage. But what if the worlds destroyed are a consequence of the harbinger, not a direct result?"

Down the tables, Mercy saw Vashti start before she caught herself. Her Aunt's lips thinned as she suppressed whatever she'd been about to say.

Cannon frowned. "All right. What else do you think it could be?"

"I don't know." Wick looked thoughtful. "The last time the galaxy knew such devastation was during the Ascension Wars."

"War on such a massive scale would require the destabilization of the entire government."

"Yes."

"From everything we hear of the Commonwealth, the Council of Sovereign Planets is solid, as is the monarchy. The King and Queen are in good health, the royal line is secure, and the Council as insufferable as ever. Their largest conflict is with us."

A chill touched Mercy. Vashti's words came back to her. *"Once this event happens, it will throw the*

Commonwealth into chaos. The monarchy will be gone. The government as it currently exists will be gone. A power vacuum will exist."

As much as she hated to admit it, with was right.

"He's right," Vashti said. She sounded defeated, her head bowed. "It's been a mistake, all these years, keeping this hidden. A terrible mistake. First, we were trying to protect the succession and prevent a panic. Lilith was so young, and the Queen's death so sudden. Neither of us was thinking clearly, I'm afraid. Later, Lilith insisted we remain silent. She said we didn't know who to trust, that anyone could be a tool of the alpha queen. If I'd spoken up, would my sister have made different choices? Would she have been a different person?" She shook herself, as though waking herself from her thoughts.

She nodded to Cannon. "Thank you for protecting me as far you have, but I must speak the whole truth." She looked at Wick, then at the others. "I am the source of the vision, the precog Cannon refused to name. I had the first vision the night my mother died. This threat, this alpha queen, killed her. Lilith and I tried to save her. We failed.

"We decided the event had to be something on the scale of a supernova, but it is correct that we should not assume that. Anything that destroys the government of the Commonwealth could be the harbinger. As Wick said, it is even possible that the destruction we saw was a consequence, not a direct result. I was a fool not to see it sooner."

Vashti, Mercy thought, had also been very young when she'd first had this vision.

"If this queen attacked and killed Kiana some fifty years ago, why has she not moved against us in the time since?" Dem asked. "Clearly, that was an attack. And, ultimately, successful. Why not follow it up with something more?"

"I don't know," Vashti said.

"I might." Mercy was reluctant to speak. She didn't want to explain how she knew this. She focused on Vashti while everyone else looked at her. "The alpha's true goal wasn't just killing Kiana. She wanted to *be* her. To take her place. Correct?"

Vashti nodded. "Yes."

"She failed. When you told me about this event, you said Lilith was knocked across the room. That Kiana shoved her out of her mind."

"She did."

"If that's true, maybe it was more than that. What if she attacked the alpha queen? What if Kiana died in some final sacrifice that wounded her? So severely that it's taken the alpha a long time to recover. Or, at the very least, it's made her cautious. She could have been active all these years, manipulating events behind the scenes. Maybe *she* pushed Veritas against us. Keep us at odds, and it makes us vulnerable. *All* of us."

"That's a lot of guesswork," Cannon said.

"It is. I don't know if it even matters. The past is less important than what is happening right now."

He rubbed a hand over his jaw. "True."

"We need to figure out how to get in touch with Veritas and extend a hand of peace. We must end hostilities before the alpha queen makes a concentrated attack against us." Before the visions came to pass, and she took control of them. Mercy thought of Lilith's theory, that the alpha queen had several others who served her, other queens she could send throughout the galaxy to do her bidding.

And that she would take one whenever she wished a younger body.

They needed a united front if they were to have any hope of defeating her.

Around the room, several of the holo projections were suddenly disrupted, fizzling out one by one amidst curses.

Mercy felt a sudden influx of hundreds, no thousands of Talented minds. So overwhelming, she doubled over, grasping at her head. She fed power to her mental shields, and the overwhelming feeling vanished. She could still sense them, but they were distant stars, held at bay by her shields. More and more minds gathered closer.

"What is it?" Cannon asked sharply.

"A fleet has jumped into the system," Sebastian said. "Veritas." He paused. "They're demanding we return their people and give them Rani, or they will open fire."

Mercy felt the blood drain from her head. She looked at Cannon. "We can't give them Rani. It's not just about her anymore. She's unstable. Knowing what we know, waking her up would be a huge security risk. She could already belong to the alpha queen."

Cannon cursed. "Something tells me they

aren't going to be pleased when they find out the condition of their people, either." He pushed away from the table. "Sebastian, sound general quarters. Let's try to negotiate, but all hands to battle stations." He looked at Mercy. "Are you ready to revisit those peace negotiations?"

ercy followed Cannon onto the lift that would take them to the CIC. She didn't realize Reaper wasn't with her until the doors were closing.

"Wait!" She lunged forward, stopping them with a hand. Reaper, already moving down the hall, turned back.

What is it?

"Where are you going?"

"I fly with my dogs," Reaper said. "My corvette is fast, maneuverable, and more heavily armored than the interceptors. I can be support to our fighters and protection for capital ships." He exchanged a look with Cannon. "If this turns into a fight."

She stepped out of the lift and gave him a quick, hard kiss. *Be careful.*

He squeezed her arm lightly, then let go and took off down the hallway. Mercy got back onto the lift, trying to control her worry. She was aware of Cannon giving her a long look as the doors closed.

"He'll be fine," he said. "He's Reaper."

"That doesn't mean he's invulnerable."

"No, but he is a damn sight harder to kill than most people." He looked down, his hands folded in front of him. "Have you thought about what you might have to do to stop this?"

"Controlling them like puppets will only make this worse, and delay the inevitable. It will piss them off, and I can't control them forever." Mercy crossed her arms. "We need to make peace."

"Be that as it may, there may be no choice."

"There is always a choice."

The lift came to a stop, and they stepped out together. Organized chaos reigned. Personnel manned duty stations in a flurry of activity, both physical and telepathic. The fleet checked in one ship after another, shields were powered, and squadrons of fighters were given their orders as they queued up to launch. Sebastian stood in the middle of it all, with his hands clasped behind his back. He'd been among the first to leave the meeting. His Talent was active, and Mercy saw it as strands of golden light emanating from him, spread out in brilliant lines that seemed to connect with every station. It criss-crossed the room in a pattern that was at once beautiful and distracting.

Mercy blinked, closing her eyes. Lilith had shown her how to let Talent fade to the background so that she wasn't blinded every time someone used it around her. When she opened her eyes, she still saw Sebastian's threads, but in a much more subdued presence.

"Report," said Cannon, striding into the room. Mercy followed more slowly. She'd never been up here when the viewport blast shield was open. She could see the entire fleet arrayed before them, ships moving into battle positions, squaring off against the incoming fleet Veritas had sent. A fleet that continued getting bigger. Large and small, flashes of incoming jumps appeared in the distance, glinting like water under starlight.

"Current count is fifteen ships," Sebastian said, "mostly cruisers and frigates, but they do have two — make that three — destroyers. And they're still coming. Range is point-zero-five light seconds. Targeting has several vectors, but they are still well outside the field of engagement."

Cannon eyed the viewport, rubbing his chin. Mercy could almost hear him thinking. If they attacked now, before Veritas had finished moving its fleet into position, they would be at a huge advantage. But they would have to close distance, and in that time, Veritas could move their ships into more defensive positions.

In space, combat involved a lot of closing distance, firing weapons, and trying to shoot the enemy's weapons down before they breached your hull. Repeat until one side capitulated or everyone was dead.

And if they started this, they could kiss goodbye any hope for peace and unity. Mercy stepped up beside him. "Cannon, let me talk to them. We need to end this peacefully."

"They came looking for a fight, Mercy." He stared into her eyes. "And how did they find us? Let me tell you: our traitor gave up our coordinates. Who knows what else he's told them?"

"You seem awfully certain the spy is male." He'd said *he* in the Core meeting as well.

His eyes narrowed. "I am almost *completely* certain."

"You know who it is," she said, cocking her head. "Why haven't you arrested them?"

"Because there is small sliver of room for a mistake. I'm giving him just enough rope to hang himself. Let's see what he does with it." There was something dark and vicious in Cannon's eyes. Right then, he reminded her so strongly of Lilith that Mercy almost didn't believe he wasn't really her grandson.

His gaze snagged on hers, and he frowned. "What?"

"Nothing. Look, whatever he's told them doesn't matter. None of this bullshit matters except *her*. She's coming, and they don't know about her yet."

"You don't know that. They might be working *with* her, for all we know."

"Or, they might have no idea that they're playing a role in a much larger battle. You agreed in the meeting that we need to join forces with Veritas to survive what's coming. Right now, you're looking at a whole fleet of the enemy you've wanted to destroy for at least the last decade. It's clouding your judgement." Mercy gestured to the growing number of ships visible through the viewport. "Let me talk to them. At least let me try."

Cannon never took his eyes from her face. "Hail them," he ordered.

"Yes, sir." A young man opened a channel, then

nodded to Mercy. She felt a polite brush at her shields. *It's open, Your Majesty. You are connected to their flagship, the destroyer* Valiant.

She barely winced at the title. *Thank you.* Nervous, she cleared her throat. Cannon touched her arm lightly and she hesitated, looking at him in question.

"*Valiant,*" he said aloud, "this is *Nemesis* actual. Her Majesty the Queen would like a word." He grinned at her.

Mercy rolled her eyes. He took far too much pleasure in calling her that.

"This is *Valiant* actual." The voice on the other end was male. "Does this mean you're ready to hand over our people?"

Mercy let out a long breath, steadying herself before replying. "Your people are safe, but currently being tended to by our chief medical officer. They escaped Birn with us, but both groups suffered casualties, which we are treating. It would be unsafe to move them at this time."

"Stalling won't help you," the voice said. "If any of our people are injured, the last place we want them is with you. You will return *all* of them to us. Feria and those from the peace summit you so *graciously* arranged, as well as the rest you have stolen. And Rani."

That was clearly out of the question. Even if Mercy had been willing, Rani was now a dangerous liability. They could not afford to wake up a young, unstable queen. She was too vulnerable.

"I'm not stalling. Surely, in that entire fleet you've mustered, you have someone capable of truth sensing. Test me."

"As Queen, you could still lie."

Could she? Well, if she could force them to stand down, she supposed she could also force them to believe her. But if they believed her capable of that, what made them think they stood a chance in this fight?

"As Queen, I could also force you to stop this. Have you considered that?"

The com was silent.

"*Valiant?*"

"You're new to your abilities. Untrained, by all reports. If you think you can stop us, try."

"That's not what I—"

"They're gone, Your Majesty. The channel is closed."

"Damn it, get them back."

After a moment, the crewman shook his head. "I'm sorry, Your Majesty. They're not responding."

"Range is point-zero-three light seconds, and closing," Sebastian said. "They're moving into attack position."

"Their weapons are powering up," another crewman said.

"You've had your chance," said Cannon. "I told you they wouldn't back down."

"We can't afford this battle," she said. *Why* could none of them understand that? "Cannon, please."

She held his gaze, nearly holding her breath.

Sebastian cursed, pulling their attention to him.

"Two more clusters of ships have jumped in. Commonwealth Navy, destroyers and...a Monarch-class. They're bearing two-point-seven-mark-five, and eight-point-three-mark-one. Flanking positions." He looked at Cannon. "Range: less than point-zero-one light second."

"Weapons hot," a crewman said.

"Closing blast shields," Sebastian said. The viewport grew smaller as the blast shields slowly moved back over it. A screen popped up, a holographic replication of the view outside. A second screen showed a map of each ship's position in relation to the pirate fleet, differentiating fleets with clear, bright colors.

"I'm sorry," Cannon said to Mercy. He turned away. "Defensive formation, and launch interceptors."

Mother damn it.

Helplessly, Mercy watched the colorful flickers of movement on the holoscreen as the Veritas fleet launched their fighters. A sense of dread filled her. *This is what she wants,* she thought. *This is exactly what she wants.*

Whatever the consequence, she *could not* allow this to happen. It was playing right into the hands of a future that would see them all but destroyed. *Fuck it,* she thought. She reached out for the strands that connected her to every pirate, to every Veritas agent, to every Talented person here.

She reached out, and hit a wall.

What the hell?

She could feel them, all of them. But she could only touch the strands that belonged to pirates. The others were closed off to her. As though they were shielded somehow. How was that possible? She tried again. And again.

It was no use. She glanced down at her wrist.

Where was Lilith when she needed her? What could block a Queen from reaching her people? They'd never covered that possibility.

Out the viewport, the first fighters engaged. Flashes of plasma and particle beam salvos strafed the space between them. Mercy felt the bright lights of Talented minds snuff out, each one like a wound gouged out of her psyche. She staggered.

Cannon caught her arm, holding her up.

"Mercy?"

Light headed, she had to let go of the strands or risk passing out.

"I tried," she said, her breaths short and too fast. "I can't control them." She looked at Cannon. "I can't stop this."

*

REAPER WATCHED the fleet power weapons on his scope. He switched his targeting view to the destroyers, and sure enough, they were moving into an attack formation that would place them on a vector for *Revenant* and two other cruisers. Destroyers carried heavy batteries of missiles at the sacrifice of faster maneuvering. However, the battlecruisers weren't nimble enough themselves to completely escape a deadly salvo. They'd have to rely on their turrets and fighters to shoot down the missiles.

Mason.

I see them. Launching interceptors.

Reaper sent a command to Ghost and the rest of his squadron. Then he followed them in with the corvette.

Boss, said Ghost. *They have a fucking Monarch.*

I see it.

It seemed Veritas had brought a few Navy ships with their personal fleet. Anyway you looked at it, the pirates were outgunned. Outgunned in space combat was almost always certain death. Too much depended on being able to launch superior firepower at your opponent. Reaper opened his Talent as his dogs engaged enemy fighters. He could see the entirety of the battle like one big organism. Weak points flashed through him, one after another.

At the moment, it looked like he was fighting on the losing side.

He felt the trap close around them the moment those Navy ships jumped in on flanking vectors. It was a risky gamble that could have cost them their fleet. One small calculation off, and it could have killed them all, both groups of ships dying in a jump disaster. But instead, the gamble paid off, and now the pirates were caught in trap that would slowly tighten around them.

Reaper felt more than saw the enemy fighters closing on his position. He fired on them even as he dropped his corvette's nose, his ship diving beneath their incoming trajectory so they passed harmlessly overhead. The dive had cost him the kill, his plasma salvo skimming by them and scoring no hits.

Below him, Jaxon fired on an enemy ship, the cockpit cracking like a shell as plasma peppered across it. Another fighter closed in behind Jax, and Reaper fired a disruptor burst. It missed, but the fighter veered off, straight into the path of Knox's weapons. A burst of fire from Knox sheered the enemy ship's stabilizer in two. The fighter spun wildly, ejected from the combat area as though thrown by some unseen, giant hand. The cockpit blew off in a pressurized burst, the pilot floating free.

Reaper left him. He was no longer a threat.

They were outnumbered nearly two to one, multiple enemy fighters engaging each of their interceptors. Reaper tried to save his Talent during ship-to-ship combat. Sometimes, a strategic strike against an enemy commander could turn the tide of a battle completely. But today he couldn't afford to wait. His own squadron and two others were fighting a losing battle. He could feel death all around him as ships were systematically trapped and destroyed by groups of enemy fighters.

He closed his eyes, seeking the minds around him. All of his dogs still lived; he felt them first. Jaxon, Knox, Titus, Ghost, and Zion. He felt other minds familiar to him: Mason's fighters and another squadron of dogs. Griffin's men, he realized, though Griffin himself was curiously absent. Reaper had never known him to miss a fight.

He marked each of these, and expanded his awareness to include others, those unfamiliar to him. They were heavily shielded, but Reaper's Talent sought out the flaws in each one. He spread tendrils of Talent to each of them...three, seven, ten, fourteen...he arrowed his Talent through the tiny flaws in their shields. Some cracked. Others shattered. Nine minds went dark as his Talent burrowed deep, killing them instantly.

Ships veered off target or collided with wingmen. Three more minds went dark.

Twelve enemy pilots were dead, but the battle had a long way to go and more fighters were already moving in to reinforce those remaining.

Boss, I'm in trouble. Ahead of him, Ghost did a hard turn trying to evade two enemy interceptors. But they anticipated the move. One of the fighters turned, angling in a way that put Ghost in a bad spot between them. Titus fired at one, but missed.

Above you, said Reaper as an interceptor arrowed down toward Titus. The medic broke off from Ghost's attackers to evade his own.

Reaper was at the wrong angle; he didn't have a shot. He turned the corvette, knowing even as he did it, he would be too late.

Ghost, eject, he said.

The pilots all wore flight suits designed to survive for a short time in the deadly vacuum of space. But oxygen was limited. Ghost would have less than twenty minutes of survivability — assuming he wasn't killed the moment he ejected.

The enemy ships fired. There was no way Ghost would clear the blast in time. The cockpit shell burst open seconds before the plasma salvos hit. Reaper didn't see Ghost as his ship tore apart.

Finally lining up the enemy ships, he fired from both batteries. They'd been so intent on killing Ghost, neither pilot had seen the threat until too late. Reaper caught them dead on. The hull of one cracked, oxygen and nitrogen venting into space seconds before the ship broke apart. The other ship went dead, power and engines knocked out. Reaper used the pilot's panic to get past his shields, killing him.

A whisper brushed Reaper's mind. *Ghost.* It was faint, but unmistakable.

Reaper looked for him, but could see no sign of the dog floating through space.

Ghost, report.

The silence dragged on. Frustration penetrated the cold cocoon around Reaper. He did a sensor sweep of the area but it was impossible to differentiate a single human form from the combat scrap rapidly filling the area. Large and small pieces of ships floated and spun in a growing field of debris.

Around him, the battle continued. Reaper couldn't afford to spend any more time looking for Ghost. He turned his attention back to the enemy fighters.

"Boss."

Shock made Reaper start violently. He turned to find his dog materializing in the copilot's seat next to him. Ghost's face was a pale smear inside his flight helmet. Reaper barely turned aside the reflexive wave of Talent that would kill him.

Ghost? What in the hell had just happened? Teleportation?

That made no sense. Teleporters were rare and limited to a powerful branch of the kinesis family of gifts, specifically telekinesis. Ghost's Talent wasn't kinetic, it was telepathic in nature. His telekinesis was so weak he could only move small objects short distances.

Ghost could never be a teleporter.

What then?

Boss! Ghost grabbed at the copilot's controls. In his shock, Reaper had allowed the battle to fade from his awareness. Interceptors were closing on them, fast.

They had nowhere to go.

*THE BATTLE UNFOLDED BEFORE MERCY. Some of the larger ships were engaged now. Before her horrified gaze, a cruiser broke apart. Pieces of the hull spun into the path of the fighters, destroying three of them as they collided with it.

She could feel them, all of them, the living and the dying.

No, no, no. How had Lilith handled this? They hadn't covered the effects of battle on the Queen.

A deep foreboding filled her. This was intensely, horribly wrong. What if this battle was the harbinger of everything to come? Of everything Vashti saw? Something or *someone* was blocking her from reaching the Veritas minds. It didn't seem possible, but that shield was very real.

Could they have another queen? Could the alpha queen be *here*?

Dimly, she heard Cannon issuing orders. Sebastian had become *Nemesis,* guiding the huge ship with his thoughts. She felt more and more minds around her burn out, flashes of Talent fading to black voids again and again.

Reaper. A frisson on awareness made her reach for him. He was trapped, his corvette taking fire. *No!*

Even as she thought the denial, a familiar ship

joined the battle, seemingly from nowhere. The fighter from Wolfgang's frigate. It strafed the ships closing on Reaper's position, destroying them.

Atrea and Wolfgang.

Thank the Mother. For a moment, Mercy closed her eyes and fought back fear and tears.

Mercy, you can't afford to be distracted. Reaper's voice entered her mind. Calm, as he always was. *Only you can end this.*

He was right, of course.

I'm trying, she sent back.

She felt him engaging more enemy ships. *Try faster.*

She closed her eyes and adjusted her scan to look, not for those she had connections *to*, but for those she didn't.

With a shock, she realized there was one mind here, aboard *Nemesis.* And like those of the Veritas ships, she couldn't touch it at all.

What the hell? That should have been impossible. There shouldn't have been a single person aboard this ship who didn't belong to her.

The unclaimed mind was in the infirmary. She glanced at Cannon and Sebastian. Both of them were busy with the battle. They didn't need her here, but if she could figure this out, maybe she could stop this whole mess.

She left while they were distracted.

She ran into Griffin as she stepped out of the lift on her way to the infirmary. His face was ashen.

"What is it?" she asked.

"Vashti. She's— I think she's had another vision. She fell in her quarters, hit her head. It's bad."

Mercy glanced down and saw the smear of blood on one of his hands. Her heart gave painful thump. Griffin didn't look injured, so that had to be Vashti's blood.

"I was going to the infirmary," he said. His eyes were glassy. "She went down hard, hit the corner of the table." His gaze dropped, unable or unwilling to meet her eyes. "I left the room for one damn minute. One." His voice was bitter. "I didn't want to move her. I need Doc, or—"

"Doc isn't in the infirmary," she said. She'd felt him in her scan of the ship. Both he and Nayla were on the hangar deck. "They're in the hangar." But they were busy helping injured pilots. She knew, however important Vashti was, however fond of her Doc might be, he wouldn't abandon the injured and dying for one person. Still, he might have someone he could spare. Nayla's gift made her a natural fit for the infirmary, but she was far from his only staff.

She frowned suddenly. "Why didn't you send for Doc telepathically?"

Griffin shook his head. "I reached out, but Doc is closed off. He does that when he's working sometimes. When a distraction might be dangerous to his work." He stared at his hands. "She was convulsing when I found her. I don't know if that was the head injury, or the vision. What if she saw something we need to know? Something about the battle?"

Mercy wondered the same thing. If the alpha queen was here, Vashti might well have seen something of vital importance. That realization shifted her priorities. Not only was Vashti hurt, but she might have information Mercy needed.

"Maybe I can help her," she said aloud. If she could borrow Nayla's gift again, as she had when Wolfgang almost died.

A small part of Mercy wavered. She still needed to find out what the *hell* was going on with her connection to Veritas. Something was preventing her from reaching them. Her connection hadn't been severed, just blocked. And the person in the infirmary, whoever it was, might have answers for her.

But it wasn't a choice. Not really. Mercy needed to go to Vashti. The infirmary, and whoever was in it, would just have to wait.

She remembered Reaper's words. *Try faster.* Everything seemed to be fighting against her right now.

"Go," she said to Griffin. "Get to the hangar. Ask Doc to spare one of his people to come help." In case Mercy failed. "I'll go wait with Vashti."

He hesitated, so she shoved at him. "Go!"

He got back on the lift, still looking dazed as the doors closed on him. Worry spiked adrenaline through Mercy. Griffin was a seasoned pirate. If he was this affected, Vashti had to be in real trouble.

Maybe dying.

Mercy had to help her. She waited anxiously for the next lift.

You still need answers. Somehow, her inner voice sounded a lot like Lilith. *One person's life isn't worth sacrificing that knowledge.*

Mercy set her jaw as the lift opened. Instinct

told her she needed to know whatever Vashti had seen if she wanted to end this. And she was damn well not sacrificing anyone. She hesitated, her hand hovering over the controls. She needed help, someone else to investigate for her. Reaper and his dogs were all flying in the battle. Every available pilot was in a ship, flying with the fleet. That included Atrea and Wolfgang.

Hell, was every single person she cared about fighting?

Wait a minute. She knew exactly who *wouldn't* be out there. And he was in the infirmary. He might be able to get the answers she needed.

Treon, she sent. *Wake up.* She touched the strand of connection she had to him, sending the command down the link. *I need your help.*

CHAPTER TWENTY-FIVE

reon woke, reaching for a bottle of *mnemosa* that wasn't there. His hand flailed for a moment, and then his brain caught up with him and he blinked, looking around. He groaned.

He was in the Mother-damned infirmary, instead of his own quarters.

The lights were dim, and the only noise came from Doc's various tech and machines, which beeped or made other odd sounds occasionally.

Where was everyone? Only one other bed was occupied. A young woman, one he didn't recognize, which immediately intrigued him. Sitting up, he reached out with his Talent, wincing at the slight headache even so small an action produced. Well, one couldn't expect to recover all at once.

To his surprise, he *did* recognize the young woman after all. Her mind, at any rate. It was the slave from the dropship, but she was now clean and wearing one of Doc's unfortunate synth-cotton gowns which he so graciously forced on patients. With a grimace, Treon realized he was wearing one himself.

He tugged at the ugly thing, hating the rasp as it brushed over his skin. Synth cotton was nowhere near as soft as the real thing. Treon hopped off his bed. This wasn't his first infirmary visit. If he remembered correctly…he pressed his hand to the drawer attached to the bed's undercarriage, and it opened to reveal his clothing, clean and folded neatly.

He hesitated, but the young woman appeared asleep. At least, her eyes were closed and her breathing even. He shrugged. Even if she woke, it wasn't as though modesty was a concern of his. Treon stripped off the offending gown and dressed, feeling more himself the moment he got rid of the horrid garment.

He cast his mind outward, careful not to stretch too far. His headache increased but was still at tolerable levels. A scattering of varied thoughts greeted him, all focused on one thing: battle. It appeared *Nemesis* was engaged in combat. How very like him to sleep through it.

"Well that explains where Doc is," he murmured to no one in particular. "And Nayla too, I suppose." Both would be down on the hangar deck, where a triage area would be set up for pilots injured in the fighting.

The most serious cases would be brought here when the worst of the battle was over. Treon would be long gone when that happened, having escaped back to his quarters, safe from Doc's lectures and admonishments.

And where he could drink *mnemosa*. Doc would have none here. The good doctor was a stickler for natural recovery. He disapproved of the overuse of stimulants.

But if Treon had any hope of helping in this battle, he was going to need some. He started for the door, then stopped. What had woken him? He had a vague impression of Mercy asking him to do something, but nothing more.

A memory came to him, of scanning the young woman on the dropship, and the intriguing feel of her mind. The hidden depths and secrets it might hold. Thoughtful, he turned back into the room and crossed to her bed.

No longer hidden behind a camouflaging layer of grime and neglect, she was younger than he'd imagined. In her early twenties, he'd guess. She had very pale skin, though some of the starkness was likely due to her condition. Her face was all sharp angles, with a wide mouth and hollow cheeks that accentuated high, slashing cheekbones. Too thin, her features would probably soften if she ate properly and put on a healthy weight.

Someone, probably Nayla, had taken the time to comb out the hopeless tangle of her long hair. So dark it was almost black, it looked dull and lackluster at the moment. It, too, would likely be improved with a proper diet and nutrition. Doc would have cut it off if left to his own devices. But his young protege, Nayla, had a soft spot for making patients comfortable and happy.

Treon wasn't yet recovered enough to mentally

scan her with any depth. But that didn't mean he couldn't get a feel for her Talent. He reached out lightly, careful not to overextend himself. A thrum of power had him pulling back.

Shocked, he realized she was at this moment actively using her gifts. He cocked his head. Was she sleeping? Or was her consciousness not currently occupying her body?

He cast his gaze around and it landed on the wall of Doc's drawers and cupboards. Treon rummaged through them until he found what he was looking for. He tore open the capsulet, examining the sharp point of the needle. Yes, that would do nicely.

Without preamble, he used it to prick the girl's finger. She came awake with a shriek, her hand reeling out to crack him full in the face.

Ouch. For someone so physically weak, she hit him hard enough that he saw stars for a few seconds.

Being startled awake should have disrupted her Talent as well. But it hadn't. He could still feel the thrum of power from her.

"Extraordinary," he said.

She stared at him wildly, then scrambled back as far from him as she could get without falling off of her bed. He held up his hands to indicate he meant her no harm, then realized he was still holding the capsulet. He set it down, then showed her his empty hand.

"I only meant to wake you. You're...well, I'm not sure what you're doing, exactly, but you are definitely doing something with your Talent. I'm not at my best, or I could tell you what, and maybe even why. But perhaps you know?" He looked at her hopefully. Nothing annoyed Treon more than a mystery he couldn't solve.

His words did not seem to comfort her. She looked around, her face pale and her eyes wide, taking in Doc's machines, the infirmary bed, her synth-cotton gown. Her mouth dropped open in horror.

"Yes, I can see what this might look like. But you're safe here. We rescued you." This was *so* much easier when he could introduce himself in the fantasy world of a telepathic landscape. No scary medical infirmaries, for one thing.

It occurred to him to wonder why she was here, when no one else from the dropship was. He'd felt Reaper's mind in his brief scan, his brother's thoughts fully engaged in the battle outside.

It was nice to know Reaper had survived and was apparently feeling well enough to go straight into combat. Perhaps the others had similarly recovered from their ordeal.

In any case, one mystery at a time. He already had one to solve, and she continued to cower away from him, gaze darting around the room in suspicion and horror.

"Let's start with something simple," he offered, his voice soft. "My name is Treon. And you are?"

She stared at him. Her eyes were still wide, still terrified. Was there something wrong with his face? Usually women found it pleasant to look at.

"My brother found you on a Commonwealth Navy ship. You were being held as a slave. We freed you. You're safe here, with us. Like you, we are Talented." Telekinesis wasn't his strong suit, but he floated a cup from the sink to his hand. "See?" The headache began to beat an unhappy tempo behind his eyes. He had to stop using Talent before he passed out again.

Still, the display seemed to have the desired effect. It calmed her. She was no longer looking at him like he might carve her into pieces at any moment. She remained sitting at the far end of her infirmary bed, but did relax enough to study him. She had eyes so deep a blue, they flashed violet beneath the infirmary lights. Interesting. He caught no glint of tech or enhancement.

Well, they were definitely not Killer blue, of that he was certain.

"Shall we try again?" he asked with a smile. "My name is Treon." He gestured. "And you?"

She hesitated, eyeing him.

"I promise, no harm will come to you here. We make a habit of freeing slaves when we find them. You're clean and cared for, which is much more than I can say for the condition we found you in." He shrugged. "I can address you as 'woman' or 'girl', if you'd prefer."

By her grimace, he thought she did *not* prefer.

She shrugged thin shoulders. "They call me Thirteen."

A ridiculous name, but he wasn't about to tell her that. Had she been a slave for so long that she no longer remembered her real name? Or perhaps she never had one. The irony never failed to amaze him, that nulls, so lacking in real power, could so easily enslave his people. Often, they indoctrinated them from infancy to believe they couldn't escape, destroying their sense of self-worth until the slave believed themselves to be utterly inferior to their head blind masters. It was infuriating.

He kept the anger from showing on his face, holding his easy smile. "There, you see? That was easy. Now, what exactly are you doing with your Talent there?"

She hesitated, and he did his best to project a harmless, comforting persona.

"I'm…gathering motes of energy and layering them. Filling in the flaws."

He blinked. *What?* "I'm sorry? You're gathering motes of energy?" What the hell kind of Talent was that?

She looked confused. "Yes. You know. You do the same thing." She gestured to him, then frowned. "But you're very thin right now. You should replenish."

All right. So the girl wasn't crazy, she was just describing things oddly. Because he *was* very thin on his reserves of power right now, and he *did* need to replenish. But what did that mean for her? That thrum of power he felt, she was doing *something* more active than pulling on her reserves.

"Could you describe that a little more?" he asked. "What you're doing, I mean. I used telekinesis to float this cup to my hand. I used telepathy to test your shields. Are you doing anything like that?"

She shook her head, then stopped, seeming to consider his words more carefully.

"Maybe. Not *testing* shields. Making them strong."

Odd. Whatever she was doing had the feel of something large scale. Strengthening her personal shields was definitely low on the list of probabilities. Was she lying to him? Being deliberately evasive? He began to grow even more irritated. If he'd had even half his strength available to him right now, he wouldn't be wondering these things.

"*Whose* shields are you making strong?" he asked.

The infirmary was completely closed in. It was built in one of the central, inner areas of the ship. No handy viewports existed with which to view what was happening outside. But she jerked her chin toward where he knew the battle was taking place.

Damn, he would kill for some *mnemosa*. Wincing in anticipation of how much it was about to hurt, Treon sent his mind out questing. Normally, reaching the battle would have been child's play, but his range was hampered by his condition. He had to strain to reach, his head throbbing with every second he tried.

Got it, he thought, triumphant. Then his head tried to split open and he groaned, falling against one of the empty beds. The girl jumped back, but he couldn't spare a moment for her.

He had the answer to his question, but it didn't matter. She was working with the enemy, strengthening their shields. And he couldn't do anything about it. *Idiot,* he told himself. He'd seen a pretty face, emaciated from starvation and ill treatment, and he'd assumed she was helpless.

Now *he* was the helpless one, the last of his reserves utterly spent.

His vision went gray, then white, and he felt himself slipping, falling. *Mother damn it*, he thought.

Then he passed out.

ercy found Vashti right where Griffin left her, lying on the floor of her quarters, unconscious. She was on her stomach, crumpled and frail looking, her face unnaturally gray beneath the fall of her long hair, the white and black strands matted with blood. A broken teapot lay on the floor beside her, its contents mixing with the pool of blood that soaked her robes.

"Vashti." Mercy went to her knees beside her aunt, carefully brushing the hair back from her face. She didn't have to check for a pulse. Mercy could feel Vashti's mind, a bright spark of warmth that pulsed faintly.

That pulse was concerning. Most of the time, the minds around Mercy were steady, bright lights. She started to reach out mentally, but hesitated. Would she do more harm than good, connecting to Vashti's thoughts?

No, best to go straight for Nayla's Talent and see what that revealed. She took a deep breath. This would be her first time "borrowing" Talent in the real world since Lillith's training. She should be able to do it without disrupting Nayla. She hoped.

She reached for the unique spark that was the young biokinetic's mind. Nayla's thoughts were focused behind her shields, bent to treating the wounded as they came into the hangar.

Surviving space battle was a tricky proposition at the best of times. Most damage that destroyed a ship also killed the pilot and crew. But cockpits were designed to protect the fragile human lives inside. Short of that, flight suits were fully space worthy, at least until oxygen ran out. During any battle there were gunships tasked with finding and recovering wounded.

Just now, Nayla was treating one of those wounded. Mercy didn't look to see how bad it was. The mental light of the man's mind was faint, so dim it was barely perceptible.

This was why she hadn't tried to pull Doc or his people to help Vashti. In the midst of a battle, it felt as though she'd be choosing one life over others. She didn't look to see who they were working on, afraid it might be someone she knew. Afraid it might divert her focus. Instead, she concentrated on Nayla. The girl's Talent burned so bright, it was blinding.

Breathe. Concentrate. Lilith's voice was an oddly soothing cadence in her mind. *Don't let yourself be distracted.*

That was new and disconcerting. Could Lilith really talk to her like this? Be in her mind whenever she wanted?

You need to assimilate the girl's gift, not worry about me.

"I am always worried about you," Mercy said aloud.

A waste of time. I am not your enemy. And you need my sister. Stop stalling.

Just as acerbic as ever. It was definitely Lilith.

But she was right. Mercy did need Vashti. Cautiously, she reached for Nayla's Talent. Each Talent had a unique feel. Reaper's was cold and perhaps the most overt, but all of them had an identifying signature. Nayla's felt sharp, like the edge of a knife.

Mercy held it carefully.

What are you doing? Take it.

Mercy ignored Lilith. She knew the fundamentals. Had practiced them in the safety of that otherworldly place with Sebastian. But this was real. The weight of that made all the practice in the universe feel shallow.

Vashti could be dying while you dither.

Don't push me, Grandmother.

Lilith finally fell silent.

Mercy took a deep breath and absorbed the Talent. She pulled it inside until her own brightness took on the same sharp-edged feel of Nayla's gift. Then she turned her attention back to Vashti.

Nayla's Talent was like putting on a new type of vision. She could see the entropy of age effecting Vashti's body. The slow, steady decline of her organs, the arthritis that sometimes made her move so stiffly.

Why hadn't she had her bones strengthened? A shot of anti-aging serum would have slowed the process, injecting her body with medical bots that would slow the entropy and restore cartilage to her joints. But there were no signs of this in Vashti's body.

Mercy set curiosity aside and turned her focus to the head wound. It was fresh, blood still sluggishly flowing to widen the pool on the floor. But blood loss wasn't the issue. Interlocking lines spread across Vashti's skull from an impact point, the bone fractured in a pattern that indicated a vicious blow to the head.

Uncertainty gnawed at Mercy. She knew nothing of broken bones and fractured skulls. Doc's words from months ago floated back to her. *You were lucky. One slip, and Wolfgang bleeds out instead of recovers.* What if she wasn't so lucky this time? She should stop and get Doc or Nayla. What had she been thinking to try this herself?

Don't be foolish, Lilith said, her voice clear and commanding. *My sister is dying in front of you, and you have the power to save her. The risk isn't in using the Talent you've borrowed; it's in waiting and letting her die.*

Even as Lilith spoke, the bright pulse of Vashti's mind dimmed. Panic made Mercy reach out instinctively.

The Talent seemed to know what to do. Tendrils of bright golden light wrapped around Vashti, threads stretching and coiling in thin filaments of light banding around her. They multiplied, one after another, overlapping until they covered her completely. Warmth seemed to emanate from them. The pulse of Vashti's mind strengthened. As Mercy watched, the blood flow from the head wound slowed and stopped. The lacework of cracks in Vashti's skull faded, the bone fitting neatly back together in its proper shape. Before her eyes, the wound healed.

Other pains healed as well. The Talent didn't seem to distinguish one hurt from another. Bruises and faint abrasions from the fall faded, soothed away by the golden threads. But the Talent didn't stop there. Bones increased in density. The connective tissue and cartilage between joints thickened, reconnecting. Arteries hardening with age softened. Her skin became more supple and elastic, lines fading. Her hair thickened and darkened until the silver streaks had faded to thin strands. The Talent burned so hot and bright it blinded Mercy. She threw a hand up as though that would protect her from the wave of heat.

What the hell just happened? Stunned, Mercy sat back, knocked onto her ass as the tendrils of Talent suddenly unwound from Vashti and retreated back to her, bringing a wave of unexpected energy with them. It faded almost immediately, draining away her strength.

The world tilted sideways as her head spun, dizziness swamping her. If Mercy hadn't been sitting already, she'd have fallen. Her hands splayed against the cool floor as she tried to anchor onto anything solid and stable. A moment later, the vertigo passed, and she was left feeling strangely empty.

She tried to stand and fell back down. Her arms and legs shook, trembling with weakness.

You used too much, Lilith said in her mind. *I've*

told you before: never expend more energy on someone else than you can afford to lose.

Irritated, Mercy scowled. "You wanted me to save her."

Save her, yes. Leave yourself vulnerable and open to attack? No. If the Alpha Queen tried to take you now, what reserves would you have to resist?

Before Mercy could frame a response — her mind seemed as sluggish as her body, slow to process and put thoughts together — Vashti moved. Her Aunt groaned, her legs shifting, tangled in her robes.

Mercy lurched forward, crawling to Vashti's side, careful to avoid the mixed pool of tea and blood. She reached out as Vashti's head turned, her eyes opening. Mercy froze and stared.

The woman who lay on the floor was a stranger. Gone was the kindly looking older woman with aged skin and long silver-streaked hair. Instead, a young woman blinked up at Mercy, her green eyes wide and confused. Her bronze skin was smooth and unblemished, her hair long and lustrous, dark without a single strand of silver. The face could have mirrored Mercy's own. More narrow, with a longer nose and fuller lips, but otherwise they might have been sisters.

"Mercy." Vashti reached out, grasping Mercy's hand. It felt wrong. The skin was supple and smooth. "Stop him."

Confused, struggling to grasp what had happened, *how* it had happened, Mercy just stared at her, open-mouthed.

How is this possible, she thought. And then, with

no small amount of horror and wonder, *what did I do?*

"Mercy!" Vashti's nails bit into her wrist. "Listen to me. You must stop him."

"Stop who?"

"I've been wrong, so wrong. How did I miss it?" Vashti's voice was bitter, full of self-loathing.

"You need to rest." Mercy placed her free hand over her Aunt's. "You almost died. That fall nearly killed you."

"Fall? I didn't fall." Vashti's mouth twisted into a grimace. "He hit me, that traitorous nephew of mine."

Adrenaline shot through Mercy. "Griffin?" she said. "Griffin hit you?"

"I *saw* him." The word had an emphasis that told Mercy Vashti wasn't talking about seeing him with her eyes. "He belongs to her. I don't know how I missed it." She tried to rise suddenly, but only succeeded in tangling herself more thoroughly in her robes. "You must stop him…before…before he takes her. Before he is gone."

Mercy was having a hard time tracking what Vashti was saying. Apparently regenerating someone by fifty years took its toll. She cast a look around the apartment. "Do you have any *mnemosa* here?"

"In the…cupboard." Vashti waved a hand in the general direction of a wall cabinet. Mercy crawled across the room, brushing her fingers across it to trigger open the cabinet. Inside, a neat row of four bottles stood together. She took one, hesitated, then grabbed another.

She hates it, said Lilith. *She won't drink it. And weak as you are, you'd best drink both yourself.*

Mercy ignored her.

"Here," she said as she crawled back to Vashti's side, bottles cradled in her arms. She popped the cap off one of them, and then wrestled Vashti into a sitting position. "Drink this." She handed her the open bottle.

Vashti grimaced. "I've always hated this stuff."

See?

Mercy grit her teeth against Lilith's smug tone.

"It's not my favorite, either, but we need it right now. Me, because I just spent more energy than I should have healing you, and you, because... well. Because." Mercy gestured vaguely at Vashti and left it at that. Did her Aunt know what had happened yet? Mercy sure wasn't ready to explain it. What was she supposed to say? *I was healing you with someone else's Talent, and I accidentally de-aged you. A lot.*

She opened the other bottle and took a long drink. *Mnemosa* wasn't bad tasting. It had a faintly sweet flavor with an underlying, tart fruitiness and a metallic aftertaste. It was that aftertaste that Mercy really didn't like. To deal with it, she chose to drink half her bottle in one go, chugging the stuff like water.

Vashti sipped hers more slowly, grimacing with each swallow. Mercy almost said something to Lilith, but thought better of it. Taunting her grandmother felt like a bad idea.

"You must go after Griffin," Vashti said. "I saw him, what he's capable of. He knows that. It's why he—" She gestured to her head.

I never liked that boy, said Lilith. *But Vashti doted on him. Treated him like a son. Foolish.*

Shut up, Mercy told her sharply.

"You had a...a vision about him?" she asked Vashti.

The other woman nodded. "He's going to betray us." Her face twisted with anger and something like grief. "He already has."

"He's the spy," Mercy said, and immediately wondered if Cannon knew. If Griffin was who he'd suspected.

Vashti looked resigned. Sad. "And he tried to kill you before," she said.

Before. There was only one *before* that held great significance.

"He blew up the lift?" The explosion had almost killed Wolfgang as well, not to mention putting the entire ship at risk.

"Yes. He's been her creature for a number of years, I think, and when you came along, another queen—" She stopped, shaking her head. Tears glimmered in her eyes.

Vashti genuinely loved him, Mercy realized. It didn't matter what he'd done, or might still do. Whether Griffin was related to her through blood or not, Vashti loved him.

"Her creature?" Mercy prodded gently. "You mean the Alpha Queen?"

Vashti nodded. "She controls him. There's something..." Her voice trailed off as her attention drifted, her eyes unfocused. Mercy reached out and squeezed her leg. Vashti blinked, looking at her again. "She has something over him, something she uses. I couldn't see more than that. But he knows once the others find out, it's a death sentence. Reaper will never let him live. He's desperate to escape, to get off the ship. You have to stop him."

Mercy reached out to Cannon, but found the effort sent her mind spinning. She took another swig of *mnemosa*, swallowing. "I just need a minute," she said. "My Talent isn't—"

"Mercy." The urgency in Vashti's voice stopped her cold. "He doesn't just want to escape. We have something his Queen wants. Some*one*. He's going to take her."

"Who?"

"Rani."

Mercy stared at her, her mind slow to puzzle through it all. "She's not here. Rani's in stasis on Ardon. He can't get to her."

Something vulnerable flickered across Vashti's face. This younger version was easier to read, somehow, than the older one had been. *Guilt.*

"What?" Mercy asked, a cold wash of foreboding prickling her skin.

"We needed to understand how they were able to replicate a clone with Talent - and not just Talent, but a queen." Vashti's voice was even and firm, no hint of apology to it. She didn't feel at all badly about using a young girl as a science specimen.

Betrayal made Mercy's throat dry. "No one told me."

In her mind, Lilith laughed. *Why would they tell you? They know you want to save her, and she can't be saved.*

Shut. Up.

"Only a select few knew," Vashti said. "To protect her, we wanted everyone to believe she was safe on Ardon."

Safe. Mercy had wanted Rani out of Veritas's hands to keep her safe. But were the pirates any better? Both factions wanted to use the girl for different reasons. And the Alpha Queen? Wanted her, presumably, for a fate even worse. Bile rose in Mercy's throat. When she spoke, her voice shook.

"Who knew?"

"Mercy—" Vashti's placating tone only made her anger burn brighter.

"*Who?*"

"Myself, Doc, Cannon, Sanah—"

"*Sanah?*" Mercy never would have guessed that Dem's empathic wife would have agreed to something like this.

"Well, yes. She's our resident cloning expert. She and Doc are working on a project that could restore reproductive capabilities to the women made barren by Matera-D—"

"I don't want to hear it."

"No harm came to the girl. She's been in stasis nearly the whole time."

"Nearly?"

Vashti shrugged. "Doc had to be able to access samples, run tests. She is only taken out of stasis for very short, controlled windows." Vashti waved a hand. "None of this matters right now. Listen to me. Griffin knows. He was the one who retrieved her during the move to Ardon and brought her back aboard. I entrusted him with the task." Her voice took on a bitter tone. "He must be stopped."

Yes, agreed Lilith in Mercy's head. *You really must stop him. A young, vulnerable queen cloned from your genetic material? Not someone you want in the alpha queen's hands.*

"Do you ever shut up?" Mercy snapped as she rose to her feet unsteadily.

Vashti eyed her in surprise.

"Not you," Mercy said. She fingered her wrist where the bracelet lay.

A smile softened Vashti's face. "And how is my dear sister?"

"Annoying. Look, Griffin already has a head start, and I'm not exactly at one hundred percent. Where is Rani now?"

"In the genetics lab."

Mercy had a vague idea of where it was. Griffin was probably already there. She needed to be certain. She reached out to Sebastian, the thought delicate, hesitant. In the midst of a battle, it might be dangerous to distract him. But the moment she brushed his shields, she felt his awareness of her.

It was more a feeling than words in her mind. A question. What did she need?

You. I need your Talent. We have a situation.

In a rush so unexpected it staggered her, Sebastian's Talent flowed and merged with her own. It buzzed faintly, like electricity.

Mercy took a deep breath, wondering what this would do to her so soon after borrowing Nayla's gift. But to her surprise, the rush of Sebastian's Talent seemed to bolster her flagging reserves, far better than the *mnemosa* had. With a thought, her awareness merged with the ship, flying down corridors, into rooms and compartments, across hangars and down lifts.

Between one heartbeat and the next, she became *Nemesis*.

More than that. She was *Nemesis*, and so was Sebastian. They weren't a ship and two minds, they were one being, one mind, one awareness.

And because of that, the whole of the ship, inside and out, unfurled before Mercy like the stretch of limbs after waking. She/They felt the thrum of nanobots flowing through her hull, the power of the drive at her core. Every footstep on her deck was unique, each life that pulsed within her a heartbeat.

Outside was the cold of space, the dark void filled with stars and planets and the dust of the universe that clung to her hull, bits and pieces picked up over decades of travel through the dark. Mercy didn't see so much as feel the other ships around her. She felt them with *Nemesis's* sensors, the heat of their weapons, the lives within their metal walls.

As one part of her assimilated the overwhelming amount of sensations and information flooding her senses, another continued the battle.

She fired on an enemy cruiser. It broke open, spilling its crew out into space. Some wore environmental suits that protected them. Others did not. Mercy felt their minds cry out in pain and terror before falling silent.

So many minds. Familiar. *Hers*. They filled the battle, so many. Warm and vivid until they went cold and dark.

Wait.

Something was wrong with this, with all of this.

She hesitated. Enemy plasma fire rocked against the shielding of her hull. *It burned, so hot, it burned.*

Stop. The word held no power. Those minds. Half of them were closed to her, shut away behind a barrier, a wall.

STOP.

The command pulsed out to every ship, every com, every soldier in a flight suit. For a moment, only a moment, it seemed everything froze. But it lasted less than an instant, a nanosecond.

That barrier had to go.

Without thinking about it, she reached out to every mind she could touch. Everyone within reach. Reaper, his Talent an icy presence. Atrea, her focus sharp, lethal. Wolfgang. Ghost. Zion. Haggerty. Dem. Cannon. Sanah…so many more. Tens of thousands of minds.

Yes… The voice was distant and faint, a thread she could barely hear, but she still recognized Lilith. *Take them.*

She did.

CHAPTER TWENTY-SEVEN

*T*reon woke to agony. His head quite literally felt as though it had split open and his insides were leaking all over the floor. Surely, that wasn't possible? The clean, medicinal smell of the place convinced him he was still in the infirmary, even before he tried turning his head to look around.

I really have to stop waking up like this.

"Don't move." The voice was vaguely familiar. The young woman. The former slave.

Treon groaned.

"Yes, I'm sure your head hurts very badly. You shouldn't have done that." Her tone very plainly said that he was an idiot.

What was it he'd done? His thoughts were foggy, floating things. Detached feeling.

Electricity jolted through him when he remembered. *She was working with the enemy.* He tried to sit up, and his head exploded. His vision went white, the pain reverberating through his entire skull, his teeth, his collarbone. Mother be damned, he'd never been this close to burn out in his life.

"You aren't *close* to burn out. You *are* burnt." A hand touched Treon's arm, steadying him, and her face swam into focus as the white bled from his vision, leaving him blinking at a blurry rendition of the world. "Are you trying to kill yourself?"

That was a ridiculous question. Of course he wasn't trying to kill himself.

"Then again," she continued, "maybe you should. You've caught her interest now, and she'll never leave you alone." Thirteen's tone held regret and a resigned weariness that went bone deep.

Treon blinked at her. What was she saying?

She sighed, looking at him, and there was no hint now of the frightened thing she'd been. Those violet eyes of hers looked older than her years.

"If I leave you like this, you could die." She contemplated him for a long moment. "I don't know if I'm doing you any favors by fixing you. But...I'm tired of watching people die."

As she spoke, Treon felt his headache ease. The pain washed away to nothing so completely he could have cried in relief. The sheer absence of it made his head feel light, as though a huge weight had lifted from him.

"What are you doing?" he rasped.

She gave him that look again, like he was being particularly stupid. His jaw clenched. It was a look she seemed inordinately fond of. He, on the other hand, did not appreciate it.

"You used so much energy, you took it from inside yourself. Your—" she hesitated. "Your spirit.

You have holes now, empty places that shouldn't be empty. I'm filling them."

She talked so strangely, this woman.

But whatever she was doing, it *was* helping. He felt his strength returning, bit by bit, layer by layer.

"Why are you helping me?" he asked. Her hand brushed his forehead, resting gently against him. She didn't answer. "Why are you helping *them*? Are you with Veritas? A spy perhaps, placed for us to find?"

She smiled. "If so, I made a poor one. I haven't even been here a day and you've already found me out."

Not a spy, then.

"Who are you?" he asked. The answer felt surprisingly important to him.

She eyed him. Some deep pain lurked in the depths of her eyes, the lines of her face. "No one. A slave."

"But you're not. We freed you."

She laughed, the sound cold and bitter. "No one can do that. Least of all, you. I told you, you've caught her interest now. She knows you exist." Thirteen shook her head. "Sooner or later, you'll belong to her. Just like I do."

Understanding hit him and he grasped her wrist. "You work for *her*. The queen."

She pulled herself from his grip, and he was still weak enough to let it happen. He struggled into a sitting position as she stood, her face turned in the direction he knew the battle to be.

"Why are you helping them?" he asked again. "Because *she* wants you to?"

Thirteen glanced down at him. She nodded once.

"You don't have to do this."

"You don't know me," she said. "Don't presume what you don't understand. One day, you will. There is nowhere in this universe where you can go to hide from her."

Treon shook his head, pleased when he was able to do so without pain. "If that were true, we'd all be her slaves already. Why aren't we? If she's so all-powerful, why are any of us free?"

Thirteen shrugged. "For a long time, she slept. When she woke, the universe had changed. There were other queens. She's been gathering her power for decades. Maybe longer, I don't know." She met his eyes. "But trust me when I say, she always gets what she wants."

"And right now, she wants us fighting with Veritas." Treon's mind raced as he tried to think why. But despite whatever she'd done to help him, he was still not at his best.

Thirteen didn't answer him. She looked back to the battle, then glanced toward the inner wall of the room, a direction that led deeper into the ship.

"I have to go," she said.

"Wait." He reached out a hand as though he could stop her. It trembled. His headache might be gone, but he was still weak. Damn it, he hated this.

She looked at him for a long moment, her expression contemplative. "For now, you're safe. Lie low, and don't do anything to draw her attention. She might forget about you for a little while."

"Listen to me," Treon insisted as she moved toward the hatch leading out of the infirmary. "We can help you. Just wait a moment."

"I don't have time for this," she said. "The longer this takes, the more people will die."

"The longer what takes?" he asked.

She looked ridiculous, standing there in one of the infirmary's ugly gowns and her bare feet. She wrestled open the hatch door, ignoring him.

Desperate, he cast about for something to say to stop her. Where was his vaunted wit? It seemed to have utterly deserted him. "Thirteen, whoever you are. Just answer me this: is it worth it?"

She stopped in the doorway, the fall of her hair hiding her face from him. Emboldened, he continued. "You obviously hate whatever it is you're doing. You yourself say you are a slave. You're not living your life. You're living at her whim, doing her bidding." She glanced at him, just the barest dart of her eyes in his direction. "What good is living, if you hate who you are? If you hate every day?" He struggled to stand, using an infirmary bed to lean against. "That's not how belonging to a queen should be. We have our own queen, now. And she is kind and caring to all her people. We could take a stand against her, this queen you follow. We could win."

She looked him full in the face at that, and her own expression twisted into a grimace. "I wish that were true," she said.

"What if it is?" Somehow, Treon felt sure that turning Thirteen from her goal could mean the difference in this battle. "What if you're wrong? I helped my brother escape her grasp once. I can do it again."

She gestured to him. "And look what it did to you. You might have saved him for now, but what about the next time she comes?"

"Next time, we'll know what to expect. We'll be prepared."

"So will she."

Frustrated, he bit back angry words. That wasn't the way to convince her.

"We are stronger than you know," he said. "We have survived insurmountable odds before. What if, together, we can resist her? Defeat her?" He held out his hand. An offering of friendship. Of safe haven. Of peace. "Don't you at least want to try?"

She stared at his hand for so long his arm shook. Finally, she shook her head. True regret shone in her eyes. "I'm sorry," she said, and walked out the door.

Treon was too weak to follow her. He couldn't even telepathically call for someone. His mind was still too fragile. But lesson learned. Instead of trying to stumble his way to the hallway, he struggled over to Doc's com system and thumbed it on. He contacted the CIC.

"We have an intruder," he said. "And she's helping the enemy."

He was shocked to receive a mental reply.

We know. We heard.

The voice, it sounded familiar, but...Sebastian? Mercy? Was his mind so muddled he couldn't tell one from the other?

We are both. The voice sounded amused. Treon shook his head violently, and soft laughter followed him.

MERCY DREW on the minds connected to her, just a tiny sip, a siphon of strength that, from so many minds, was so faint no one noticed. But it filled her reserves back to the brim.

She felt Sebastian handling *Nemesis* in the battle. He maneuvered the capital ship to protect the rest of the fleet. But from this perspective, Mercy saw the whole of everything. The battle. The people within *Nemesis*.

She realized something.

The space battle could have no point, no endgame except destruction. It wasn't the end goal, then, but something else. A distraction.

Tracking Griffin proved ridiculously easy. Mercy knew where he was within *Nemesis* the instant she concentrated on him.

She was unprepared to find Octavia with him.

The two were pushing Rani's stasis pod down a hallway. Most of the able bodied personnel were either flying in the space battle, or at duty stations. They had a clear run all the way to the hangar. But that didn't seem to be where they were going.

How did they expect to escape the ship?

Then it clicked. Octavia was a teleporter. She could take at least one person with her. Rani? So, Griffin was meant to stay behind? Why? He knew it meant his death to stay.

She heard Sebastian's thoughts as though they were her own. *He means to sacrifice himself to do this.*

It was a shock. Why would he do that?

I don't know. Sebastian sounded puzzled as well.

He belongs to you, Lilith said, impatient. *Just order him to stop. Force him to. This is well within your capabilities as his Queen.*

She was right, of course. Mercy didn't like it, but it was the simplest solution. She reached for Griffin's mind.

And found it closed to her. Like Veritas, there was a shield, a barrier around it. She could not touch him. Shock coursed through her, rippling through Sebastian as well. The ship shuddered around them.

Careful. Sebastian's voice was a whisper.

Sorry. This being the ship thing was tougher than she'd anticipated.

But she knew the source of that strange barrier now. The slave, the woman Reaper and the others had rescued. Thirteen, Treon had called her. She was moving through the ship like she knew exactly where to go, confident and sure.

She was going to Griffin.

Mercy couldn't touch her mind. "Thirteen," she said, using the coms of the ship.

That seemed to give the woman pause. She stopped, looking curiously around.

"You should have listened to Treon," Mercy said. "It's not too late. Join us."

The woman sighed, looking weary and irritated. "There is only one way this ends," she said. "You should save yourselves the trouble and just let her go now. Before more lives are lost."

Mercy didn't have to ask who she meant. *Rani.* "Why does the alpha queen want her?"

A ripple of surprise and something that might have been amusement startled a laugh from Thirteen. "The alpha queen? Is that what you call her? Mother will enjoy that." She shook her head. "Don't ask me things I can't answer. The girl is useless to you. A broken clone. Just let her go, and your people will live."

"I won't do that."

Thirteen started walking again. Mercy/Sebastian shut the emergency doors at either end of the corridor.

"You won't escape," Mercy said as Thirteen examined the doors. "You're trapped until I let you go." For good measure, she triggered the doors in the corridor around Octavia, Griffin, and Rani as well.

"This is a mistake." Unnatural calm settled over Thirteen's features. "What is this girl to you? What am I? We have been nothing but your enemies. Are we worth the lives of your people?"

"Giving the alpha queen what she wants feels like a bad idea. I'm not going to do it."

Mercy could see Thirteen's face clearly. She could see the sorrow that washed over her. "You don't understand. Mother always gets what she wants. The only choice you have is how much it will cost you to give it."

"I don't believe that."

Thirteen closed her eyes. "I'm sorry," she said. The words were so soft, Mercy almost missed them.

For what? She'd only thought the words when an oath from Sebastian pulled her attention outside of *Nemesis*. Ships were dying in suicidal collisions, pilots flying them into one another deliberately. Not just fighters. As she watched, a dreadnought broke against a cruiser, their hulls crumpling like paper as they crashed against one another. Talented minds died in a wave of thousands. Mercy sucked in a breath, the loss so staggering she would have fallen free of Sebastian had his mind not held to hers.

He clung to her. *What is happening?*

I don't know.

"I told you. You think all of these minds are yours?" Thirteen shook her head. "Mother is everywhere. Some of your people have been hers for years. Decades. Long enough to foment a war. Long before you tried to claim them."

Is she talking about Veritas? Sebastian asked.

I think — I think she's talking about all of us, Mercy answered, feeling sick.

"How many?" she asked. How many of the pirates, of Veritas, were not hers? How many belonged to the alpha queen?

Thirteen shrugged. "I don't know. Enough. She will force them to die, all of them, until she has Rani. And she'll make them take others when they do. Minds you've claimed. Ships will ram other ships, killing hundreds, even thousands of people. Is that what you want?"

No. Mercy thought of all of the lives out there. Of the people she loved who might already be dead.

Give up the girl, Lilith said. Her voice sounded tired. *This battle is lost. We cannot fight her today. We are too divided. Give up the girl, and we live to fight again.*

I can't.

Mercy. That was Sebastian. Pleading.

Being Queen means making hard choices, Lilith said. *I told you that.*

Mercy said nothing. As she watched, a corvette crashed into a gunship. Frantically, she reached for Reaper. She felt him, the familiar coldness of his mind. *Still alive. Thank the Mother.*

Be a Queen, Lilith said. Her voice was hard. Cold. *Or don't, and let our people die.*

Fine.

"How has she hidden from me?" Mercy asked Thirteen. "Before I give you Rani, I want to know how she had my people. How I missed it."

"She wouldn't want me to tell you that."

"That's my price. It's your job to make sure this happens, right? To get Rani back to her? Tell me what I want to know."

Thirteen laced the fingers of her hands together. "You're a young queen. New to your power. She is old, and sly. She sank her hooks deep, into the deepest part of their minds, from the mental plane. Even they didn't know she was there, until she wanted them to. Your —" Something flickered across her face. "Your planewalker. He can look and tell you if she's there. His Talent is strong enough. He can teach you to do it."

"Planewalker?"

"The man in the infirmary."

Treon.

"How do I know you're telling the truth?"

Thirteen spread her hands. The barrier around her mind abruptly dropped. "Look for yourself. I'm not lying."

Her mind was completely open to Mercy for that moment. Long enough to see the entirety of her thoughts. So much pain and conflict. So much weariness. But she was telling the truth.

Then the barrier was back.

"Do we have a deal?" Thirteen asked.

Mercy hated herself in that moment. "Yes," she said.

CHAPTER TWENTY-EIGHT

It was the hardest thing Mercy had ever done, letting Thirteen go. Letting Rani go. Letting them all go.

It started with Thirteen. Mercy and Sebastian dropped the emergency doors, freeing her. They watched as she met up with Griffin and Octavia. With Thirteen in charge, they seemed to abandon their plan to teleport out. They changed direction and went to the hangar.

"Give us a ship," Thirteen said. "A dropship will suffice."

That was good, since dropships were about the only class still sitting in the hangar. They loaded Rani's stasis pod. Doc protested, and Griffin warned him back. Mercy reached out to the doctor's mind, something she was reluctant to do. But she was well acquainted with Doc and his temper. The last thing she needed was a complication like that.

Doc, she said. *Let them go.*

Mercy? But—

Let them go. It's the only way this ends right now.

He stopped arguing, watching with bafflement as Octavia and Griffin boarded the ship with the stasis pod.

"We didn't agree for you to take them," Mercy protested.

"They are hers," Thirteen said. "And she will not give them up. Be glad you can keep the people you have."

Silent tears ran down Octavia's face, and Mercy felt sick. The girl had been nothing but a pawn this whole time. No wonder she'd struggled to fit in here; she'd never truly been free.

We will get them back, Sebastian said softly in her mind, where only she could hear him.

Damn right, we will, Mercy agreed, her jaw tight. Today they might be losing a battle, but this was merely the opening salvo in what would surely be a war. One Mercy didn't intend to lose.

The dropship's engines spooled up. Mercy watched it launch with a tightness in her chest. She brushed her mind against Octavia's. *We will come for you,* she said, the words a whisper.

There was no reply.

Once free of *Nemesis,* the Viking jumped, and they were gone as quickly as that. The barrier that kept Mercy from touching the minds of the Veritas fleet fell. At the same time, other ships began jumping out. One, three, seven. Ships from both fleets followed the Viking. More from Veritas than the pirates. But enough from both sides that both Mercy and Sebastian watched in shock.

No! I never agreed to this!

But it was too late. Was it a blessing, that those the alpha queen had taken were fleeing to her side? Or a harbinger of what was to come? In Vashti's vision, it was only a matter of time before they all followed her.

I will not allow that to happen, Mercy thought.

No, Lilith agreed. *We will not.*

For perhaps the first time in her life, Mercy and her grandmother were in complete agreement.

It occurred to Mercy then that she had specific people to worry about. How did she know that some of them hadn't belonged to the alpha queen? Frantic, she searched for the ones she loved most. Reaper. Atrea. Wolfgang. Reaper's dogs. Max. Cannon. Dem. Sanah. Tamari. Nayla. Doc. So many.

They were there, all of them. Relief flooded her.

Had there been children, in those ships? Don't think about it. She couldn't think about it now, or she'd fall apart.

Be strong for your people, Lilith said.

For all of them, Mercy thought. In the confusion following the exodus of ships, the battle halted.

Sebastian, Mercy said. *Broadcast a message. All ships, stand down. A new enemy has entered the field. This battle is over.*

✦

FERIA STARED at the holoscreen Cannon placed in front of her, an unreadable expression on her beautiful face. The words scrolling across the screen were an agreement. Something more than a peace treaty, something less than a merger.

It was an alliance. It promised an end to hostilities, open trade, a sharing of information and technology between the pirates and Veritas, both of whom were swearing fealty to Mercy.

Like it or not, she was going to be Queen to them both. It was the only way Veritas would even consider signing. They needed to belong to a queen, if they hoped to survive what was coming. Rani wasn't an option. And they would not take orders from Cannon. Not now. Not ever.

It didn't matter that much of the hostility between them in recent decades might have been created and fostered by the alpha queen and those who followed her. Those old wounds might never completely heal, though Mercy was hopeful.

Not long ago, it had looked like this alliance was impossible, too. But circumstances had a way of changing things. All in all, the pirates and Veritas had lost a staggering twenty percent of their respective forces when those ships had jumped out of the system and fled to their true queen. That loss, that truth might have inspired this alliance, but it also meant that trust was in short supply with everyone.

Cannon had spent the past three nights awake and combing over the lists of people lost. Mercy knew he'd been studying those names, asking himself if there was any way he could have known. Telling himself he *should* have known.

It didn't matter. Not anymore. They had to put the past behind them if they wanted to move forward. Their survival depended upon it.

Feria looked at Mercy, then Cannon. She looked behind her, at her own people arrayed around her. Then, without a word, she reached out and pressed her hand to the pad beneath the holoscreen, wincing when it extracted a tiny amount of blood and DNA. She passed the screen to Cannon, who repeated the action.

Mercy felt a ripple of anxiety. Now, both the pirates and Veritas were sworn to her.

This is nothing, said Lilith. *A mere formality. I don't understand why you even bother. They already belong to you.*

Mercy didn't try to explain it. She barely understood, herself. She cupped a hand around the bracelet. She really needed to figure out how to shield against Lilith. The idea of her grandmother popping into her mind whenever she wished was more disturbing than all the sworn alliances in the universe.

A faint snort from Lilith had Mercy gritting her teeth.

Either you help me figure out how to shield from you, she said. *Or I take this off and never put it on again.*

A long silence answered her. Mercy, as Feria and Cannon exchanged a reluctant and perfunctory handshake, reached down and began pulling the bracelet off.

Fine. I'll stop checking on you whenever I wish.

Mercy kept her hand on the bracelet. *Not good enough.*

I have to be able to reach you. What if you'd had me blocked during the battle? What might have happened then?

I survived just fine before you, Mercy said. *And I'll survive just fine without you again.*

Did you?

Mercy tugged the bracelet free of her wrist. It felt odd as it pulled away from her skin, detaching itself from her. Not painful, but not exactly pleasant. Like removing a bandage from freshly healed skin. Both freeing and oddly vulnerable. She began to pull it over her hand, sliding her fingers through it.

Wait! Lilith's panicked voice stopped her. *Oh, very well. You can... disconnect your mind from the bracelet at any time, effectively preventing me from speaking with you. However, you won't be able to access the blade, either.*

I can live with that, said Mercy. She slid the bracelet back into place.

Please don't do it all of the time. I'm — it's very alone, being inside an object.

I thought Sebastian visited you?

He does, said Lilith with fondness in her voice. *But he's often busy, and there is no one else.*

A trickle of sympathy moved through Mercy despite her best efforts. She shoved it aside. Lilith had shown no such emotion to her parents.

Still. She did need her. *I still need training,* she said after a time. A peace offering.

Lilith could have said a hundred different things. Mercy expected a scathing evaluation of her abilities in reply. But instead, uncharacteristically, her grandmother said simply, *thank you.*

You're welcome.

An uneasy silence fell between them.

The meeting dragged on. Now that the alliance

was formed, it was time to strategize their next move. How best to prepare for the coming destruction Vashti had foreseen.

It was Feria who suggested that Vashti's vision might be more symbolic than literal. Mercy's first instinct was to protest. Vashti and Lilith had spent years analyzing the visions; surely they'd have considered this.

But to her surprise, her Aunt spoke before she could.

"It's possible. I don't know if it matters."

"Of course it matters," Feria said with her old arrogance. "A supernova is a destructive force we cannot hope to prevent or defeat. Something else that it merely symbolizes, though, we may have more luck with."

Vashti frowned. On her new, younger face, the expression looked pensive rather than disapproving. It was still a shock, seeing her like this. For everyone. Core members kept sending furtive, uneasy glances her way. And Vashti herself looked more uncomfortable than Mercy had ever seen her.

She'd used her age like a shield, Mercy realized. Projecting a picture of frailty so that others would keep their distance. And, perhaps, underestimate her. She seemed unsure how to navigate this new reality. Doc kept scanning her, not even trying to hide his efforts as he analyzed the results and then scanned her again.

And Mercy hadn't seen Cage anywhere. He'd been keeping to himself since his brother's betrayal. It was the first time she could remember seeing Vashti quite so alone.

"Even if the first wave of destruction is not a supernova," Vashti said, "it will still be something on the same scale. Something difficult to predict, that will destroy the Commonwealth's power structure and plunge the core worlds into chaos."

"Perhaps," Feria agreed. "But that doesn't mean we have to sit back and let it. I've already got my people working on possible scenarios—"

Vashti cut her off with a harsh laugh. "You think I haven't run all of the possible scenarios already? What is it you think Lilith and I were doing over the past fifty years?"

"I wouldn't know," Feria said with a deceptively charming smile. "But I'm sure having more minds working the problem can't hurt. Perhaps we'll come up with something you missed."

Her tone was nothing but sugary sweetness and oh-so-helpful. Beside Mercy, Cannon's arm flexed, his hand clenched against his thigh.

You should kill her, said Lilith.

For Mother's sake, I told you to stop doing that.

I know, but you really should. She's a threat.

Mercy bit back a sigh as she stood up. This alliance was already off to a fantastic start.

"Enough." Everyone looked at her. She looked at Feria. "Don't be a condescending bitch. The empaths in the room can feel it." She pointed to Vashti. "She's been studying these visions for the whole of her life. Which is a lot longer than you might think. You would be stupid to waste that resource." She looked at her Aunt, barely keeping herself from flinching. For some reason, Mercy felt a lot of guilt over what she'd done when healing Vashti. "Feria and her people are good at what they do. Don't waste that resource, either. Maybe we can see something new by working together."

Vashti nodded, the move reluctant, but firm.

Mercy looked around the room. She met Cannon's gaze first. A lot of emotion simmered there, but she'd known he'd struggle with this treaty. It was going to be rough going for these first few months, at least. But he nodded. She moved on to Reaper, feeling nothing but his support, and a reassuring indifference to the undercurrents in the room behind his cool gaze. Sebastian smiled at her when her gaze rested on him, an approving sort of smile that made her want to return it. Wick looked sour, but then he always did. Dem was thoughtful. Doc was still so focused on whatever scans he was studying that he barely looked up from his datapad. And Treon had been in his own brooding world for much of the meeting. Reaper had warned her that his brother wouldn't react well to losing.

That was Reaper's word for Treon's burn out and the subsequent vanishing act of Thirteen, whom he'd felt was his responsibility. She supposed it fit. He *had* lost, perhaps for the first time in his life. And he was *not* reacting well. He snarled at anyone who dared speak to him, sipping at his *mnemosa* and glowering.

Still, Mercy met each and every gaze in the room. Some chairs stood empty. They'd lost a few Core members to recent events. Either to the battle, or the exodus. One of their first orders of business would need to be filling those positions.

Whatever was coming, it was happening soon. They needed to be strong.

The rest of the meeting was a lot of talk that generated more research and not much else. Finally, Mercy called it. She was tired, and tempers were beginning to fray. It was time to be done for the night.

She watched Feria and her people go with mixed emotions. Some of the Veritas people were staying here, and some pirates would be retuning to the Commonwealth with them. They were trading resources and knowledge. But no one was wholly comfortable with either, yet.

"You're tired." Reaper voice in her ear had Mercy turning to smile up at him.

She nodded. There was no use denying it. The past few days had taken a toll she wasn't fully recovered from yet.

"None of these problems will be solved in a night. Let's go eat."

She let out a breath. "All right."

"I thought we might eat with Wolfgang and Atrea," he said. She raised an eyebrow. Reaper rarely liked sharing their private time with anyone. He shrugged. "You like spending time with them."

She snaked her arm around his waist. "Thank you."

His arm settled over her shoulders, pulling her against him as people filed out. "I've also invited Sebastian."

She went still, then risked a glance up at his face. His expression was relaxed, easy. He met her gaze. "You like spending time with him, too. And you should start figuring out if that's all it is, or if he's going to become a consort."

She kept expecting Reaper to react differently. Maybe it was time she stopped putting her own expectations on him. He clearly had no problem with the idea of multiple consorts. She was the one reluctant.

"Maybe," she said. Across the room, Sebastian was talking with Dem, an easy smile on his face.

Reaper brushed his lips across her hair. "There's no rush."

Even as he said the words, unease scuttled down Mercy's spine. The alpha queen had Rani. She had a force the strength of which they did not fully know or understand. Time was the one thing they might not have.

She'll be coming, she thought. Reaper, of course, heard her.

"Yes," he said simply. "She will be."

EPILOGUE

THREE MONTHS LATER

*A*kyra adjusted the collar on her palace uniform. It itched uncomfortably, something in the fabric rough against her skin. She dropped her hand back to her side right before another guard came around the corner of a hedge row. They exchanged formal nods as they passed each other. Idly, she wondered who she looked like to him. Desmon had spun an illusion and attached it to her shields. It fogged her real face and encouraged other minds to fill in the blank. Instead of her shoulder length black hair, pale skin, and icy blue eyes, they'd see someone else, someone they knew.

Stop fidgeting. Desmon's voice was sharp. *Every extra movement you make is a risk.*

I know, she sent back. He always worried about his illusions breaking. But they never did. People *wanted* to see what they expected. They'd done this dozens of times, and Desmon always worried. *It's fine. I dropped my hand before he turned the corner. Relax.*

I am relaxed! You're the one about to walk through mechstone walls two meters thick and into two battalions of elite guards. If things go wrong, you'll be trapped.

They won't go wrong. They'd prepared for this mission, practiced it hundreds of times. Besides, Akyra's Talent would guide her. She didn't feel worried, she felt confident. Her muscles were loose, her mind eager with anticipation. She was ready.

Desmon was right about one thing: the palace walls *were* two meters thick, with windows too high up and too narrow to easily access. It was less a palace and more a fortress. This place had been built during the Ascension Wars. It was designed to withstand any attack, even an orbital assault. If the palace was razed to the ground, it still had caverns and tunnels built deep into the earth, a safe haven to retreat to. The Commonwealth had chosen its capital with that in mind; it wanted the monarchy safe.

Security was tight. Only authorized personnel could enter, and they had to submit to a full body scan each time they passed through the inner gates. There was no way she could pass that scan.

Not unless she could walk through walls.

Despite its functional structure, efforts had been made to beautify the palace. The mechstone, in addition to being so strong it could survive an assault from a capital ship, was infinitely customizable. The palace had 'seasons'. Each one featured a different look, complete with landscaping and customizable weather.

This was summer. The palace was white right

now, an opaque, pale stone with flecks of blue, green, and gold shimmering beneath the sun. Outside the walls of the outer courtyard, the early morning was dreary with fog and rain. But in here, the sun shone brightly overhead.

It wasn't real, of course. But it looked and felt real. Akyra felt the warmth against her skin, and if she glanced up, she'd have to squint against the brightness.

Manicured groundcover in deep brown with tiny, bright green flowers covered the entire lawn, with sculpted hedges forming a geometric pattern throughout the courtyard. They had small leaves in a deep red color, with white, star shaped flowers sprinkled throughout. More mechstone laid in whimsical walking paths spiraled through the maze of landscaping.

A manmade brook ran freely under a footpath bridge that covered the main walkway, winding its way around the palace in a moat that was purely cosmetic, shallow and filled with bright, flashing bits of silver, orange, and teal. Fish that were probably holographic, rather than real.

Delicate Starlotus trees were planted every five feet along the walls, forming a cover of fragrant, violet blooms against a backdrop of the trees' silvery leaves. In Fall, they would be replaced with something more robust, more suited to an earthen palate.

But for now, these trees formed the perfect screen for Akyra to slip behind. She followed one of the mechstone paths. Her Talent was active, filling her with icy calm, and tracking moments of vulnerability around her. She timed her strides on the path so that when it spiraled close to the branches of a Starlotus tree, no one was watching. Ducking behind the wall of foliage, she leapt over the cosmetic moat and came face to face with the white palace wall.

All right, Koal, she sent. *You're up.*

Beside her, the air shimmered faintly, her unseen companion letting her know he was still with her. He'd shadowed her steps, silent and invisible, and now he would get her where she needed to go.

Her Talent was killing. On her own, she could never get through these walls. But Koal was a ghost walker. He could scout invisibly, project himself behind locked doors, and yes, even walk through walls. And he could take others with him when he did it.

They were a Wraith squad. A team designed for infiltration and elimination. Once, they'd numbered four. But their fourth was off on a mission of her own, so this was left to the three of them. Akyra wasn't worried. They were efficient and practiced, and nulls were easy targets. Even royal nulls.

She held out her hand, feeling nothing when Koal took it. But he must have touched her, because a moment later she watched her own form fade to translucent, then to nothing.

Wait, she cautioned, scanning with her Talent. Two null minds were close by in the hallway beyond. Servants, gossiping as they strolled past. Akyra waiting until they'd been gone for a count of twenty before giving the go ahead. *Now.*

Koal pulled her through the wall. It felt cold, like a winter wind passing over her, lasting for roughly three breaths. Then she was stepping onto the stone floor of the corridor. He dropped her hand and she became visible again. Just a palace guard on an errand.

She accessed the layout she'd memorized, and then took off at a brisk walk toward the royal apartments. She checked the time on her implant. Less than ten minutes to complete her mission before word of the Council's fate would reach the palace and everything would go into lockdown.

Assuming the teams dispatched for the councilors were successful, of course. Akyra wasn't worried. She knew they would be.

She'd chosen the wall with the closest entry point to the apartments. She reached the entrance to the family's private wing in under two minutes. The moment she saw the palace guards stationed at the end of the hall, she let her Talent pull her under.

Icy cold washed over her. She'd always imagined this to be what space felt like, a cold so deep nothing could penetrate it. No emotion. No distractions. Just an endless void. She activated her soul blade, the ring on her right hand. She didn't call the weapon into existence yet, but held it poised to appear.

She walked up to the guards casually, her gait relaxed. She wore a smile, knowing they would see a face they expected.

"I have an urgent message for His Majesty," she said as she approached, ready in case either of them displayed any suspicion or alarm. But why should they? Nothing out of the ordinary happening here. They waved her through with friendly nods and a casual greeting.

She was almost disappointed.

Akyra went to the nursery first. It was her most difficult target.

Sereya was a paranoid King. Gossip said he believed his cousin had been assassinated. The ship that carried his family to their deaths had been no accident, but planned sabotage. He chose not to have children in the usual way. Instead, he used the controversial incubation and stasis practices that many of the Innova political party subscribed to. They were a tech-focused group that believed in embracing a future of AI and what they called 'clean reproduction'.

Why be messy and have all of those family problems, when you could just have your children raised in safe isolation, educated while they slept?

The room was guarded, of course, and no random person would be allowed entry. She slowed her gait as she turned down the corridor. The guards were alert, but not alarmed when they saw her. Both carried plasma rifles. A man and a woman. One of them called out to her, a name Akyra didn't know.

"What are you doing here, Viv?" the woman asked.

Akyra tensed, but the male guard didn't react to the name. Sometimes multiple people saw different faces. That could have been a complication, but it appeared both guards saw the same person. It was possible the female guard's use of the name Viv had solidified the illusion for her counterpart.

Akyra shrugged as she closed the distance between them. "The King had a bad feeling. He wants a report on the nursery." She spoke softly, low enough that the guards would have to strain to hear her. Desmon's illusions could mimic sound, but not well or easily.

Twenty steps separated them.

The two guards exchanged glances. "We sent him one an hour ago," said the man. "Right on schedule."

"Why didn't he just call down?" asked the woman.

Fifteen steps. "I just follow the orders I'm given," Akyra said. A screen lock was on the wall behind the woman. *Damn.*

The female guard studied her with a frown. "You sick, Viv? Your voice sounds odd."

The illusion was breaking.

Ten steps. Akyra burrowed into the woman's mind, tearing past the tattered excuse of a mental shield she had. She rifled through a thousand useless pieces of information, looking for the one she needed. The guard gasped, eyes wide. Beside her, the male guard started to lift his rifle.

Seven steps. Searching, searching...*there*. She threw out a blast of telekinesis, knocking the man back.

Akyra called her soul blade into existence. It shimmered into her hand, a faint smoke outline in the air. She leapt across the remaining distance. Her blade slammed into the woman's chest, stopping her heart. Akyra jerked it sideways, cutting across the woman's body. White smoke rose from the line of her cut, dissipating into the air.

The male guard's eyes were wide, his mouth

hanging open in shock. But he was well trained, recovering in seconds to bring his rifle to bear. Those seconds were all Akyra needed. Her blade cut in a downward arc, across his neck and through his body. He jerked, the synapses in his brain telling him he was cut, telling him the wound was mortal, his spinal cord severed. He dropped to the floor, white smoke rising from his body.

Akyra eyed the lock on the wall, a small screen with the dual requirement of a predetermined shape and genetic screening. She checked the time. Five minutes left.

She reached down and lifted the woman's body. She had to use telekinesis to help hold the body at the right height. Taking hold of the dead guard's hand, Akyra pressed the woman's index finger to the lock's screen and drew the shape she'd pulled from her mind. The door hissed open.

Inside the room, three incubation pods were lined against one wall. The occupants inside were held in a kind of coma, their brains attached to biotech that fed them a database of knowledge and experience. The pods were reinforced with nanogaph armor plating, the kind used for ship hulls. It made them almost as impenetrable as stasis, with nearly indestructible enclosures. She could pick up one of those plasma rifles outside and shoot at the pods as much as she wanted. If she was lucky, one of them might scuff the surface. A weapon from a capital ship could destroy them, but being safely tucked inside the palace, that was an unlikely form of attack.

The King's children, the Commonwealth heirs,

raised in a virtual environment of the monarchy's choosing, safe from any prospective violence or assassinations. Theoretically.

Even without her Talent, Akyra would have felt nothing as she disabled the alarm, and then cut the power to each of the pods. They weren't real people, they were a lab experiment. The nulls should be thanking her for removing them from their monarchy's order of succession.

Manifesting her soul blade, she went to each pod and thrust her blade into the occupant inside, stabbing them through the brain. The pods might be unassailable by physical weapons, but soul blades attacked the mind.

Just to be thorough, she cut through the pod controls. Soul blades could disrupt any electrical current, be it organic or tech. They sparked and smoked, and the panel went dark.

The first part of her mission complete, she banished her blade and moved on to the King's apartments. He and the Queen were creatures of habit. He rose every morning just after dawn, and then followed all of the newsfeeds while he ate the breakfast tray his staff would have left in the hall outside. The Queen would rise toward the end of this breakfast period, and the two would discuss their calendars for the day before parting to go about their respective duties.

It sounded positively dull. Akyra couldn't imagine wanting to rule.

She reached the door to the King's apartments, smiling at the palace guard stationed outside of it. He returned the smile, relaxed and unwary. While he might have waved her past, she could take no chances. As soon as she was close, she summoned her blade and stabbed him through the throat. A faint gurgle escaped him, muffled by the telekinetic shield she placed over his mouth. Akyra lowered his body to the ground, using telekinesis to let it fall soundlessly.

She could hear the newsfeed faintly from behind the door. Two minutes left. Perfect timing. She dismissed her blade.

Akyra pressed against the door, feeling with her Talent. Yes, there was the King. He was worried about recent reports of elevated pirate activity on the fringes. She smiled. Nulls had such poor shields, it was child's play to reach past them. She did not have the Talent of some of her kind, to kill the mind with a thought. Her bloodline was, regrettably, impure.

She had to resort to more kinetic methods. She gripped his brain with telekinesis and squeezed. A thud sounded on the other side of the door, the King's body falling to the floor.

The sound woke the Queen, who rose from her bed, confused and blinking away sleep. She could have reached for the alarm next to the bed, but didn't, her sleep fogged brain uncertain of what had woken her. Her shields were more substantial. Akyra took a moment to study them. The Queen, it seemed, was Talented. Latent, untrained Talent, but it meant it took actual effort for get past her shields. It took longer. Precious seconds ticked by. Finally, Akyra was in.

The Queen's body joined the King's on the floor.

Done, and with just over a minute to spare.

Akyra exited the palace the same way she'd come in, moving as quickly as she dared. Koal was leading her out through the palace wall when the clock ran out.

Right now, Akyra knew, an urgent ansible message would be incoming to the palace. They would try to rouse the King, and he would fail to answer the summons. Shortly after that, the bodies would be found.

She and Koal had left the sunny display of the palace grounds and were five blocks away in the dreary cold of the city when the alarm began to sound. Akyra shared a glance with Koal, who was visible now. He held her hand, so they looked like a couple. He was barely fifteen to her eighteen. They looked like kids. No one to be alarmed about.

"The King is dead," she said, unnecessarily. The ice of her Talent was thawing, slowly leaving her.

Koal nodded solemnly. "Long live the Queen."

ABOUT THE AUTHOR

Carysa Locke has been writing stories since she started with horrible Star Wars fanfic in the 6th grade. (Trust me, it was bad!) Her Telepathic Space Pirates series is based on a series of role-playing games her best friend ran which introduced her to this universe and concept, although many aspects changed as the books have taken shape, but some of the central characters and the core of the space pirates themselves were created by her friend, MaLea Holt, for those games.

I would LOVE to hear from you and get
feedback on
Pirate Consort

Never miss out on a new release - sign up
for my newsletter, *The Pirate Fleet!*

A note from the author: reviews are the word-of-mouth authors rely on. Not only do we love reading our reviews, but they help sell more books. Please take the time to leave a review, either where you purchased the book, or on places like Goodreads.

You can also find me in these places if you want to drop in and tell me in person what you thought:

www.carysalocke.com
https://www.facebook.com/carysalocke/
carysalocke@gmail.com